Anna Bartlett Warner

The Star out of Jacob

Anna Bartlett Warner

The Star out of Jacob

ISBN/EAN: 9783337042165

Printed in Europe, USA, Canada, Australia, Japan

Cover: Foto ©Andreas Hilbeck / pixelio.de

More available books at **www.hansebooks.com**

THE

STAR OUT OF JACOB.

BY THE AUTHOR OF

"DOLLARS AND CENTS."

"I am the root and the offspring of David, and the bright and morning star."—Rom. xx. 16.

NEW YORK:

HURST & COMPANY, Publishers,

122 Nassau Street.

PREFACE.

A PREFACE is an impertinence, where one has nothing
to say. I will but remind the reader, that upon almost
all Palestine questions great authorities are divided, and
that it is impossible for the most careful and candid ex-
aminer to follow one, without seeming to slight another.
A very evident fact, but one sometimes forgotten.
Partly to show 'how doctors disagree,' I have given
various opinions on two or three points, in Notes at the
end of the volume.

There is also an Index of Illustrations, which the
reader will do well to consult. My sister and I are exceeding careful in this work to take *nothing* for granted,
—and by no imagination of ours does even a flower
bloom upon the hillside, or a particular bird wing his
way across the sea.

I have tried to keep fancy out of the book, altogether
It is not that, I hope, to think out things as they might

have been, with at least some one authority for every point.

' The secret things belong unto the Lord our God: but those things which are revealed belong unto us and to our children for ever, that we may do all the words of this law.' Deut. 29 : 29.

A. W.

The Island, Dec. 21, 1867.

Note.—The Illustrations in this volume, were executed by the Engraving Class at the Women's School of Design.

INDEX OF CHAPTERS.

INDEX OF ILLUSTRATIONS.

The Star out of Jacob.

Chapter I.

INTRODUCTION.

By a small window looking towards the sunset, stood our four children. The bright rays — stripped now of their warmth, for it was November — yet shone lovingly upon the young heads and faces, and the old room looked fair and kindly in their light. Ours is not a city house, you can see that at a glance; the stamp of the town is not upon one of its belongings. Outside there is no high flight of marble steps, leading up to splendour; but only a single flat doorstone, grey and time-worn, and trodden with the feet of many friends. Some of these stand even now upon the Mount Zion, — some pass up and down yet in the dust of this world.

The old clapboards, which once were red and once were white, now in their faded strife of colours shew no kin to a brown stone front. Neither are there church steeples in sight, nor 'palatial' dwellings; but tall green cedar spires instead, and a

bird's nest or two laid bare by the falling leaves
and the chirp of crickets for the busy hum of men.
The stream of life that we see is a sparkling river;
while a fair, fair outline of swelling hills bounds
our visible world, and almost our earthly desires.

Within doors the difference is quite as great.
Small windows, glazed long before plate glass came
in fashion; low ceilings, and doors with old revo-
lutionary hinges; a wide fireplace, wherein the oak
sticks have sunk down into a heap of glowing coals
and white ashes, — all say very plainly, 'this is
not in town.' And the entire absence of velvet
furniture, satin curtains, and all *useless* pretty
things, says it too.

The children at the window, gazing out at the
sundown, wear neither silk frocks, nor sashes, nor
embroidered jackets. Frocks of dark crimson stuff,
little white ruffles, and aprons to suit the fancy of
the wearer, deck the girls; while Cyril is in grey
from head to foot.

I said the four were at the window, but indeed
Gracie has a window all to herself; not watching
the sunlight, but catching its last rays upon her
book. Gracie is a true bookworm, going over her
beloved pages with a slow, patient devouring. She
reads enough for two children, and remembers
enough for three or four. There never was such a
child, I believe, for searching out and applying
knowledge.

Cyril likes knowledge, too, but in a much more
dashing, boyish way. Shining deeds catch his eye,

but he is not half so particular as Gracie from what quarter the light comes. Mabel, on the other hand, cares most where it *falls;* and will question this, and disparage that, just to be rid of some uneasy pressure on her conscience. But our little Sue is still in that Paradise of life, whither the tempter has not yet brought shame nor fear.

These three are in deep discussion. Some important matter is on hand, apparently; for the young ones speak low and with much eagerness, every now and then glancing back into the room at mamma. Ah, our mother!—perhaps you will think that I should describe her too; but how can I? If you, with a poor little paint-brush, will fashion me the velvet leaves and dewy freshness and heart-satisfying fragrance of a perfect rose, then will I draw for you my mother's picture. She sits here near me, pulling lint in the fading light; an ample white apron almost covering her black dress, a little transparent white cap half veiling her brown hair. I am in black, too, do you see? since the week before Richmond; but mamma was too anxious to keep all gloom from the children's hearts, to put any on their dress. Only as Gracie petitioned with her quiet tears that they 'might at least wear mourning as a soldier's children,' you can see that there is a little band of crape upon each small left wrist, and on Cyril's arm. How earnestly they talk! and louder now.

'You see, Cyril,' Mabel says, with her emphatic gesture, 'we *must* have them.'

'I don't see it at all,' Cyril answers. 'We must have bread, I suppose, but there's no need of butter.'

'O, don't you think so,' said little Sue.

'Yes, he does,' said Mabel; 'he likes butter as well as anybody. But we're talking of books, not butter.'

'It's all one,' said Cyril. 'You'll see. Butter or books — it makes no difference. Things we can do without, — that is the point.'

'But I'm talking of what we *can't* do without.'

'Well —' said Cyril. 'Then you'll have to learn.'

'How you do talk!' said Mabel excitedly. 'Look at Grace now — will *she* ever learn, do you think?'

'Gracie,' said mamma, ' come away from the window. You are spoiling my precious eyes.'

Grace laughed, but obeyed instantly; and coming up to our mother curled herself down at her feet on the rug.

'How many pairs of eyes have you, dear mamma?'

'About — five pair, — besides my own,' said mamma, laying her lint straight.

'I don't believe you know anything about it, Cyril!' exclaimed Mabel at the window. 'Now we'll ask mamma. Mamma! — Sue, you tell her what we were talking about.'

'Mabel always wants a deputy,' observed Cyril.

'Tell her, Sue,' Mabel repeated.

Little Sue climbed into mamma's lap, quite displacing the lint manufacture ; and happily unconscious of any connection between books and butter, stated the case with great simplicity and clearness.

'Mamma, are you going to buy us a great many new story books this winter?'

'I never meant *all* story books,' corrected Mabel.

'Are you, mamma?' said Sue.

'It is a good winter to read over the old books, Sue,' said mamma.

'But we've read them all, dozens of times,' said Mabel. 'Dear mamma, why do you say it is a good winter for that?'

'Because books are so very dear, that it is a bad winter to buy new ones.'

'Are *story* books very dear?' said Sue, counting mamma's buttons with her small fingers.

'Very dear. I shall make my old ones do.'

'But we've read ours so often!' said Mabel disconsolately. 'I know every one of mine by heart.'

'And by head too?' inquired mamma.

'What is the difference, ma'am?'

'All the difference that there is between knowing the words, and understanding what they mean.'

'O I know what all the words in my books mean,' said Mabel.

'I suppose you could give me an account of each story, and tell me what was the name of the best girl and the worst boy, and all that they did, and where they lived?'

'Yes, mamma.'

'And how about the meaning of the story itself?

the truth hid away in it, the lessons to be learned
from the joys and sorrows of this girl and boy ? '

'Why — I don't suppose I could tell quite so
much about that,' said Mabel, hesitating. 'I always think most of the story.'

'But *that* part is the most interesting of all, I
think,' said Gracie. 'Only it puzzles me sometimes.'

'There isn't much worth remembering in their
books, you know, mamma,' said Cyril. 'They're
just about boys and girls, as you said.'

'Then I am to understand that *you* know your
books more thoroughly ?' said our mother. 'You
know the cut of Cæsar's robe, I suppose, as well as
the list of his battles; and you can describe the
make of the dagger that stabbed him, and the sort
of pavement on which his blood dripped down.'

But it was Cyril's turn now to hesitate.

'No mamma, — I was thinking only of the deed
itself, not how it was done.'

'Ah, you see how easy it is to know and yet not
know a story, a history, or a life.'

'But mamma!' — began Mabel and Cyril.

'Mustn't we have *any* new books, then ?' said
Sue.

'We'll see,' said mamma, stroking the sunny
little head that lay on her breast. 'We'll see
about that when Christmas comes.'

'Mamma,' said Gracie, looking up and speaking
for almost the first time; 'if books are so dear I
don't think you ought to get us one. And then I

was remembering our pleasant time every afternoon — when we read. And mamma — don't you
think, perhaps, you would tell us stories, — if we
have not books ? '

Gracie had been studying the matter very gravely, and there was a little twinkling light on her
eyelashes that told of a struggle. Mamma's other
hand went down to her, and was at once caught
and held fast. There was deep silence for a few
minutes.

'I had been thinking of telling you stories — a
sort of stories,' answered mamma at length; 'or of
reading them over with you. There is one particular story that we have all read, and yet I know
might read again with great pleasure. If we
should go it over together, slowly; a little bit every
night ; and I should tell you besides all the stories
and history of every kind that help to explain it, —
how would that do ?,

'Why splendidly, mamma,' said Mabel, while
Gracie gave the hand she held a silent squeeze.
'But what story can you possibly mean ?'

'It's one of my histories, I suppose,' said Cyril.
Mamma, Sue could never understand that.'

'Yes I could — when I'm grown up,' said Sue.

'Sue can understand this now,' said mamma.

'Is it my book of animals ?' asked Mabel.

'It is not a new story,' said our mother; 'but it
tells of the most interesting places in the world,
and of the most wonderful things that ever were
done. Nothing was ever so fine as the way in

which the story is told, and every word of it is
perfectly true.'

'Why mamma,' said Cyril, 'have we got it in the
house?'

'I know what it is,' said Gracie, raising her
head; 'it's the Bible. That is the only book in
the world that is perfectly true.'

'The Bible!' said Mabel, — 'but, mamma,
there's nothing at all new about that.'

'Wait till we begin to study it, — you have no
idea how new it will seem then.'

'Which story in the Bible, mamma?' said little
Sue. 'I like the Bible!'

'We will begin with the story of the life and
death of our Lord Jesus.'

Sue sat up and looked into the fire as intently
as Gracie had done.

'Mamma,' she said, 'will you tell us all about
my Jesus, and the people that loved him, and how
they followed him in the little ships?'

'Yes, Sue; and what sort of ships they were,
and how the people were dressed.'

'And about the temple, mamma?' said Cyril;
'and the river Jordan, and the Romans? I shall
like that.'

'O mamma,' said Gracie, 'will you begin to-
night?'

'Too late for to-night,' said our mother. 'I
must get together my books and maps, and then
we will try and begin to-morrow.'

Chapter II.

IN THE BEGINNING.

THE hour before sundown was to be the story hour; which would, as mamma said, leave us the twilight to talk it over in. So when the next afternoon shadows began to creep across the lawn, the children came trooping into our little sitting room, eager to begin the promised pleasure. You might notice that Gracie brought her Bible with her, — as usual she was going into the matter in earnest.

As for mamma herself, she had long before made her preparations. Books and maps of various kinds lay on the table, ready for use ; and her own Bible — a Bagster's quarto — lay there, too. What further preparation she had made had been secret and unseen; yet you could read it in her face when she came in, a little while before the children, with her white apron and lint. But this other work was on her heart; for now and then the white hands and the white threads dropped together, and mamma sat looking through the window with a deep gaze that I think saw not our sunset moun-

tains.   I think she was seeing the far-off hills of
Palestine, visited long ago in company with one
who was now in the holy land on high.   I too, a
little child then, had made that journey; bringing
back childish recollections of camels and palm
trees and wild-looking Arabs.   I thought I could
read mamma's face now: until something like a
reflection from the pearly gates of heaven fell upon
it; and then I could look no longer.

The children, gay with the thought of their new
study, came singing along the hall; making the
old house echoes ring with their full chorus:

'O Canaan, it is my happy, happy home!
I am bound for the land of Canaan."

And then as they came in, Gracie broke out with one of her joyous solos —

"If you get there before I do——"

But catching sight of her mother's face, the child dropped like a skylark, nestling down on the floor at her feet.

Mamma had hastily taken up her work at the first sound of the singing, but now she put it by, and turning to the table opened a great atlas which lay there. And I thought I had never heard anything so sweet as the voice with which she began.

'Children, we are to study the story of the Promised Land, — of its purchase for us, of its free gift to us; of its King, its glory, and its joy; — that we may learn to be not faithless, but followers of them who through faith and patience inherited the promises.'

'I thought,' said Cyril, 'that we were to study Palestine, and the life of Christ. I didn't know it was to be heaven.'

'The land is on high,' our mother answered, 'and there was the deed of gift executed; but the purchase money was paid here; and the land of Canaan on earth is but a type of the heavenly Canaan: it is one of the "patterns of things that are in the heavens." And here were laid all the scenes of our wonderful story.'

2

'Mamma,' said Mabel, 'I can't get used to your calling it a story.'

'There is a certain German tale,' answered our mother, 'which as if it surpassed all others in the world, is called, "The Tale of tales." That is only a fancy. But in the truest and deepest sense, the Gospel account is "The Story of stories." There was never another like it, nor shall be again. It was written by men taught of God; and who were eye-witnesses of these things, or had perfect understanding of them. It was written that we "might believe that Jesus is the Son of God, and that believing, we might have life through his name:" it is the story of good news to sinners, — the history of things of which even angels desire to know more.'

'Where are you going to begin, mamma?' said Cyril.

'Why it begins at Bethlehem, don't you know?' said Sue. 'That is where my Jesus was born.'

'But where was our Jesus before he came to Bethlehem?' answered mamma. 'We must learn that first.'

'I've been trying to think where you would begin, too, mamma,' said Gracie; 'for all the four Gospels begin differently.'

'Which one of them is dated the furthest back?'

'Matthew begins at Bethlehem, with the birth of Christ,' said Mabel; 'at least that is the first thing I remember.'

'And Mark with the coming of John the Baptist in the wilderness,' said Cyril, who had just been after his Bible.

'And Luke with the promise of his coming,' said mamma. 'Where does John begin?'

Gracie, down on the floor, was already studying it. Mabel peeped over her shoulder.

'Mamma, John begins further back than all!—in heaven, I think.'

'Yes, John has a sort of preface to his history, and dates the first words as far back as the thought of man can reach: "In the beginning." '

'That is the way the whole Bible begins,' said Cyril. "In the beginning God created the heavens and the earth." '

'And it is of him who was in the beginning, that John's preface tells. In the beginning of all things; before earth or sky or sun or stars were made; "In the beginning was the Word, and the Word was with God, and the Word was God." '

'That seems to be a description in three parts,' said Cyril, considering the verse.

'So it is. The first is like the words which the Lord Jesus himself afterwards spoke to John in a vision: "I am the first and the last." And what does the second say?'

'Mamma,' said Gracie, turning over the leaves of her Bible, 'the second is like those other words of Jesus — here, — "And now, O Father, glorify me with thine own self with the glory which I had with thee before the world was." '

'Why that is it exactly!' said Cyril, — 'how could you find it so quick?'

'And for the last part,' said mamma, 'hear these words in Hebrews: "Unto the Son he saith, Thy throne, O God, is for ever and ever."'

'Mamma,' said Mabel, 'how do people know who is meant by the Word, in that verse?'

'Why because Jesus is called by that name in other places in the Bible,' said Gracie. 'I know one, in Revelation: "And he was clothed with a vesture dipped in blood: and his name is called The Word of God."'

'Yes, and in the first epistle of John, where he says: "There are three that bear record in heaven, the Father, the Word, and the Holy Ghost: and these three are one."'

'One, and yet three,' said Gracie; 'and so "the Word was with God, and the Word was God." Mamma, was Jesus called the Word, because his is the name above every name? — the one word that we *must* know?'

'The reason's plain enough,' said Cyril. 'The Bible says somewhere, don't it, that God has spoken to us by his Son.'

'And he said, "Hear ye him,"' remarked little Sue.

'A great monarch,' answered our mother, 'has very little direct intercourse with his subjects; it must all be carried on through another. Even if they thrust their petitions into the king's own hand, the answer will be given them by some one else. In public affairs it is the same. The English queen is said to open parliament, but her speech is often read for her by one of the officers of state; and so in France, where the keeper of the seals speaks in the king's name, at his bidding. But this is especially the case in Eastern lands. When an ambassador has audience of the sultan, every reply to his words is given through the vizier, who is the sultan's prime minister: the grand seignor never speaks directly to his guest. In China, the emperor hardly even allows himself to be seen by the common people. In Abyssinia, also, an old traveller tells us, the king kept himself out of sight and hearing. He sat within a sort of balcony, all enclosed with curtains and latticed windows. On public occasions, when a criminal was on trial or an ambassador craved audience, the king took his seat by a particular window which overlooked the court of judgment and of audience. In this window was a hole covered with a curtain of green stuff, and close by the curtain, on the outside, stood an officer of state called kal hatzé; through him the king sent his answers to the ambassador, or his questions and commands to the judges at the council table. The kal hatzé was one to stand between the king and the people.'

'That seems like the veil which Moses hung before that part of the temple where the glory of God was,' said Gracie. 'Mamma, what does kal hatzé mean?'

'It means, "the word or voice of the king."'

'"For by him hath God spoken unto us"' —
Gracie repeated, 'O mamma, that is it, that is it!

'But Jesus is the King, too,' said Sue.

'Yes,' said mamma, 'the kings of the earth speak
by some one of their subjects, but God hath spoken to
us by his Son. "The Word was God:" although
to do this work and to fulfil this office, he took on
him the form of a servant.'

'But,' said Mabel, 'God didn't speak to the people so in the Old Testament times.'

'Well he spoke a great deal,' said Sue. 'He
spoke to the sea and the birds and the earth. And
to Moses, too.'

'Yes, but that was not Jesus,' said Mabel.
Then our mother answered:

'"In the beginning was the Word, and the
Word was with God, and the Word was God. All
things were made by him; and without him was
not anything made that was made."'

'But you don't mean that it is he the first chapter of Genesis tells about?' said Mabel.

'O mamma,' said Gracie, 'was it *Jesus* who said,
"Let there be light"?'

'I always thought that it was God the Father
who created everything,' said Cyril.

'The Bible says that by him, — by his Son
whom he hath appointed heir of all things, — God
made the worlds. Not merely our little earth, but
the *worlds:* all things were made by him. And
if you study that first chapter of Genesis, you will
find in almost every verse the Word who was in the

beginning with God. God said, "Let there be light," — "Let the waters bring forth," — "Let the dry land appear." "And he spake, and it was done; he commanded, and it stood fast." For the Word was God.'

'And so every bit of our world tells of Jesus,' said Gracie, — 'I am so glad!'

'But, mamma,' said Mabel, 'who was it spoke in that other verse — I mean that other time — about making man, you know? That is a little different.'

'"Let us make man in our image" — that is the Lord Jesus still.'

'It sounds,' said Cyril, thoughtfully, 'it sounds just as if two were consulting together.'

'Remember first what is said in this verse: "The Word was with God, and the Word was God." Then turn back to the glorious saying of Isaiah, when he prophesied of the coming of the Lord in human form: "Unto us a child is born: unto us a Son is given. And his name shall be called Wonderful, Counsellor, The Mighty God." And now you are ready for those other words: "God said, Let us make man in our image."'

'That lights it up splendidly!' said Cyril. '"Counsellor," — that name always puzzled me before. I never could understand what it meant.'

'It's very strange,' said Mabel. 'Why I thought it was only the New Testament that told about Jesus.'

'From the beginning of the world,' said mamma,

'the Son of God hath declared the Father. All through the Old Testament times he was the Word of God. But when the fulness of time was come, "the Word was made flesh and dwelt among us:" the Voice of the Old Testament is the Incarnation of the New.'

'There again!' cried Gracie, — 'I never understood that verse before. "The Word," seemed just a name; I never thought of its meaning the Voice from heaven that people had been hearing for so many, many hundred years.'

'In our English Bible,' mamma said, 'that name is never given to the Lord except in the New Testament. John is the only one of the sacred writers who calls Jesus the Word; and he but four times. But in the old Jewish Targum it is constantly used.'

'Ah, I am glad to hear about the Targum,' said Cyril; 'I came upon that word the other day, and couldn't find what it meant.'

'When the Jews were carried away captive into Babylon, and dwelt there for seventy years, they lost the perfect knowledge of their own native tongue. The orders given them by their conquerors, the speech they heard on every side, were in another language. And so by degrees they ceased to speak or to understand pure Hebrew, and learned a sort of mixed language, which was neither Hebrew nor Chaldee, but made up from both. Then when at last Cyrus sent back the remnant of Judah to their own country, and the temple was rebuilt, and the priests began to read aloud to the people that law of the Lord which they had not heard for so many years; then it appeared that the people could not understand it. For the law — the five books of Moses which bore that name — was written in the pure ancient Hebrew. So the priests, who almost alone had kept their learning, "read in the book of the law of God distinctly, and gave the sense, and caused them to understand the reading."

'That is, they translated it out of the pure Hebrew into the people's mixed language, I suppose,' said Cyril.

'Precisely; adding also a word or two here and there, to explain the meaning. And after a while these explanations and translations were written down, and called a Targum, — from an Arabic word which means translation. This was on the Pentateuch — the five first books of the Bible. Then as other books were written, — of history, of prophecy; the Psalms of David and the Proverbs of Solomon, — there came to be Targums upon them also: the habit of explaining to the people was still kept up. One read aloud the sacred words, and another gave the explanation.

'Why did not the reader himself do that? asked Cyril.

'I do not know, unless it was to guard the truth from mistakes and misrepresentations; so that in the mouth of *two* witnesses every word might be established. Just as St. Paul said to the church at

Corinth: "If any man speak in an unknown tongue, let one interpret. But if there be no interpreter, let him keep silence." Even as it was, mistakes crept in after awhile; and some of the later Targums are in part very fanciful and untrustworthy. Yet they were in general use; and the dying words of our Lord himself, as they are told in Matt. xxvii. 46, are from the Targum or Chaldee version of the Psalms. But this first Targum of all, on the Pentateuch, being the oldest Jewish writing upon the Scriptures, was always held by the Jews as of the highest authority; and proves how those to whom the law was first committed, understood its words. And now we come back to our starting point. In this old Targum, the word which in our English translation is Jehovah, the LORD; this is generally explained by Memra — the Word. Thus *Memra* created the world, *Memra* went before the Israelites in the pillar of cloud and of fire; appeared to Moses on Sinai, and to Abraham at his tent door.'

'And so this is our story, mamma,' said Gracie after a pause, — 'this is what we are to study: " The Word was made flesh." Mamma, until you begin to think and know a little what that name really means, the text seems like nothing, in comparison. Why it is one of the most glorious verses in the whole Bible!'

'Yes, just think!' said Cyril, — 'the Word that created heaven and earth, and that called to Moses out of the burning bush, and that gave the law on

Sinai, — that very Word "was made flesh and dwelt among us!"'

'It seems odd that John chose just that name for the very beginning of his gospel, though,' said Mabel, 'instead of some of the grand splendid titles from the Old Testament.'

'The names of our Lord Jesus are very many,' said mamma, 'and it is hard to call one grander than another; although some may be more precious to us. They are like the many crowns which John in the Revelation saw resting upon his head. But each of the four writers who were to tell the story of his life upon earth, chose first some name which teaches the work he came to do. In Matthew it is "Jesus Christ, the Son of David," and in Mark, "Jesus Christ the Son of God;" while Luke says simply "Jesus," and John takes his peculiar name "The Word."'

'Mamma,' said Gracie, who had been in a profound study down on the floor, 'in this place in Revelation it says the Lord had another name, which no man knew. What does that mean?'

'I suppose it means, how little we yet know of Him who is from everlasting. "Clouds and darkness are round about him;" and we know him only through clouds and mists, and by reflected light. "Wherefore is it that thou dost ask after my name?" he said to Jacob, — and again to Manoah, "Wherefore askest thou thus after my name, seeing it is secret?" "His name shall be called Wonderful," said the prophet Isaiah.

"There shall no man see my glory, and live," said the Lord to Moses; and so no thought of man can conceive what yet the saints shall know. And perhaps of all the promises to them who shall stand in the heavenly Jerusalem, there is not one of more grand fulness than this: "I will write upon him my new name."'

'"They shall see his face, and his name shall be in their foreheads,"' Gracie repeated, — 'O mamma!'

'But how do all those other names tell of the Lord's work on earth?' said Mabel. 'They're just names.'

'Just names that mean something. They are not English words, you know, most of them, but they have a meaning. If you put every word of that first verse of Mark into English, it will read something like this: "The beginning of the good news of the Saviour, the Anointed, the Son of God."'

'Ah that's beautiful!' said Gracie. '"The beginning of the good news." — O how glad they must have been to write it!'

Then our mother answered in her sweet voice:

'"How beautiful upon the mountains are the feet of him that bringeth good tidings, that publisheth peace; that bringeth good tidings of good, that publisheth salvation; that saith unto Zion, Thy God reigneth!"'

The glorious words sounded through our little room like a strain of music; and I saw Sue look up at her mother's face, as if wondering whether the sudden light and sweetness came from thence.

'Mamma,' she said, 'sing!' — and softly at first, then with the joining voices of all her young choir, our mother sang, —

> "How sweet the name of Jesus sounds,
>   In a believer's ear!
> It soothes his sorrows, heals his wounds,
>   And drives away his fear."

Chapter III.

THE LAND.

'AND now,' said Sue, as she climbed into our mother's lap, and established herself in great comfort, 'now we're going to Canaan! Mamma said so.'

'Canaan is an ugly name,' said Mabel; 'it sounds so old fashioned.'

'Very old fashioned, indeed,' answered mamma; 'nearly as old as the Deluge and the Tower of Babel. Canaan was Noah's grandson, — the fourth son of Ham; and when the Lord confounded the language of those proud builders in the Plain of Shinar, and they were scattered abroad upon the face of the earth, "after their tongues, in their countries, and in their nations," — then Canaan and his sons settled in this land, which we call Palestine. They were thereafter its possessors, and Canaan is its first Bible name.

'Three hundred years passed by, and then God gave the land to Abraham and his seed, by promise, while yet they possessed not a foot of ground within its borders; and so Canaan became the Land of

Promise : "The land which God sware unto Abra-ham." '

'Mamma, how long was it only the promised land?' said Gracie.

'Between four and five hundred years. Then Abraham's seed, delivered from their bondage in Egypt, marched into the land and took possession; and Canaan once more changed names, and became the Land of Israel.'

'Is Palestine a Bible name, too?' asked Cyril.

'Yes; though in the Bible it is applied to only a part of the land, a district on the southwest, that was peopled by a wandering colony from Africa. They were called Philistines, and their land was Philistia, or Palestine, — a name which was after-wards used for the whole country. Then it was " the Glorious Land," to one of the prophets; and to another, " the Holy Land; " because there God had made known his truth and declared his pres-ence as in no other country of all the world. It was " Jehovah's Land," — claimed by the Lord of the whole earth, in some special manner, as his own. He demanded its tithes, its first fruits were sacred unto him. " The land shall not be sold for ever," he said to the Israelites, " for the land is mine." Long before our Lord Jesus had really come, it was called " Thy Land, O Immanuel; " and now since he has dwelt there; since Palestine alone, of all the earth, has been trodden by him, it must be for ever both glorious and holy to us.

'See,' said mamma, turning to her map, ' it lies

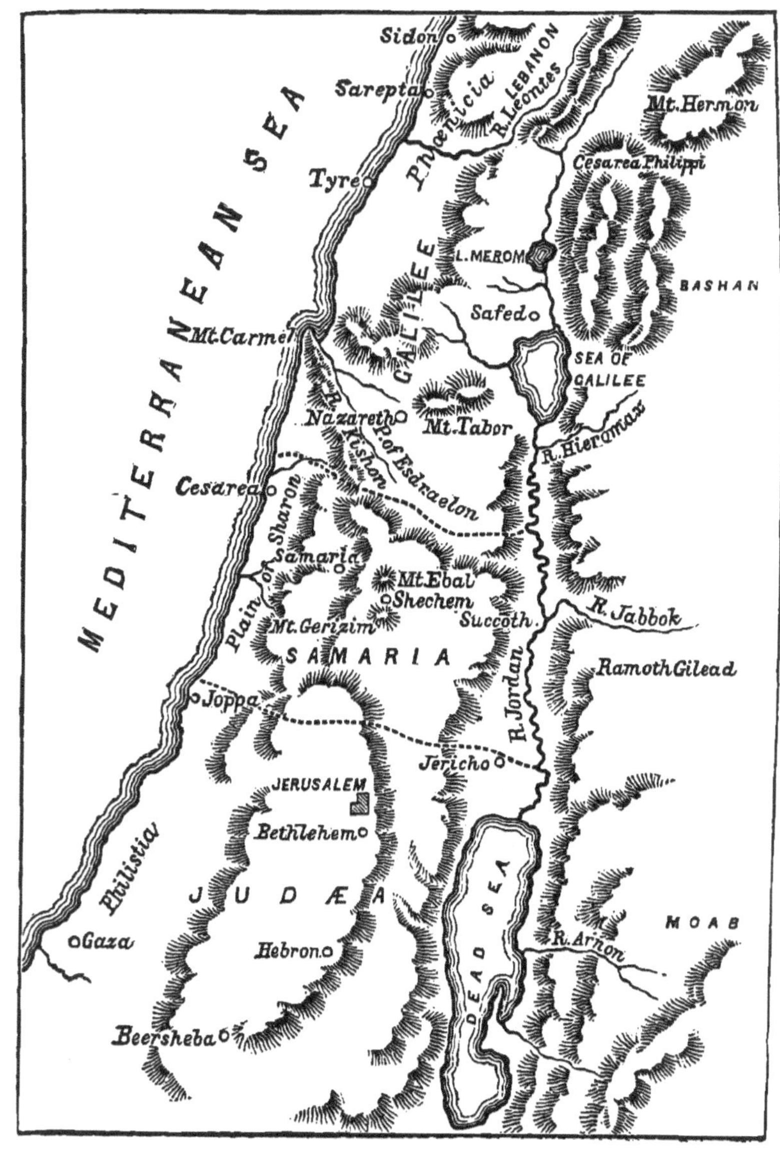

MEDITERRANEAN SEA
Sidon
Sarepta
Phoenicia
R. Leontes
LEBANON
Mt. Hermon
Tyre
Cesarea Philippi
GALILEE
L. MEROM
BASHAN
Safed
Mt. Carmel
SEA OF GALILEE
Nazareth
R. Kishon
Mt. Tabor
R. Hieromax
Cesarea
P. of Esdraelon
Plain of Sharon
Samaria
Mt. Ebal
Shechem
Succoth
R. Jabbok
Mt. Gerizim
SAMARIA
Ramoth Gilead
Joppa
R. Jordan
Jericho
JERUSALEM
Bethlehem
Philistia
JUDÆA
DEAD SEA
MOAB
Gaza
Hebron
R. Arnon
Beersheba

here, in the eastern hemisphere, on the west edge of the great continent of Asia. A little strip of country, not larger than the two States of Massachusetts and Connecticut, cut off and set aside, as it were, from all the world. On the north rise the snow-capped ranges of Lebanon ; on the south lie the parched deserts of Arabia ; the Mediterranean Sea divides it from Europe on the west ; and on the east another desert, three hundred miles wide, comes between it and the rest of Asia. On this side, too, the deep, deep valley of the Jordan forms a yet more difficult barrier, so that whatever part of the territory of Israel at any time lay to the east of Jordan, might be considered as outside of the natural limits and defences.'

'I should have thought,' said Cyril, 'that the Lord would have chosen some great country in which to dwell, — and Palestine is only a mere strip, as you say.'

'Yes, we should have thought,' mamma answered; 'but our thoughts are not like his. And you will find, all through the gospel story, that the Lord did not choose great things, either for himself or his people. His kingdom is not of this world.'

'And no subject who loved his king would want to be stationed in a foreign country,' said Gracie.

'He might be stationed there for a time, on duty,' said mamma, smiling; 'but his reward must be in the presence of his king. It is the subjects who " seek their own," that are *rewarded* with foreign service. Yes, Palestine is very small, and yet it is the glory and wonder of the world. "I have set Jerusalem in the midst of the nations round about her," said the Lord by his prophet. The oldest nations of the world were on either hand: Greece, with her arts and learning, and Old-World civilization; "the broad wall of Babylon," "the pomp of Egypt;" but "in Judah was God known: his name was great in Israel." And now every inch of the ground is sacred, every rock and hill has a history touching the people of God; their foes, their weakness, their strength. Somewhere in the deep bed of the Jordan, lie the twelve stones that mark where the priests stood, when Israel passed over before the Lord; somewhere in the valley of Elah is the pebble that smote Goliath to the earth. The rocks have been altars; the hilltops mounts of sacrifice. The stones where Abraham bound his son, stretching forth his hand to slay the lad, are there still; and those other stones where Jacob dreamed his wonderful dream. The earth has drunk the blood of whole "armies of the aliens;" of hosts "fighting for the Lord against the mighty;" the old pathways are worn with the footsteps of the twelve tribes of Israel; the well-curbs are cut deep with their bucket ropes. Here, mingled with the common earth, or hidden in the caves on the hillside, is all that earth could keep of Abraham, and Jacob, and Joseph; of David, the man after God's own heart; of Deborah, and Gideon, and Samuel; waiting till the trumpet of recall shall sound. Small as Palestine is, it is yet the

most varied of all lands, and must once have been
exceeding lovely. Now, in the time of its forsaking and degradation, we can but guess what it was
when God called it, above all countries of the
earth, " My Land." It was " a goodly land," then,
and a " pleasant ; " but no one can tell now what
special light and beauty hung around it, in the
days when it was : " A land which the Lord thy
God careth for : the eyes of the Lord thy God are
always upon it, from the beginning of the year even
unto the end of the year." Now, it is " utterly
ruined and spoiled." '

'How do the Jews feel about it, now ? ' said Cyril.

'Ah, it is still the centre of the world to them ;
the one spot of all the earth. Still they call it by
that proud Jewish name, " the Land." Denying
the Messiah, whose coming was its chief glory, they
look back to the old times when the unseen presence of the Lord dwelt there within the veil. They
count its very stones and dust and air, sacred ; and
from every corner of the world whither they are
now scattered, they wander back, poor, despised,
unknown, — to die and be buried in the Promised
Land. For the Lord shall yet inherit Judah, and
shall choose Jerusalem again.

'If you look on the map, you will see that a broad
range or platform of hills runs quite through Palestine, from north to south, with but one break, where
at the lower edge of Galilee the great plain of Es-
daelon cuts through the hills, and opens a highway
from Jordan to the sea. Dr. McLeod compares the

range to a broad, flat-bottomed boat, with corrugated sides, turned upside down in the midst of the land.'

'What are corrugated sides?' said Cyril.

'Corrugations are wrinkles. The sides of boats are sometimes ridged, or wrinkled, to add to their strength; but the deep, deep wrinkles in the sides of this great platform, are made by ravines and water-courses to the lowland, worn by the torrents of six thousand years. Its top ridge is the water-shed of the country.'

'Well, I don't know what a water-shed is,' said Mabel.

'Carry out Dr. McLeod's image, and suppose the boat to have a narrow keel, do you see how all the rain which fell upon this keel would not lodge there, but would run off down to the low country on either side? The water-shed of a country, or of a continent, is that highest ridge of land from which the rains pour down on either side after this fashion. At the foot of the Palestine hills, there is on each side a broad border of lowland; on the west the sea-coast plain, which is in some places ten or fifteen miles wide, and to which the platform hills slope down through another range of gentler heights and broad rich valleys. But on the east, the edge of the hill country stands like a dark wall, steep, precipitous, with wild clefts and gorges, overlooking the valley of the Jordan, some ten or fifteen hundred feet below.'

'How broad is this platform, mamma?' said Cyril.

'Fifteen miles in some places, twenty in others, while the breadth of the whole land is nowhere more than ninety miles, and its extreme length a hundred and fifty-eight. More than half of this area lies west of the Jordan, and there almost all the scenes of our wonderful story were laid, — in the original Promised Land. So near are the boundaries, so wonderfully clear the air, that from many a hilltop the surrounding countries are in sight. From almost every point you can see the purple mountains of Moab, rising up in a long straight wall beyond the Jordan valley ; and when you turn to the west, there is the blue sea line, with its border of white sand. So may David's gaze have passed from the one to the other when he sang : "The sea is his, and he made it ; the strength of the hills is his also." '

'Mamma,' said Gracie, 'it is just like the Holy Land where believers live ! — there is the world on one side and eternity on the other. And God careth for it always.'

'Gracie's imagination !' said Cyril, with a laugh. 'What becomes of the other two boundaries, poetess ?'

'Why, the desert is the way by which we came up out of Egypt, — sin and slavery lie there. And the ranges of Lebanon are " the hills unto which I .ift up mine eyes," ' added the child, gazing out at our own mountains, all tipped with the sunset glory.

'I don't see what that has to do with Lebanon,'

said Mabel; 'I dare say the mountains of Moab were a great deal prettier.'

But our mother answered, in her sweet way, —

'"Will a man leave the snow of Lebanon, which cometh from the rock of the field? or shall the cold flowing waters that come from another place be forsaken?"' and Gracie laid her face down on mamma's hand, and was still with pleasure.

'Mamma, what did you mean by its being a *varied* land?' Cyril asked.

'I mean a land with the utmost variety of climate and production, as well as of surface. At one time snow, at another fierce tropical heat; the northern boundary always snow-clad, the Jordan valley often like a furnace: a country where the cold-loving oaks, and walnuts, and maples, are as much at home, as the orange trees and bananas that glow and ripen in the plain of Sharon. It is hard to tell, at first, whether one sees more of such old friends as apples and plums and nuts, or of such new acquaintances as olives, figs, and pomegranates. Almost everything will grow there with proper care. It is just so with the animals, too, — familiar little sparrows chattering upon the house-tops, and tall camels striding away across the sand. Nowhere, in all the world, are so many distinct regions represented, as in this little country of Palestine; and thus the allusions and illustrations and images of the Bible, are in a sort familiar to "every nation under heaven." Desert plains and snow-clad mountains; cultivated fields, wild val-

Chapter IV.

THE OLD PRIEST.

THE children had gathered round the table and were poring over the great map which lay there. Then mamma opened another book, and shewed us two or three smaller maps, with different divisions.

'At the time when our Lord came upon earth,' she said, ' the land was all cut up into Roman provinces. It had once been portioned out into twelve lots, as you see it here, for the twelve tribes of Israel; it had been gathered first into one monarchy, then into two, as here; it had been conquered by the Assyrians, and ruled by Persian satraps; had been subject to the Greek empire, under Alexander the Great, and to Egypt and the Ptolemies. After that, the people roused up and gained their independence for a while; but not being at peace among themselves, Rome sent her legions, under Pompey the Great, and settled all disputes by taking the whole country into her own hands. This was about sixty three years before our story begins. The divisions now were three: Judæa to the south, then

Samaria, then Galilee; while the land east of Jordan was portioned out into five more. Each province was governed for Rome, though the governors were not always themselves Romans; and thus it happened.that a young Edomite boy, named Herod, was first made ruler of Galilee by Julius Cæsar, and then was put by Antony in command of Judæa, with the title of king.'

'Was that Mark Antony, who fought in Egypt and married Cleopatra?' said Cyril.

'The very same.'

'Edom was Esau, wasn't he, mamma?' said Gracie.

'Yes; and so it came to pass that Herod, the descendant of Esau, was set to rule over the descendants of that very Jacob who had bought Esau's birthright, and stolen his blessing. This was a little more than thirty years before our Lord came. To the Jews, Judæa was the most sacred part of the whole land. Here was Jerusalem, the holy city, and in Jerusalem that temple of God whither all the tribes had gone up to worship for hundreds of years. And although the first temple, built by Solomon, had been long ago destroyed by invaders, yet to the second, rebuilt upon the same place, the Jews gave much of the old reverence and devotion. One of the first things Herod did to gain favour, and to cover the cruelties with which he had established his throne, was to build anew some parts of this temple; enlarging, and adding, and adorning, until it covered twice as much ground as ever before. And though the Jews were a conquered people, still they kept up the temple service; and there was the daily sacrifice, and the throng of priests, and all the old ceremonies, with which their heathen conquerors thought best not to interfere.

' " Now there was in the days of Herod, the king of Judæa, a certain priest named Zacharias, of the course of Abia." '

' Ah! that sounds like business,' said Cyril; 'what was "the course of Abia," if you please, ma'am ? '

' The priests you know,' answered mamma, ' were a company of men set apart for the temple service and all things connected with it. They had the temple itself in charge; they prepared the shew bread, they offered the sacrifices.'

' Yes, I know,' said Cyril; 'and they were all from the tribe of Levi. Aaron was the first; he was high priest; and then his sons were other priests.'

' In the early times,' said mamma, 'while Aaron's descendants were yet few, they could all be employed together in the various duties of the priesthood. But by the time King David came to the throne, the priests were a multitude, and could not possibly all serve at once. So David divided them by lot into twenty-four sets or courses, each one of which should serve in turn, a week at a time; and each course was named after one of its chief men. If you turn to the twenty-fourth chapter of First Chronicles, you will see how the courses were

arranged; and there you will find that the eighth
course came to Abijah, the Abia of whom Luke
speaks here.'

'And did the whole course serve together?'
asked Cyril.

'At first, I suppose. But when the number of
priests had again increased too much for even this
arrangement, then each course was divided into
seven families; and each of these families took a
single day of that week of service which belonged to
the whole course. The new course always came in
at midday on the Sabbath; the morning sacrifice
was offered by the outgoing set of priests, and then
the next set were there all ready for the evening
sacrifice at night. This priest, Zacharias, was an
old man. He and his wife were both well stricken
in years, and his wife was of the like noble lineage
with himself; " she was of the daughters of Aaron,
and her name was Elisabeth." But far better than
that, " they were both righteous before God," —
righteous in his eyes who looks not on the outward
appearance, but on the heart; for they walked " in
all the ordinances and commandments of the Lord,
blameless." '

' Then they were a fine old couple, that's all,' said
Cyril.

' Cyril! ' said Mabel, — ' how disrespectful to speak
so of anybody in the Bible ! '

' Mamma,' said Sue, ' how can people walk in
commandments ? '

' When day by day, and hour by hour, in every

little or in every great thing, they try to know the will of God and to do it.'

'That must take a great deal of time,' said Mabel.

'Nay,' said mamma, 'there is no loitering in such a life. David even said, "I will run the way of thy commandments." It came to pass in those days of which we were speaking, that the course of Abia came up to Jerusalem for its week of service; and while Zacharias executed the priest's office before God, in the order of his course, "his lot was to burn incense when he went into the temple of the Lord." For as the different offices were very many, and some were counted more honourable than others, they were always distributed among the priests of each family by lot.'

'Mamma, why do you never like to have us draw lots ?' said Cyril.

'Because casting lots is either an infidel or a religious thing, — not to be used at all in the one sense, nor ever carelessly used in the other.'

'Religious, and infidel !' said Cyril, — 'why I thought it was just chance.'

'There is no such thing in the world,' said mamma; 'it is just as heathenish to talk about chance, as it is to talk about Mars and Venus. When the old Greeks put their dice or pebbles, their black and white beans, or their little clods of earth into a vessel, for the drawing of lots, first of all they made supplication to the heathen gods to direct them, and all lots were called sacred to Mercury. Among the Jews, on the other hand, it was purely a religious service. They decided everything by lot: the choice of soldiers for an expedition, the dividing of the spoil when the fight was done. The land was divided among the tribes by lot; every man's inheritance being in the place where his lot fell; and in all difficult cases of crime and judgment, the matter was decided by lot.'

'Well, then it seems to be a very good thing,' said Mabel.

'Listen, and see how they did it: "Ye shall be brought according to your tribes," said Joshua; "and it shall be, that the tribe which the Lord taketh shall come according to the families thereof, and the family which the Lord shall take shall come by households; and the household which the Lord shall take shall come man by man." "Saul said unto the Lord God of Israel, Give a perfect lot." "And the disciples prayed, and said: Thou, Lord, which knowest the hearts of all men, shew whether of these two thou hast chosen. . . . And they gave forth their lots, and the lot fell upon Matthias." '

The children were somewhat in a muse at this, being like most children, fond of the forbidden amusement; and Mabel said, half under her breath, —

'But we never prayed over it, — of course *that* would be different.'

Mamma answered, —

' "The lot is cast into the lap, but the whole disposing thereof is of the Lord." '

'And so God disposed it that Zacharias should burn incense that day,' said Sue. 'What was the incense, my pretty mamma?'

'The incense used in the temple service, and long before that in the tabernacle, was made of four particular sweet spices, and in a special way, exactly according to God's commandment. It was "a perfume, a confection after the art of the apothecary, tempered together, pure and holy." No one might make any like it for his own use or pleasure; it was for the Lord's service, and that alone. "It shall be unto you most holy," said the Lord to Moses. Jewish tradition declares that there was one particular family of priests whose duty it was to prepare the incense; and one special part of the temple was set apart for the work, and called "the house of Abtines," from the family name of these priests. There constant watch was kept, that the incense might be always ready. So to this day in some of the great temples in India, there is kept a man whose business it is to distil sweet waters from flowers, and spicy oils from the scented woods, for the heathen services in the temple.'

'To burn before their idols!' said Gracie. 'Mamma, they must have learned that from the Jews.'

'Very possibly; and as it was death for a Jew to make any of this holy incense for himself, so in certain parts of India it is high treason for any subject

to use the best sort of a certain sweet spice or com
pound ; it must be kept for the king.'

'Mamma,' said Sue, 'what did the incense mean ?
what was it for? Did God like it?'

'Everything in the old temple service meant
something,' answered mamma; 'and by studying
the use we can sometimes get at the meaning. See
how it was with the incense. It was perpetual.
Day by day the fragrant cloud went up from the
altar of incense, the sweetness of the morning lingering in the temple until the censer was brought
in at night : fit emblem of the pleading of him who
ever liveth to make intercession for us ; and as he is a
priest upon his throne, so the golden altar was mounted with a crown and touched with the blood of atonement. But " no strange incense " might be offered
there, there is no other name given whereby we
may be saved; neither might any other offering
be added to it : our trust must be in Christ alone.
This was the " perpetual incense," — ever ascending before the mercy seat ; for through him only we
have access unto God, — and this its constant, daily
use. Then on the great day of atonement, that
one time in all the year when the high priest
went into the Most Holy Place, the incense must
be his surety and defence. "He shall take a censer
full of burning coals of fire from off the altar before
the Lord, and his hands full of sweet incense beaten
small, and bring it within the vail: and he shall
put the incense upon the fire before the Lord, that
the cloud of the incense may cover the mercy seat

that is upon the testimony, that he die not." Such was the old command. Or if the sins of the people had brought down judgments upon their heads, then again the incense brought deliverance. "Take a censer," said Moses to Aaron, " and put fire thereon from off the altar, and put on incense," "for there is wrath gone out from the Lord; the plague is begun." And Aaron did so, and ran in among the congregation, and " stood between the living and the dead, and the plague was stayed." '

'It's the same old word, mamma,' said Gracie: ' " If ye shall ask anything in my name, I will do it." And oh, *that's* what it means in the Revelation! — " There was given to the angel much incense, that he should offer it with the prayers of saints." But why was the altar of incense *outside* the veil ? '

'Because " the way into the holiest of all was not yet made manifest;" the time was not come. Then, the priest trembled to approach the mercy seat, even with the pleading cloud of incense in his hand; but now, we may all " come boldly." Yet only through Christ, — there must be no " strange incense," no other offering.'

'Well, mamma,' said Mabel, ' the old priest went into the temple to burn incense.'

'Yes, it was his lot; and as a special blessing was thought to belong to this office, so special care was taken that it should come to every priest in turn. Twice each day the incense was offered; at the time of the morning and of the evening sacri-

fice. Every morning, as the dawn came on, a crowd
of priests began the daily service in the temple.
One trimmed the lamps, and another cleared away
the cinders from the altar of incense; while others
swept the temple courts, and yet others chose out a
lamb for the burnt offering, and killed and prepared
it to be laid on the great brazen altar.'

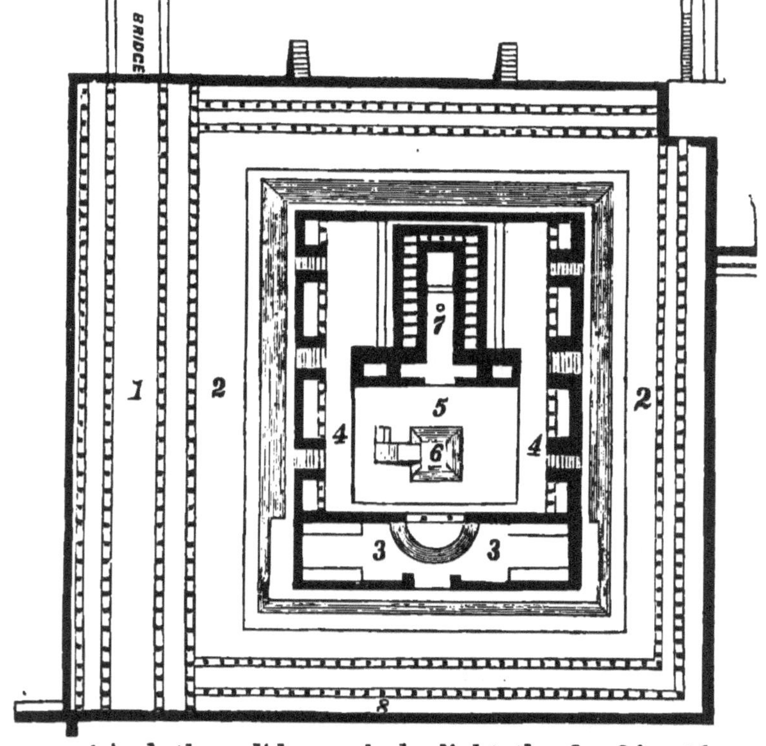

'And then did somebody light the fire?' said
Sue.

'The fire on the brazen altar was kept always

burning; but some of the priests brought fresh wood and laid it on, that all might be ready for the sacrifice. Then another priest went to the house of Abtines for a golden phial full of incense, and carried it into the Holy Place; and a second followed him with a silver shovel of live coals, taken from the altar of burnt offering.'

'Where was the incense burned, mamma?' said Cyril; 'I don't quite understand.'

'Look at this plan of the temple,' said mamma. 'These outer enclosures, the spaces between these first lines, were different courts, divided from each other by rows of columns, and surrounding the place where stood the body of the temple itself. You see in this central space of all, what looks like a long hall in two parts. On three sides of it were small rooms, used by the priests for different purposes, and on the fourth side, the entrance. And directly in front of the entrance, in this square, open court, stood the brazen altar, or altar of burnt offering.'

'And what was the hall for?' asked Mabel.

'The hall was the Sanctuary itself. The long apartment, the one nearest the porch, was called the Holy Place; and beyond that, divided from it by a thick veil or curtain, was the Inner Sanctuary — the Most Holy Place. There, within the veil and hidden by it, was the mercy seat, over which continually rested the glory of God; and just outside the veil, in the Holy Place, stood the altar of incense. It was made of wood, and overlaid with

pure gold on every side. Hither came the priest
with the great golden dish which held the phial of
incense,.and setting it down, he bowed towards the
Holy of Holies, and went out; and then came the
other with his silver shovel of coals, and pouring
them into a smaller shovel made of gold, so that
some of the coals were spilled, he placed this on
the golden altar; then, bowing reverently, he too
went out, and the priest whose lot it was to burn
incense entered alone.'

'Mamma,' said Gracie eagerly, 'why did they
bring more coals than enough? Was it to shew
that "grace doth much more abound"?'

'You may see that in it, at all events,' said mamma; 'the love and pity and forgiveness at which
all hearts in the world might be kindled, but which
very many despise and tread under foot.'

'But why did they take so much trouble about
the coals?' said Mabel; 'they might have lighted
it from the lamps, just as well.'

'Not "just as well," when the Lord's command
was different. To use "strange fire" was a great
offence; and two of Aaron's sons were struck dead
in a moment for presuming to do it.'

'There must be no intercession but Christ's, and
his only through his blood, just as it is now,' said
Gracie; 'I see it so plain.'

'Mamma,' said Mabel, 'I think Grace runs off a
great deal! What did the priest do then?'

'He cast the incense on the fire; "and the whole
multitude of the people were praying without at

the time of incense." It is supposed from this, that the day here spoken of was the Sabbath, for on other days there were generally but few people at the temple service ; but this time the whole multitude : each praying silently in his heart; for the time of incense was one of profound stillness all through and around the temple.'

'I don't see why they were praying *without*,' said Cyril ; 'I should think they would have been praying within. That's the way in our churches.'

' But everything about God was far off then, for the one true and living way into his presence was not yet fully made known ; and so though people went up into the temple to pray, yet they never could venture near the mercy seat. Even David himself might not, but must worship at a distance, chosen king of Israel though he was. " I will pay my vows in the courts of the Lord's house," he said : " My soul fainteth for the courts of the Lord." And now at the time of incense, even the space between the brazen altar and the porch was cleared ; and the people stood and prayed either quite outside the temple, or in some of its outer courts.'

'But, mamma,' said Sue, raising her head, ' if they couldn't go near the mercy seat, what did they do ? Because that's what my hymn says.'

'What does it say, darling ? '

'Why, about the mercy seat,' said Sue, — 'don't you know ?—

> "From every stormy wind that blows,
> From every swelling tide of woes,
> There is a calm, a sure retreat,
> 'Tis found beneath the mercy seat."

Didn't people have any troubles then, mamma?'

'But, pet,' said Mabel, 'that means the mercy seat in heaven. This was only a place in the temple.'

'The mercy seat in the temple was a sign or figure of the one on high,' said mamma; 'with the veil that hung before it, beyond which the people might not go. For until Jesus came, or except to those who fully believed in his coming, God's mercy was a hidden thing. It is "the blood bought mercy seat" before which we lay all our fears, and all our sorrows, we who sometimes were far off, but are now made nigh by the blood of Christ.

'So the multitude were without, praying; and the priests stood ready with their slain lamb; and other priests were there, with their silver trumpets. Overhead, in the open sky above the temple, the glory of sunrise was just beginning to appear, as the priest whose lot it was to burn incense passed into the Holy Place, alone; and taking the phial of incense, poured it out upon the live coals upon the altar. Then as the cloud of sweetness rose up and filled the room, floating in before the mercy seat, and as the heart cry of many a sinner and many a saint went up to God as silently from the multitude without, Zacharias too said his prayer, and bowing in adoration towards the Most Holy Place, was just going away, when "there appeared unto him an angel of the Lord, standing on the right side of the altar of incense; " shining out through the ascending clouds of intercession, a messenger with tidings that the Desire of nations was at hand.'

'Oh, I'd like to see an angel!' said little Sue. 'Mamma, did he have wings?'

'Why, he must have had, or Zacharias wouldn't have known who he was,' said Mabel.

'Nay, there are other angelic tokens beside wings,' said mamma, with a smile; 'and I suppose in this case there was such a bright glory about the stranger, that Zacharias could not doubt for a moment who it was. But for what had he come? The old priest "was troubled, and fear fell upon him."'

'I should think he was too old a man, and had seen too much, to be scared at an angel,' said Cyril.

'But what I wonder at,' said Gracie, 'is that he wasn't delighted. Why, even people who are only going to heaven are beautiful, — but an angel who had just come from there!'—

'Nevertheless, Zacharias was troubled. Had the angel come to charge him with some sin? to smite him for not offering the incense with a pure heart?'

'And then the angel said, "Fear not." Mamma,' said Gracie, 'when people really fear God, I suppose they need never be frightened.'

'Never: and now the angel added to that comforting "fear not," these words of joy: "Thy prayer is heard."'

'Well, I do think,' said Cyril, who had been studying the passage while mamma spoke, ' it was a very queer time and place for a man to pray that he might have a son.'

'I think that was not his prayer,' said mamma. 'Years before he had prayed that, very often; but he was an old man now, and had so long ago given up all hopes of a son, that he was not ready to believe such a promise, even on the word of an angel. But I suppose there was one prayer of which his whole heart was full when he went in to burn incense, — the great national prayer that Christ would come. For the land was trodden under foot of strangers, the people paid tribute, the holy city was a conquered city, — where was that "rod out of the stem of Jesse," whose dominion should be "from sea to sea, and from the river unto the ends of the earth?" who should "stand for an ensign of the people," who should "sit upon the throne of David, to order and to establish it?" When should the fountain be opened for sin and for uncleanness? and the shadow of the great Rock stretch out across that weary land? This was in the old priest's heart as he stood before that veiled mercy seat, and the Desire of nations was on his tongue. It often happens,' mamma continued, ' that God answers many prayers in one; and so here. The angel just touched upon the private, personal joy, — " thy wife Elisabeth shall bear thee a son,"—and then went on to the glorious work that son should do, the glorious herald that he should be. " Thou shalt have joy and gladness," but also " *many* shall rejoice at his birth." " He shall be great in the sight of the Lord," — " And many of the children of Israel shall he turn unto the Lord their God, and shall go before Him ! " '

' Mamma, please stop ! ' said Gracie, ' it is almost too much to think of. Jesus had never come then, the people did not know him, — and now he was coming : " the Lord their God." '

' Zacharias couldn't have cared so very much about it, I should think,' said Mabel, ' or he'd have believed it.'

' Ah,' said mamma, ' it is just the Lord's greatest mercies that most try our faith ; and Zacharias shewed his weakness here, like the rest of us. For a moment he forgot the glad tidings he had heard ; he forgot the glorious promise that his own son should be the first to proclaim them : for a moment he could think of nothing but his old disappointments : and unbelief took them up, and asked, querulously, " Whereby shall I know this ? " '

' I wonder he wasn't struck dead then,' said Mabel.

' The Lord's patience was great then, as it is now,' answered our mother, ' for how often do we read the promises of God with these words hid away in our hearts : — " Whereby shall I know this ? " '

' Well Zacharias did get pretty well punished, said Cyril. ' But I don't see how Gabriel, even though he was an angel, should have dared to tell him he should be dumb. I thought only God could do that.'

'Only God can; but sometimes it pleases him to put honour upon his message, by directing his messenger to pass sentence upon those who will not believe. So Elymas the sorcerer was struck blind at the word of the apostle Paul. And now at the word of the angel, Zacharias became dumb, until the promise which he had doubted should be fulfilled.'

'Mamma, angel means messenger, doesn't it?' said Gracie.

'Yes, Gabriel told at once his glory and his office,—"I stand in the presence of God,"—"I am sent." To stand in the presence, to stand before a king, is an Eastern form of speech, which implies constant, close personal service. "Happy are thy servants," said the Queen of the East to Solomon, "which stand continually before thee." "Seest thou a man diligent in his business?" said the wise king himself upon another occasion: "he shall stand before kings; he shall not stand before mean men." So King Rehoboam "consulted with the old men, that stood before Solomon his father," and then forsook their counsel, and consulted with the young men, "which stood before him." All the officers of the king, whatever their rank, were called servants, and all "stood" when they were in his presence.'

'Mamma, is everybody made dumb who won't believe?' said little Sue.

'Not just in the way Zacharias was. They can speak some things, but have no voice to tell the

loving kindness of the Lord ; and, instead of proclaiming the glad tidings of great joy, they are, like
Zacharias, "dumb, and not able to speak."

' " And the people waited for Zacharias, and marvelled that he tarried so long in the temple." For
a sort of terror hung about that veiled mercy seat,
and the people were always alarmed if the priest
who went in to burn incense made any delay ; fearing he might have done something presumptuously,
and perhaps been struck dead for his crime, bringing judgments on all the nation. Therefore it was
the habit of the priest to stay but a very little
while, to make but a short prayer, and then hasten
out to the people. And now when he tarried, they
marvelled. And when at last he came, he could
not tell them what was the matter, for he was
speechless.'

' Did the people think that was a judgment ? '
said Mabel.

' The old priest made signs to them, — signs of
joy and not of fear, — and they perceived that he
had seen a vision ; no such unheard of thing in those
days. And then the temple service went on ; the
sacrifice was consumed upon the brazen altar ; and
as the smoke rose up into the clear blue sky, the
priests sounded a burst of joy and praise on their
silver trumpets. For that was the daily custom,
as soon as the priest whose lot it was to burn incense came out from the Holy Place. But how it
must have sounded to the heart of Zacharias that
day ! for *he* knew that it was the first flourish of

trumpets that announced the herald of the long promised Messiah, the King of Israel. The Jews have a tradition that this sounding of the silver trumpets could always be heard as far as Jericho; but it seems as if on that morning it might have echoed round the world! until again "the morning stars sang together," and "the mountains and all hills praised the Lord."'

'You say this was at the *morning* sacrifice, mamma?' said Cyril.

'I said that, for it always seems to me as if the first announcement of the Light of the world must have been at daybreak; but the Bible does not tell. It only says that when Zacharias had accomplished all the days of his ministrations, he departed to his own house.'

'Mamma,' said Sue, suddenly looking up with her very studious little face, 'did Zacharias wear a black coat?'

'Why no, Sue!' said mamma smiling, — 'as far from that as possible! On the contrary, he wore a white one; and it was not what you would call a coat at all, but a long white robe which reached to his feet. It had long, loose sleeves, and was bound around the waist with a broad girdle of linen, woven in a sort of scale pattern, and embroidered with flowers in purple, scarlet, white, and dark blue. This girdle was passed twice round the waist, then tied in a knot in front, leaving ends which hung down nearly to the floor. The priest's feet were bare, and on his head was a sort of linen cap or mitre. But this dress was only worn when he was ministering in the temple, and never anywhere else. The priests came to the temple in their ordinary dress, and put on the linen robes there, and put off their shoes; for even in Egypt, among heathen people, it was a sign of reverence for the priests to perform their service barefoot.'

Chapter V

THE MESSAGE TO MARY.

'MAMMA,' said little Sue, when we were all together the next afternoon, 'I want to hear some more about the angel. Didn't he ever come again?'

'He came again in six months.'

'Oh, to see the old priest?' said Sue, looking very much interested.

'No, not to Zacharias this time. Zacharias, you remember, was in the temple at Jerusalem, in Judæa, when the heavenly visiter came to him; but now "the angel Gabriel was sent from God unto a city of Galilee,"—the most northern province of all.'

'Gabriel, again,' said Cyril. 'I wonder if all the other angels were as busy.'

'Those who "alway do God's commandments" are not likely to be idle,' said mamma; 'and those who "minister to the heirs of salvation" will find enough to do; but there was one special piece of work on earth that seems to have been always entrusted to Gabriel,—it was to proclaim the coming of the Lord Jesus.'

'He told the old priest that his little boy should go before the Lord,' said Sue.

'That was not the first time Gabriel had come to earth on his particular mission. More than four hundred years before that morning when he stood by the altar of incense, Gabriel had appeared to the prophet Daniel, in Babylon, and told him how soon the Lord should come.'

'I didn't know there was anything about angels in the book of Daniel,' said Cyril.

'He is called simply "Gabriel," and "the man Gabriel," for "he had the appearance of a man." Daniel saw him first in a vision; and then one day, as he was speaking and praying and presenting his supplication, "the man Gabriel, being caused to fly swiftly," came to the prophet and talked with him about Messiah the Prince, and told him just how long it would be, until the Lord should come and make an end of sins, and bring in everlasting righteousness.'

'And when four hundred years had passed,' said Gracie, 'then Gabriel was sent again. How he must have longed for the time to come! And then he told Zacharias that his son should be the Lord's herald. Gabriel must be a happy angel, mamma.'

'He was a highly honoured one too; the only angel who is often mentioned by name in the Bible. And strangely enough, people who do not believe the Bible, nor worship Jesus, yet know this story, and give honour to Gabriel because he was the Lord's servant and announced his birth. There is no angel so popular among all the Moslems of the East.'

'Why, who do they think Jesus was?' said Mabel.

'A great prophet, — nothing more. Both Persians and Turks give him a sort of reverence; and thereupon claim the special friendship of Gabriel, and suppose this particular angel to be the special enemy of the Jews.'

'But they reject the Lord just as much as the Jews did,' said Cyril. 'I don't see the difference.'

'There is none,' said mamma: 'to reject Jesus as the Son of God, is really to reject him altogether; but some think they may believe and give honour in their own way, and not according to the word of the Lord. So the Turks and Persians call Gabriel their friend, and the Persians give him a name which is doubtless very grand in Eastern ears, though it sounds strange to us; they call him "the Peacock of Paradise."'

The children all laughed at this, except Sue, and she said, indignantly, —

'I guess *they* don't see angels much! Mamma, when Gabriel went to Galilee, what did he do?'

'He went into a city of Galilee which is called Nazareth, to the house where a poor girl lived, named Mary.'

'Why, mamma,' said Cyril, looking up from his Bible, 'how do you know she was poor? — if you please.'

'I know from other things in the story; and

here it tells that she was espoused — or betrothed
—to a man named Joseph, — and he was a carpenter.'

'I thought espoused meant married,' said Mabel.

'Not always: among the Jews espousal meant
much the same as our word betrothed, or engaged;
only it was more formal, and held to be as binding
as the marriage itself. The contract was made between the friends of the bride and the friends of
the bridegroom, with a feast, and with gifts and
solemn oaths; and after that the parties were considered man and wife, though ten or twelve months
generally passed before the marriage. A betrothed
woman might not give away her property, nor the
man choose another wife, unless the contract of espousal was done away by a regular divorce. Thus
Mary — or Miriam, for the names are one — had
been espoused to Joseph; a man of the royal blood
of the house of David, though by trade he was but
a carpenter; and before the time came for the marriage, while she was living quietly there in Nazareth, unknown and unheard of in the great world,
the angel Gabriel was sent from God direct to her.
And the angel said: "Hail, highly favoured, the
Lord is with thee: blessed art thou among women." '

'Mamma,' said Mabel, 'I used to think it would
be nice to see angels; but in the Bible everybody
seems to be frightened.'

'I think Mary was more perplexed than frightened,' said mamma; 'it was his *saying* that

troubled her, — not his appearance. "She cast in her mind what manner of salutation this should be," for it was different from any she had ever heard. People always gave each other religious greetings in those days, but the usual form was a sort of wish or prayer: "The Lord be with thee"—or, "Blessed be thou of the Lord," and Mary would have understood such a salutation well enough. But the angel spoke to her as to one towards whom the divine favour was not only certain, but also very great and special: "Joy to thee, highly favoured, the Lord is with thee" — "thou art blessed." Mary was well accustomed to be passed by and overlooked; perhaps not one of her rich neighbours had ever sent her so much as a message of courtesy; and now on a sudden such words from the King of kings, brought by a special messenger, were almost overwhelming. No wonder she was troubled at his saying.'

'And then she went to thinking directly what it might mean,' said Gracie. 'I suppose that is what we should do always with God's words, whether they trouble us or not.'

'Always. But there was another reason why Mary pondered. Ever since the promise of joy God gave in Eden, — that the seed of the woman should bruise the serpent's head, — ever since then, from age to age, many a righteous woman had hoped that her son might prove to be the promised Deliverer. The promise at first was indistinct, — "the seed of the woman," — it should be one of

Eve's descendants, that was all. Then God said to Abraham, "In thy seed shall all families of the earth be blessed," — salvation should be of the Jews. Then Jacob, taught by the Lord what should "befall his twelve sons," declared that from the tribe of Judah should He come, unto whom the gathering of the people should be; and still later the Lord said, "David shall never want a man to sit on the throne." Henceforth the Messiah was looked for from David's line alone, — "the rod out of the stem of Jesse," which should stand for an ensign of the people. And now when the angel said to Mary — herself of the tribe of Judah and the house of David — "Blessed art thou among women," — no wonder she mused; for of whom should that be true, but of the mother of him so long hoped for and expected. And the thought was so full of amazement, so full of awe, that Mary might well have sunk almost fainting at the angel's feet. But the angel said, "Fear not, Mary, for thou hast found favour with God." '

'Gabriel wanted her to think of that first, I suppose,' said Gracie. 'Like the old words, mamma, "The joy of the Lord is your strength." '

'But who can tell how the words fell on the ear and sunk into the heart of her who listened, as the angel unfolded his message! "Thou shalt bring forth a son, and shalt call his name JESUS." And then, as he had done with Zacharias, the angel went on to give the promise in detail; but how different this one from the other! That child should

indeed be great, and should do wonderful things;
but of Jesus it was said, "He shall be great, and
shall be called the Son of the Highest : and the
Lord God shall give unto him the throne of his
father David; and he shall reign over the house of
Jacob for ever; and of his kingdom there shall be
no end."'

'No end — no end!' Gracie repeated. 'Mamma,
it does one good just to say over those words.'

'I guess Mary was glad then,' said little Sue.

'She was so glad, and so humble, that it never
seemed to enter her mind to say how many women
there were in Judæa more worthy of this wondrous
honour than she.'

'So humble, mamma?' said Mabel. 'Why, I
should think being humble would have made her
say it.'

'I do not call it being humble to think we know
better than the Lord,' said mamma; 'and Mary
had just been told that he had chosen *her*. The
humility which shrinks back from God's appointment is often but the coldness of heart which
slights the honour, or the sloth which dreads the
work. The angel said unto Mary, "That holy
thing which shall be born of thee shall be called
the Son of God," — "for with God nothing shall be
impossible." And Mary answered: — "Behold the
handmaid of the Lord; be it unto me according to
thy word." When God puts honour upon us, the
most humble thing we can do is to accept it.'

'And then the angel departed,' said Gracie; 'and I dare say he sang all the way back to heaven.'

'Mamma,' said Sue, 'I'd like to see the house where Mary lived when the angel came. Was there a big, big window for him to go through?'

'Ah I do not know, Sue, how he went in,' said mamma, while the rest laughed. 'Some people think Mary was not in the house herself when the angel came, but that she had gone to the fountain to draw water, and met him there.'

'And what do you think, mamma?' said Mabel.

'I think the Bible words seem to say she was in the house. But the place matters little, for God can speak, and angels can come, to us, anywhere. One thing more the angel said before he departed; he told Mary of the great joy which had come to Zacharias and Elisabeth; and "in those days" — that is, in the days that followed soon after the coming of the angel — Mary set off on a journey to see Elisabeth, to hear and tell all the wonderful things which had come to pass.'

'Elisabeth was her cousin,' said Cyril.

'Did she go in a carriage, mamma?' asked Sue.

'No, not in a carriage; we may be sure of that. Mary, you know, was living up in the northern province of Galilee; and between her and the hill country of Judæa, lay a distance of a hundred miles. Not miles of railway, nor of smooth, well made road, but of rough hills and deep valleys; with narrow, rugged paths winding up and down, in just the way the camels and donkeys thought best. For in some parts of Palestine they are the chief road-makers. No carriage could be used there then, as none can now: the traveller either journeys on foot, or rides a horse or a donkey, and at a very slow rate. Even the horses cannot trot over much of the road, but go at a sort of fast walk of two or three miles an hour. Mary went "in haste," making what speed she could; yet instead of whirling down to the hill country in a few hours, she must have been several days on the way.'

'But why was it called the hill country,' said Cyril, — ' if there were hills all along?'

'It was the hill country of Judæa, — the hill country which had been part of the inheritance of the tribe of Judah, and which is the south end of the long mountain ranges of Palestine. It is a wild, desolate region now; for " Jerusalem is ruined, and Judah is fallen: because their tongue and their doings were against the Lord, to provoke the eyes of his glory;" and no other land, once cultivated, has ever become so barren and forlorn. The rounded hills, with dry watercourses between, are gray with limestone rocks and low shrubs and herbage; for the forests of Judah have long since disappeared. Ruined terraces, reaching quite to the summit of the hills, yet mark the place of the old vineyards and gardens; and on almost every hill top are the broken walls and fallen buildings of the fenced cities of Judah, towards which the pathway, deep worn in the limestone of the hill, goes

winding up like a white thread. Here and there
you see a town which is yet inhabited, and where
olive trees and vines stand loaded with their rich
fruit ; but neglect and ruin mark all the rest.'

'What are terraces ? ' said Cyril.

'In a country where there is but little level
ground,' said mamma, 'the people often make terraces to get place for their fruit trees and gardens.
A garden planted on the mere face of a steep hill
would soon be cut up and washed away by the rain,
and so the people build walls on the hillside, and
fill the earth in behind them all smooth and level,
and the wall keeps the earth in its place. On
many of those hills of Judah the terraces run round
and round, from the bottom to the very top. There
are the old walls yet, and the broken down watch-
towers ; but in the places where " Judah bound his
foal to the vine," there is little else now but silence
and desolation.'

'Mamma, it didn't look so in Mary's time ? '
said Mabel.

'No, not so ; though just how fast the ruin has
gone on, we do not know. But once, long, long

ago, when "also in Judah things went well," this hill country was the stronghold of the tribe. Then there were forests and palm trees and myrtles among the rocks and caverns; then the streams and springs were more abundant; and the slopes of each city-crowned hill were covered with vineyards and olive groves, and the terrace walls stood strong and perfect. Every vineyard had its watch tower, and Judah "washed his garments in wine, and his clothes in the blood of grapes." '

'Mamma, I shouldn't like to see it now,' said Gracie; 'I would rather think of it as it used to be. Isn't there *anything* left of its old glory?'

'Anything?—yes, one thing,' said mamma,— 'the flowers. It seems as if no curse from heaven or earth could ever rest on them; and in spring time the whole land glows and shines with their wild beauty. Flowers peculiar to Palestine, and in such profusion as I can hardly describe; seeming more like a spread-out cloth of crimson or white or gold, than like little separate blossoms. The spring grass on hill and valley is but thin and short, and over and among that bloom multitudes of daisies, blue hyacinths, and the white star of Bethlehem, with pale brier roses on their prickly stems. But most striking of all are the red flowers,— poppies, wild tulips, anemones; until in some places the land is "a blaze of scarlet," and the anemones "run like fire through the mountain glens." '

'Oh!' the children cried, with a long breath of eager admiration.

'These crimson anemones of Palestine,' mamma went on, 'have gained for themselves a strange name: they are called "blood-drops," — "the blood-drops of the Lord."'

'And that is all that is left of the glory of Judah!' said Gracie mournfully, — '"the blood-drops of the Lord!"'

'Mamma,' said Mabel, 'won't you let it be spring time when Mary went to see Elisabeth? I like to think of her riding among the flowers.'

'We will suppose it was, if you like,' said mamma; 'and along the glowing, dazzling hill-sides, and through the deep flower-strewn ravines, Mary went with haste, to one of those hill-top cities of Judah, not then ruined and cast down. And she entered into the house of Zacharias, and saluted Elisabeth. And even as she spoke, the Spirit of God came with power into the heart of Elisabeth, and she broke forth with the very greeting of the angel: "Blessed art thou among women!" declaring at once her joy, and her unworthiness of so high an honour. Once, the old priest's wife may have thought it an honour to her poor young cousin to come and pay her a visit, but now things were changed. "And whence is this to me," she cried, "that the mother of my Lord should come to me?" Seldom before, perhaps, had those two words — "my Lord" — been so spoken: the whole Bible up to this time gives but one instance. They had been said often enough as a title, as a mere rendering of praise and reverence, a mere form of address; but now with that sense of personal love and possession which only a believer in Christ can know. And as Elisabeth ceased, Mary answered in like words: "My soul doth magnify the Lord, and my spirit hath rejoiced in God my Saviour." Sweeping with a glad hand that "instrument of ten strings," and sounding first the Lord's work, and then his power and goodness, and then those promises which "stand fast for ever." There has been many a thanksgiving among God's people from age to age, and many an outburst of joy and faith; but I think never such a one as was heard that day, in the unknown city in the hill country of Judæa. "And Mary abode with her about three months, and returned unto her own house."'

'Mamma, what was that "one instance"?' Gracie said, as mamma closed her books.

'The only one I remember;— When David said, "The Lord said unto my Lord, Sit thou at my right hand, until I make thine enemies thy footstool."'

Chapter VI.

IN THE HILL COUNTRY.

'WHEREABOUTS in the hill country did Zacharias live, mamma?' said Cyril, leaning his elbows on the table and poring over the map. 'The Bible don't seem to tell.'

'And therefore we do not certainly know; scholars are divided on that point. But far down here among the mountains of Judah, and just where the hill country borders upon the desert, are the ruins of Juttah, — one of the cities of the priests in former days. The hill is partly covered with the buildings of the modern Moslem town of Yuttah; but among and around these lie old walls and foundations, once the dwellings of the worshippers of the true God; and here, it is supposed (by those who should know best) lived Zacharias and Elisabeth. Here, then, was born that child so especially set apart for the service of God, and filled with the Spirit of God even from his birth. Elisabeth's neighbours and friends came to rejoice with her; and when the child was to be named, "they called him Zacharias, after the name of his father." But his mother knew that her son had been already named from heaven, — "Thou shalt call his name John," said the angel, — and now she repeated the words, and answered, "Not so; but he shall be called John." '

'Well that was a great deal prettier name than Zacharias,' said Mabel.

'But in those days, as now, people thought more of pleasing some friend or relation than of giving the baby a pretty name. "They said unto her, There is none of thy kindred that is called by that name." And then, as Elisabeth did not give up her choice, they appealed to Zacharias himself, and made signs to ask how the child should be called.'

'And then Zacharias asked for a writing table — so he was dumb yet,' said Cyril.

'Mamma, why did he ask for the table? — why didn't he just go and sit down and write?' said Sue.

'O that was not what we mean by a table,' said mamma; 'it was a writing *tablet*. People did not know how to make soft sheets of letter paper in those old times, and had to use other things instead. Sometimes they wrote their words upon pieces of metal, sometimes upon slabs of stone; using a hard graver's tool for a pen: such were the two tables of the law which God gave to Moses in Mount Sinai. Sometimes they used long strips of prepared leather, which when they were full could be rolled up and tied, — all the early copies of the books of the Old Testament were written in this way. But the ordinary writing tables were bits of lead or smooth thin strips of wood, sometimes used singly and sometimes tied together, and answering much the same purpose as our slates.'

'But the writing can be rubbed off our slates,' said Cyril.

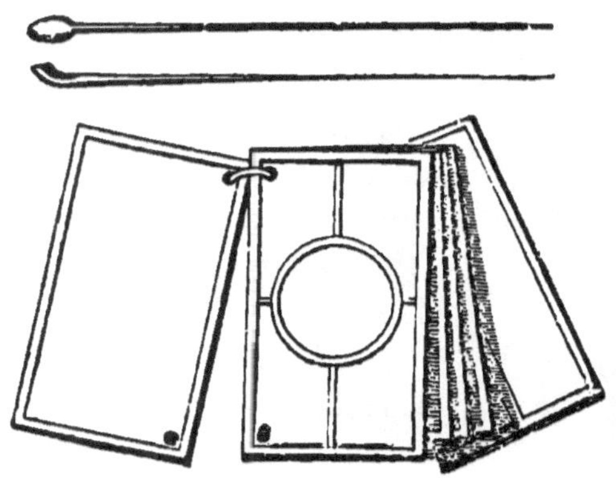

'So it could from these. From the lead tablets it was beaten out, to leave a clear surface for the next occasion; and the chalk marks on the wood were rubbed or scraped off. This is the only sort of slate used in Greek schools to this day. Often the wooden slabs were coated with wax, in which the letters were traced with a sharp steel pencil. See, here is a picture of one. On such tables, it is said, the Old Testament prophets used to write their visions and prophecies; setting them up then in some public place for all the people to see. "Write the vision," said the Lord to the prophet Habbakuk, "and make it plain upon tables, that he may run that readeth it."'

'It must have taken a great while to write so,' said Cyril; 'and I don't see how they could put *any* thing on one of those little tablets. Why, when we go scratch, scratch over the paper, two or three words would fill a line like that.'

'They did not go scratch, scratch, as you call it,' said mamma. 'It was a slower kind of writing, with a different language and a different alphabet. Look at this word "Hebrew"—you see the characters are just such as could be easily made with a sharp, hard point of steel.'

עִבְרִי,

'Well, which sort of table did Zacharias use?' said Mabel.

יוֹחָנָן

'This one in the picture. It is called by the very same word now in Greece that St. Luke used for it eighteen hundred years ago. Just such a writing table as this was brought to Zacharias, with one of those long, sharp steel pencils; and in the soft white wax he traced these words: "His name is John." The people who stood by marvelled; but for Zacharias, with the writing of that word the last sign of his unbelief was swept away: "His mouth was opened immediately, and his tongue loosed, and he spake and praised God."'

'Mamma, how did it show his faith to write that?' said Gracie.

'To give his child the name which the angel had ordered, was to acknowledge that the promise brought by the angel had been fulfilled. "John" means "the gift or mercy of the Lord," — and the old priest had doubted whether such a gift could come to him. But now he acknowledged that this child was indeed "Jehovah's gift" — his mercy: and not only as any child might be, but that he was a sign of that "unspeakable gift" which should follow, — of that mercy of the Lord which is from everlasting to everlasting.'

'And when he had openly set to his seal that God is true,' said Gracie, '*then* his faith was worth something. It was not enough to hide it away in his heart; for he must have believed, as soon as the child was born, — and it was eight days old now.'

'I don't see why the people marvelled,' said Mabel.

'It was perhaps an uncommon name, in the first place,' said mamma. 'So far as we know, but few people had ever borne that name before; the Bible tells of not one. And even the old "Johannan," or "Jehohanan," which means the same as John, had been little known. Perhaps, too, these neighbours and friends were of those who knew the promises, who remembered that God had said, "I will send forth my mercy," — "I will give to Jerusalem one that bringeth good tidings." Long, long had the hand of the Lord been stretched out in anger over

the land, until even his faithful people had said,
"Is his mercy clean gone for ever?" And now as
Zacharias took the writing table, we can fancy how
those around him looked over his shoulder; how
they watched the long steel pointer as it traced out
the words: how those who could read spoke out the
tidings to all the rest, — "His name is John," —
the gift, the mercy of the Lord. What manner of
child should this be? for those who trusted the
Lord most fully had but seen the promise afar off.
But Zacharias knew; and in such words of praise
and rejoicing did his faith now declare itself, so
publicly did he make it known, that fear came on
all that dwelt round about; and these sayings were
noised abroad throughout the whole hill country of
Judæa. From mountain top to mountain top, — to
Hebron and Maon and Carmel and Ziph, — the
tidings spread; and all that heard them laid them
up in their hearts, saying over and over again:
"What manner of child shall this be?" And the
hand of the Lord was with him, — the power and
presence and love of God.'

'It seems as if Zacharias couldn't stop speaking
when he had once begun,' said Mabel, bending
down by Grace.

'But he says it all as if the thing were already
done!' said Cyril. ' "God hath visited" — "God
hath raised up." That can't be spoken of John,—
and Jesus wasn't born yet.'

'The shout of faith is always a shout of victory,' said our mother. 'To faith, things *are*, when

God has once promised them. And besides, Zacharias spoke by special divine inspiration. No, the words were not spoken about John: already the greater had overshadowed the less. It was "the horn of salvation," the deliverance from our enemies, the fulfilment of God's covenant promise, over which Zacharias poured out his heart. Even his long wished for son was but a very secondary joy. Standing there by the side of his child, the present cause of gladness almost disappeared before the thought of the glory which should follow.— "Thou, child, shalt be called the prophet of the Highest: for thou shalt go before the face of the Lord to prepare his ways." To give knowledge of salvation, to declare the tender mercy of God, to proclaim the coming of the Dayspring from on high, which should give light to them that sit in darkness, and guide our feet into the way of peace. O what words to be spoken over a helpless child! But the time of his work was not yet come. Now, he must "grow and wax strong in spirit," — as every child must who would do work for God.'

'And did he go to live in the deserts so as to have more time for study?' said Cyril.

'Many people have thought so, though I see not how the Bible warrants it. Children in general were under the mother's care until they were five years old, when their regular education began, under care of the father. Then, when old enough, the boys were often sent away to the charge of some priest or public teacher. But as Zacharias himself was a priest, and as Juttah was just on the borders of the desert, the words here may mean nothing more than that in this wild region of country, unknown and unnoticed, John passed his years of preparation for the work he was to do. For when people are strong in the Lord, and in the power of his might, they can live just as separate from the world in it as out of it: like some of those rivers which flow into the sea, and through it, and yet never mix with it, nor lose their fresh colour and sweetness in its salt waves.'

'Mamma,' said Sue, 'if the words *did* mean something else, where would John have lived then?'

'Then, as soon as he was old enough, he would have lived in some one of the caves of which those wild regions by the Dead Sea are full, — lived a hermit life, "till the day of his shewing unto Israel."'

'Mamma,' said Gracie, 'I don't understand all these words of Zacharias. It's easy to know what is meant by our enemies, and to see how as soon as the Deliverer comes to our help we can "serve him without fear," — *that* means, "sin shall not have dominion over you." But what is "a horn of salvation"?'

'I can tell you something about that,' said Cyril; 'I found it out when I was studying the texts about Darius and Alexander. A horn is one of the Bible symbols of power and strength.'

'And Jesus is "mighty to save,"' said Gracie; 'O yes!'

'Then it is often used as an image of glory and dominion,' said mamma: ' "The horn of Moab is cut off," — " I will cause the horn of Israel to bud." And there is yet another meaning. On each corner of the brazen altar was a little point or projection called a horn : to these were bound the animals brought for sacrifice, and they were daily wet with the shed blood. Even the golden altar of incense had its four horns, which once every year must be touched with the blood of atonement. When a criminal fled to the temple for refuge from the law, he laid hold of the horns of the altar and was safe : so by Jesus, our horn of salvation, we lay hold on eternal life, and there is no more condemnation. No wonder there was rejoicing in the house of Zacharias that day, for the promise which had been given since the world began was now near its fulfilment.

'Meantime, away up in Nazareth, the news of some of these things had come to the ears of Joseph. But when he heard of Mary's joy; when he learned that she was to have a child, and that she believed this child would be the long-expected Messiah; then Joseph was troubled. He did not believe, I suppose, that this promise had really been brought by an angel; he did not believe that this child should be called the Son of God; but he thought that Mary had deceived him, or was deceived herself, and that the whole thing was a made-up story. Yet he was a just man, unwilling to do any one the least wrong; and he decided with himself to keep the matter secret, so far as he could. He would put her away privily, — they would separate, but there should be as little said or known about it as possible. While he thought on these things, with much doubt and sorrow of heart, and being one day — or one night — in a weary sleep, behold the angel of the Lord appeared to Joseph in a dream, and brought him counsel.'

'Was that Gabriel, too, mamma?' said Sue.

'So it is supposed, but the Bible does not tell.'

'But I thought dreams never really meant any-thing?' said Cyril.

'You forget that God can make anything mean something: there is no way, as there is no place, in which he cannot speak to us. And in former days, he often made his pleasure known "in a dream, in a vision of the night, when deep sleep falleth upon men." "God is departed from me," said Saul, after his wilful disobedience, "and answereth me no more, neither by prophets, nor by dreams." '

'And did people know that God made the dream?' said Sue.

'They were pretty sure to know that, even when they did not understand the meaning of the dream itself. Sometimes it was plain enough, as when Jacob's favourite son dreamed that the wheat sheaves of his brethren made obeisance to his sheaf: sometimes it needed an interpreter. Pha-raoh dreamed of the seven full ears of corn, and the seven blasted ears, but knew not till God's servant told him, what they meant, nor that God had

shewed him what he was about to do. So Danie
was called upon to interpret the dream of the king
of Babylon, being himself taught of God in a night
vision what to say. And I think we can see
several reasons why God chose this way of instruct-
ing Joseph. Mary had doubtless told him of the
visit of the angel, and Joseph perhaps laughed at
the idea. He had never seen an angel himself, —
how then should she? So men reason. And then,
as Mary persisted in her story, we can imagine
him saying in utter unbelief, "She must have
dreamed it." But when the angel of the Lord not
only came to Joseph himself, but came in a dream,
then Joseph had no more to say: the words of his
betrothed wife were proved true. In silence and
wonder he listened to the voice of the angel, that
told him not merely what name the child should
bear, but also its glorious meaning: "Thou shalt
call his name JESUS: for he shall save his people
from their sins." In complete submission and obedience, he followed the command he had received,
and "being raised from sleep, did as the angel of
the Lord had bidden him, and took unto him his
wife."

'It came to pass in those days, soon after this,
"that there went out a decree from Cæsar Augustus, that all the world should be taxed."'

'Cæsar Augustus was the Roman emperor,' said
Cyril.

'He was the Roman emperor at that time; and
not content with the subject condition of Palestine,

he had a mind to put the people yet more under foot, and make them pay tribute. So he issued this decree; and whether it included the whole Roman empire or not (for history leaves this uncertain), in Palestine at least "all the world"—that is, everybody—must be taxed. And first of all, to this end, everybody must be registered; their names and age and amount of property must be written down. As soon as the decree went forth, the work of registering began; though the whole matter was not finished and the tribute actually imposed, until ten years after. This taxing was first *made*, or completed, when Cyrenius was governor of Syria. Syria was a region of country lying to the north of Palestine.'

'That registering must have been a little like our census, mamma,' said Cyril.

'Yes, in some points. But our census-taker goes about from house to house, asking questions and noting down replies; while in this case the people must all go to the registrar and give in their own names. And a troublesome piece of work it was; for by Roman as well as Jewish custom, each man must be taxed in his own city; not the city where he lived, but the one which had been the headquarters of his tribe or family,—the city where he belonged by descent and birth. So the whole land was put in commotion. You can think how it would be here,—people going from Boston to New York, and from New Orleans to Cincinnati, and from the far off States of Idaho or

Oregon back to some little village in New England; and though Palestine was but a small country in extent, yet you must remember that there were no steamboats or railroads to make the miles seem short. People could not travel faster than two or three miles an hour. And so with Mary riding some slow, sure footed mule, and himself probably on foot by her side, Joseph went up from Galilee, out of the city of Nazareth, into Judæa, unto the city of David, which is called Bethlehem. Because he was of the house and lineage of David.'

'Why does it say "went up"?' asked Cyril. 'It looks *down*, on the map.'

'Bethlehem is really one of the high points of the country. But besides this, it was near Jerusalem; and towards Jerusalem, their glory and their joy, the Jews *went up* from every part of the whole land; from Egypt or from Assyria. It was the highest part of the whole earth to them.'

'Because God's name and presence were there,' said Gracie. 'But now, mamma —

> "Not from Jerusalem alone,
> To heaven the path ascends." '

'Thus journeying on,' said mamma, 'first through the richer province of Samaria and then among the swelling hills of Judah, I suppose that Joseph and Mary came to Jerusalem; and passing in at one of its twelve gates, crossed the city, and went out through another gate on the south side which

looked towards Bethlehem, — then about six miles
— or two hours — off on the Hebron road.’

‘Mamma, did you see those gates?’ said Sue.

‘There is nothing left of the old gates now,’ said
mamma, ‘nor of the old walls. Jerusalem that
was is all passed away. Nothing more than a
few foundation stones here and there remains of
her former greatness; and instead of twelve open
gates, there are now but five. Yet these probably
stand in the places of some of the old ones, leading out to the great highways which approach
Jerusalem on different sides. The “Damascus
gate,” as it is called, is on the north, opening
upon the very road along which Joseph and Mary
came that day; and the Bethlehem, or Hebron,
gate is on the south side of the city.’

‘Was Bethlehem in sight, mamma?’ said Gracie.

‘No, not in sight, and yet almost that; for as
they wound down into the deep valley, and then
up along the steep ascent, they had but just lost
the line of the city walls and the sheen of the glittering temple, when in full view before them lay
the little village of Bethlehem, on the ridge of its
limestone hill. God had chosen a new place and a
new manifestation for his glory, — “not of this
world,” was written upon every step of our Master’s
life, as it should be upon that of his servants. In
everything “he humbled himself;” and so his
birth was to take place not in that glorious city of
Jerusalem, the joy of the whole earth, but in a

small suburban town, little thought of and never distinguished. The temple — built of white stone and in many parts covered with plates of gold — shone in the distance like "a hill of gold and of snow," dazzling as the kingdoms of this world and the glory of them : but the two wayfarers left it behind, and journeyed on to the humble town which had been chosen for the birthplace of that child, whose name should be called " Immanuel: God with us." '

' Is it a pretty place, mamma ? ' said Sue.

' It is a wonderful place, Sue, — no, I doubt whether you would call it pretty ; but the old town has a very striking appearance as you see it from almost any point. It is built on a narrow rocky ridge, which slopes sharply down to the east from the platform of the central hills ; and is a complete specimen of the hill towns of Judah : with one main street that is half a mile long, and houses all built of the same white limestone as the hill itself. The town is neat, for the East, and the houses are well built ; and the hot glare of the limestone is softened by the vineyards and olive groves and fig trees, which grow in terraces quite to the top of the hill ; sweeping round its sides like a regular stairway. Far off in the eastern distance lies the Dead Sea, with its desolate shores ; and still beyond falls the purple shadow from the long mountain wall of Moab. It is a wild, bleak scene now, although the terraces on the Bethlehem hill are green and fruitful and in perfect order ; but once the surrounding

BETHLEHEM.

hillsides were terraced and fertile like its own; and the valleys between, but little cultivated now, were once a mere waving cornfield, and gained for Bethlehem its name: Ephratah, "the fruitful:" Bethlehem — "the house of bread." '

'Ah it can never lose its name now!' said Gracie, — 'since the bread of life was first seen there. Mamma, how beautiful it is, the meaning of Bible names. But why don't they cultivate the fields still?'

'The country is overrun with wild troops of Arabs, and no crops are safe at any distance from the town. But Bethlehem must have been wonderfully beautiful in those old times when it bore its two-fold name of plenty, and was called Bethlehem-Ephratah. And it was one of the very oldest Bible towns; already built and inhabited when Jacob came back with his family and flocks from Padan-Aram, and met his first great sorrow almost beneath its walls. For Rachel died "in the way, when there was yet but a little way to come unto Ephratah." Long after that, the town was fortified by King Rehoboam; but tower and wall have disappeared, and the town has been destroyed, and all the buildings there now are new. Nothing is left of the Bethlehem that was, except the associations and the hill outlines and the valley sweep. But here David was born, — here, by the gate, was the well of water for which he longed when the Philistines held Bethlehem, and David and his men were in hiding in the caves below. It is half a mile from the gate now.'

'The very old well, mamma?' said Cyril.

'The very well; to which the three mighty men charged up the hill, "and broke through the host of the Philistines, and drew of the water, and brought to David." At the foot of the hill lie the broad cornfield valleys where David's great grandmother, Ruth, gleaned after the reapers at the time of barley harvest; and on the neighbouring heights David kept his father's flock, and fought with the lion and the bear that came up out of those wild ravines and caves, of which the hill country of Judah is full. Hither came the prophet Samuel, to anoint a new king over Israel, in place of Saul, whom the Lord had rejected; and they called David from keeping the sheep, and anointed him. And then humbly going back to his charge, and valiantly leaving it again to fight in the Lord's cause; even after he had slain the Philistine giant, David gave no higher account of himself than this: "I am the son of thy servant Jesse, the Bethlehemite." '

' "Lowly in heart," the Lord's Anointed, a King and a Shepherd too,' said Gracie. 'In how many ways Christ was the son of David!'

Chapter VII.

BETHLEHEM.

I COULD see how mamma had us on her heart as she went on with the gospel story. I could see it when she first began; and now as we came nearer and nearer to the great centre and light of the whole, the feeling grew very deep. She did not even take up her work this afternoon, while waiting for the children to come in from their walk; but sat with the open Bible before her, her face resting on her hands. And the sweet unhidden lines of the mouth told all. How tender, how pleading they were at times, — how they trembled and gave way, as once more the young voices came in with a song : —

> " Hark ! the herald angels sing, —
> Glory to the new-born King ;
> Peace on earth and mercy mild,
> God with sinners reconciled.
> Joyful all ye nations rise, —
> Join the triumphs of the skies ;
> With angelic hosts proclaim, —
> Christ is born in Bethlehem."

'O the angels ! the angels !' said Sue, climbing into mamma's lap; 'we're going to have ever so

many angels to-day!' and Sue wrapped her arms
round mamma's neck, and gave her kisses as if she
thought certainly *one* angel was already in our little
room. And mamma leaned her fair cheek against
the child's sunny head, and began softly, in a low
voice:

' " And she brought forth her first born son, and
wrapped him in swaddling clothes, and laid him in
a manger; because there was no room for them in
the inn." It is said in Proverbs, that "a man's
gift maketh room for him," — but when our Lord
Jesus came to give his own life for his people, the
people said: " No room." '

' But I suppose there really was not,' said Mabel. ' Inns do get very full sometimes.'

' Yes, inns do, — and so do hearts,' said mamma;
' until there is no room for Jesus. But when do
mere worldly thoughts and desires fail to gain ad-
mittance? And if Mary had come with a long
train of servants, and Joseph had proclaimed the
promised birth of some great earthly prince, who
would not have found room then? Every private
house would have been thrown open, every guest
would have offered his apartment, and the whole
inn would have been thought too small. But
again, " Not of this world." There were perhaps
a thousand people in that crowded inn, — strong,
sturdy men, accustomed to spend nights as well as
days in the open air; yet not one gave up his place.
Already began our Lord's humiliation upon earth;
and now for the first time he was despised and re-

jected of men : " he came unto his own, and his own received him not : " and the poor mother, weary and sick, could find no place of shelter but the very meanest in all the town.'

'Mamma,' said little Sue, 'why didn't Joseph go to another inn, if that one was full ? '

'Because, little Sue,' said mamma, ' there was but one in all the place. These Oriental inns are not in the least like ours. In the thinly settled countries of the East, where tracts of desert land are frequent ; and where, because of the heat, people can travel but a short distance without rest, there are great public places of shelter built here and there along the road ; and always, if possible, near a well or fountain. Some of them are in the towns, some on the wild roads between. These inns, or khans, or caravanserais, are " untying places " — " lodging places for the night ; " for here the traveller stops and unloads his camel, or takes the saddle from his donkey, and gives himself a night's rest.'

'And gets a good supper too, I suppose,' said Cyril.

'If he has brought it with him,' said mamma, — 'not else. At most of these inns there is no landlord and no servants : the traveller must take care of himself ; provide his own bed and cook his own provisions. Often the khan is a mere walled enclosure, from which the animals cannot stray while their master rests, and where the weary rider himself can find a shadow from the heat ; but some-

times the walls are built up strong and thick, and
twenty feet high; with flanking towers, and loop-
holes; to defend the caravans and their rich treas-

ure from the roving troops of Arabs or other ma-
rauders. Such khans have much more elaborate
accommodations, and look in the distance like a
small fortress.

'Passing in through a great arched gateway, the
traveller enters a wide open court, that is maybe a
hundred yards square, and as full of noise and bustle and confusion as it is possible to imagine. On
one side stand a long row of camels, jingling their
little bells; on another are horses and mules; some

tied, some running loose, and kicking and biting to suit their own fancy. Mingled and mixed up with these, and filling the court, is a crowd of people, — muleteers and camel drivers and pedlers and merchants, dressed in all dresses and speaking all tongues. In the centre of the court is the well; or sometimes a long raised platform, while the well is at one end; and on this platform the men sit and smoke and talk, or even sleep, in the mild summer nights. All round the sides of the court runs another platform, on which are the lodging rooms, with a sort of arched piazza in front of each; and as the partition walls come quite out to the edge of the piazza, it is divided into as many small open spaces as there are enclosed rooms. Each traveller has for his own use the bit of piazza in front of his room, as well as the room itself; and in fine weather he lives out here much of the time, just using the room as a lock-up place for his goods. This platform is raised up three or four feet above the court.'

'I can see how it is,' said Cyril, looking at the picture. 'I can see the archways, and the people, and all.'

'Back of these rooms,' said mamma, 'between them and the outer wall of the khan itself, but down on the level of the court, is a long arched gallery of stables. You see it runs along the outside of the khan, looking a little like a long shed. Into this shed or gallery, the floor of the platform extends out a little way, beyond the back wall of

the rooms, making a sort of shelf all along; and
as the side walls of each room are carried out here
just as they are in front, only not so far, the head
of each stall becomes a sort of shallow recess, with
this shelf or bench at the end.   Here the muleteers
lodge in bad weather, and the poorer sort of travellers; or indeed any sort, when the inn is full: the
broad shelf serving to hold the mule's bag of corn,
and also as a place of rest for the rider.'

'What a horrid place!' said Mabel.   'Mamma,
how are the real rooms furnished?'

'Not at all, — the khan supplies nothing but
water and shelter: unless here and there a new
one, with "modern improvements."   The traveller
spreads his carpet, or his bed if he have one, and
the room is furnished.   There had been one of
these khans at Bethlehem from very early times, —
"the habitation" — or hostel — "of Chimham," as
it is called by Jeremiah; for rich men sometimes
built them, as well as monarchs and town authorities; and probably enough this was yet standing,
or at least one in the same place.   It was a very
large inn — in Jeremiah's time it had held a great
many people — but now it was crowded; not only
with the ordinary stream of travellers passing that
way, but with all those of the house and lineage
of David who had come up thither to be taxed.
Every one of the little rooms was taken; the open
court was thronged with guests; and the broad flat
roof of the lodging rooms was covered with those

who had gone up there to enjoy the air or to sleep.
"There was no room in the inn."

'Joseph, I suppose, had journeyed slowly, for
Mary's sake; and as traveller after traveller passed
him on the road, I can well believe that he began
to feel anxious about this very matter of lodgings.
Then as the day declined; as the round shadows
of the Judæan hills grew longer and deeper, and
the heights of Moab shone in the setting sun; we
can guess how glad he was, when at last he turned
the mule's head towards the great entrance of the
habitation of Chimham.

'We can imagine it a little,' mamma went on,
speaking softly : 'we can think how Joseph led his
charge through the archway into the open court,
and then stood still, uncertain what to do. We
can fancy how the people resting in their piazza
rooms looked down on the new comers, and thought
them hardly worth even a look. We can feel how
she before whom an angel had bowed his head in
salutation, waited in that noisy throng, while Joseph listened to those who told him there was " no
room ; " and then how he took up the bridle once
more, and leaving the court, turned off at one of
the corner doorways into the long stable, and there
found shelter for his wife in one of those shallow
recesses that were but the leavings of other people's
rooms. " Ye know the grace of our Lord Jesus
Christ, that though he was rich, yet for our sakes
he became poor." '

' Mamma ! — I don't like to imagine it,' said Gracie.

' To understand any place, any situation, in this world,' said our mother, ' we must look up to the sky that is over our heads, as well as to the ground beneath our feet. *Nothing* can be seen in its true light if heaven be kept out of view, — the shadow of earthly glory is often up there, and the glory of mortal night.

' " There were in the same country " — in the little plain spread out at the foot of Bethlehem's hill, or in some of the wild valleys and hillsides of the wilderness of Judæa which lay yet further to the east — there were " shepherds abiding in the field, keeping watch over their flock by night." It was at that time of year when the flocks are abroad on the hills for pasture ; and instead of being securely shut in the fold, in charge of one shepherd and near home, they were out in the open starlight. Perhaps a hedge of tangled thorns was piled up round them, and a poor dog or two may have given that protection by a bark which he would hardly have done by a bite, — for Eastern dogs are worth little ; but the sheep's real defence was in the faithful band of shepherds. They kept watch. "And, lo, the angel of the Lord came upon them, and the glory of the Lord shone round about them;" and through the darkness of the night there broke such a flood of overpowering splendour as mortal eyes could hardly bear. "They were sore afraid." But using Gabriel's words, the angel — who was probably Gabriel himself — said unto them: "Fear not."'

'It is always "Fear not," when they are telling about Jesus,' said Gracie, — 'we are to be delivered from *all* our fears, mamma.'

'Think how the shepherds must have listened then,' said mamma, 'when like cold waters to a thirsty soul there came this good news from the land that is very far off. Think how the deep music of those words must have sounded through the still night. Every other sound was hushed, every earthly voice was silent; darkness and stillness rested on the whole hill country of Judæa; only in that one field near Bethlehem there shone the dazzling glory of the Lord. "Fear not: behold, I bring you good tidings of great joy, which

shall be to all people. For unto you is born this day
in the city of David a Saviour, which is Christ the
Lord.''   Children,' said mamma, leaning her brow
on her hands, ' we have heard of these good tidings
all our lives, until the most of the world forget what
the words mean.   It is only as the message comes
anew to each repentant sinner, and it is said to
him, " unto *you* is born in the city of David a Saviour " — that the great joy is really understood.
Small comfort would it have been to the shepherds,
little would it have stirred their hearts, to hear of
the good tidings for all people : just as men now
know that Jesus is the Saviour of the world, and
care nothing about the matter.   Joy comes into
no heart that does not lay hold of the promise for
itself. But I suppose these poor shepherds had
long felt that they were sinners, had long prayed
that the Deliverer might come ; and now it was
said — not merely " to all people " — but " unto
you.''

' " And this shall be a sign unto you," said the
angel. " Ye shall find the babe wrapped in swaddling clothes, lying in a manger." '

' They must have been very much astonished
then,' said Cyril. ' They never could have guessed
that the Deliverer would come in that way.'

' But I guess it helped them not to be afraid,'
said Sue. ' Because he was a baby then, and so
poor. Mamma, were they just like my little
clothes, that I had when I was a baby ? '

' Ah not a bit like,' said mamma : ' a baby in the

East is tied up till it looks just like a small mummy.'

'Tied up!' said Sue.

'Yes, in swaddling clothes, to keep it straight. That is the notion. The child is bound round and round, from head to foot, with bands of purple and white linen — if it's a rich baby — till it is perfectly firm and solid, — a little hard, stiff bundle, with neither hands nor feet, but only a head. And the head is tied up too: sometimes in a soft shawl, bound across the forehead, or in a quilted silk cap, with bands across the forehead and under the chin. The caps are trimmed with gold coins. Then the little bundle is wrapped in a striped silk robe over all; and looks like — you can imagine what!'

'And the *poor* babies, mamma?' said Sue.

'They are all "poor" babies, I think, to be in such a condition,' said mamma; 'but when the parents are poor too, then the little child wears only the swaddling clothes; and they are made of coarse blue cotton, bound round with narrow strips of red leather. At least I have seen such among the poorer Arabs. The rich baby, in its silk robe, is put to sleep in a splendid cradle, and half smothered with silken quilts; and the *poor* baby — now, as eighteen centuries ago — is merely wrapped in swaddling clothes, and laid in a manger.'

'How disappointed the shepherds must have been!' said Mabel. 'It sounded so mean to be sent to such a place.'

'Disappointed!' said Gracie, who had been in a trance of imagination and interest: 'disappointed in Jesus? O no! — Mamma, they *could* not have been!'

Mamma's eyes flushed. '"It is enough for the disciple that he be as his Lord,"' she said. 'No, they could not have been disappointed in *him*. Yet they may have wondered at first, or even doubted, for it is hard for mortal eyes to understand anything but mortal glory. Our sight often fails at the very moment when there is most to see. But just at that point — just at those words which have "sounded mean" to many a human ear, — the irrepressible joy of heaven broke forth. "Suddenly there was with the angel a multitude of the heavenly host," — a throng of the innumerable company of shining ones, — "praising God." It was not enough to praise him in heaven; but here on earth — here where their Lord had come to be "made a little lower than the angels for the suffering of death," — here suddenly was heard that burst of joy and triumph and praise, the music of which shall ever sound, high and clear, above all the discords of earth. "Glory to God in the highest, and on earth peace, good will toward men." The King of glory, the Prince of peace, had come. Four thousand years had passed, since by one man sin entered into the world, and death by sin, — four thousand years of wars and fears and pain and sorrow; of delayed hope, of eager longing. But now at last was fulfilled that promise, "The mountains shall bring peace to the people;" and among the wild hills of Judæa was born that day a Saviour. How few welcomed him then,—how few receive him now! But "O hope of Israel, the saviour thereof in time of trouble, why shouldest thou be as a stranger in the land, and as a wayfaring man that turneth aside to tarry for a night?"'

The children sat hushed and grave, for a minute,—then little Sue broke the silence.

'I should have been real sorry when the angels went away, if I'd been the shepherds,' said Sue, twining her arms round mamma's neck.

'Nay, those who find Jesus need not grieve over the departure of angels,' mamma answered. 'And so the shepherds said one to another, "Let us go even unto Bethlehem, and see this thing which is come to pass, which the Lord hath made known unto us."'

'I don't see how they knew where to look, mamma,' said Mabel. 'The angel just said "in the city of David."'

'And "in a manger,"' said Gracie.

'And those two things were just enough,' said mamma. 'If we went into a city to look for some stranger, we should first of all search in the hotels and public houses; and so I suppose did the shepherds. They crossed the plain, and climbed the Bethlehem hill, and went with haste to the great inn. And when there, they had no need to ask any questions, no need to inquire at any of the room doors,—the manger could be in but one place. So when they entered the broad gateway, they doubtless turned at once into the long gallery behind the inn, passing on from stall to stall; until in one of the small recesses — no larger, no better than all the rest, they found Him whom their souls sought. "They found Mary, and Joseph, and the babe lying in a manger." Perhaps, as some of the old painters fancied, there was a visible light and glory shining all around the child, and so they were the quicker guided to the spot.'

'Was the manger like ours in the barn?' said Sue.

'I do not quite know,' answered mamma. 'It might have been merely that platform shelf at the end of the stall; to which the animals were tied, and on which their provender was laid; or there may have been such a manger as the people in Palestine often make now, — a sort of box or trough, either chiselled out of a solid stone, or built up with smaller stones and mortar. Such mangers there sometimes are, both in the stable of a khan, and in the houses of the people. For in many of those strange Palestine dwellings, the principal room belongs to the family and the cattle, in about equal proportions. The floor of the family side is raised two or three feet above the rest, till it is nearly on a level with the heads of the horses and mules; but there is no partition; and when the animals are all away, the mangers are often cleaned out, and then used as a crib for the chil dren. Something of this kind, filled with soft fod, der, may have been in the stall, but I cannot tell you exactly, because the Bible does not tell us. The crowds of people in the inn were sleeping, and talking, and telling tales, according to their fancy; knowing nothing, heeding nothing of that wonder which had come to pass. So it was then, and so it is now, — the world goes on its own way of business or pleasure, and it is but a few here and there who give ear to the good tidings and seek to find Jesus.'

'Mamma,' said Gracie, 'don't you suppose the people did attend and believe, when the shepherds told them?'

'They heard, no doubt: the shepherds could not keep that great joy to themselves: but the Bible says only, "they that heard wondered." A great many people content themselves with wondering. They like to hear good news, it interests them, but they do not act upon it. Only Mary, that we are told, kept all these things, and pondered them in her heart. And without that heart-pondering, even news from heaven is of no avail.

'Glorifying and praising God for all the things that they had heard and seen, the shepherds went back to their flocks, — the knowledge, the sight of Christ should only make us more diligent in business; — and the most wonderful night this world has ever seen, or shall ever see, was over.'

Chapter VIII.

THE PRESENTATION.

'MAMMA,' said Gracie, as we came round the table the next afternoon, 'it seems so strange to me that the morning after that wonderful night should have been just like all other mornings, — and yet I suppose it was.'

'Yes,' said mamma, 'we have no reason to believe anything else. The little town of Bethlehem wore no holiday dress; the hills and the sunshine and the birds, were bright with only their every-day beauty. All over the world men were sacrificing to idols, and striving for conquest, and fighting — "kingdom against kingdom;" and though He had come "whose right it is," he who "must reign till he hath put all enemies under his feet," no one knew it but a mere handful of poor believers. The kingdom of God came not with observation. Even the Lord's ancient people — "whose were the promises" — yet looked for their fulfilment in the coming of a Deliverer who should bring national glory, not personal salvation, to Israel; and were not ready to receive him in any other way. But the angel had said to Joseph, "Thou shalt call his name JESUS : for he shall save his people from their sins." '

'Was that a new name too?' Mabel asked.

'No, it is only the Greek form of the old Hebrew name, Joshua. Joshua was a great type of Christ, — the leader and captain of the Israelites when they passed out of the desert into the land of Canaan ; and for some such leader as he had been, the Jews hoped now. But they shaped the promised blessing according to their own wish and fancy, and so could not recognize it when it came. Just such a Deliverer should the Lord Jesus indeed be ; but all in a heavenly, spiritual sense. No visible triumphs, no earthly greatness, did he promise his people : but he came to be the captain of their salvation ; he came to lead the true Israel — both Jew and Gentile — out of the wilderness of wandering ; to fight for them and with them against all the hosts of hell ; to lead them by faith over the river of death, and into the promised land on high. "Jesus" means "a Saviour" — or "the help of Jehovah," — "I have laid help on one that is mighty," said the Lord by his prophet : and now "when eight days were accomplished for the circumcising of the child, his name was called JESUS." '

'And nobody took any notice,' said Gracie.

'Well there was not really so much to attract people's attention, just at first,' said Cyril.

'Very little,' said mamma, 'except to that faith which catches the least token of God's covenant-

keeping love. Faith is quick sighted, and traces
out her way through the wilderness by even a bent
leaf or a broken twig ; following the steps of Him
in whose path not the smallest thing is without a
meaning. But the eye of sense misses all these
sure indications of the Lord's work, ever seeking
for a cleared road and a great highway; for some
visible splendour, for outside greatness. And so
after all the report of the shepherds, and all the
wondering that followed, most people could see
nothing in that manger at Bethlehem but an ordinary Jewish child. "A root out of a dry ground,"
to some ; but to others, " the Branch of the Lord,
beautiful and glorious;" such was the Redeemer
of the world, even from his birth.'

'It's strange, too,' said Cyril. 'I should have
thought he would be such a splendid child, mamma, that people could not have helped seeing, —
whether they liked it or not.'

' "Thy holy child Jesus," ' — Gracie repeated
softly.

'Yes,' answered mamma, 'that most exquisite
of all beauty the Lord had, for he was without sin.
No other baby's face was ever heavenly like his.
We talk of the pure faces of our little children, before they have grown up to know and to practise
sin ; but Jesus was "of purer eyes than to *behold*
iniquity :" nothing in his mind would ever answer
to it, nothing in his heart but would always turn
from the very thought of it. There is no such
child in the world now,' said mamma with a little

sigh, and folding Sue's small hand in her own.
'But in every other part of his human nature the
Lord was just like the little ones he came to save.
"When the fulness of time was come, God sent
forth his Son, made of a woman, made under the
law, to redeem them that were under the law." In
every age, in every way, in every point, God's creatures had broken his law; they had disobeyed, they
had slighted it: but now Jesus came to honour and
fulfil that law to its least particular in his life, and
by his death to bear its penalty; that his obedience
might be accepted for us, and his life-blood pay our
life-ransom. And as to do this work "it behoved
him in all things to be made like unto his brethren," therefore "he took not on him the nature of
angels, but he took on him the seed of Abraham,"
and was born with all the weakness and infirmity
of every other child. He "bore our griefs, he carried our sorrows," — there is no trouble nor suffering of any sort in even a child's little life, which
Jesus does not understand. We may tell it all to
him: grown-up human people may forget how a
child feels, but Jesus cannot.'

'Though it's such a great, great while ago — '
said Sue, looking up wistfully in mamma's face.

'Jesus never forgets,' mamma answered softly.
'He was to stand for us, to be our substitute, and
so he began his life on earth as we all do. So to
even the outside ceremonies of the law he was
obedient, and submitted to the sign of the covenant God made with Abraham. He was circum-

cised the eighth day, receiving his earthly name then; just as children do now when they are baptized.

'For a month after this, the Bible tells us nothing about Bethlehem. Everything, I suppose, went on in its usual way, and people even ceased to wonder at the strange things they had heard, and never watched to see what might follow. Only Mary kept all in her heart, waiting for the fulfilment of all the Lord's great promises; and very careful, the while, herself to fulfil all his least commandments. So when the forty days were ended, Mary and Joseph took the young child up to Jerusalem, to present him to the Lord; according to that word of the Lord which had been long ago spoken by Moses. For as a confession that she was a sinner, and that her child was a sinner by birth, every mother among the Jews was ordered to appear before the priest when the baby was a few weeks old, and to offer a sin offering. Those that were rich brought a lamb and a turtle dove; but the poor only a pair of doves, or two young pigeons. This was all that Mary could afford.'

' But *her* child was not a sinner,' said Mabel.

' He was made in the likeness of sinful flesh,' said mamma, 'and as a man he came of a sinful race. So his mother must offer her sacrifice; and as this child was her first-born, he must be presented in the temple, and solemnly bought back or redeemed. Long, long before this time, when the Israelites were in bondage in Egypt, the Lord slew all the first-born of the Egyptians to set his people free; and as a sign and remembrance of that, every first-born of man or beast among the Jews was declared to be the Lord's only. The clean beasts were sacrificed, the unclean were redeemed or else killed, — not in sacrifice, but as cut off from man's use, — and every first-born child was redeemed with a sum of money. This might be done when the child was a month old, or might be delayed yet ten days longer, until the mother went to offer her sacrifice. "Made under the law," ' — mamma repeated thoughtfully, — 'we have to study those words a great deal, to understand such strange things! A sacrifice presented for the birth of Him who came to take away sin; the Redeemer of the world bought back with a sum of money.'

'I should think Mary would have been afraid to do either one or the other,' said Mabel. 'Because *she* believed who her child really was.'

'It is not faith, but presumption, which decides when — and when not — it is for God's glory that he should be obeyed,' answered mamma. 'Faith is very humble; very sure that God knows best, and never afraid to follow his word exactly. It asks no stronger reason than this: "Thus saith the Lord." Faith takes it upon trust that "the law of the Lord is perfect;" and according to the law of the Lord, Mary now went up to Jerusalem.

'I cannot tell you what loveliness as well as glory there is to me, about all that little journey. Mary,

very likely, riding upon a mule, as she had done
when coming from Nazareth; and Joseph on foot,
carrying the money, and probably too a basket with
the turtle doves; and in Mary's arms that child at
whose name every knee shall bow. "The Lamb
of God" — "The Lion of the tribe of Judah:"
Jesus, "the help of Jehovah," the Saviour of the
world! Truly, "it is the glory of God to conceal
a thing," and "his thoughts are very deep."

'The road from Bethlehem winds round the head
of a long valley that stretches off eastward, towards
the Dead Sea; then mounts up and up to the
crest of another ridge which overlooks the valley
of Rephaim; and there, to the north, "one sees
the white line crowning the horizon, and knows
that it is Jerusalem." Then down into the plain
again, and along this, until suddenly the road descends into the deep ravine of the Valley of Hinnom,
mounts swiftly up on the other side, and passes
"through the gates into the city."

'If you look again at our plan of the temple,'
said mamma, opening the book, 'you will see that
next to these great open cloisters, or colonnades,
the first court is that of the Gentiles. Here might
come all foreigners and strangers of every nation,
but none but Jews might go any further. Between this court and all the rest of the temple,
was a beautiful marble screen or barrier, four feet
and a half high, made like a balustrade; and upon
it here and there stood little marble pillars, graven
with inscriptions in Greek and Latin, forbidding

any one but a Jew to pass beyond, upon pain of death.   Beyond this balustrade was the wall dividing the court of the Gentiles from the court of the women, with a great gateway of entrance.   A few steps led up to this; and on the other side of the court of the women, fifteen steps more led to the wall and gateway of the court of Israel.

'Across the court of the Gentiles went Mary and Joseph, with the child Jesus; then up the two or three steps, and through the magnificent gateway or portico into the court of the women — or the outer court; for the court of the Gentiles was not held to be really within the temple.   The court of the women was small, extending only across one side of the temple; but it did not belong to the women alone.   Men came there with their wives, and others who had brought no offering, as well as all the women of Israel; and the women could never go beyond this court, unless when they were to offer a sacrifice.   Never had Mary gone further than this : but now, she passed through the court of the women, then up three or four steps to a sort of circular platform, and from there by fifteen steps more to the next gateway, which opened into the court of Israel.'

'I don't understand about these gateways,' said Cyril.   'You speak of them as if they were *places* — not mere entrances.'

'So they were,' said mamma; 'for over each was built a great gatehouse, with a space of forty or fifty feet within, and side rooms built up like towers.

This one that led into the court of Israel had folding doors that were sixty feet high, so that it took
twenty men to open and shut them ; and the doors,
with the posts and lintel, were of bronze, overlaid
with thick plates of gold and silver.

'In this great gateway Mary paused.   Before her
lay the inner court — the court of Israel ; set apart
for the men alone ; and within that, surrounded by
a low dividing wall, was the court of the priests
and the great brazen altar.   Still further on, she
could see the temple itself, and the golden glitter
of its first entrance way.   She stood still, not ven-
turing to approach nearer, yet holding in her arms
Him who should make an end of sacrifices, and take
away the veil from the mercy seat, and make manifest the way into the Most Holy Place : by whose
blood all — both Jews and Gentiles, men and women and little children — should have boldness to
enter in.

'And now one of the priests came forward, clad
in his long white robe ; and taking the doves from
her hand, he went back into the court of the priests
and stood by the brazen altar.   He chose one of
the two for a sin offering, and wrung its neck, and
sprinkled of its blood upon the side of the altar,
wringing out the rest of the blood upon the ground
at the altar foot.   It was a sin offering.'

' Mamma,' said Gracie, ' did Mary know then of
that other blood of sprinkling which all this signified ? '

'Not clearly, as we do, I think.   But every Jew

knew that without shed blood there could be no
remission of sins; and all the believing ones looked
forward to some better atonement than the blood
of their daily sacrifices, and took that as a mere
sign. The priest took the second dove, and wrung
its head quite off, laying that upon the altar fire;
and he wrung out the blood at the foot of the altar,
and plucked away the crop and the feathers, casting them upon the ash heap. And then cleaving
the bird, but not dividing it in two, he burnt the
whole upon the altar: "a burnt sacrifice, an offering made by fire, of a sweet savour unto the
Lord." '

'That is such a strange expression,' said Cyril, —
'and yet I've seen it often in the Bible. How was
the savour sweet, mamma? I should think it
would have been very disagreeable.'

'Sweet, for what it signified,' said mamma.
'Sin is hateful in the Lord's eyes, and disobedience and unbelief he cannot away with. But when
Noah after the flood offered burnt offerings, acknowledging God's justice, beseeching his mercy,
promising to do his will; "the Lord smelled a
sweet savour." Almost all the sacrifices were in
one sense burnt offerings, but their meaning was
different. There was the simple sin offering:
there were "the sacrifices of joy" — the thank-
offerings; and there was the burnt offering proper
— "the sacrifice of righteousness." For while the
first meant only atonement for the sinner; and the
second was a joyful acknowledgment of mercy;

the burnt offering was an offering of obedience, of dedication. The *whole* of this sacrifice was con sumed, — the whole was laid on the altar and ascended to God ; for the Hebrew word is one that signifies " ascends." Abraham was commanded to offer up Isaac, not as a sacrifice for sin, but as a burnt offering of obedience. And God said unto him, " Now I know that thou fearest God, seeing thou hast not withheld thy son, thine only son, from me." So the apostle says: " I beseech you that ye present your bodies a living sacrifice:" so Jesus gave himself for us, " an offering and a sacrifice to God for a sweet smelling savour; " making not only a perfect atonement, but yielding also perfect obedience. The first dove was the sin offering, its blood only was wanted : the second was the sign of obedience and consecration, and it was all laid on the altar. There must be no divided heart in serving God, — the burnt offering was always consumed whole.

' After this, another priest came forward and received the child Jesus into his hands, and asked Mary if this was her son. And when she answered yes, he said, " Have you never had any other child ? " — and she said no. " If so," said the priest, " this child as the first-born belongs to me. If you desire to have him, you must redeem him." And Joseph, holding out a cup with money in it, answered : " This gold and silver is offered to you for that purpose."

' Then the priest, turning towards all who might

be within hearing at the time, said : " This child, as the first-born, is therefore mine, according to this law, — 'all the first-born of man among thy children shalt thou redeem,' — but I am content with this in exchange." And giving back the child, he took from the cup five shekels, the redemption price.'

'What's a shekel?' said Sue.

'An old Jewish coin. These five shekels were worth two or three dollars of our money.'

'So little!' said Mabel.

'It was only a sign, you know. We can give the Lord no real *price* for anything, — we can but shew our obedience, and acknowledge that we owe what we can never pay.'

'But, mamma, here's another thing,' said Cyril : 'I don't understand this sign at all. Why did they want to buy back their children from the service of the Lord?'

'Not from his service, certainly, in one sense,' said mamma. 'But from any special, set-apart service, which would prevent their engaging in common worldly business. Instead of that, God chose out the whole tribe of Levi, to serve in their place; and the first-born of all the other tribes, being redeemed and having a substitute, were released from all special service; either as priests, or in any business closely connected with the priest's office.

'Now there was in Jerusalem at this time, a just and devout man named Simeon, — one who waited for " the consolation of Israel ; " according to the words of the prophet Isaiah : " Comfort ye, comfort ye my people, saith your God. Speak ye comfortably to Jerusalem, and cry unto her, that her warfare is accomplished, that her iniquity is pardoned : for she hath received of the Lord's hand double for all her sins." For him who should make an end of sins, Simeon was watching ; and it had been made known to him by the Spirit of God that he should not die until this his desire was fulfilled. And now, " when the parents brought in the child Jesus, to do for him after the custom of the law," then Simeon took him up in his arms and blessed God, — gave him thanks and praise, — for this great joy. Simeon had not a wish left, not a doubt unanswered : " For," said he, " mine eyes have seen thy salvation." '

' But wouldn't he have been saved if he had never seen Jesus ? ' said Sue.

' O yes,' mamma answered, ' for he had heard about him, and believed : Simeon had seen the Lord by faith, long before this. People were saved in that way before Jesus came down to earth, just as they have been ever since he went back to heaven. But no beautiful Gospel story had been written then, Sue ; the blood which cleanseth from all sin had not been shed ; and the sure promise of God in which believers trusted, yet seemed dim and afar off. They longed to see the salvation — the means of salvation — which the Lord had prepared. So Jacob, near two thousand years before, could say : "I have waited for thy salvation, O Lord !" So David, in the fulness of his heart, exclaimed : "Oh that the salvation of Israel were come out of Zion !" For the Lord's promise was "I will place salvation in Zion " — "Say ye to the daughter of Zion, Behold, thy salvation cometh." '

'No wonder Simeon was glad !' said Gracie, 'O mamma, what joy ! '

' And Simeon rejoiced not for his own sake only, but for all the world. He took no narrow view, as did many of the Jews, — this was not to be a mere earthly deliverance, neither for them alone : now the message was — "Look unto me, and be ye saved, all the ends of the earth." This child, so unnoticed, was to be " a light to lighten the Gentiles," as well as " the glory of Israel." But it was a wonderful thought for a Jew to entertain. Hitherto, for age after age, the knowledge of the true God had been almost entirely confined to the Jews : to them he had especially revealed himself. But now was come the fulfilment of that word of prophecy concerning the Lord's Anointed : "It is a light thing that thou shouldest be my servant to raise up the tribes of Jacob, and to restore the preserved of Israel : I will also give thee for a light unto the Gentiles, that thou mayest be my salvation unto the ends of the earth." And as Joseph and Mary marvelled to hear such things, Simeon blessed them — that is, saluted them, gave them the ordinary greeting — " Blessed be ye of the

Lord;" and then went on to warn Mary against
any doubtful thoughts, and to tell her through what
reproach and gainsaying the work and the glory
must be brought to pass. " Behold, this child is
set for the fall and rising again of many in Israel,
and for a sign which shall be spoken against." As
said the prophet Isaiah long, long before, — " He
shall be for a sanctuary ; but for a stone of stumbling and a rock of offence to both the houses of
Israel." '

'What does that mean, ma'am ? ' said Cyril, —
' " the fall and rising again " ? '

' It means,' said mamma, ' that " the ways of the
Lord are right, and the just shall walk in them :
but the transgressors shall fall therein." " Unto
you which believe, he is precious," said the apostle
Peter; " but unto them which be disobedient, a
stone of stumbling." And for Mary herself, who
kept all these things in her heart, she indeed should
see the glory, but should see it through tears of
bitter grief. " A sword shall pierce through thine
own heart also," said Simeon. For King of kings
as Mary knew that child to be, yet in his human
nature he was still her child and she his mother;
and she who at the promise of his coming had cried
out with joy : " My spirit hath rejoiced in God my
Saviour : " she should see the work finished, standing amid the darkness by the death cross of her
Son.

' There came in,' said mamma, steadying her
voice, and drawing one long, deep breath, — ' there

came into the court at that instant, another of those who waited for the consolation, — one of the people to whom age is not weakness but glory; who are as "a shock of corn in his season." It must have been in the court of the women that Simeon met Joseph and Mary, for this new comer was a woman; Anna, of the tribe of Aser — or Asher — a widow, and very old; but still a prophetess, one to whom the Lord spoke in special revelation. And she, serving him day and night, lived altogether in the temple. Now, coming into the court of the women, she too gave thanks unto the Lord, and spake of him — told what she had seen and knew — to all those in the whole city of Jerusalem who looked for redemption. Seven hundred years before, God had said : " The Redeemer shall come to Zion," — . and from age to age one and another had answered: " I will wait for the Lord, and I will look for him." Now he had come. Now rang out in each believing heart the glad words of the prophet Isaiah : — " O Zion, that bringest good tidings, get thee up into the high mountain; O Jerusalem, that bringest good tidings, lift up thy voice with strength; lift it up, be not afraid; say unto the cities of Judah, Behold your God !" '

'That was splendid work to do,' said Cyril.

'It was, and it *is*,' said mamma. 'That is the very work all those who have found Jesus must do.'

'And now as then there are always some who are waiting for him,' said Gracie.

'Always: and those who are waiting for him

are ready when he comes.　So it was then, — so it
shall be at his second coming: the longing and
the fearing dwell close together, the trimmed and
the untrimmed lamps stand side by side.'

Chapter IX.

THE WISE MEN.

'WHERE now, mamma?' said Cyril, the next afternoon. 'We've got out of the temple, I suppose, — do we stay in Jerusalem?'

'No, we go back to the city of David, for so did Joseph and Mary: either to prepare for returning to their Nazareth home, or — as some think — to make arrangements for remaining at Bethlehem. Joseph was likely enough to wish to stay in the place where he had seen and heard such wonderful things, if only he could find work there.

'It was in the days of Herod the king. Four thousand years had passed since the garden was planted in Eden for the first man and woman; and more than a thousand since David was anointed king over all Israel; and seven hundred and fifty years since the building of Rome, — that great city which had now stretched forth her sceptre of power even over the Holy Land.'

'Well what year was it, mamma?' said Mabel. 'What year of our time, I mean, — I don't know much about Rome and David.'

'Why it was at the beginning of our time,' said

Cyril. 'That was the Christian era, and we date from that. So the days of Herod the king were 1864 years ago.'

'These last days,' said mamma. 'Herod had already reigned more than forty years; and all the days of Herod the king were stormy and cruel. He was first made ruler over Judæa by Rome, then driven out by other invaders; came back afterwards and reconquered the province, styling himself its king; and since then had been trying in every way to make his throne secure. Sometimes it was by seeking to please the Jews; rebuilding and adorning their temple: sometimes by putting to death different members of his own family whom he suspected of wanting the crown. His wife and two sons perished thus, among the rest; and as he grew older, and became infirm and tortured with illness, cruelty was his pastime. Knowing that he had not very long to live, fearing perhaps that even this little remnant of his life might be cut short by some one of the oppressed people, Herod seized and imprisoned a great many of the principal Jews, giving strict orders that the moment he himself should die, these men should all be slain. Thus the people would fear to kill him, and when at last his life was at an end, the land would be filled with mourning. For tyrant as he was, Herod did not choose to have it said that there were rejoicings at his death. In such days as these, our Lord Jesus was born, — he who came to be Prince of Peace.'

'It's a great wonder the people were not glad to see him,' said Cyril.

'Mamma, wasn't *anybody* glad?' said Sue,— 'besides the shepherds, and the two people in the temple?'

'It is one of the joyful, blessed things which we know,' said mamma, 'that although so many disregard the Lord's word, and fail to observe his working, yet that in every age — and perhaps in every country — there are always some who believe. They may have but little knowledge, their faith may be very dim; yet towards that distant light which, like Christian, they but "think they see," their hearts are turned with the intensest longing. And this is one sense in which Jesus is called the Desire of nations; for many a time people long for him, for something to supply their great need, before they have ever heard his name spoken by mortal lips. So a poor African woman of one of the wild native tribes, interrupted the missionary in his first talk to them about the love of Jesus, exclaiming: "Yes — I know that, — this is the One who spoke to my heart long ago." So a Hindoo, dragging himself along a weary pilgrimage to propitiate some idol, with heavy irons fastened to each foot, stopped to hear the preaching of a white man at the street corner. And as he heard of Jesus, and of his precious blood, the Hindoo threw off the weights from his feet, and ended his pilgrimage there; crying out: "This is what I want!" Such things are found in many a heathen land; and so from the time that Jesus appeared upon earth, there began to come to him from all parts those whose weary hearts had been fainting for his salvation.'

'Like Simeon and Anna,' said Cyril.

'Yes, most of all from among the Jews; but not from them only. "Now when Jesus was born in Bethlehem of Judæa, in the days of Herod the king, behold, there came wise men from the east to Jerusalem, saying, Where is he that is born King of the Jews?"'

'From the east,' — said Cyril. 'That's pretty indefinite.'

'The east,' said mamma, turning to her map, 'was a general name for all this region of country that lies east of the Holy Land: Mesopotamia, Chaldæa, Arabia, and Persia. Sometimes, too, it was used very indefinitely — meaning an unknown great distance in that direction; for so the vast continent of Asia stretched away towards the sun-rising, and no one knew how far. Idolaters lived there, and fire worshippers, and worshippers of the sun and moon: nations which having once had the knowledge of the true God, had yet forsaken him and lost it all.'

'I should say these were very wise men, to leave such countries and come to find the King of the Jews,' said Cyril.

'Yet you must not suppose these heathen people were like some we hear of now-a-days,' said mamma. 'Other things they knew, — it was only the

wisdom which is from above that they despised.
They were no wild tribes, sunk in ignorance and
barbarism, but were the oldest nations of the world;
the most civilized, the most learned. Solomon in
the height of his glory was compared with them,
and said to be " wiser than all the children of the
east." To but one sort of learning were they indif-
ferent — " they did not like to retain God in their
knowledge; " and so all their study and acquire-
ments were laid at the feet of false gods, and these
countries became in the sight of the Lord, " a
region of darkness and the shadow of death," where
the very light was as darkness.

'Chief among all men at the courts of Babylo-
nia and Persia, was a certain sect called Magi — or
Magians : men who gave their lives to study and
divination. They were astronomers, learned in all
the courses and movements of the stars; and they
were astrologers too, — trying to read in the heavenly bodies the destinies of men. In difficult
times the king called upon them for counsel : they
interpreted his dreams, they foretold success or
failure to his enterprises; and no sacrifice was
thought complete, unless some of the Magi were
present, chanting prayers. Daniel, you remember,
when he was a captive in Babylon, was made chief
of all the wise men; for the king proved him to be
" ten times wiser than them all." '

'That was because God told him what to say,'
said Gracie.

'It is glorious to think of,' answered mamma,

'how even then, living at a heathen court, head of a band of heathen sorcerers, Daniel was yet a burning and a shining light to the glory of the true God. His lamp never grew dim, even among the idolatrous damps and fogs of "that great city." And doubtless other lights were kindled at his, and others learned to look for the time when " Messiah should be cut off, but not for himself; " and so for all the six hundred years since then, there had perhaps ever been some, even in those dark regions, who waited for salvation ; forsaking the worship of that visible sun which God himself had placed in the heavens, and watching to see the Sun of Righteousness arise. And now when the time was fully come, " there came wise men from the East to Jerusalem, saying, Where is he that is born King of the Jews? for we have seen his star in the east, and are come to worship him." '

'But how did they know the time was come ? ' said Cyril. ' That puzzles me.'

' Why they saw the star, — it's plain enough,' said Mabel. ·

' Mamma,' said Sue, ' which star was it ? '

' To begin with the star,' said our mother, softly patting Sue's little hand, ' we never saw one like it, Sue, nor ever shall. It was no common star, which may be seen every night, but that is about all we know. Many learned men have made out theories, and chosen stars, and said a great deal that was both curious and ingenious on the subject ; but nothing of it all seems to suit the Bible words.

It was "*His star*," — something which even astronomers had never seen before ; a brilliant, wonderful sign in the heavens of His coming, who is
the light of the world. For nothing is too hard for
the Lord.'

' What made people think of a star in connection
with his coming, anyhow ?' said Cyril.

' That was an old, old tradition, dating back, it is
supposed, even to the time of Balaam, two thousand
years before. Balaam, himself a sorcerer from the
East, was brought over by the king of Moab (with
whom Israel was at war) to pronounce curses
against their victorious hosts. And then, standing
on some of those heights of Moab while Israel rested in the plains beneath ; yet unable to speak one
word about them which the Lord did not permit ;
Balaam poured out blessings instead of curses ; fore-
telling in prophetic words the future glory of Israel :
and he said : " There shall come a Star out of Jacob, and a Sceptre shall rise out of Israel." These
words were always explained by the old Targums
as one of the prophecies of the Messiah ; and so it
became a current tradition among the Jews that a
star should be the sign of his coming. To that
point indeed did this belief go, that an impostor
who came, calling himself " the son of a star," en-
snared and led away the whole nation for a time.
Doubtless Balaam's prophecy was reported among
his own people too, the children of the East ; and
even from that far away time, it may be, there had
been a constant watch kept ; and wise men and

star-gazers of the East were ever on the lookout for
some token in the sky which should tell that the
King of the Jews was born. And now at last these
had seen the star, and were come to worship him
who should bear the sceptre.'

'Did these men come from Babylon?' asked
Cyril.

'We do not know, — the Bible does not tell; yet
some things in the story seem to prove that they
must have come from a still greater distance, and
that it was only at the end of a very long journey
that they arrived in the land of Israel. As a matter of course they bent their steps first towards the
capital city of the land, to seek for its King; and
as if they had quite forgotten the powerful Edomite
monarch who held the throne, they passed along
the streets of Jerusalem repeating their strange
question : " Where is he that is born King of the
Jews ? " No one could be *born* King of the Jews,
who was not of David's line; but for four hundred
and fifty years none such had been in Jerusalem,
and only the Lord's promise kept the royal succession unended. And now here were strangers come
to announce that fulfilment of his word, which as
yet his own faithless people did not know. The
appearance of the wise men, their foreign dress,
above all their questions, must have stirred men
strangely : " all Jerusalem " was troubled. And
not only Jerusalem, but her usurper king, as soon
as the rumour reached his ears. Here was a new
danger, and one very difficult to meet, for the sign

and the inquiries could have but one meaning. Herod had not lived among the Jews so long without knowing their expectation of the Messiah, — indeed numbers had refused, in the face of all perils, to take the oath of allegiance to him, for the very reason that they looked for their own King; and now he had come. A new star to herald his birth, and the great ones of the earth already hastening to pay him homage. Herod was troubled — and all Jerusalem with him.'

'I should think Jerusalem would have been glad,' said Mabel.

'People who live under a tyrant's rule,' answered mamma, 'learn to dread any new stir or commotion; as almost any one is sure to be the excuse for new deeds of oppression. And so in this case the fears of the Jews got the better of their faith; and instead of welcoming the news, the glad tidings of great joy, they could think only of fresh cruelties on Herod's part: new executions, new imprisonments, perhaps a new war.

'Herod at once took counsel. Calling together the chief priests and scribes, — those head men of the nation who were most learned in the law and the prophets, — he demanded of them where Christ should be born. This King of the Jews, now so suddenly asked for, could be none other than that Messiah whom from age to age the prophets had foretold, — where should he be born? in what part of the land was it declared he would make his appearance? this Christ, the Anointed King over the

house of David and the nation of Israel? And the
chief priests and scribes, well knowing, answered
at once: " In Bethlehem of Judæa; for thus it is
written by the prophet, And thou, Bethlehem, in
the land of Juda, art not the least among the princes of Juda: for out of thee shall come a Governor,
that shall rule my people Israel." '

'Well there was some good stuff in them,' said
Cyril, ' or they would never have dared speak so
plainly to such a king.'

'Yet they were not of those who waited for redemption in Israel,' said mamma : ' not one of them,
so far as we know, set out to seek and follow their
new Ruler. But even wicked Jews had great respect for the written law ; and the scribes, who had
it in charge to read and explain to the people, took
jealous care of every word and letter. I can imagine
too, that to the proud Israelites there was great
satisfaction in for once asserting their national
glory, to the face of the tyrant who seemed to have
them under foot. We are not thy slaves, O king,
— we are God's chosen people : and he will provide us a Governor. For thus it is written.'

'Mamma,' said Grace, ' what does " the *princes*
of Juda* " mean? Judah had but one throne.'

'The local governors, those who were set· over
oue city — or ten cities — sometimes bore that
name; and here it is transferred from the men
to the cities they ruled. Bethlehem was " little
among the thousands of Judah," — one of the
smallest of the governor-cities ; and yet from her

should come forth a Governor who should rule the whole.

'Herod seems never to have doubted for a moment the truth or authority of those words of the prophet, now declared to him. But I dare say he dismissed his council as if the whole matter were of very slight importance ; and then privately, lest others should see and follow his example, he called the wise men, and eagerly inquired how long ago the star first appeared. How long had this new Ruler been hid away in the kingdom ? how much time was there to do anything ? The wise men answered ; and then Herod, his wicked plans already laid, sent them away to Bethlehem with a fair pretence : " Search diligently for the young child," he said ; spare no pains to find him ; and then bring me word, that I too may come and worship.'

'The wise men must have thought they had come to a queer country,' said Cyril. 'Kept waiting all that time, and finding no one that even knew the King was born ; and then talked to secretly, and sent off alone to find him !'

'But they must have been too happy to think much about that, now they were so near finding what they had sought so long,' said Gracie.

'I don't see how they came to think they had anything to do with the King of the Jews, any way,' said Mabel.

'They were of God's people Israel, strangers though they might be, and from a strange land,' answered mamma ; ' " for he is a Jew which is one

inwardly ; " and the glad tidings were *to all people.*
But I doubt if they felt very happy when they left
the king. For their faith had been sorely tried.
They had seen the bright star in their own eastern
land, before they set out, and must have travelled
on across the desert expecting to find the land of
the Jews musical with rejoicings from one end to
the other. But all was silent; the people wore
their every-day look of business or fatigue or discon-
tent or sorrow; the very capital itself was unmoved;
and as they went through the streets of Jerusalem
putting their eager questions to one and another
person whom they met, men gathered round them
in groups — laughing, jeering, and disbelieving.
Then they had speech of the reigning monarch,
but even he had heard of no new pretender to his
throne; and now at last they were sent away from
ruler and capital, and bid to go and search diligently to see if they could find the King of the
Jews, in a little obscure town in the neighbouring
hill country! I can well believe that their faith
had almost given way, — that they were well nigh
ready to turn back to their own land and their
idolatrous worship.'

'But they didn't do it, mamma,' said Sue. 'I
guess God wouldn't let them.'

'Those who are really seeking the Lord,' said
mamma, 'are sure to find him; and never have
their faith tried beyond what they are able to bear.
"What man is he that feareth the Lord? him shall
he teach in the way that he shall choose." If we

can see but one step before us, yet take that step
in faith, God will clear a way for the second.
" When they had heard the king, they departed;
and, lo, the star, which they saw in the east, went
before them." They had seen nothing of it since
they left their own country, but now it. appeared
again. It was near nightfall when the wise men
left Herod, — a whole day or more they had spent
in fruitless inquiries, and now at evening they set
forth to begin their search anew; moving slowly
along the hilly road towards the city of David.
Half way between Jerusalem and the high ridge
from which you go down into the Bethlehem valley, there is, in the very middle of the road, a
spring. The water is cool and pleasant, and any
day you may see women there with their pitchers,
and get from them a draught of the fresh stream.
This is the well of the Magi : for the legend says,
that as they plodded doubtfully along towards
Bethlehem, they stopped at this spring to drink.
As they bent over it, dipping in hands or cups, suddenly they saw reflected there the herald star which
they had seen before in the east ; and looking up,
lo, it was shining in the sky above their heads.
" When they saw the star, they rejoiced with exceeding great joy," — all doubt, all unbelief were
gone : and rising up quickly they followed the star,
which was not stationary now as they had seen it
in the east, but " went before them, till it came and
stood over where the young child was." '

Sue clapped her hands,

'Just over the very house, mamma?'

'Just over the very house. And "when they had entered the house, they saw the young child with Mary his mother, and fell down, and worshipped him."'

'Then it must have been a peculiar star, certainly,' said Cyril, 'or they never could have recognized it so.'

'Mamma, is that a true story about the spring?' said Gracie.

'It is an old legend,' said mamma, — 'that is all I know.'

'But I don't see why it says "in the house,"' said Mabel. 'It was in the stable.'

'Are you sure?' said mamma. 'It is well to be quite sure, before we venture to criticise even the smallest Bible words. You know as soon as the taxing was over, the crowd must have cleared away, and so there would be plenty of room in the inn itself. But I doubt if they were in the inn at this time. Joseph seems to have taken up his abode in the city of his fathers; perhaps finding work more plenty there than it had been at Nazareth; and then he would have removed from the inn to some small house in the town where he could pursue his trade. But however that might be, and wherever the place was, the star came and stood over it, hanging its signal light above the house.'

'If it had been at the inn, they wouldn't have needed a guide, any more than the shepherds did,' said Cyril: 'they would have gone straight there

in the first place, to lodge and make inquiries.
Well, mamma?'

'At this house — whatever it was — the wise
men entered in. And there, with no royal robes,
with no glittering train of servants, in something
no finer than a carpenter's house, " they found the
young child, and Mary his mother,"— she was his
only attendant : and they fell down and worshipped
him, — prostrating themselves to the very earth
before him, after the fashion of Eastern nations ;
having no doubt that this
was indeed the very King
of the Jews.'

'Did they fall quite
down, mamma?' said
Sue.

'Quite down. Some-
times this prostration was sudden and complete at
once ; but in cases of special ceremony, or of adoration, it was gradual ; the person falling first on one
knee, and then bending lower and lower until his
forehead touched the ground : as Abraham " fell on
his face " when God talked with him. So they
worshipped him ; and then opening their treasures
— some precious load which they had brought with
them on their camels — they presented unto him
gifts, — a gift is the next mark of homage, after
prostration. And in the East, nothing is done
without gifts, — there are fifteen different Hebrew
words to express this one thing : the one word
meaning something given to an inferior, as by a

king to his subjects, and another something given by the subjects to their king, and so on. The criminal gives to the judge, and the debtor to the creditor; and without a gift no one in the East can be born, or married; can either rejoice, or pay a formal visit, or make a bargain: and thus the wise men came with full hands before him who was born King of the Jews. "They presented unto him gifts: gold, and frankincense, and myrrh."'

'Well what was it they *gave* him?' said Sue, knitting her small brows at the hard words, and bestowing her emphasis with true childish irregularity.

'Gold, — you know what that is: and frankincense was a precious resinous gum from Arabia or India; and myrrh another Arabian gum, said to come from a thorny acacia-like tree.'

'What strange gifts!' said Cyril.

'No, the costly natural productions of a land were very often so used; and the wise men brought the very two things perhaps most generally held precious in the East: gold, and perfumes.

'They presented their gifts. And then God, who knows the secrets of the heart, sent them word in a dream that they should not return unto Herod. Their first audience of the King of the Jews was over; they had found the desire of their hearts; and now, wearied with their long journey, were asleep in the old khan, their camels tied before them. Doubtless they intended to return to Herod the very next morning; but in their sleep

God spoke to them and gave his orders, counter-
manding those of the king; and like true wise men
they made haste to obey. Rising from sleep, they
prepared to set out at once. An Eastern traveller
does not undress for the night, or at most throws
off but a single upper garment, so they were soon
ready; and in the open court of the khan, where
there was neither gas nor lamp, the beautiful Bethlehem stars looked down and gave their light. The
camels were loaded and untied, and the men once
more set forth. I suppose they had come by the
great caravan route through Bagdad, and so down
to Jerusalem from the north; but now they departed into their own country another way: passing
down through Hebron, and across the desert to the
head of the Persian Gulf, and so avoiding Jerusalem altogether.'

'And didn't they ever see Jesus again?' said
Sue.

'I think not — till they went to heaven.'

'Well that certainly is the strangest story!' said
Cyril. 'The unbelief of the Jews, and the faith of
these strangers; and the star, and the dream, and
all! It's grand, but it's queer.'

'Ah, mamma,' said Gracie, 'I think people were
very happy in those days, when they could go and
find the Lord, and see him face to face!'

'The promise stands yet,' answered mamma, —
'"Seek, and ye shall find." And then shall you
see him. Not as he was here, in his humiliation;
not despised and rejected of men: but "thine eyes

shall see the King in his beauty ; " with ten thousand times ten thousand angels round his throne.
And for gifts, you shall cast your crowns at his
feet.'

'And then,' said Sue, drawing a long childish
sigh, and folding her little hands together ; 'then
we'll never have to go away from him any more,
for Herod nor anybody else.'

Chapter X.

HY couldn't dreams mean something now, mamma?' asked Mabel.

'They might,' answered mamma, 'because all ways of teaching are still open to the Lord; but now that we have the written word, now that "in these last days he hath spoken to us by his Son," visions and dreams and prophecy, and the open ministry of angels, seem to be laid aside. Angels do their work still, but we do not see them; and God speaks to us, but it is silently in our hearts; and though he leads us every minute, and guides every step of our way, there is no pillar of cloud or of fire before our eyes. Our life now is by faith and not by sight.

'But in those old times it was different. Hardly had the wise men taken their departure, in obedience to the command from heaven given in a dream; the soft, noiseless tread of their camels was maybe even then passing down the Bethlehem slope; when another sleeper in the old town was aroused by a heavenly message. The angel of the Lord — perhaps the very same who had brought the magi their orders — appeared to Joseph in a dream, saying: "Arise, and take the young child and his mother, and flee into the land of Egypt." No rest might he find, who had come to give his people rest: the changes to which their lives are subject came in full measure upon him; at evening worshipped by the Eastern sages, and before dawn compelled to flee for his life. "Be thou there until I bring thee word," said the angel to Joseph; "for Herod will seek the young child to destroy him."'

'Foolish man!' said Cyril, 'to think he *could* do anything against the Lord's Anointed!'

'The wisdom of the world is foolishness with God, and he taketh the wise in their own craftiness. Herod thought he had laid his plans so well, and behold God knew them all. Like the man in the cornfield, there was one direction in which Herod forgot to look.'

'What man, mamma?' said Sue.

'The man who went into a cornfield to steal. He looked this way and that way, to see if anybody was in sight, and then jumped over the fence and began to pick the corn. But his little boy reminded him: "Father, there is one way you forgot to look, — you didn't look up." And so it was with Herod now, — yet the Lord was watching every thought and intent of his heart. God's servants may always trust the perfect knowledge of each one of his commands, — there cannot be the least mistake in them. "Arise," said the angel — and Joseph arose, and took the young child and his mother by night — that same night, for there must be uo delay — and departed into Egypt. Joseph and Mary needed all their faith, not to feel cast down. How strange it must have seemed to them! this child, the King of the Jews, the Son of God, obliged to escape into a distant heathen land from the fury of an Edomite king. Could not God keep his own in some other way?'

'Well why couldn't he?' said Mabel. 'It seems so, I'm sure.'

'Doubtless he could,' said mamma, 'but if this had not been the *best* way, God would not have chosen it. A sufficient answer to all the unbelieving questions which we ask about things that befall ourselves sometimes. They departed into Egypt. It was not needful to wait to get money for the journey, — the costly gifts of the wise men would amply supply all their need in that respect: the mule was tied at his manger under the same roof with themselves, after the fashion in poor Eastern houses; Joseph had not even to go out of the house or speak to a single person until all was ready for the journey. Then silently they went forth by night, and before the day broke were well on their way towards Egypt. The road they took,' said mamma, opening the map, ' was probably this. First down the highway to Hebron, and then through the rocky passes of the hill country across to Gaza. There they might join themselves to some set of merchants going to Egypt, for in the East people generally travel in companies. Gaza

10

was a sort of frontier town, where the caravans took in their last supplies before entering the desert: here Joseph could buy a stock of provisions and whatever else was wanted; and then, under guard, convey his precious charge along the sea-coast road through the desert, into the land of the Pharaohs.'

'How far was it, mamma?' said Gracie.

'It is three long days' journey from Bethlehem to Gaza, in the first place; and then from Gaza to Cairo is two hundred and forty-eight miles, which at the slow rate of caravan travelling would take between two and three weeks.'

'And did they go to Cairo?'

'Cairo was not built until six hundred years after that. But tradition says (and in this case it is probably true) that they went to a very ancient town called Heliopolis, about six miles — or two hours — from where Cairo now stands. A great many Jews lived in and about the city, while a whole Jewish town lay some twelve miles to the northward. Heliopolis was one of the oldest cities in the world. Never a large place, by all accounts, but it was Egypt's city of learning — her University; and from the midst of its little cluster of houses rose up a magnificent temple of the sun, that was built when Jacob, the great head of the Jewish nation, was but a boy in his father's tent.'

'Mamma, what is a temple of the sun?' said Sue.

'A temple built and set apart for the worship of the sun. Egypt had forsaken the Lord, and served

other gods ; and thus Heliopolis got its Bible names :
On, the city of the sun, and Beth-shemesh — the
house of the sun. Here Jacob's son Joseph found
a wife, for Pharaoh gave him "the daughter of Pot-
ipherah, priest of On :" here, according to Jewish
writers, Jacob himself came to dwell, and Moses to
be educated. And in later times Heliopolis was
the birthplace of Pliny, and the school of Herodotus.'

'But I wonder *this* Joseph did not go to the
Jewish town, instead of that heathen place,' said
Cyril.

'He may have done so; the two were not far
apart, and the Bible says nothing about it. But
the Palestine Jews were not very friendly to this
Egyptian settlement, because the people had built
a temple and appointed a priesthood of their own,
to the forsaking of the one at Jerusalem. However, according to all the traditions, it was in or
near Heliopolis that this Joseph took up his abode ;
but of course tradition tells a great deal else. For
instance, outside the city there is a strange, twisted,
bent old sycamore tree, under which it is said the
holy family rested on their way ; the tree miraculously bending down its branches to shelter them,
and then miraculously living on until this day. It
is called the Virgin's tree, even yet. And near
by is the spring of " Ain Shems," a willow-shaded
pool that once belonged to the great temple of
On. Tradition says the water was salt at first ;
but that when Mary came there with the young

:hild to drink, he commanded the spring to become
iweet.'

'Is it true, do you think, mamma?' said Mabel.

'I think not — nay, I am *sure* not; for the Bible
says that the *beginning* of the Lord's miracles was
at Cana of Galilee, — so it could not have been here
in Egypt. It is likely enough that he drank of the
spring, and that the little party rested under some
former tree in that same place.'

'Mamma,' said Sue, 'who is tradition?'

The children gave a great shout at this, all except poor Sue herself, who looked more demure
than ever. But mamma said with her reassuring
smile, —

'Tradition is a great many people. History,
you know, is a written account of people and events.
But tradition is an account told by one set of persons to another, from age to age, without being
written down; and often though the foundation of
the story may be quite true, yet by the time it has
been told and told a great many times, and for a
great many years, it gets twisted and changed until
there is no truth left. One person forgets a little
here, and another — given to exaggeration — adds
on a little there; and so tradition is seldom to be
trusted.'

'I'll go to see that tree though, when I am in
Egypt,' said Cyril. 'Is Heliopolis a learned city
now, mamma?'

'It is no city at all. "He shall break the images of Beth-shemesh," said the prophet Jeremiah,

" and the houses of the gods of the Egyptians shall
he burn with fire;" and so it has been done.
Where once Heliopolis stood is marked by low

mounds of rubbish; the place is a ploughed field
and a planted garden; and of the splendid temple
of the sun but two relics are left. One is the pool
of " Ain Shems," the former spring for the temple
use; the other is a solitary obelisk. See, here is a
picture of the old place as it looks now. Once
there were great buildings, and avenues of stone
sphinxes, and numbers of obelisks here and there;
but this is the only one left; and it is the oldest in
the world. It rises up in the midst of the gardens, a shaft of red granite sixty-eight feet high
above the pedestal; and stands there looking off
across the desert and the green fields of Egypt, to

the distant Pyramids, as it did four thousand years ago. It saw the Midianites pass by with Jacob's favourite son Joseph, when his brothers had sold him into Egypt; it looked down afterwards on his splendid marriage procession; and threw its long shadow across the sand when Moses fled from the face of Pharaoh.'

'Well there's no doubt I shall go to see *that*,' said Cyril.

'Here then, to this region, we may suppose the fugitives came,' said mamma; 'and here they abode until the death of Herod: "that it might be fulfilled which was spoken of the Lord by the prophet, saying, Out of Egypt have I called my Son."

'It is not very easy to make you understand these words, but I must try. The Israelites, you know, were in bondage in the land of Egypt, for a great many years; and then God called them to come out of Egypt, and set them free. And this is a great type or image of the bondage of sin, and of the deliverance from it which only God can give. The true Israel, God's people in heart and not merely in outward name, they are all at first the servants of sin. But when they hear and obey the word of the Lord to come up out of that region of evil wherein they dwell, then — though they are poor and weak and fast bound — the Lord himself strikes off their chains and strikes down their enemies, and makes them freemen for ever. From that time he becomes to them, "The Lord thy God, which brought thee out of the land

of Egypt, out of the house of bondage." And it is
of God's love to do this, as he said: " When Israel
was a child, then I loved him: and called my son
out of Egypt." Now our Lord Jesus, for whose
dear sake all mercy and all deliverance comes, was
made in all things like unto his people, that he
might be a merciful and faithful High Priest for
them; that he might feel all their sorrows, and prove
all their temptations, and touch with his atonement
and his sympathy every step of the way that they
must go. He could not suffer the bondage of sin,
for in him was no sin; but when he was a child he
went down into the real Egypt, and passed through
that bitter servitude in a figure. " In all their
affliction he was afflicted." They were exiles and
strangers in that land, far from their Father's
house; and he too went into banishment, the better to lead them home.

' Meanwhile, Herod found out that he was mocked
of the wise men. They had slighted his command,
and not heeded his wish; and were gone off into
their own country another way. Herod was not
used to being treated in that fashion, and he was
" exceeding wroth," — not merely for the slight,
but for its probable consequences. Clearly the wise
men must have found what they sought, or they
would have come back to get new directions; and
perhaps they had guessed his intent, and had given
warning, so that the young child was already beyond his reach. If they had only brought back
word to the king at Jerusalem, it would have been

easy enough to have this young pretender to his
throne put to death ; but the wise men with their
guiding star had disappeared, and nothing was
left for Herod but sweeping measures. "He sent
forth, and slew all the children that were in Bethlehem, and in all the coasts thereof, from two years
old and under."'

'Mamma! — how many?' said Sue, nestling
her face against her mother's breast.

'The number of children of that age is generally
about one fifth of the whole population,' said mamma. 'If then the people in Bethlehem numbered
as many as they do now, there must have been
more than a thousand of these little ones whom
Herod slew.'

'But why did he kill children of two years old?'
said Cyril. 'I thought this was just after the pres-
entation in the temple.'

'It would seem not,' answered mamma, 'for it
is said that Herod did this "*according to the time
which he had diligently inquired of the wise men.*"
They lived far off, and must have been long on the
way, so it was some time since the star first appeared to them ; and Herod had found out this with
great exactness. Then his fears would make him
go further than the real need. If it was more than
a year since the star appeared, he would kill all the
children that were two years old and under. And
in the same way, it was not enough to do this in
Bethlehem only, but it must be also in all the
coasts thereof.'

'I was going to ask what that means,' said Cyril.

'It means so much of the surrounding country and villages as belonged to Bethlehem. In the division of the land in Joshua's time, we read of " Gaza with her towns and villages — Ashdod with her towns and villages," and so on. Round about Hebron at the present day, are first open suburbs, then gardens and fields, with little watch towers where many of the people go to live in the summer time; then beyond these are the dependent villages, or " daughters of the city," as they are called. Sixteen such villages even now, in Hebron's fallen days, are under the rule of her Sheikh. Coast, is a Bible word for border, — the hills near Tyre were *the coasts of Tyre and Sidon;* and so the " coasts " of Bethlehem were the neighbouring hills and valleys, with their clustering hamlets and scattered houses. All over that fair portion of the hill country, wherever there were little ones with their sweet voices and unsteady steps, there came Herod's executioners: catching the baby from its mother's arms, and the child of two years old from her knee, and leaving them slain at her feet; until the sweet hillsides of Bethlehem and all the coasts thereof were strewed with withering blossoms.'

But at that, there came such a pitiful childish sob from Sue's full heart, that mamma could not say another word; and the room was in an utter hush. Then our mother spoke again, softly, and in the words of old Matthew Henry : —

' " These were the infantry of the noble army of

martyrs ; shedding their blood for Him who came
to shed his blood for them." '

' The first martyrs for Jesus ! — it is glorious to
think of now,' said Gracie, brushing away her
tears : ' but oh, then ! ' —

' Then,' said mamma, ' we cannot even imagine
what it was. The mother gone with her baby to
the well, or teaching her little ones at the house
door at home, or watching their play, or mounting
the hill path with one in her arms and another
holding fast to her dress, all bereaved in a moment;
and on the blood-stained floor, or the blood-sprinkled stones at the well, or the crimsoned path in the
white limestone rock, only the lifeless forms of her
darlings left. Here,' said mamma, her voice drop-
ping again, ' in this Western world, people suffer
silently; and those who feel the deepest sorrow
generally tell it the least. But with the people of
the East all is outspoken ; and both men and women " lift up their voices and weep," in a way that
we here have no conception of. I never heard anything like it anywhere else. We were at Tibnîn,
in the north of Galilee, and the Pasha had come
there to draw conscripts for his army. It was a
wild stormy day, the Pasha with his armed escort,
and the Prince of Tibnîn with his people, sat in a
sort of upper balcony ; and down below in the open
court were the men from all the region round about,
among whom the lot was to be cast. With them
were their mothers and wives — the women of the
villages, who had followed on foot through the pelt-

ing storm, and now stood without shelter, waiting to know the lot. All of them were breathlessly still, and only the wild voice of the storm could be heard. But when the names of the conscripts were drawn, and it was made known who were to go, there burst forth such a cry as I never heard, — moans and shrieks and exclamations of utter distress.'

'And I suppose that was the way at Bethlehem,' said Mabel. And our mother answered tenderly:

'Then was fulfilled the word of Jeremiah the prophet, "In Rama was there a voice heard, lamentation and weeping, and great mourning, Rachel weeping for her children, and would not be comforted, because they are not." '

'And the poor mothers did not know for whose sake their children were killed,' said Gracie.

'No — they did not know,' said mamma with a long sigh; 'and they did not know him as we do: so how they lived through that bitter wave, I cannot tell.'

'But what does "Ramah" mean?' said Mabel. 'It ought to be Bethlehem.'

'Some think that the cry was heard even as far as to Ramah, which is on the other side of Jerusalem; and some that one of the stricken villages bore that name. But as the same word is used for a hill or high place, it may be no special name here, but only a general term for the region round about Bethlehem: so that we might read: "In the *hill country* was there a voice heard." This prophecy, like many others, referred to more than one event. Rachel, you know, was Jacob's favourite wife; and when she died he buried her close by Bethlehem, — her tomb is there to this day. Long after that, Nebuchadnezzar king of Babylon invaded Palestine, and carried away captive great numbers of the Jews. The bands of prisoners were mustered and led forth from Ramah, and there it is said were many slain who were too old or too feeble for the journey; but the rest were marched down past Rachel's tomb to their long weary captivity. • Many Benjamites were among them; and so in a double sense by a sort of poetical image, Rachel, the mother of that tribe, was said to weep over the loss of her sons and to mourn with her daughters, when the people were carried away out of their own land. This was the first fulfilment of the prophecy.'

'Rachel wasn't the mother of many of the tribes,' said Mabel.

'Of only two. But in the East the head wife takes the lead in all things. Rachel was Jacob's favourite wife, — and the Jews. of whatever tribe, call her "Our mother Rachel," to this day. Rachel's tomb is no longer the "pillar" which Jacob set up, but the site is unquestioned; and the Moslems have built a little white tomb there, after their fashion, and on all sides there are Moslem graves. It may be that in former times, before the Moslems had possession, the Jews themselves used to bury there; and if so, then these slain little ones were probably laid to sleep in the green valley round Rachel's tomb; and the poor mothers came to weep and lament near her who had once said: "Give me children, or else I die!" They could not be comforted.'

'Well they ought to have been,' said Sue, 'because Jesus had taken their babies. And we'll see all those little children in heaven, mamma, won't we?'

'Yes, they are all there,' said mamma softly, — 'all there before the throne.' But she broke off abruptly, fluttering over the leaves of her Bible as if looking for something she could not see.

'Was Bethlehem a Benjamite city?' Cyril asked. 'O no — I remember — it was one of the thousands of Judah.'

'It was close by the inheritance of Benjamin, — the boundary line between the two tribes ran just south of Jerusalem, crossing the Bethlehem road. But both tribes belonged to Judah as a kingdom.'

'What sort of a place is Bethlehem now, mamma?' said Gracie.

'It has passed through all sorts of changes since the days of Herod the king,' answered mamma. 'Within a hundred years from the time when the surrounding hillsides echoed with that bitter cry, one of the Roman emperors planted a heathen grove on the very place where Bethlehem stood; ploughing up the ground and scattering the foundations. That was the Emperor Hadrian.'

'What in the world did he do such a thing for?' said Cyril.

'Out of hatred to Him who had been born there, I suppose. It was "the offence of the cross," — a new thing then in the world, but of which the world will never again be free, until the Lord shall come in his glory. There too Hadrian built a heathen temple; and the temple and the grove remained for a hundred and eighty years. Then about A. D. 330, the Emperor Constantine cut down the grove, and tore down the temple; building up instead a great church, which remains to this day, — probably the oldest piece of Christian architecture in the world. An immense pile of buildings, altogether; for joined to the church there are now three great convents, stretching out along the ridge of the hill. The nave of the church just shews faint traces of its old splendour. The Corinthian pillars are there yet, and the beams of cedar from Mount Lebanon; but the gilding is worn off, and the mosaics are faded; and the place and the services are all now in the hands of those who put themselves under useless, ignorant bonds, when they might be the Lord's freemen. The old Church is full of lamplight instead of sunlight; and the monks shew a marble manger and a stone cave, instead of the old inn of Chimham. And though they pretend that it stands on the very spot where the Lord was born, I think no one who really loves his name would wish to believe it. The cave of the Nativity, as it is called, is a grotto beneath the church altar, with steps leading down to it from either side; but there is nothing in the grotto itself, or the winding passage to it, or in the silver lamps and pictures and coloured hangings with which it is decked, to make one feel or believe that here was the manger where Mary laid her first-born son, " because there was no room for them in the inn." All traces of that time have passed away.

'The town is neatly built, very clean for an Eastern town, with houses of sparkling white limestone; and the sides of the hill are well terraced, and covered with figs and olives and vines, their soft shadows toning down the white rock soil. It stands even higher than Jerusalem, — 2,400 feet above the level of the sea. On the west, down in the valley, is Rachel's tomb; on the east a fertile plain where it is said the shepherds watched their flocks on that wonderful night. The people are lively and stirring; the women very handsome, the men strong and spirited, very troublesome to their Turkish rulers.'

' Are they all Jews?' asked Gracie.

'Not one, — there are no Jews in Bethlehem. The people are almost all Christianized Arabs, of the Catholic, Greek, and Armenian churches. Many of them shepherds and husbandmen, many more carvers and makers of pretty trifles out of the Red Sea mother-of-pearl, and the coloured marble of Jerusalem, and olive wood, and asphaltum from the Dead Sea. The old enclosing wall of the city has been broken down, but there are gates at the entrance of some of the streets; the houses are all flat roofed ; and along the hillside paths are little huts of unhewn stone, and roofed with branches, such as perhaps once filled " the coasts " of Bethle-hem.'

NAZARETH.

Chapter XI

NAZARETH.

THE children were busy with their Bibles when mamma came in, next day; grouped together in a stream of golden light that slanted in from the west.

'I like those next words,' said Cyril, — ' " Now when Herod was dead." Such men ought to die.'

'It was pretty bad for him, though,' said Sue gravely. 'But I guess it was good Herod couldn't go to heaven, because he'd have frightened the children.'

'Frightened the children?' said mamma, as she took her seat and drew Sue into her arms, — 'do you think anybody can be frightened where Jesus is, where they can see his face? Why even in this world the little ones who believe in him need never be afraid. "He gathers the lambs with his arm," — either on earth, or else up to heaven.'

Sue looked up shyly, with her deep, wistful glance ; but our mother's eyes grew dim and turned away. I think she had not got over the thought of the little ones at Bethlehem.

'How long did Herod live after he had killed the children, mamma?' said Mabel.

'But a few months, I believe. Yet the time must have seemed long to Joseph and Mary, waiting in Egypt, and knowing nothing of events in their own land: no daily papers full of reports, no mail every few hours to bring tidings. But the orders were plain: — "Be thou there until I bring thee word:" and Joseph had only to obey them to the letter. And just as soon as Herod was dead, without waiting till some slow caravan should carry the news, there came the promised despatch from heaven. Joseph, far down in Egypt, probably knew of the king's death before half the dwellers in Jerusalem. An angel appeared to him in a dream as before, saying: "Arise, and take the young child and his mother, and go into the land of Israel: for they are dead which sought the young child's life." People never make mistakes when they do exactly what the Lord bids them, because he knows everything. When he says Go, they may set forth fearlessly, — when he says Stay, it is at their peril if they stir a step.'

'I guess Joseph was glad that the Lord said Go, this time,' said Sue.

'No one not a Jew can know *how* glad he was,' said mamma; 'for to be out of the land of Israel and cut off from Jerusalem, was the most sorrowful thing in the world for a true son of Israel's race. We can just imagine a little with what longing eyes Joseph and Mary looked across the desert sand, beyond which, far out of sight, lay the mountain of the Lord's house and the sweet hill country

of Judah. With what glad haste did they arise
and prepare for their going home, when at last
the command came ! and then they journeyed on
their way, following the desert road in its windings,
until they had crossed the river boundary line of
El Arish, and were in Judah's land once more.
Then up the coast road to Gaza, with sand hills
between them and the sea, and the road itself no
better than a camel track in the sand. But towards
the hill country on the east, they could see ploughed
fields and grassy plains, and flocks.'

'I should think the camel track would become a
broad road, with so many caravans travelling it,'
said Cyril.

'The road is not so exactly marked out as that,
— each string of camels or asses seems to choose
its own ; and in the space of sixty yards there will
be twenty of these tracks crossing and interlacing
each other. But they make the way plain enough,
quite up to Gaza.

'At Gaza Joseph was to meet tidings of another
sort. I suppose he pitched his tent outside the
city, as is the custom now, and then went in among
the people ; eager to see and hear the men of his
own land once more. And there, perhaps from
some caravan just in from Jerusalem, he heard bad
news : Herod indeed was dead, but "Archelaus did
reign in the room of his father;" and Joseph was
afraid to go thither, — afraid to advance a step further into the country.

'Again God came to his help ; again in a dream

he was told what to do. He must not go across the
hills to Bethlehem, the city of his fathers; but must
journey on and on through the sea-coast plain, towards the north, and then turn aside into Galilee,
where Archelaus had no authority nor power.'

'I think it was very nice to be directed so all
the time,' said Mabel.

'Do you?' said mamma, — 'the promise stands
yet: "I will instruct thee and teach thee in the way
which thou shalt go." But then it is upon one
condition: "Be ye not as the horse, or as the
mule; which have no understanding: whose mouth
must be held in with bit and bridle." We must
follow, if we would have God lead. So did Joseph.
He was afraid — afraid to go into any part of the
land of Israel; "notwithstanding, being warned of
God in a dream," notwithstanding his fear, he went
on.'

'Sometimes in joy, sometimes in sorrow, sometimes in fear, — always in obedience!' said Gracie.
'So it is, mamma.'

'Was this another dream?' asked Mabel.

'I think so; while Joseph tarried at Gaza, troubled at the news he heard, and not knowing what
to do. The great caravan route from Egypt to
Damascus,' said mamma, pointing it out to us on
the map, 'went first as we have seen to Gaza, and
then along the beautiful sea-coast plain — the Shefelah — and the narrower plain of Sharon, almost as
far north as Cæsarea. Then turned off to the
north-east across the great inland plain of Esdraelon.'

'That is the plain that cuts the hills in two,' said Cyril.

'Yes. This is not the place to tell you much about the Shefelah, — its sandy strip of shore whereon stood the old coast cities of the Philistines; and its boundless fields of grain, — without a fence, without a break, almost without a stone, — that stretched back from the sands, "an ocean of wheat," to the wall of Judah's hills, full fifteen miles away. Here and there on a bit of rising ground there was a village, or one of Philistia's inland cities; set in a frame of gardens, with orange groves bearing immense fruit, and pomegranates brilliant with scarlet blossoms. From the Shefelah the road passed on into the plain of Sharon; and then through that rent in the hills twelve miles wide, the caravan route turned eastward. Even so Joseph went on through the Shefelah and the plain of Sharon; and then leaving the caravan route at the foot of Esdraelon, he literally, according to the Bible words, "turned aside into the parts of Galilee." '

'Then the caravan road did not go quite to Nazareth,' said Gracie.

'No, it crossed the south border of Galilee, going east; and there Joseph must have turned into the great northern highway, going towards Nazareth, his former home.

'Of all the provinces of the Holy Land, Galilee is the wildest, the richest, the most beautiful. Very different from the rolling hill country where Judah "bound his foal to the vine;" for the jagged heights of Galilee, wilder, higher, and more broken, held yet in their recesses rich upland valleys; while at their base lay broad plains of unbroken fertility. Here the tribe of Issachar "saw that rest was good, and the land that it was pleasant:" here Naphtali dwelt "like a hind let loose;" "satisfied with favour, and full with the blessing of the Lord." Here Zebulon was "for an haven of ships," and "rejoiced in his going out;" "and he sucked the abundance of the seas, and the treasures hid in the sand;" while of Asher it was said, "Let him dip his foot in oil:" "his bread shall be fat, and he shall yield royal dainties." The mountain ranges of northern Galilee are but spurs of Lebanon; with grassy plains far up on their heights, and forest glades, and glens opening out east and west. Here are thick woods of evergreen oak, and clumps of cedar, and myrtles and orange groves and olives. The hills are full of vineyards, the valleys of cornfields; and everything will grow in that wonderful climate, from the Caspian walnut to Egypt's palm. Streams from Lebanon pour down the ravines, and grass and flowers and birds make Galilee the garden of the Holy Land.'

'Is that *now*, or *then*, mamma?' said Cyril.

'It is a garden still,' said mamma; 'though now it is neither half settled nor cultivated. But we can just guess what it must have been. High up among these ridges that slope down from Lebanon, is a little crescent-shaped valley, a mile long and a quarter of a mile broad, stretching off east and

west, and with branches that run up among the
ravines like so many fingers. Fifteen rounded hill-
tops surround it on all sides ; white limestone hills,
but tinged with the colours and flecked with the
shadows of scattered figtrees and wild shrubs and
patches of grain. The valley itself is rich with verdure and cultivation. Thick grass — that rarity in
Palestine ; gardens hedged with prickly pear ; fruit

trees, cornfields, and multitudes of flowers, make
a brilliant mosaic of nature's own pattern. Figs
and oranges and mulberries and olives are among
the trees ; and the grass is embroidered with daisies
and tulips, lilies, poppies, anemones, and tall hollyhocks growing wild. The earth, where it shews,
is red and white with the crumbling limestone and
the rich soil ; and the golden gleam of citrons, and
the purple hue of grapes, shine in the summer sun.'
  'A valley among fifteen hills !' said Cyril. 'And
how high up, mamma ?'
  'About 1,300 feet above the sea ; and some of the
roads are rough enough. Approaching from the
south, after crossing the great plain, you come to a

rocky ledge a thousand feet high. No stranger would imagine that the way lay there, — Mr. —— said he should as soon have thought of riding up the Palisades of the Hudson River. But our guide declared that there was a " firstrate road," and up we went. Up among rocks and grassy ledges, where I think only Syrian horses could have kept their feet. The path was much of the time in the solid rock, sometimes mounting up by rude ledge steps for thirty feet or more, — just rock, with here and there a few flowers, or a low bush, nestling in the crevices. Then we turned round great masses of rock which not even our ponies would climb, and so came into the main road which finds its way to the plain through a ravine some distance to the west of where our path began. But such a "main" road! Slippery descents of rock, and sharp ridges, and loose stones, and holes ; and the ravine very narrow in some places.'

'Mamma,' said Sue, 'did your pony throw you off ? Weren't you afraid ? '

' My pony carried me up like the splendid little fellow he was, and neither slipped nor stumbled nor threw me off. And I was not afraid, Sue, — I had too much else to think of. For this was the old, old road to Nazareth; and up and down these very ledges of rock must Jesus have walked many and many a time. The wild ravine was full of his presence. And there is nothing like that,' added mamma softly, ' to make every road — whether of life or of Palestine — seem safe.

—'"Let me but see
Before me in the toilsome way,
The form of Him once slain for me · –
I'll sing and triumph all the way!"'

How clear and sweet the words came out! what though the voice fainted a little,

'Whichever path from the plain Joseph and Mary may have taken, when they came back from Egypt,' mamma went on, 'they came presently into this main road up the ravine; mounting slowly up: and then at a sudden bend in the hill Nazareth in its mountain nest — the fairest village in all Syria — lay before them. Fifteen hills, as I told you, circle it round. That to the north is the highest, rising up four hundred feet above the valley, and covered with herbage. The side towards the valley is steep, and seamed at the base with ravines; and in these ravines, and on the ridges between, lies the town : the white limestone houses holding fast to the rocks, and hiding in the glens, or standing on some point of higher ground to overlook the valley. People say that the old foundations shew that the whole town once stood well up on the hillside, but it is creeping down yet more and more into the valley now. Neatly built houses, flat roofed of course, and so shining white that one forgets the dirty lanes that lie between, — till one tries to go through them in wet weather. And then it is just as much as anybody can do.'

'O mamma!' said Gracie, — 'why don't they keep it clean?'

'I never saw a clean Oriental town,' said mamma. 'It's not the fashion of the East; and the people of Nazareth are no worse than others in this respect.'

'Are they Arabs too?' said Cyril.

'Yes, settled Arabs; like the people of Bethlehem. A bold, hardy, independent set; standing their ground well against all encroachments. The women are tall and well-shaped, and have a great

reputation for beauty; but not content with their natural advantages, most of them tattoo their faces and arms, and blacken their eyelids with kohl.'

'Tattoo their faces!' said Cyril. 'I thought only savages did that.'

'It is a savage custom,' answered mamma, 'and heathenish too, in its origin; for among some nations the tattooed marks on the forehead or hand were a mark of service to some heathen god; just as soldiers in certain armies were branded with a sign of allegiance to their prince.'

'And as the people in the Revelation who wore

shipped the beast were marked with his name,' said Gracie.

'The people of Nazareth use tattooing only as a beautifier now,' said mamma: ' its old meaning, if it once had one among them, has quite passed away. All the Arab women tattoo themselves more or less. So with blackening the eyelids : the custom was not thought respectable among the Jews. But the wicked queen Jezebel, a Phœnician, " painted the eyes ; " and her example was followed first by others like her, then by more respectable people ; and most Egyptians and Syrians do it yet. The *kohl* is a sort of lampblack prepared from burnt resin or almond shells. It is kept in a little glass vase ; and then with a small stick of wood or ivory or silver, dipped first in rose water and then in the kohl, the Syrian beauty marks round the edge of both the upper and under eyelid, and " puts her eyes in paint." '

'What horrid people ! ' said Mabel.

'I do not see that kohl is much worse than the little black patches English ladies wore on their faces in Addison's time,' said mamma. ' And for that matter, my dear, *every* face is marked in some way : stamped with the seal of God, or marked with the spot of the world. And this is a short way of deciding many a doubtful question, — will it mark me as belonging to the world, or to Christ ? '

'What sort of people in other respects are those at Nazareth ? ' said Cyril.

'About three fourths belong to the Greek and

Roman Catholic churches; and there are a thousand Mohammedans, a very few Protestants, but not a single Jew. No Jews seem willing to live in either Nazareth or Bethlehem. One of the prettiest places to see the people is at the Fountain of the Virgin, — the old living spring which supplies all Nazareth with water. It is outside the town, a little to the north-east; a stone-built fountain, with several openings through which the water flows out within sight and reach. Tradition says that here Gabriel came to Mary with his wonderful tidings; but though there is no reason to suppose that true, yet the fountain bears her name to this day. And hither she must have come, very, very often, with the child Jesus by her side. It is the same old fountain still, — the springs of an Eastern city are never lost sight of, though the city itself may pass away; and down the same path come all the girls and women of Nazareth now, to draw water. Come in bands of twenty or thirty at a time, — at some hours there is such a crowd that it is hard to get near the fountain. I used to sit there often, to watch the women as they came up, bearing their 'all earthen pitchers on head or shoulder, and then stopping to laugh and gossip and play round the old stone troughs. All brunettes, with black eyes and hair, and all of Arab blood. There are none "of the house and lineage of David" at that fountain now.'

'Mamma, how were they dressed?' said Mabel.

'In full trousers, and over that a long white

FOUNTAIN AT NAZARETH.

shirt; and then a long open robe of striped cotton
or Damascus silk, bound round below the waist with
a broad girdle. Some wore anklets of silver, and
all had bracelets — silver, gold, or glass; sometimes
with a jewelled ring on the finger, fastened to the
bracelet by a chain. On their heads they wore first
a tight linen cap, and in front, coming down each
side of the face like·the chains of a dragoon's helmet, was a thick linen roll covered with silver coins
as close together as they could be put on. A long
white pointed veil hung down the back; and over
the lower part of the face, and across the brow, were
the folds of a muslin shawl; leaving only the wearer's eyes to be seen. In the house these lower folds
are pushed down beneath the chin.'

'How large coins, mamma?' said Gracie.

'As large as a crown, or half crown — those worn
by the women; the children's were not larger than
a shilling. The girls will not sell one of these coin
rolls, for any price. Now and then at the fountain,
among the busy group, a few men might be seen;
wearing their long dressing gowns of silk and cotton, gayly striped with red and purple, or violet and
yellow, or purple and white; and girdled with a
shawl, or with a broad leather belt stitched full of
pockets and purses. And every man wore on his
head the red and yellow Arab shawl.'

'Well it wasn't polite to wear their dressing
gowns out where people could see them,' said Sue
with grave disapproval.

'Ah that is all the coat they have,' said mamma.

'I called it a dressing gown, for it looks like one; but it is really their *dress*.'

'Mamma, are any of the old Nazareth houses standing yet?' said Gracie; 'or is it all new, like Bethlehem?'

'All new: I suppose that very few of the building stones even, of Mary's time, remain. That soft white limestone soon crumbles away when exposed

to the weather; and the houses, if not cared for
and kept in repair, very soon go to ruin. Nazareth
has been once and again sacked and deserted, and
probably the stones of the house where Mary lived
are but dust in the highway now. The Romish
monks pretend that they have the whole house safe
at Loretto, — and the Greek church shew it in
equally good repair somewhere else; but the real
little house at Nazareth has for ever passed out of
sight.'

The children sat thinking, as mamma ceased, —
musing over the strange customs and scenes of that
far off land; — all but one little heart. Gracie suddenly broke forth with almost a cry.

'Mamma! — how can one escape that dreadful
mark!' —

Mamma laid her hand tenderly on the child's
head.

'Listen, Gracie,' she said. '"And I looked, and .
lo, a Lamb stood on the mount Sion, and with him
an hundred forty and four thousand, *having his
Father's name written in their foreheads.*" Where
that seal is set, neither earth nor hell shall have
power to place its own.'

Chapter XII

GOING UP TO THE PASSOVER.

'S that is Nazareth!' said Cyril, leaning his elbows on the table and studying the little photograph which mamma had laid before us. 'And here Joseph and Mary came to live. "They came and dwelt in a city called Nazareth."'

'And there my Jesus lived too,' said Sue.

'Yes,' said mamma, ' "when they had performed all things according to the law of the Lord." They had gone through all the required ceremonies at Jerusalem, had been exiles in Egypt at his command; and now coming back again by his permission, "they returned into Galilee, to their own city Nazareth." "That it might be fulfilled which was spoken by the prophets, He shall be called a Nazarene."'

'Mamma,' said Gracie, 'I've been trying and trying to find those prophecies, and I couldn't find one! I couldn't see that even the word Nazarene is in all the Old Testament.'

'Ah I dare say,' answered mamma; 'it is not in our English translation; but if you could have searched the Hebrew Bible, you would have had better success. Nazareth is now called by the Arabs En-Nâzirah; but the real name in Hebrew is Nêtser, — and Nêtser means a shoot, a sprout. Now turn to the 11th of Isaiah : " And there shall come forth a rod out of the stem of Jesse, and a Branch shall grow out of his roots." The word used there for Branch, is Nêtser. And in other places the same image though not precisely the same word is used. Jeremiah says : " Behold, the days come, saith the Lord, that I will raise unto David a righteous Branch," — and Zephaniah, " I will bring forth my servant the Branch " — " the man whose name is the Branch." '

' Mamma,' said Sue, ' I don't understand it one bit ! '

' You would know what I meant if I called my little Sue a flower ? ' said mamma.

' O yes,' said Sue.

' Well in the Bible kings and great men are often called trees. Now when a tree dies, or is cut down, after a long while the old root which is in the ground sends up a new shoot; or sometimes the branch of a living tree bends down and takes root. And if some king was spoken of as the tree, then this shoot or branch would mean his rightful heir and descendant. But a piece of any but the royal tree would not be called a branch at all. Now king David had been dead a long, long time; and there had not been a prince of David's line for a great many years. But the Lord had promised;

and then Jesus came: "a rod out of the stem of
Jesse" (David's father), and a Branch from the old
root. For his mother was of the royal family of
David. "And he came and dwelt in a city called
Nazareth ; that it might be fulfilled which was spoken by the prophets, He shall be called a Nazarene." He shall be a Nêtser, — a Branch, — and
"the Lord God shall give unto him the throne of
his father David."

'Quick and constantly now, from this time forward, went on the fulfilment of all that the prophets had foretold concerning this wonderful One.
"The child grew, and waxed strong in spirit," —
strong in the Lord and in the power of his might :
"and the grace of God was upon him." "Grace is
poured into thy lips," so it had been written of him
long before, and now all was accomplished. "The
Spirit of the Lord shall rest upon him, the spirit of
wisdom and understanding, the spirit of counsel
and might, the spirit of knowledge and of the fear
of the Lord ; and shall make him of quick understanding in the fear of the Lord." '

'But he was the Lord himself,' said Mabel.

'And the Son of man too : "made a little lower
than the angels for the suffering of death," and
therefore receiving grace, and needing comfort, and
feeling pain, like any other man. Thus every bit
of his human nature and of his human experience
is a lesson for us. "He left us an ensample that
we should follow in his steps." '

'How, mamma?' said Cyril. 'I should have

thought that just these things which you were telling were beyond being copied.'

   ' Listen to what the Bible says,' replied mamma.
' " The fear of the Lord is the beginning of wisdom :
a good understanding have all they that keep his
commandments."   " 'Thou, therefore, my son, be
strong in the grace which is in Christ Jesus."
Think how the first twelve years of his life passed
on, and what fruit they bore !   " The grace of God
was upon him," all those years.

   ' " Now his parents went to Jerusalem every year
at the feast of the passover." '

   ' I don't understand much about the passover,'
said Cyril.   ' The Bible's full of it, too.'

   ' Fifteen hundred years before this time of which
we have been speaking,' said mamma, ' there was
" a night much to be observed unto the Lord," —
the night wherein he brought out the children of
Israel with a strong hand from their bondage in
Egypt : " this is that night of the Lord to be observed of all the children of Israel in their genera-
tions."   He bade each family choose out a spotless
lamb, and kill it, and sprinkle its blood on the posts
and lintel of the house door ; and then they must
roast the lamb whole, and gather round and eat it,
with unleavened bread and bitter herbs ; each one
dressed for a journey, with staff in hand, and in
haste.   So, after this manner, in silence and by
night the children of Israel kept the first passover.   And at midnight the Lord passed through
the land of Egypt, and smote with death the

first-born in every house; but when he saw the blood-sprinkled doorposts where the Israelites dwelt, the Lord passed over those houses, and suffered not the destroyer to go in. Therefore this feast was ordered to be kept by the Israelites for ever; in memory of their great deliverance, of their liberty and new life: everything henceforward should date from that. "This month shall be unto you the beginning of months: it shall be the first month of the year to you," said the Lord, — the month Abib: for on the fourteenth day of Abib, at even, the feast of the passover was kept.'

'What month was Abib?' said Cyril.

'It answers to our April — or rather part of April and part of March. Abib means, the month of ears of corn; for the barley harvest began then. And the children of Israel kept the feast year by year, through all their wanderings. But when they were settled in the Holy Land, and the temple was built, then it was ordered that the feast should be kept at Jerusalem by all the assembled people; and so every year at that time, all the men of the whole nation went up for the feast, to the place the Lord had chosen.'

'And not the women too?' said Mabel.

'The women might go or not, as they chose; and the devout ones usually went, if no home duties were in the way. So Hannah, the mother of Samuel, went to the feast; and so Mary, year by year. And when the Lord Jesus was twelve years old, he too went up to Jerusalem at the time of the feast, with Mary and Joseph. This was the custom among the Jews, — at the age of twelve a boy was taken to the passover for the first time.'

' Well what became of the fields and everything while the men were away ? ' said Cyril. ' Enemies might have come and conquered the whole land.'

' What becomes of anything, which we leave to God's care, at his command ? ' said mamma. ' Is it neglected, do you think ? As for enemies, the Lord had made a special promise about that : " neither shall any man desire thy land, when thou shalt go up to appear before the Lord thy God thrice in the year." For there were two other pilgrimage feasts, besides the passover.'

' That was first-rate,' said Cyril. ' Why of course it was just as good to have God lay his hand upon people's hearts, as to have him stretch out his hand and cut off their heads.'

' Just as good !' — said Mabel, — ' isn't that a boy's speech ? Mamma, why do you say *pilgrimage* feasts ? '

' Because each one was kept at Jerusalem, and crowds of people went up to them from every direction. Nothing like those feasts has ever been seen in the world since then ; nor will be, until the time of that holy convocation when all the general assembly and church of the first-born shall meet together in heaven, — in " Jerusalem which is above." As the day of the feast drew nigh, the people of each town and village set off together, joining themselves to other little companies by the way ; until the roads were filled with long processions of men, women and children, their faces all towards the holy city.

'Imagine what the scene would be, in some mountain village of Galilee for instance. It is now two or three days before the passover, and the people have made all their preparations and are ready for the journey. The scattered travellers on the hillside have come in, and the people of the town have shut up their houses; and it is night, and all stand waiting in the streets for the first breaking of the day. Then as the dawn comes softly up in the sky, the little company sets forward : first the elders of the town, and the priests, if any dwell there; then the people — on foot, or on camels and asses; while scattered here and there through the crowd are the Levites with their musical instruments. And as the people move forward at the slow caravan pace, the Levites begin to chant; and through the grey morning twilight, and among the glorious hill-tops of Tabor and Hermon, and over the old plain of Esdraelon, sound forth the notes of the psalteries, and the chorus of voices, young and old : —

'"I was glad when they said unto me
   Let us go unto the house of the Lord.
   My feet shall stand within thy gates, O Jerusalem.
   Jerusalem is builded
   As a city that is compact together.
   Whither the tribes go up,
   The tribes of the Lord, unto the testimony of Israel,
   To give thanks unto the name of the Lord."'

'O grand!' said Cyril. 'It makes one wish one's self a Jew.'

'Mamma,' said Gracie, softly, 'it makes one think how St. Paul desired to depart, and be with Christ.'

'Ay!' mamma answered, with the flush mounting on her pale cheek, — 'and of that day when "the redeemed of the Lord shall return, and come with singing unto Zion." No heart can conceive what that music will be. And few things on earth could ever be compared with this, its great type, of which I have told you. The glorious words of the psalm, the full voices, the long train of pilgrims, — some going up to Jerusalem for their first, and some for their last passover. Then as they went on, leaving further and further behind them their houses and possessions which the Lord had promised to guard while they were away, again the song burst forth : —

"'I will lift up mine eyes unto the hills
From whence cometh my help.
My help cometh from the Lord
Which made heaven and earth.
He will not suffer thy foot to be moved ;
He that keepeth thee will not slumber :
Behold, he that keepeth Israel shall neither slumber nor
sleep."'

'Mamma,' said Sue, 'how could the people sing when they were riding ?'

'Because in a caravan everybody moves slowly, at a slow foot pace ; not more than two or three miles an hour; so that those who ride go no faster than those who walk. Ever nearer and nearer to the holy city, resting at midday because of the heat, spreading their mantles for carpets, sharing their stores with one another, thus the procession moved on. From one direction came a company well supplied with honey, — another came loaded with clusters of raisins; and each gave freely of such things as they had. Even as the pilgrims who are journeying to the Celestial city, give help and refreshment to each other: "every man according to the measure of the gift of Christ."

'And now at length, on the third or fourth day, they drew near to Jerusalem, and every eye and heart were eager with expectation. All other things were forgotten for the time, and the people chanted as they went: —

"How amiable are thy tabernacles, O Lord of hosts!
  My soul longeth, yea, even fainteth for the courts of the
    Lord.
  My heart and my flesh cry out for the living God.
  Blessed are they that dwell in thy house —
  Blessed is the man whose strength is in thee —
  A day in thy courts is better than a thousand."

'On and on, over the swelling hillsides and through the deep valleys, with such haste as they could make. The sun was declining, throwing the wild hill country into exquisite light and shade; and the still spring air caught and held and prolonged the rich music, as once more the Levites began their song, and the people joined in.

" Great is the Lord, and greatly to be praised,
  In the city of our God, in the mountain of his holiness.
  Beautiful for situation, the joy of the whole earth,
  Is Mount Zion, on the sides of the north, the city of the
      great King.
  We have thought of thy loving kindness,
  In the midst of thy temple, O God,
  According to thy name, O God,
  So is thy praise unto the ends of the earth :
  Thy right hand is full of righteousness.
  Let Mount Zion rejoice,
  Let the daughters of Judah be glad,
  Because of thy judgments.
  Walk about Zion, and go round about her.
  Tell the towers thereof:
  Mark ye well her bulwarks,
  Consider her palaces ;
  That ye may tell it to the generation following.
  For this God is our God for ever and ever :
  He will be our guide even unto death."

'The psalm was begun with every voice joining
in ; but before it ended many a one was silent, with
heart and thought too full of joy and expectation.
And as the last words were sung, the Levites prolonged the notes on their instruments, but the people were still as death ; and only the soft footfalls
of the camels and the hushed tread of the crowd,
could be heard.   Suddenly from those in the front
rank burst forth the cry — " Jerusalem ! — Jerusalem ! " — " Jerusalem, thou city built on high,
we wish thee peace ! "   For there in the distance
rose the white walls of the city, gleaming in the setting sun ; and up into the clear air there mounted
a light cloud of smoke from the evening sacrifice.'

'Mamma,' said Gracie, 'it will be so, will it not, when the other pilgrims get home? and they'll see first the gates of pearl, and "the light most precious;" and then the sacrifice that bought it all. And they'll sing a new song then.'

Mamma bowed her head in answer, but she did not speak: some thought of the discords and pain of earth made the thought of that music too deep for words. But Sue, striking her little hands together, sang with her clear voice:—

> "There we shall reign and shout and sing,
>   And make the heavenly arches ring;
> When all the saints get home—
>   When all the saints get home."

And the other children caught up the refrain and repeated it, till it sounded through my very heart. Then mamma spoke again.

'Thus, in this manner, our Lord Jesus went up to the passover when he was twelve years old; but though the city was thronged, with twenty times its usual numbers, yet for once every house was open to him, as to other strangers. For at the time of a pilgrimage feast, no dweller in Jerusalem counted his house his own. Even so, all could not lodge within the city; and white camps were pitched on every side. That of the Galilee pilgrims was always to the north, on the Mount of Olives.'

'I suppose the people who came first got the houses, and the people who came last took the tents,' said Cyril.

'I suppose so; though many might prefer the tents, even if there was room elsewhere. Jerusalem was a wonder of beauty by night, at such a time. In the city people were all up on the roofs of their houses, taking supper; and lights and feasting were on every hand; while in the valleys beyond the walls, and on the surrounding hills, the white tents of the pilgrims gleamed out bright in the moonlight. Every now and then a burst of music was heard in the distance — cymbals and trumpets and song — as some new caravan came up; arriving late because of its longer journey or rougher road; and so the thirteenth of Abib — or Nisan, as the month was called in later times — came to an end; and the next day was that of preparation for the passover. One part only, of the preparation, was made this evening. After supper, the master of the house with his younger guests — each bearing a torch — went in grave procession from room to room of the whole premises, searching for leaven; opening each closet and cupboard and drawer, to make sure that none of the forbidden thing was concealed there. The master himself carried a dish and brush; and every little crumb of leavened bread, every particle of leaven in any shape that he could find, was carefully swept into the dish. The search was so minute and careful that it sometimes lasted two hours; and then when every nook and corner had been examined, the dish was carefully locked up, the householder saying these words the while; "Whatsoever leavened thing there is in my house, which I have not seen nor put away, may it be scattered in pieces and accounted as the dust of the earth." '

' Why did he say that, mamma ? ' asked Sue. ' Why did they do all that ? '

' God had ordered that they should eat only unleavened bread all the days of the feast, and they wanted to be quite sure that there was none other in the house, and to protest that if there, it was without their knowledge. Leaven was taken for a type of sin, — a sign of people living in worldly abundance and servitude ; and therefore God's people must put it away. Even the sign must not be allowed when they kept this memorial feast, in token of the blood that saved them and set them free ; but they must eat the bread of haste and simplicity, as pilgrims who seek a country. And as they searched for even the least speck of leaven, so might God search their hearts. As David said : "Cleanse thou me from secret faults," — "that which I see not, teach thou me."

' The day of preparation came. All the families took an early meal, to have time for the needful arrangements ; and then the women baked a supply of unleavened bread, and the furniture and vessels and floors in every house were washed, and all things put in the neatest order. At noon a slight repast of the thin white cakes of unleavened bread was set out under the palm trees in the inner court of each house ; and when this was over, a fire was made in the garden, and the locked-up dish of leaven was solemnly brought out and burnt.'

'What was the unleavened bread like ? said Mabel.

'Something like thin crackers, — made of flour and water, and baked in flat cakes which were pierced full of little holes, lest the least fermentation should take place.

'And now, about the eighth hour — or two o'clock — the trumpets sounded a long blast from the temple, and said to every one who heard, that the passover had begun ; while from streets and tents and houses a thousand horns answered the signal. Immediately every man who was at the head of a family set out for the temple ; either bearing a lamb on his shoulder, or having it driven before him by a servant ; and the throng became presently almost impassable. By degrees, however, the men were gathered in the court of Israel, dividing themselves into three great bodies ; and there they waited until the evening sacrifice should be over. It was offered an hour before the usual time, on this day ; and as soon as it was laid on the altar, when the lamps were lighted in the holy place, and the incense was mounting up to heaven in a fragrant cloud, then the gates into the priests' court were thrown open. At once the first division of the men went in there, and with three blasts of the trumpet the gates were closed again, and the work of sacrifice began. On this day only, each man killed his own. The priests stood in two long rows, reaching from the people to the altar, one row bearing basins of gold and the other basins of silver. Then each

Israelite in turn brought forward his lamb, and first telling how many were to partake of it, he drew his knife across the creature's throat. The priest nearest to him caught the blood in his basin, and handing it to the next priest took his empty basin in exchange; and thus the basin that held the blood was passed along, until the priest who stood next the altar received it, and threw out the blood at the foot of the altar in a single jet. Meantime each man of the people stepped aside as soon as his lamb was killed, and began to skin it and take off the fat, which another priest carried away and laid on the altar. The work went on with great quickness; and when one division of the people had finished their work, the gates were opened and another set took their place. Not silently was all this done, but with singing and praise: the Levites, standing on the fifteen steps between the court of Israel and the court of the women, sang the great Hallel, as it was called, — the Psalms from the 113th to the 118th; and at each Psalm there were three blasts of the trumpets. Then when all was done, and it began to grow dark, the people went home; and the priests carefully cleansed the temple courts, and burned the fat of the lambs with incense upon the altar.'

'Mamma, how many were there of these priests and Levites?' said Cyril.

'In the time of King David there were twenty-four thousand Levites engaged in the temple service alone, besides the singers and musicians; and these numbered four thousand more. So you may think what the great Hallelujah was in those days, sung by four thousand trained voices; but the priests alone blew the trumpets, on any occasion. Of the priests there were so many, that tradition says it had never fallen to the lot of any priest in latter times to burn incense twice.

'While the men were thus busy at the temple, on the day of preparation, the women at home had other work to do. Tables were set and ovens heated, and all made ready for the feast. The ovens were holes in the ground, two and a half feet wide, but five or six feet deep. The sides were faced with stone, and the fire was kindled at the bottom, and kept up until the stones were very hot. Then the whole lamb was put in to roast: a spit of pomegranate wood thrust through it from end to end, and a second shorter piece run across from shoulder to shoulder, and thus it was suspended in the oven until thoroughly done.

'It was now the fifteenth of the month, for the Jewish day begins at sundown. Every house was brilliantly lighted, the members of each family were assembled, all dressed in their best clothes. Children as well as grown people, the servant with his master: on this night all were equal. "In Christ, there is neither bond nor free." Only no foreigner, — none who were not of Israel might come to the feast: they had no part in the great deliverance, no faith in the blood of sprinkling. But there were Jews of every nation, — from Egypt, Cyprus, and Babylon.

'The supper room was sweet with perfumes, and in the midst of it stood a low table, placed out of order and set as if in haste; and round it stood the family, all dressed as if for flight; sandals on their feet, and staves in hand, and their costly robes girt close about them. And first of all, the master of the house took a wine cup, and as he filled it he blessed the Lord who had given them that day. Then tasting the wine, he passed it round the table; and after another blessing spoken, all the company washed their hands. The roasted lamb was now set on, with the unleavened bread, the vinegar, and the sauce of bitter herbs; and each one took some of the herbs, dipping them in the vinegar.

'At this moment the mistress of the house made a sign to one of the little ones there, and the child spoke out, asking the meaning of all these strange things. And at once the father answered, — telling how God had redeemed Israel out of the house of bondage; how for the sake of the sprinkled blood of the lamb the destroying angel had passed over their dwellings; how from thenceforth they had been the Lord's peculiar people : telling also of the haste with which they fled out of Egypt, having only time to take with them their kneading troughs of unleavened bread. Then each one eat of the bitter herbs, singing afterwards the 113th and 114th Psalms. Another washing of hands followed, and the cup was again blessed and sent round. Then they eat of the unleavened bread with the herbs and vinegar, and the lamb was carved, but so as not to break a bone nor divide a joint.

18

'With joy and singing the feast went on, until an hour before midnight : it must not continue after that. After prayer, and another washing of hands, and another cup blessed and drunk, they sang Psalms 115th to 118th : once more washed their hands, once more drank of the cup, and the feast of the passover was ended. But whatever portion of the lamb was not eaten, was burnt that very night : it might not remain until the next day.'

' It sounds just like a great, beautiful parable,' said Cyril. ' I wish you'd explain it, mamma.'

' It is easily explained,' mamma answered, ' for the whole was a wonderful type of Christ, and of the soul's dealings with him. We were in the bondage of sin and darkness, and "Christ our Passover was sacrificed for us." And as each soul must accept and rest in that sacrifice for itself, so each householder must slay his own lamb : on this occasion not even the priest might do it for him ; for in Christ we are made priests unto God. The lamb was roasted whole, for the sacrifice is one, and Christ's people are one : and no part of it might remain until the next day, because as the Redeemer's work is a finished work, so must be the believer's acceptance. We must be all Christ's, or we are none of his ; for no man can serve two masters. The feast began with blessing — "I will take the cup of thanksgiving, and call on the name of the Lord." And the washing of hands was a sign of purification, of putting away sin from the daily life. "I will wash my hands in innocency," said King David.'

'Mamma, I don't see what the bitter herbs should mean,' said Gracie. 'Seems to me everything ought to be just sweet at such a feast.'

'I think they had several meanings,' said mamma. 'They were a sign of that repentance, so bitter and yet so wholesome, which every soul must know before it is ready to receive Christ; they were a remembrance of the bondage which had made the life of every Israelite a bitter thing. And as much as either of these, perhaps, they were a token of the persecutions, the afflictions, which yet awaited them. Those who come to Christ do not leave all sorrow and trial behind them, only they have the assurance that one day their sorrow shall be turned into joy. "In the world ye shall have tribulation," said the Lord to his first disciples; "but be of good cheer: I have overcome the world."

'The unleavened bread was a sign of entire, simple heart-devotion to God. No reservation was there, no hidden half work; for the least speck of such leaven would soon leaven the whole lump. Leaven has in itself the seeds of corruption and dryness and mould; but unleavened bread will be sweet and pure for any length of time. It was a sign of haste too: not the provision of ease and worldly indulgence, but "the unleavened bread of sincerity and truth." And the half-prepared table, and the sandals, and the staff in hand, were just a reminder of the word that comes to every dweller in sin: "Escape for thy life!"—and so escaping, so fleeing from bondage to Christ, he is thenceforth a pilgrim ; his loins always girt, his light always burning ; his feet shod with the preparation of the gospel of peace, ready for the Lord's service. And as he journeys on, from time to time the cup of salvation is in his hand, and the great Hallelujah — one part of it or another — is ever sounding in his heart, making melody to the Lord. Sometimes it is this : " Not unto us, O Lord, not unto us, but unto thy name give glory : " sometimes this ; — " I love the Lord, because he hath heard my voice and my supplication, — Return unto thy rest, O my soul, for the Lord hath dealt bountifully with thee." Oftenest of all, the memory of what Christ has done : " Open to me the gates of righteousness " — " Bind the sacrifice with cords, even unto the horns of the altar." " O give thanks unto the Lord, for he is good : for his mercy endureth for ever."

' " And his mercy is unto children's children of them that fear him," ' said Gracie hiding her face and hands in mamma's lap.

And our mother answered, ' Amen ! '

Chapter XIII.

THE YEARS AT NAZARETH.

'M*AMMA*,' said Mabel, 'it keeps seeming strange to me that the Lord himself should have done all those things you told us of yesterday. All that feast and shedding of blood was nothing to *him*.'

'Ah it was something to him!' said mamma, — 'the appointed sign of his own perfect sacrifice, now so near at hand. Besides that, he came to fulfil the whole law, to obey its least demands. He went up to Jerusalem after the custom of the feast. Now the feast of unleavened bread lasted for seven days; but whoever chose might return home after the third day was past. Those who were more devout, or who were rich and could afford it, having neither harvest nor flocks to call for their care at home, remained through the whole week.'

'What was done?' said Cyril.

'All through that first evening while the people kept the feast, the priests were hard at work cleansing the temple; sweeping and washing and putting in order, after the throngs of men and animals that had crowded it that day. Then they too eat the

passover, and a little after midnight the temple was
lit up and the gates were opened. Soon after that
all Jerusalem was astir. The watchman on the temple wall stood looking for the dawn; a priest asking him from time to time, "Does it begin to be
light towards Hebron?" And when he could say
yes; when the morning light was not only in the
eastern sky but was tinging the hills towards Hebron; by that time the streets were filled with people in their gayest dress. For the temple was
never so crowded during the whole year, as on the
morning after the passover. Then came first the
usual morning sacrifice, after that special offerings
and sacrifices peculiar to the feast; with the singing of the Hallel; and on this day the whole body
of priests were in attendance, not merely a single
course. Offerings were made for all the people,
and after that each one brought his own.

' At the evening sacrifice there was the ceremony
of the wave-sheaf: sheaves of barley, the first fruits
of the harvest, specially cut and bound in some one
of the fields about the city, were now carried to the
temple and presented to the Lord of the harvest.
Then some of the grain was roasted and ground,
and on the next day this meal was salted and
mixed with oil, and burned upon the altar, a thank-
offering unto the Lord. After this came a special
sacrifice, and then all those who needs must went
home, to carry on the harvest so solemnly begun.
But many remained at Jerusalem throughout the
week.

'So, it is supposed, did Mary and Joseph at this time; for they fulfilled the days, the days of unleavened bread, and as they returned, the child Jesus tarried behind in Jerusalem; and Joseph and his mother "knew not of it." They had set off with the Galilee caravan, but the child Jesus presently left them; and they supposing that he was somewhere in the company, wandering about as a boy will do, went on a day's journey without him.'

'A whole day's journey, mamma?' said Sue.

'The first day's journey of a caravan, Sue, is generally very short; not more than two or three hours. They set out, get fairly away from the city, choose a good camping place, and halt for the night; so that if any important thing has been forgotten, any needful stores not laid in, the matter may be found out and set right before they are too far away. So the Galilee pilgrims went on a few miles, perhaps to Beeroth; and then when they were encamped and night drew on, and still the child did not appear, Mary sought him among all her kinsfolk and acquaintances. And when he was not to be found, she turned back to Jerusalem, seeking him there; and there at last she found him, after three days. After three days,' — mamma repeated, — 'that is an Eastern form of speech. When I first reached Gaza, the health officer said we must be four days in quarantine; but the day we arrived counted for one, and the day we went away for another, — we were really shut up but two. And so at Hebron, a quarantine of "two days," meant only remaining over night.'

'Then the three days here, means over two nights,' said Cyril.

'Yes. They did not reach Jerusalem probably till in the night, or even till the next morning. All that day they sought — in the house where they had been staying, or on the north hill where the Galilee camp had been, and in the houses of all their friends; but to no purpose; and it was not till the next day that they found Jesus in the temple. They had looked perhaps in its great courts, before; but now, either directed by some word, or searching as one seeks in even unlikely places at last, they went through the various rooms in the outskirts of the temple, and found him there.

'Among the Jews many learned men took upon themselves the office of public teachers; and while some had private lecture rooms, and others taught in the synagogues, there were others still who occupied class rooms in the temple itself. Here they kept a sort of school for those boys who were themselves destined to become scribes and teachers. At thirteen, every boy became as they said a child of the law; bound to study its precepts and to obey them; but for most boys the synagogue teaching in their own town or village was thought enough, and their learning seldom went beyond the texts written on their phylacteries. But when a boy was devoted to the calling of the scribes, then he went up to Jerusalem and joined some one

of these other schools. There the younger boys
sat on the floor and the elder on a bench; while
the Rabbi, mounted on a high chair, told forth all
the wisdom with which his own mind was stored,
and a sort of interpreter — or crier — repeated it
to the boys. There were also several assistant
teachers. There was little book learning, few book
lessons, in those days: the master questioned the
boys, and they questioned him, — proposing difficult questions, inquiring after hidden meanings.
Deep questions sometimes, touching the law of
God and the life of a true Israelite; or often about
things of mere ceremony and surface work.

'In such a class did Joseph and Mary find the
child Jesus, "in the temple, sitting in the midst of
the doctors, both hearing them, and asking them
questions." We know not what these questions
were; but it is easy to imagine how the Lord
would bring up word after word from Moses and
the psalms and the prophets concerning himself;
proving that the kingdom of God was at hand;
and how the scribes in turn, drawn on by his wonderful words, would ask hard questions of him, —
striving in vain to be anything that day but learn-
ers. "And all that heard him were astonished at
his understanding and answers;" for as had long
ago been foretold, "the Lord God had given him
the tongue of the learned."

'So Mary and Joseph found him, and were astonished with the rest. But either forgetting for
a moment who her child really was, or else with a

secret pleasure at thus claiming him before the great ones of the land, Mary ventured on a reproof: "Son, why hast thou thus dealt with us? behold, thy father and I have sought thee sorrowing."

'With a sudden assertion of his work, his power, his divine authority, Jesus answered: reproving her in turn. "How is it that ye sought me?" he said: "wist ye not that I must be about my Father's business?" Not to be her child, not to do her pleasure, had he come to earth; but to finish the work of God, to fulfil his counsel, to carry out his plans. Joseph and Mary understood not what he said to them; but according to her old custom Mary "kept all these sayings in her heart," waiting to understand. And he, "learning obedience" for our sakes, left the temple, and "went down with them, and came to Nazareth, and was subject unto them."

'So eighteen years passed by, and of them all we have but one short record: "Jesus increased in wisdom and stature, and in favour with God and man." Like other children in the steady growth and development of both mind and body; but in the constant increase in the favour of God, O what child is like unto him!'

'I wish the Bible told us something more,' said Mabel.

'Something less, do you mean?' said mamma.

No, it tells only that Jesus' time was not yet come; and he was unknown, unnoticed by the world, dwelling humbly at Nazareth, subject to those who were called his parents, busy I suppose with their servile calling and occupations.'

'What was their calling?' said Cyril.

'Joseph was a carpenter; and as the fashion is now in Galilee, he probably travelled about from place to place, doing his work. So small a town as Nazareth would give him not very much to do, in that land of stone houses and unchanging fashions; and he would naturally go round the country, repairing a roof here, or mending furniture there; and perhaps even as far as to Tiberias, to work at the fishing vessels on the lake: following his trade now in the houses and now in the open air, as his various customers might demand. And doubtless He who was called in later times "the carpenter's son," went with him, "and was subject unto him;" helping in the work. Daily gaining favour with men by the pure beauty and shining of his every day life; daily hearing in his heart those words from heaven which were afterwards spoken in the ears of all: "Thou art my beloved Son, in whom I am well pleased."

'This is only a little talk, mamma,' said Gracie, as our mother closed her book.

'We are late to-night,' said mamma. 'Yes, a little talk—but a great deal to think of.'

Chapter XIV.

JOHN THE BAPTIST.

'IT generally happens,' so mamma began next day, 'that God's purpose is accomplished in a very slow, quiet and unseen way. Men delight to make a stir and a bustle with all they do; but the Lord guides Arcturus silently, and his footsteps are not known. "He that believeth shall not make haste;" for God's work is sure, and his time the best.

'Nearly thirty years passed by after the return of Joseph and Mary from Egypt, and still nothing was heard of Him who had been born king of the Jews. The generation that slighted the tidings of his birth had all passed away, and of the few who had welcomed the good news hardly one was left alive. Simeon and Anna, Zacharias and Elisabeth, were doubtless all gone: probably Joseph too; and Mary — alone perhaps of all Israel — still "kept these things in her heart." The rest of the world forgot or did not know. Herod was dead, and Archelaus was dead, and so was the emperor Cæsar Augustus; and now under Tiberius Cæsar, one of his successors, Pontius Pilate was

go\ ernor of Judæa, and another Herod was tetrarch
of Galilee. John, of whom such great things had
been predicted, was hid away in the desert, at-
tracting no attention ; and Jesus himself was living in a little Galilean town, subject to his mother,
and working I suppose for his daily bread. But
the testimonies of the Lord are very sure. You
remember the wonderful eclipse which we saw
lately, and how the people looked and waited as
the time drew near ; watching for the first edge of
that shadow which should hide the sun.'

'Yes, and they got very impatient too,' said Cyril ; 'and some of them said they didn't believe
there would be any eclipse.'

'But just when the time came,' said mamma,
'just at the very moment which astronomers had
foretold; one little, little point of shadow fell —
and then swept on. Something so, I think, must
angels have been watching at this time of which
we read ; watching to see not a shadow, but light
break over the world. Men had too little knowledge, or too little faith and patience ; saying,
"Where is the promise of his coming? — for all
things continue as they were;" — but angels knew,
and waited with the intensest interest for the first
stir in that action which was to change the world.
Thirty years before, they had proclaimed glory and
good will and peace, and yet the world went on its
old course; but now "the Lord awaked as one out of
sleep" — and the stone was cut out without hands,
which should become a mountain, and fill the

whole earth. "When the fulness of time was
come," — not one minute before, not one second
later, — "God sent forth his Son."

'It was the fifteenth year of the reign of Tiberius
Cæsar. Pontius Pilate was governor of Judæa,
and Herod — a son of Herod the Great — was
tetrarch of Galilee; Philip, or Herod Philip — his
half brother, was tetrarch of Iturea and of the region of Trachonitis, lands lying to the east of Jordan and Galilee; and Lysanius was tetrarch of
Abilene, a country between Lebanon and Damascus. All Syria and Palestine were under the iron
heel of the Romans; though at Jerusalem, the
Jews — fierce to maintain and defend their law —
were still allowed to keep up their sacrifices and
temple service. Yet the conquerors had interfered,
even here; and Annas, the regularly appointed
high priest, had been deposed by them some years
before, and Caiaphas his son-in-law installed in his
place; but the Jews still held to Annas: therefore
"Annas and Caiaphas were the high priests."
And so it was, that while the rulers of the Jews
were set up and put down by a Roman emperor;
while the darkness of unbelief and oppression
brooded over the whole Jewish land; on a sudden
there broke forth a gleam· of the day-spring from
on high, and this strange cry arose: "Prepare ye
the way of the Lord, make his paths straight."

'In those Eastern countries,' mamma went on,
'it is the custom to send some one on before the
traveller, to see that all is ready for his reception;

to choose a village where he shall pass the night,
and then either a house or a camping ground; to
provide refreshments; to prepare everything that
he may need. And when the traveller is a king,
all the roads are put in order, the bridges are
mended, and everything is smoothed and beautified
for his journey through. Even in riding through
the streets of a town, a man often runs on before
to clear the way. And now that the Lord himself
was at hand, "there was a man sent from God
whose name was John;" according as it was written by the prophets: "Behold, I will send my
messenger, and he shall prepare thy way before
thee." '

'Mamma,' said Sue, ' was the man sent right from
heaven, as the angels were?'

'Why, it was John the Baptist,' said Mabel.

'No, he did not come from heaven,' said mamma, 'but his orders did, and he was in the wilderness until they came: "the word of God came to
John the son of Zacharias, in the wilderness," in
the deserts, as the word is in another place. "He
was in the deserts until the day of his shewing to
Israel." '

'He must have been glad to get out of 'em, I
should think,' said Cyril.

'The wilderness of Judæa is not exactly what
you understand by a desert,' said mamma; 'the
Arabic name comes from a word signifying "to
'ead to pasture." It is a wild, uncultivated region,
with no settled inhabitants, — even in Judah's

populous times there were but six cities in the wi.-derness, — and now there is neither village nor road. The wandering tribes of Arabs drive their flocks up and down among its deserted solitudes, and pitch their black tents for a day or a week wherever there is a spot of grass or a pool of water. It is a long strip of country, nowhere more than nine or ten miles broad, but reaching from Jericho down to some forty miles away. East of it lies the Dead Sea; and on the west, rising up abruptly with a swift ascent, is the hill country of Judah. All its plants and shrubs are peculiar; not a hill-country leaf or flower decks the wilder-ness; and the ground is seamed with deep, wild ravines, the rocky sides of which are full of caves. At some seasons of the year there is a good deal of pasturage, and a sort of smile of blossom and freshness lingers there for a little while; but then it all fades beneath the fierce heat of the sun: the water brooks dry up, the grass turns white, the flocks live only by browsing; and their wild own-ers roam from place to place, seeking hollows in the rocks where "the rain has filled the pools." Every one of these throughout the whole wilder-ness, is known to them; and an Arab guide will tell you of one miles away, where the gathered drops of the spring rain linger the longest. Neither rose nor olive nor oak will grow here; but dry artemisias and bitter rue, with tamarisks, thorns, salsola, fagonia, zizyphus, and alhagi. Here and there, in the spring-time, there are small patches of cultivation, but with no owner living near. The planter dares' not stay by his crops, but comes again at harvest time to carry home his grain, if perchance some Arab tribe have not saved him the trouble. It is a region of valleys — the beds of winter torrents, seaming and cutting their way down the " innumerable round-topped hills, crowded one behind another, of the wilderness of Judæa. A true wilderness, but no desert, with the sides of limestone ranges clad with no shrubs larger than a sage or a thyme — brown and bare on all the southern and western faces, where the late rains had not yet restored the life burnt out by the summer's sun, but with a slight carpeting of tender green already springing up on their northern sides. Not a human habitation, not a sign of life, meets the eye for twenty miles." *

' In this wilderness, dwelling either in one of the old towns, now dwindled to a mere hamlet, or perhaps living hermit-like in a cave, John passed his years of silent unknown preparation for the work before him ; until at last he received his instructions, and was sent forth — a prophet and messenger and witness for Christ. The word of God came to John the son of Zacharias in the wilderness.'

'I should have thought John would have been living at Jerusalem, near the temple,' said Gracie.

'Jerusalem had changed : it was no more like the old city of David. Roman power had brought

* Tristram.

14

in Roman luxury, with its theatres and games.
Heathen soldiers walked the streets, and heathen
standards had been seen there ; and although the
Jews still kept up the old customs of their law and
nation, yet for the most part these were but a
form. " They said they were Jews, but were not."
John would have found a much fairer field for the
consecrating preparation for his life work, in a cave
in the wilderness, than in Jerusalem itself. He
was a Nazarite, pledged even before his birth to a
life of the strictest purity, and could have had little
in common with the Pharisees who filled the temple; and his time to rebuke them was not yet
come. Perhaps too his seclusion was ordered on
another account; for the messenger was not needed
till the king was ready to appear.'

'Did God send an angel to tell him when to
go ? ' said Sue.

'I do not know,' said mamma. 'That phrase,
" the word of God came," is used in the Bible for
those special messages which God sent the world
from time to time, by the mouth of his prophets.
"The word of God came to Nathan " — " the
word of the Lord which came to Jeremiah " —
" the word of the Lord that came unto Hosea."
But never had any man brought such a message as
was now sent by John. " Thou, child, shalt go
before Him " — such had been the promise at his
birth ; and now he came " preaching in the wilderness of Judæa, and saying, Repent ye : for the
kingdom of heaven is at hand."

'He was a strange looking preacher. No minister, in trim black garments; no priest, in flowing robes of spotless white; but a man rough and uncourtly to look at, with long hair and beard that had never been cut, and clad in a coarse sack of camel's hair, bound around his waist with a leathern girdle. Some such sack or shirt was the ordinary working dress of the common people; but theirs were generally of wool or cotton; while John wore rough haircloth, the garb of the ancient prophets. Thus Isaiah wore sackcloth; and Elijah was "a hairy man, girt with a girdle of leather:" so the two prophet witnesses in the Revelation were clothed in sackcloth. And many a false prophet has put on this dress, trying to pass for what he was not: you will meet even now in that same wilderness, starting up out of one of those same caves, men making this pretence. Wretched creatures who know nothing of God, who do nothing but evil, yet who wear a shirt of haircloth and a girdle of leather, and call themselves prophets. Zachariah told of a good time coming, when he spoke of that day when people "shall no more wear a rough garment to deceive."

'John therefore came in the dress proper to his calling, with his raiment girded for work; and his meat was locusts and wild honey.'

'Well, what is wild honey?' said Sue. 'Don't the bees make it all?'

'Yes, and wild honey is made by wild bees. Some bees you know live in hives in a garden or on a farm; but others live far away from men's houses, and put their sweet store in such places as they can find: in hollow trees and clefts of the rock. Sometimes they even hang their combs from the tree branches. Arabia and India are full of wild bees: and Palestine used to be "a land flowing with milk and honey," — honey was a chief article of food, and not merely a dainty, as with us. The people kept hives near their houses; and multitudes of bees were at work for themselves, in the woods, and to the furthest corner of the wilderness; filling the hollow trees and lining many a hillside cave with sweets. " Honey out of the rock," "brooks of honey," such were some of the promised riches of Canaan. " Judah traded in honey," and the men of Samaria had " treasures in the field " of honey; and honey was one of the gifts that Jacob bade his sons carry down into Egypt. When Saul fought the Philistines, and drove them before him, the people came into a wood in Mt. Ephraim, " and there was honey on the ground," — the trees were so filled with the bursting combs, that " the honey dropped." '

' I think I should like that,' said Cyril. ' I believe I'll go and live in Palestine.'

' And make yourself sick eating honey,' quoth Mabel.

' There might be some danger,' said mamma; for the quantity found is often a temptation. " Hast thou found honey ? " wrote King Solomon; " eat so much as sufficeth thee: " that is, eat no

more. Honey was never offered in sacrifice, but
the first fruits of it were brought as regularly as the
first fruits of harvest, and being first presented
before the Lord, became then the portion of his
priests.'

'But I don't see how anybody could *live* on
honey,' said Mabel.

'Not on honey alone. Eastern people, however,
eat sweets much more freely than we do. Butter
and honey is a favourite dish with them; and the
Arabs dip their dried fruits in honey, and their ripe

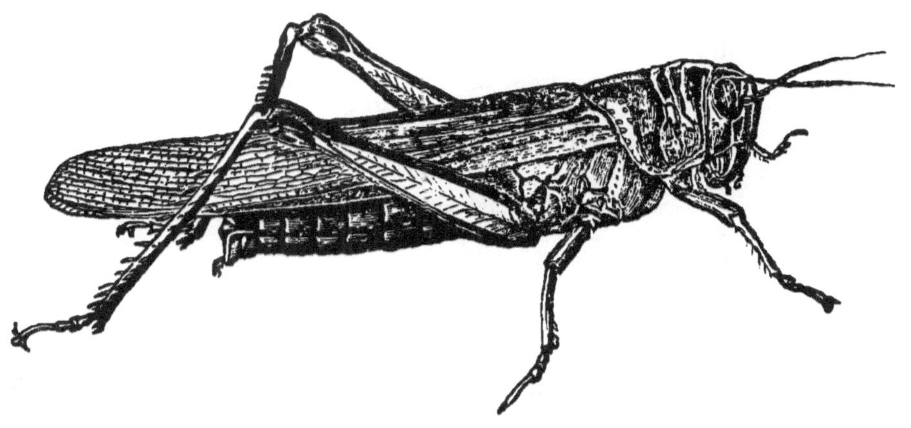

nuts. But John the Baptist had neither butter
nor fruits to relish his meal; "his meat was
locusts and wild honey." Do you know what
locusts are?'

'Mamma,' said Gracie, rather slowly — 'I've
been hoping they weren't just like ours!'

'Very much like,' said mamma smiling; — 'rather more like our large flying grasshoppers.'

'O that's disgusting,' said Mabel.

'No,' mamma answered, 'not at all disgusting: not half so bad as eating snails, and I cannot see why it is much worse than eating frogs.'

'But, mamma,' said little Sue, 'pussy eats grasshoppers!'

'And pussy eats chicken, too, if she can get it. Locusts are a very important article of food in the desert regions of the East; and if you have ever watched pussy when she was eating a grasshopper, you know pretty well how an Arab manages his locust; only the cat eats hers raw, but the Arab throws his into boiling water and salt. Then the wings and legs are pulled off (you know what a little heap puss leaves on the gravel walk), and the locusts are first dried in the sun, and then packed away in sacks, ready for use. Sometimes they are pounded fine and mixed with flour and water into cakes.'

'Locust cakes!' said Cyril. 'Well of all wild cookery!' —

'You can have them smoked if you prefer it,' said mamma; 'or they may be broiled, or roasted, or fried, or stewed in butter, and then spread upon bread as we spread anchovy paste. They taste a good deal like shrimps. The plain dried locusts are never served up as a dish, but each person goes to the sack and takes a handful when he chooses.'

'Just as if they were sugar-plums!' said Sue.

'O they are a great deal better than sugar plums, for hungry people,' said mamma.

'But I don't think it's pleasant to think of—that John should have eaten them, after all,' said Gracie.

'Quite pleasant,' said mamma. 'They are fit to be eaten, for the law delivered to Moses gives express permission to eat them—therefore they must be both good and wholesome; they are sold in the market of every town in Arabia, tied on strings, in the old, old fashion. In the sculptures at Nineveh there are figures of men carrying locusts to the king's feast. See, here is a picture of one, with the dried locusts tied upon sticks.'

'What queer things!' said Cyril. 'I don't know whether they look most like rabbits or kittens.'

'Then I suppose,' said Gracie looking at the picture, 'that John dipped his locusts in honey, as you say the Arabs do with their nuts, mamma.'

'Very likely. It is poor sort of food enough; despised by those who can afford better things; but in that wild region John would find—as the Arabs do now—not much else to eat.

'Such then was God's chosen messenger, sent to prepare his way: "As it is written in the book of the words of Esaias the prophet, saying, The voice of one crying in the wilderness, Prepare ye the way of the Lord, make his paths straight. Every valley shall be filled, and every mountain and hill shall be brought low; and the crooked shall be made straight, and the rough places plain.”

‘ Such proclamations are not uncommon in the East. When the Sultan has once or twice sent word that he was coming to Syria, all the sheikhs and petty rulers issued a general order to the people to prepare his way; and at once they assembled along the road he was to travel, and began to clear the stones away, and to fill up the hollows, and level the heights, and straighten the crooked bends.’

‘ Yes,’ said Cyril, ‘ it’s easy to understand *that*. But how can men prepare God’s way ? ’

‘ What stands in the way of his triumphal progress through all the world ? ’ said mamma.

‘ Why — sin, I suppose,’ said Cyril.

‘ And what hinders him in our hearts ? ’

‘ Sin again,’ said Cyril with a shake of his head.

‘ And John came preaching, “ Repent.” Let the heights of pride be levelled, and the hollows of unbelief be filled up: let the crooked ways of deceit be made straight, and all roughness and hardness be cleared away. Then shall all flesh see the salvation of God. The things of this world have had dominion long enough, — behold, the Lord of the whole earth is here. “ Repent, for the kingdom of heaven is at hand.”

‘ So preaching, so passing along with that strange warning cry, John went on through the wilderness to the lower part of the Jordan, close to where it reaches the Dead Sea, and taking his stand by the

sweet flowing waters of life, with the Sea of Death
so near, he preached the baptism of repentance for
the remission of sins. Were any ready and willing
to forsake their sins, to change that mind which
had hitherto served the world? — let them come
and receive the sign of baptism, and enrol themselves under the standard of repentance. It was
time to throw off their allegiance to earth, for the
kingdom of heaven was at hand.'

'What does that mean exactly, mamma?' said
Grace.

'In the book of the prophet Daniel,' answered
mamma, 'are these words: "In the days of these
kings shall the God of heaven set up a kingdom,
which shall never be destroyed: and the kingdom
shall not be left to other people, but it shall break
in pieces and consume all these other kingdoms,
and it shall stand for ever." Now was that kingdom to be set up, now was its Prince to appear and
claim his own. Yet he would take it at first by
little and little, but "he must reign till he hath
put all enemies under his feet."

'Therefore John warned the people to become
his friends,' said Gracie.

'Ay,' said mamma, 'that was the word — that
is the word now: "Be ye reconciled to God." It
was not for nothing John had his girdle drawn, for
he was in vital work and earnest. Not a sermon-
izer to interest them, not a philosopher to make
this or that theory more clear; not a dainty speak-
er to delight their fancy; but a cry! Of warning,

of entreaty, of agonized life or death ! No wonder
it echoed far and wide, — the people poured forth
at its summons. "Then went out to him Jerusalem, and all Judæa, and all the region round about
Jordan," — the multitude was so great, that it
seemed as if the whole country, smitten with a
sense of guilt, was gathered there upon the river
shore; and they "were baptized of him in Jordan,
confessing their sins." '

'What good did the confessing do?' said Mabel.

Then mamma answered: "He that covereth his
sins shall not prosper, but whoso confesseth *and
forsaketh* them shall find mercy." John came
preaching "Repent!" — change your lives, — set
your faces towards the kingdom; and the people
owned that they needed to be changed; and were
baptized as a sign or pledge that they would live
no longer as they had done. It was no new thing
among the Jews, this outward token of the inner
life : from the earliest times men had thus re-
nounced the defilement of sin in a figure, when
they were resolved to be clear from its real pollu-
tion. "Put away the strange gods that are among
you," said Jacob to his idolatrous household; "and
be clean, and change your garments." "Sanctify
the people to-day and to-morrow, and let them wash
their clothes," said the Lord to Moses when the
law was to be given from Mt. Sinai. So David
said, "I will wash my hands in innocency," — and
you know we use the same figure now. Even

among heathen nations this sign was known; and
people washed before prayer, and before offering a
sacrifice, and after a battle, and before they would
touch any sacred thing. The Jewish priests always washed when they were going into the temple or near the altar to minister; the heathen
priests of Egypt bathed twice every day and twice
every night as a preparation for their work. And
thus when John came preaching the baptism of
repentance, it was like an echo of words spoken
long before by the prophet Isaiah: " Wash you,
make you clean; put away the evil of your doings
from before mine eyes; cease to do evil; learn to
do well." '

' And were many of this multitude in real down-
right earnest?' said Cyril.

'Very many, I doubt not. John could not read
their hearts, to tell who were the real and who the
unreal penitents; but he went on to apply sharp
tests, that so each man might know about himself.
Differences of dress and appearance made it easy
to divide the throng into classes, and to these
classes he spoke in turn.

'First of all were the Pharisees and Sadducees,
the two leading sects among the Jews; each hostile to the other, and only alike in thinking themselves better than all the rest of the world. The
Pharisees had earned their name two centuries before, when one of the Greek rulers of Palestine had
set himself to break down the barriers between the
Jews and his other subjects, to change Jewish cus-

toms and clear away Jewish law. Then certain of the Jews made stand against him, resolving to maintain their law and customs even to the smallest point. And as this was called " the time of the mingling," so these men who would not mingle were called " Separatists ; " and from the Hebrew word which means to separate, came the name Pharisee. They are supposed too, to be the same sect with the Assideans mentioned in Jewish books, — that is, godly men, saints. But this good beginning had soon passed away. A holy life was found to be a difficult mark of separation from the rest of the world, — it was far easier to be peculiar in a thousand little trifles ; and the Pharisees sunk into a sect of mere formalists. They burdened the truth with so many useless laws of man's making, that the law of God beneath it all was in danger of being quite forgotten ; separating themselves from others by their dress, their ablutions, and a conscience whose scruples reached only to outward things. To bear them out in all this, the Pharisees pretended that when Moses received the written law on Mt. Sinai, there was given to him at the same time, by an archangel, an oral law, —one that was never written down, and never meant to be ; but which had been kept as it was given, by word of mouth, and preserved from age to age in memory and by tradition. In this oral law of course they could find what rules they pleased. Yet they held firmly to many great points of truth . the sovereignty of God, the immortality of

the soul, and the existence of angels, both good and
bad. But they held too, that for Abraham's sake,
because of his obedience, God was pledged to make
all Jews partakers of the Messiah's kingdom on
earth, and for ever happy in the other world.'

' I suppose the Jews liked *that* doctrine,' said
Cyril.

' Very much : the Pharisees were extremely popular; and the highest offices in both State and
Church were filled by them.

' The Sadducees, on the other hand, were a sect
who not only lived at ease, but made it their profession. They were the wealthy and noble class,
— a sort of priestly aristocracy; having their descent as was supposed from Zadok, a chief priest in
the time of King David, and a very noted and
faithful man. From this Zadok — or Sadoc — the
Sadducees were thought to have their name ; the
old Hebrew books call them Sadocites : and as
Sadoc means righteous, they like the Pharisees
began well. But they had gone yet further astray.
The Sadducees did not want even the burden of
religious forms ; and shaped their belief according-
ly. They denied the overruling power of God;
denied that there were angels or evil spirits ; and
declared that the soul of man died with his body.
They scouted the oral law of the Pharisees, profess-
ing to believe only the written law, or what they
chose to find there.

' Thus the world's two great classes were well
represented in the multitude that went forth to

hear John the Baptist : on the one hand, those who lived as they liked, denying any future account or present accountability for the life that now is ; on the other, those who hid their life with a religion of forms, and made holiness to consist in outward works and not in a changed heart.

'But John had no silver words for either of them. He knew the Pharisees by their peculiar dress, and the Sadducees by its richness ; and looking on them he sounded his cry with even more vehemence than before, telling both Pharisees and Sadducees their common ancestry : — "O generation of vipers" — descended from that old Serpent the Devil — "who hath warned you to flee from the wrath to come?" You Sadducees, who say there is no future life, no endless death; you Pharisees, who teach that the fringes of your garments and the number of your prayers can make you accepted of God; what has alarmed *you?* But if indeed ye are in earnest, then prove it: bring forth fruits meet for repentance, and shew a changed life springing from a changed heart. Think not to say within yourselves, We have Abraham to our father; trust not that God is pledged for the salvation of every Jew — "If ye seek him, he will be found of you; but if ye forsake him, he will cast you off for ever," and of these very stones on the hillside will raise up children unto Abraham. He can give to the poor and the despised and the down-trodden of earth the very birthright of your proud nation, if he will.

Already is justice armed, — "the axe is laid at the root of the trees: therefore every tree which bringeth not forth good fruit is hewn down and cast into the fire :" that fire to which you, O Pharisees, think no Jew can be condemned, and in which you, O Sadducees, do not believe.'

'Mamma,' said Gracie, 'I shouldn't think the people could have breathed! — '

'I guess nobody doubted what the preacher meant, for once,' said Cyril.

'No,' said mamma, 'his trumpet gave forth no uncertain sound; and the multitude — wondering, stirred — "asked him, saying, What shall we do then?" And again John's words rang out sharp and clear, testing their sincerity. This putting an extra border on your garments for religion's sake, is one thing; but now "he that hath two coats, let him impart to him that hath none; and he that hath meat, let him do likewise," — a very different matter from the punctilious washing of hands before eating it yourself. Then came to him publicans, probably from Jericho, which was not far off, stepping forth from the crowd to be baptized, and asking for a word of special direction : "Master, what shall we do ?" '

'Did they think themselves worse than anybody else, that they could not take general directions? said Cyril.

'Other people thought they were,' said mamma; 'their very name was hateful to the Jews, for it was a sign of foreign rule and extortion. The Ro-

man government *farmed out* its revenue in Syria,
— that is, it gave up the right of taxation in one
part of the country to one man, and in another to
another, for which right each man paid down a
certain sum of money, and then collected the taxes
to repay himself at his leisure. These upper tax
farmers, to call them so, these chief publicans, were
often rich and honourable men; but they in turn
farmed out their districts to several others; and
the lower publicans, the under tax-gatherers, made
for themselves a very bad name.'

'Mamma, why were they called publicans?' said
Gracie.

'Because they agreed to pay a certain sum *in
publicum* — the Latin word for treasury. And
having thus paid, of course so much they must
have back from the people at any rate; and whatever they could get beyond this, was all clear gain.
John struck at the root of their greatest temptation as well as of their commonest offence, when he
answered: "Exact no more than that which is
appointed you."

'Then came up soldiers, passing through the
Jordan valley on their way to Petra, where there
was an Arab insurrection just then; and attracted
by the crowd they too stopped to hear the preacher; asking him: "And what shall we do?" — we,
whose very work is in blood. But John was ready
for them. "Do violence to no man," he said:
fight only in a just cause and in a just way:
"neither accuse any falsely; and be content with
your wages." 15

' With such stirring words, with such searching
counsel, John came into all the country round
about Jordan; and the whole country went forth
to hear him. And the prophecy of the angel was
fulfilled: "Many of the children of Israel shall
he turn unto the Lord their God" — making ready
a people prepared for the Lord. For when people
do truly repent of their sins, then and not till then
are they ready to welcome Jesus — a Saviour.'

Chapter XV.

BY THE JORDAN.

'But if John was sent to prepare the way of the Lord, why didn't he tell the people about him?'—Thus Mabel, while mamma sat silent a few minutes before the afternoon talk, and the other children pored over their Bibles.

'If you were a fireman, rushing into a burning house at night,' said mamma, 'you would not talk to the sleeping people about some strong ladder just placed against the wall; even though you knew that the stairs were burned away: first of all you would wake the sleepers up. This was precisely what John had to do; to stir up the consciences of the whole nation; for the men were in a sort asleep, nor even knew their need of a Saviour.

'From the earliest times, from that very day in Eden when God softened the curse with the promise of deliverance, it had been known that a Deliverer would come. From age to age, to Abraham, to Moses, to David, by the mouth of one prophet after another, had the promise been repeated; while to Daniel had even been told the time of its

fulfilling; and learned men, counting up the **days**
and interpreting the weeks spoken of by Daniel,
were sure that now the time was at hand. So deep
and earnest was this belief, as we have seen, that
many men even braved Herod's anger, rather than
acknowledge him for king; and in some form or
other the hope of the near approach of the Messiah
was almost universal. But oppressed by the Romans, their land "desolate and overthrown by
strangers," the pure service of God almost forgotten among them; the Jews looked for their Deliverer as one who should bring earthly triumph and
worldly honour. They remembered the promise,
"In his days Jerusalem shall be saved and Judah
shall dwell safely;" forgetting that this was the
name whereby he should be called: "THE LORD
OUR RIGHTEOUSNESS."

'And thus it came to pass, that John's trumpet
words seemed to many like a call to battle against
the Romans; a summons to enlist under a banner
which should lead them on. Was it Messiah himself who spoke? "The people were in expectation,
and all men mused in their hearts of John, whether
he were the Christ or not."'

'That was a fine chance, for any man who was
ambitious enough,' said Cyril.

'Ay, but John had "waxed strong in spirit."
He was not one of those weak ones who wish to
attract human eyes, or to have a party in the
church called after their poor mortal names. The
grace of God never let him forget for a moment

that he was but " the prophet of the Highest." At once he answered their questioning looks, their half-spoken words, saying unto them all: " One mightier than I cometh, whose shoes I am not

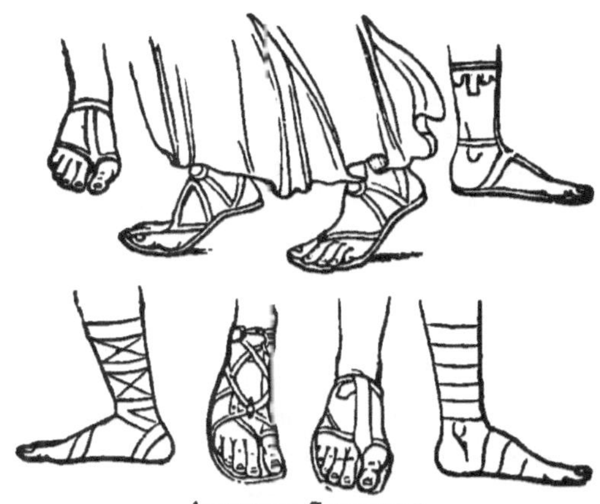

ANCIENT SANDALS.

worthy to bear — the latchet of whose shoes I am not worthy to stoop down and unloose." I do not deserve to be even his servant, — look not at me, but make ready for him.'

' What's a latchet?' said Sue.

' The shoe worn in those times,' said mamma, ' was only a sandal, — a mere sole of wood or felt or leather, bound to the foot with a long leather or cloth strap: this strap was the latchet. You see in the picture how the strap crosses the foot and is wound round the ankle, keeping the sandal firm in its place. In the East it is still the custom

to change your shoes on entering a house, or to
throw off the outer-shoe, if one is worn; and even
these sandals were taken off at the threshold.
Where a man was rich enough to have a servant
follow him about, it was the servant's business to
unloose the latchet of his shoes; and if the master
went into the temple, or to pay a visit, the servant
not only took off his sandals at the outer door, but
also bore them about after him, until the master
was ready to put them on again. Disciples sometimes did this for their teachers; but the old
Rabbis advised them not to do it where they were
unknown, lest they should be mistaken for servants. The very same customs prevail in Palestine now, though sandals are used no longer.
When Dr. Bonar went to the Turkish mosque in
Jerusalem which stands where once the temple
stood, a poor Arab boy followed him as shoe bearer;
untying the Doctor's shoes at the gate of the
mosque, and then bearing them after him, from
place to place, until he came out into the street
again. "Do you think *I* am the promised One?"
said John to the musing people: I am not
worthy to do for him even the office of a servant.
"I indeed baptize you with water; but he shall
baptize you with the Holy Ghost and with fire."
Through him shall "the Spirit be poured on you
from on high:" "a new heart will he give you,
and a new spirit will he put within you." "Behold, the Lord whom ye seek shall suddenly come
into his temple" — but take care that you are

ready; for " he shall be like a refiner's fire." So
searching, so powerful, shall be his work, that
nothing false or evil can stand before it: it will
purify all, or it will burn all. " Judah and Jerusalem shall be purged by the spirit of burning; "
and he " will bring the third part through the fire,
and will refine them as silver is refined, and try
them as gold is tried." His baptism shall be the
renewing power of God in your hearts — mine is
but the sign and preparation for that; as it is
written : " Turn you at my reproof: behold, I will
pour out my spirit unto you." " And the Redeemer shall come to Zion, and unto them that
turn from transgression in Jacob." " Repent, for
the kingdom of heaven is at hand."

'So spoke the fearless preacher, — bringing up
doubtless the old prophecies, the old promises, with
which all were familiar; and the people listened.
Before them rolled the swift river, silent witness of
the power of God; for thrice near that very spot
had its rapid tide been stayed, for his people to
pass over; and the Jordan — the Descender —
stood still, at the word of the Lord.

'The stream rushed on in its old course yet, with
fringed banks of willows and reeds and tamarisks
and oleanders; and Jericho was there — not the
old but the new town; its fertile plain full of
harvest fields from which many of John's hearers
had no doubt just come. John knew it well, even
if the plain itself were not in sight, and few
preachers have ever had at hand such a wonderful

scene to preach from. The broad plain; the site
of the old city and the buildings of the new; the
glorious harvest work that was going on all around.
Here were men cutting the grain, and others

THRESHING FLOOR.

gleaned after the reapers, and others tossed the
ripe sheaves into heaps like hills; while long lines
of loaded camels went constantly from these heaps
to the threshing floors, where yet other workers
were beating out the grain after the fashion of the
East. A Palestine threshing floor is not in a
clean well-swept barn, as we have it here; it is
merely a large round spot in the open field, from
fifty to a hundred feet broad, levelled and trodden

quite hard and smooth, and always kept for just
this use : so that the different threshing floors near
a city come to have their own special names.

'On this broad earth floor the sheaves are laid in a
circle, and then a horse or a yoke of oxen is driven
round and round upon them, dragging over the
spread-out grain a heavy board with sharp stones or
bits of lava imbedded on the under side. This is the
mowrej, or threshing machine; and it not only
beats out the grain, but also crushes and chops up
the straw into mere chaff. Then grain and chaff
together are all thrown into the middle of the floor,
and fresh sheaves are laid out all round the edge.
When the whole is threshed — and the heap in
the middle is by this time higher than a man's
head — the grain is fanned, or winnowed. The
fan is a flat wooden shovel, called raha. And first
of all, the husbandman fans the clear space on the
floor, to blow off all the dust which collects there
during the threshing : then when the floor is quite
clean he takes up a shovelful of the mixed grain
and chaff, and pours it out against the wind, so
that while the sound wheat or barley drops back
upon the floor, the light chaff is carried away by
the wind, and falls at a little distance, making another heap.

'Looking off towards the glowing plain, — possibly near enough even to see the wind's work and
the flying chaff, John burst forth again. I do not
know your hearts, — such was his thought now: I
cannot tell which of you is in earnest; "but one

mightier than I cometh." "Whose fan is in his hand, and he will throughly purge his floor, and will gather the wheat into his garner; but the chaff he will burn with unquenchable fire." For when Jesus comes into the world, or into any heart, searchingly, all that is not purified by the fire of his power and holiness must be consumed.'

'I wonder the people could understand John, he used so many images,' said Mabel in her discontented way.

'They were old images, very familiar to every Jew,' answered mamma; 'the books of the law and the prophets were full of just such. "The ungodly are like the chaff, which the wind driveth away." — "They are as stubble before the wind," — "as chaff driven by the whirlwind." Neither was that fire a new idea. "The day cometh," said the prophet Malachi, " that shall burn as an oven; and all the proud, and all that do wickedly, shall be as stubble : and the day cometh that shall burn them up, saith the Lord of hosts." No image could be more forcible. The utter dryness of the chaff, its helpless drift before the wind, the fierceness of its burning, all shadowed forth the words : " If mine hand take hold on judgment, I will reward them that hate me." No human power could stay a fire once lighted there, — if the flame be kindled it makes thorough work. We can imagine how John reminded the people of these old warnings, going back ever and anon to his own special message : " Repent." '

'Mamma,' said Sue in her plaintive voice, 'I want to hear some more about "Jesus loves me!"'

'Jesus was close at hand then,' said mamma, wrapping her arms about the child; 'for "in those days" — on some one of those very days when John was preaching, he came from Nazareth to Jordan unto John, to be baptized of him. Not by special appointment, with a day set apart for him alone and the riverside kept clear from the crowd, — not as a king did Jesus come to be baptized, but as a servant; made in all things like unto his people, and "separate from sinners" only in heart. Down amid the self-righteous Pharisees, the careless Sadducees, the despised publicans; pushed and jostled by all, unknown even to the true penitents, He came, in whose sight even the heavens are not clean. "He was in the world, and the world was made by him, and the world knew him not."

'One eye alone recognized him; one heart alone sprang forth in eager welcome: the rough-clad preacher at the river brink looked up and knew his Lord. "I have need to be baptized of thee," he said, "and comest thou to me?" — and he forbade him, overwhelmed at the mere thought. With gracious, kingly condescension the Lord answered John's scruples; not denying that they were well founded, but waiving them by his royal will. "Suffer it to be so now," he said; for thus must he "fulfil all righteousness," even the outward ceremonies of righteousness, who is to "bear the sins of many."'

'And John had Mary's kind of humility, and took the honour God gave him, without a word,' said Gracie.

'Without another word, apparently. "Then he suffered him," — "and Jesus was baptized of John in Jordan." '

'Mamma, do they know the place?'

FORD OF THE JORDAN.

'No, but it was probably at one of the fords near Jericho; where there is a break in the steep banks, and the shore slopes gently down, and the river is clear of jungle for a little way; so that the multitude could stand at the water's edge. At some one of these spots I suppose John took his stand, perhaps out on the stepping stones of the ford, a better footing than the soft shore, and where the people could come to him one by one without crowding. It seems that all the other comers, for that time, had been baptized already; "And Jesus, when he was also baptized, went up straightway out of the water," and stood on the riverside, praying; when of a sudden "the heaven was opened unto him"—was rent or torn, the word is; "and the Holy Ghost descended in a bodily shape like a dove," and lighted upon him, "And, lo, a voice from heaven, saying, This is my beloved Son, in whom I am well pleased."

' "And Jesus began to be about thirty years of age." This was the age at which the scribes, having finished their preparatory training, were sent forth to teach; being first solemnly ordained by the laying on of hands, and publicly declared to be ready for their office. "I admit thee," said the chief Rabbi, "and thou art admitted to the Chair of the Scribe." But our Lord Jesus received authority from God himself; and upon him the Holy Spirit rested: "the spirit of wisdom and understanding, the spirit of counsel and might, the spirit of knowledge and of the fear of the Lord." '

' Mamma,' said Sue, ' who spoke?' Then mamma answered—

' God the Father spoke, to God the Son; upon whom came down the visible presence of God the Holy Spirit: these three persons of the one true God, who wrought together at the creation of the

world, and now again for its redemption. It was
the sign from heaven, the divine assurance, that
this was the Promised One—the Messiah. "Thou
art my Son," said God a thousand years before, by
the mouth of David; and again three hundred
years later, by Isaiah the prophet: "Behold my
servant, whom I uphold: mine elect, in whom my
soul delighteth: I have put my Spirit upon him."
This should be his office, this his consecration, —
His, "who being in the form of God," "took on
him the form of a servant," and was "found in
fashion as a man." At thirty years of age, too,
the priests began their work; and now, called by
a voice from the excellent glory, sealed and con-
secrated by the Holy Spirit, Jesus went forth, to
teach those who would "learn of him;" "to make
reconciliation for iniquity, and to bring in everlasting righteousness." The Son of God with
power, he was also — as really, as truly — the Son
of David.'

'But that's just what I don't understand!' said
Cyril.

'How can you?' answered mamma: '"the mystery of Christ manifest in the flesh," faith can receive, but no mortal reason can explain. John
tells first of the Lord's divine nature; but two of
the other evangelists give the long human gene-
alogy; tracing back his royal descent as a king
from David, and shewing the line unbroken, and
the title perfect to the throne. Matthew in his account gives the lineage of Joseph, the supposed

father of Christ, from whom in the eye of the law
he received the inheritance; but Luke gives the
title by blood, through the ancestors of Mary his
mother; although (according to Jewish custom)
her name does not appear. "Being (as was supposed) the son of Joseph, which was the son of
Heli," etc. Heli, it is understood, was Mary's
father; and as a woman's name might not have
regular place in any Jewish record, unless in special cases, her husband's name was generally put
there instead. Thus the long line goes back from
point to point, like that of any other child of
earth; now shining with the name of one who was
"a man after God's own heart," and another who
was called "the friend of God;" now falling into
the deep shadow of some one who "did exceeding
wickedly;" rising to the throne of worldly splendour with David, or sinking to the level of poor
Rahab of Jericho: back step by step, "in all
points like as we are," even to Adam.'

'Mamma,' said Mabel, 'did John stop preaching
then, as soon as he knew that Jesus had really
come?'

'No, indeed,' said mamma; 'but he went on to
preach Jesus as he never had done before. Jesus
himself did not stay among the people then, but
"returned from Jordan;" and even as he went,
John began to declare him to the throng around.
"This was he," he cried, " of whom I spake, He
that cometh after me is preferred before me: for
he was before me." This One who was here

among you, whom even now you see in the distance, is no man like me, — "he was before me :"
his goings forth have been from of old — from
" the days of eternity."   " And of his fulness have
all we received, and grace for grace."

' Everything that we have or hope for,' so mamma went on, closing her book and turning towards
us, ' comes to us through Christ; for " it pleased
the Father that in him should all fulness dwell."
" In him are hid all the treasures of wisdom and
knowledge ; " " in him dwelleth all the fulness of
the Godhead bodily : " " in everything we are en-
riched by him."   He is " the Light of the Morning "
to one in darkness ; he is " as showers that water
the earth " to one in need.   He is " a hiding place
from the wind " of God's displeasure, " a covert from
the tempest " of sin and death ; " the shadow of a
great Rock in the weary land " of sorrow and toil
and pain.   " A strength to the poor " — " the hope
of his people ; " his very name " is as ointment
poured forth."   Grace for grace has God given to
us through him, as if one mercy were but the foundation for another.   Moses indeed was commanded
to give us the law, said John, the list of those
things " which if a man do, he shall live by
them ; " but grace and truth came by Jesus Christ.
From the beginning he never appeared save in
mercy ; and now at last he has come once for all,
to put away sin by the sacrifice of himself, to make
known the gift by grace.   In him every promise
is fulfilled : **grace and truth come by the Saviour,**

the Anointed One, the Son of God. And then John went on to tell them that this Mighty One was no stranger among them, but that all they had ever known of God they knew through him. "No man hath seen God at any time," said the preacher; — as he spake unto Moses, "there shall no man see my face and live:" no mortal eyes could bear the transcendent glory of that holy presence. But some manifestation you have always had: "the only begotten Son, which is in the bosom of the Father," — in his secret counsels, in his deepest love, — "he hath declared him." Sometimes by a voice, as to Adam; or as an angel, to Abraham; or as in human form, to Jacob. To Moses he shewed himself in fire, and to the Israelites in a pillar of cloud: "he is the image of the invisible God." This is he of whom I spake.'

16

Chapter XVI.

THE TEMPTATION.

'CHILDREN,' said mamma, 'at every step of this wonderful story you must remember the perfect divine nature and the complete human nature of our Lord Jesus; else you can never understand the displays of his mighty power, or the prayers of his human need. "The Word was made flesh, and dwelt among us:" He to whom it had been said, "Thy throne, O God, is for ever and ever," was "made a little lower than the angels, for the suffering of death." At every point you will see these two.

'His work on earth was now begun. Having first shewn himself among the people for a little, he received baptism at the hands of John, and was "anointed with power from on high;" thus "numbered with transgressors," yet declared to be that One "in whom is no sin." And having stood among the throng of guilty ones; having come near to our pollutions, to our need, he was now to encounter alone our great adversary. "Immediately the Spirit driveth him into the wilderness." It seems,' mamma went on, 'as if to each person of the Godhead was reserved some special power or influence over man; and this of which we speak has always been put forth by the Holy Spirit. "As soon as I am gone," said Ahab's messenger to Elijah, "the Spirit of the Lord shall carry thee whither I know not." Go seek thy master, said the sons of the prophets to Elisha "lest peradventure the Spirit of the Lord hath taken him up, and cast him upon a mountain, or into some valley." "The Spirit lifted me up and took me away," said the prophet Ezekiel; sometimes by visible means — "he put forth the form of an hand, and took me by a lock of mine head, and lifted me up;" or only in seeming — "In the visions of God brought he me into the land of Israel." So in later times "the Spirit of the Lord caught away Philip" from the eunuch's side, "and he was found at Azotus," thirty miles away.'

'All that is never done now?' said Cyril.

'Not in an outward, visible way, and yet just as truly,' said mamma. 'There is no vision of glory or of duty comes into any heart but by the Spirit; and often now some Philip "is found at Azotus"—brought there he himself cannot tell why nor by what impulse, to do the Lord's work: "for as many as are led by the Spirit of God, they are the sons of God."

'So "Jesus was led up of the Spirit into the wilderness," to consecrate himself utterly to the work he came to do; to count its cost, to meet all that human weakness or hellish skill could urge against it. If sin had been there, too, we should have been lost for ever; but that blessed One "could not look upon iniquity."

'He was led into the wilderness — into the wild desolate border of the Dead Sea, most probably, with its jagged cliffs and black ravines, and utter solitude: "he was with the wild beasts," — none else. And there he fasted forty days and forty nights; his life preserved by a miracle, yet with the need of food keen and unsatisfied. Twice in the Bible we are told of such a fast. When Moses was in Mt. Sinai to receive and write down the law, for forty days he did neither eat bread nor drink water; and when Elijah, fleeing for his life from Ahab's wicked queen, was fed by angels, "he went in the strength of that meat forty days." So in the strength of his divine love and purpose, receiving for men not the law but free grace, our Lord Jesus fasted forty days and forty nights in the wilderness. Fasting was a sign of complete submission of the will, of supplication, of humiliation, of deep mourning, — Jesus kept that fast for our sins.'

And mamma's face dropped on her hands, with a gush of such bitter-sweet tears as moved even our wilful Mabel.

'He kept it,' mamma went on presently, 'through the miraculous power of his divine love. He was in the wilderness forty days, and in those days he did eat nothing. Great fasts were ordered in former times, when whole cities or nations be-

sought God to turn away his anger from them;
but Jesus made intercession for the sins of the
whole world, in all ages; assuming them, confessing them, devoting himself to the world's redemption.

'The world knew nothing of it: the multitudes
away off by Jordan dreamed not of the mighty
conflict even then beginning, through which they
too might be more than conquerors; but the devil
knew, and prepared himself for battle. If, through
the human nature even then fainting from the
long fast, he could gain entrance into that sinless
heart; if he could interrupt this consecration, this
humiliation for the world's sake, and put ease and
comfort before love, it would be a great point
gained. And this was a sure way of approach,
as the devil knew from long experience. With
the pleasant look and sweet taste of an apple he
had bought Adam and Eve; with a mess of pot-
tage he wiled away Esau's birthright; with the
mere thought of the fish, the melons, and the
cucumbers of Egypt, he had filled the hearts of
the Israelites with murmurs against that God who
had delivered them from the house of bondage.
"The lust of the flesh" — bodily ease and indulgence and pleasure — had always been a powerful
weapon in Satan's hand. Now to prove its weight
again.

'"If thou be the Son of God," he said, "command that these stones be made bread," — Divine
Power has before now "spread a table in the wilderness."

'So spoke Satan, — the adversary of God and man; but no human selfishness answered his appeal. Jesus never forgot us, nor that he had come to deliver us from evil, according to the will of God. He would not shorten by a moment nor lighten by a touch his time of humiliation and suffering. "It is written," he answered, "that man shall not live by bread alone, but by every word that proceedeth out of the mouth of God." To do his will, to take what he sends and when he sends it, *that* is man's life.'

'Mamma,' said Sue, 'was the devil really there? and did he talk out loud?'

'He was really there,' said mamma, 'but whether he shewed himself and spoke out loud I do not know.. But I think, Sue, he kept himself hid, and only whispered, as he does to us. So I think it was only in imagination, perhaps, that he next brought Jesus to Jerusalem, and set him on a pinnacle of the temple; filling his mind with thoughts and suggestions, as he does ours. "The lust of the flesh" had failed, and now Satan tried another favorite weapon called "The pride of life." "If thou be the Son of God," he said, "cast thyself down from hence:" there will be no danger; "for it is written, He shall give his angels charge concerning thee: and in their hands they shall bear thee up, lest at any time thou dash thy foot against a stone." '

'There might be little danger, but what use?' said Cyril.

'The pride of life,' answered mamma; 'ambition, self-assertion. For thirty years had Jesus lived in the world, unknown save as the carpenter's son: now came the temptation to shew himself to

VALLEY OF JEHOSHAPHAT.

the people as he really was: to come among them suddenly in some startling and splendid manner. The pinnacle of the temple was I suppose the battlement or raised edge — which by law must surround every roof — on the south wing of the tem-

ple, overhanging the valley of Jehoshaphat. This wing was a part of the magnificent cloisters built by Herod, and was called the royal porch. It was in fact a triple porch, resting on four rows of immense columns : fifty cubits, or seventy feet high at each end, but in the middle rising to double that height. From its outer edge the valley went sheer down five hundred feet, so that according to Josephus, " one could not see the bottom," and he who looked over would turn sick and dizzy. To this pinnacle, either really or in imagination, was the Lord Jesus brought; and the devil said to him, Cast thyself down. The valley is deep, but safe ; for angels shall bear thee up. I know what is written, too. And I think,' said mamma, ' that Satan, who is extremely well read in history, referred here to an old Jewish tradition: to wit, that when Christ should come to restore Israel to her glory, to judge those nations that had oppressed her, the gathering point should be this same valley, and the Lord, the Judge, should stand on the Mount of Olives beyond. If then (so reasoned Satan) the promised Deliverer should descend into this valley as it were from the very skies, all men would at once receive him ; not one could doubt for a moment. And then there would be just so much time saved. But Jesus answered, "It is written, Thou shalt not tempt the Lord thy God." '

'Mamma, what does that mean ? ' said Gracie. ' How can one do that ? '

'We can tempt God in several ways,' said mamma. 'One is by denying his power, — open unbelief may tempt the Lord to assert his sovereignty in open judgment; but another much more common tempting of God is by want of trust, — that secret unbelieving fear which lies hid in many a heart. So the Israelites tempted God, doubting his promise and power: "They limited the Holy One of Israel," saying, " Can he provide flesh for his people ? " — "Is the Lord among us or not ? " — they tempted him to forsake them, and not provide. So they tempted him in the wilderness again, saying in their fear, " Would God we had died in the land of Egypt ! — wherefore hath the Lord brought us into this land ? " And then the Lord uttered those terrible words : " As ye have spoken in mine ears, so will I do unto you " — " and ye shall know my breach of promise." And so yet again, when having with hearts full of fear refused to fight the Canaanites at God's command, they then against his orders gave battle, — and the Lord left them to fight alone, and to suffer terrible defeat. To doubt the power, wisdom, and mercy and truth of the Lord ; to be unwilling to wait his time, and to accept his pleasure, and to follow him *anywhere*, that is to tempt him. Satan seemed to say nothing very bad — it was but proposing to save time and trouble, and to make a splendid appearance in the eyes of men ; but Jesus answered, "Thou shalt not tempt the Lord."

'Again the devil changed his weapon, and came

armed with "the lust of the eyes," — with earthly power, desire, and gain. In a moment of time, from some imagined lookout, he set forth all the kingdoms of this world, and the glory of them; saying, " All this will I give thee." '

' Why he couldn't do that, could he ? ' said Sue.

' " The Lord maketh poor and maketh rich," ' said mamma, ' and " by him kings reign ; " but sometimes such power is put in Satan's hands, and he gives worldly good — not indeed " to whomsoever he will " — but to whom the Lord permits.'

' So that if people are too eager for gold,' said Cyril, ' and tempt God by trying for it in unlawful ways, God lets the devil give it to them.'

' Yes, I think so,' said mamma; ' but Satan always makes the same condition : " If thou wilt fall down and worship me." '

' The devil might have had more sense that time,' said Mabel.

' He had so seldom been refused,' said mamma, ' it was such a dazzling offer to human eyes, " the devil, which deceiveth the whole world," for once deceived himself.'

' Didn't he know that my Jesus wouldn't sin, for anything ? ' said Sue.

' I suppose he hoped in spite of what he knew. Adam was a sinless being when Satan tempted him, but he fell; and the divine strength and grace which were in the second Adam, Satan had yet to learn. Perhaps he was trying to find out if this was really the Son of God. And now he was in no doubt; as He whom Satan had hoped to lead captive at his will, ordered him from his presence with that voice of power which nothing earthly nor heavenly nor in hell can withstand. Jesus answered, "Get thee behind me, Satan — get thee hence : for it is written, Thou shalt worship the Lord thy God, and him only shalt thou serve." Satan had presented himself as an angel of light (he can do that) either visibly, or by the plausible nature of his words, but now he knew that he was known ; and could no more resist the Lord's command, than he had been able to hide himself from the eyes of the Lord's omniscience. " He departed for a season," — baffled, but not yet slain ; having great wrath, because knowing that now "he had but a short time." '

'And then came the real angels,' said Sue.

'Then came softly sweeping in a troop of white-robed angels, and ministered to the wants of Him who was in all points tempted like as we are, yet without sin.'

'How in all points ?' said Cyril. 'I don't see that. There were but three temptations — and I thought we had about five hundred.'

'Try,' said mamma, — 'see if you can find any one of the five hundred which does not hinge upon bodily ease and comfort, ambition, or gain; each wrapped up as they all must be, in unbelief.'

'And I suppose,' said Gracie thoughtfully, 'that the devil has always some special end of his own to gain, — it's not the mere evil for its own sake

that he cares about. So if he could have persuaded
the Lord Jesus to give up his humiliation and obedience and suffering for us, then we never could
have got free.'

'Yes,' said mamma, 'Satan well remembered
that after the permission, "Thou shalt bruise his
heel" — came the assurance; "He shall bruise thy
head." '

'It must have been a grand sight to see, though
—just for once,' said Mabel slowly; ' "The kingdoms of this world and the glory of them!" '

Then mamma answered:

' "The world passeth away, and the lust thereof.
but he that doeth the will of God abideth for
ever." '

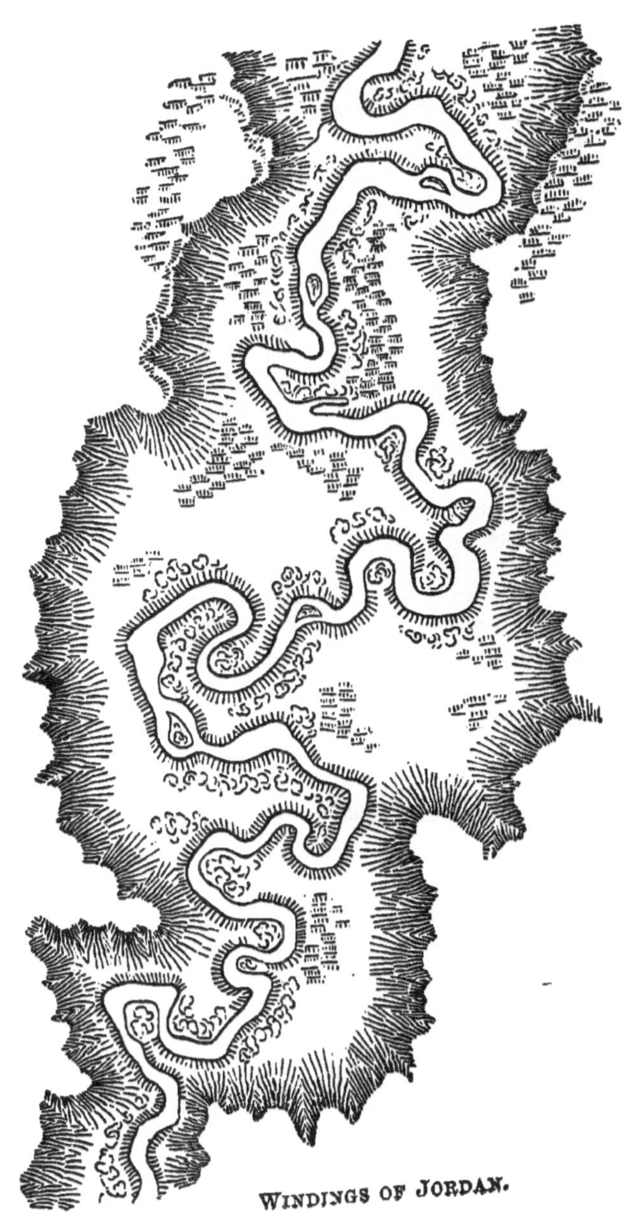

WINDINGS OF JORDAN.

Chapter XVII

BY THE JORDAN.

'IN all the world,' said mamma, unfolding her map, 'there is no river like the Jordan, no valley like that through which it flows; for it lies below the level of the sea.'

'What is the level of the sea?' said Mabel.

'The great lakes and seas of the world,' answered mamma, 'almost all communicate with each other; so that while some fill a deeper hollow than others, the surface level of all is about the same. If you take an apple, and stick on it bits of wax or bread for the dry land of the world, with its mountains and valleys, the skin of the apple will represent what we call the ocean level, — our fixed measuring point for the height of different parts of the land surface. We say a mountain is so many feet high, meaning that the top of it rises so far above the ocean level; although the height from its adjoining valley may not be half so much. Now most rivers rise among the hills, upon high ground, and then flow down towards the sea and pour out their waters at its level. But the Jordan soon reaches that level; and then rushes down and down into the earth as it were, through a deep rent in the earth's surface, until it is as far down as the deepest mine in Cornwall; and empties itself into the Dead Sea more than thirteen hundred feet *below* the ocean level.'

'What sort of a queer place does it rise in, to begin with?' said Cyril.

'At the foot of Mt. Hermon; among its spurs, fed by its melting snows, and passes through three lakes on its way; first the little Phiala, then through several miles of marshy ground it enters Lake Hûleh — the "Waters of Merom," and then sweeps on: sometimes broad and placid, sometimes foaming and hurrying between steep banks, until it glides softly into the Sea of Galilee. There was an old tradition that the waters of the river did not mingle with those of the Lake, but kept on their course straight through; and this much at least is certain, they bring out no more than they brought it: the river is just as large where it enters the Lake, as where it leaves it. Hurrying on its course now, — winding, turning, roaming about; now shooting like "a silver arrow," between its banks, then circling about in a green meadow, then clasping a little island in its swift embrace, or dashing in sheets of foam past cliffs of white limestone and black ledges of volcanic rock: fretted by the stones in a hundred rapids, leaping down in as many falls. For its bed is a constant swift descent; the river falls more than thirteen hundred feet in its course, well earning its name of the Jordan — "the Descender." But I cannot begin to tell you how crooked it is, — "it wriggles here, there, and everywhere;" * and to go an air line distance of sixty miles will travel two hundred.

'The long valley through which the Jordan flows is from six to twelve miles wide, walled in by mountain ranges on either hand: on the east the straight line of Moab, five thousand feet high; on the west the lower hills of Samaria. Here and there is a rent in this wall, and some mountain stream makes its way down to join the river, its course lying like a green ribband upon the shoulder of the hills; or a deeper cleft marks the edge of a ravine scarce fifty feet broad, with sides rising sheer up for a thousand feet. From these heights to the river there is a regular succession of descents; most of all near the lower end. Low cone-shaped hills edge away from the foot of the mountain range, their pale yellow or white slopes rolling down in billowy confusion to the edge of the first terrace. The second terrace, undulating and shrubby, lies two hundred feet lower; then fifty to a hundred feet lower still comes a flat jungle of tamarisks and willows. Through this, with banks five to ten feet high, flows the Jordan; wandering along in a sort of broad crack in the plain, fringed with living green, decked with a multitude of flowers. So hidden, so wrapped in its own verdure, that often you cannot catch a gleam of the

* Tristram.

water until you are at its very brink. "You are riding through a cloud of dust, hot ashes and blinding sulphur ; a mountain wall in front and on your flanks ; not a tree, not a shrub, not a blade of grass in sight; no more sign of vegetation round you than you would expect to see in a furnace ; when suddenly, with a start, your feet are among wild plants and your shoulders pressing against green boughs."' *

'Is it so hot there ?' Cyril asked.

'Hot? — I can hardly tell you about it,' said mamma; 'that is, at some seasons of the year. The valley — "the Great Plain" of the Jews, the "Ghor" of the modern Arabs, — lies so low, is so shut in, that the heat is withering. And the climate there is not like ours, with its cool nights and frequent rains : the sky is cloudless and glaring from the early dawn till night; the heat "enough to madden you," the light intolerable. No clouds, no shadows; only shining white limestone heights beyond the dazzling plain.'

'At some seasons, you said, mamma ?'

'At some seasons. At others the plain is a wilderness of blossoms and fruit. Here "a yellow sea of grain," there, the banks clothed "three feet deep with flowers."'

'O what sorts, mamma?' said Gracie.

'Many sorts, — varying from place to place. In one, for instance, are mullein-shaped flowers of a fine crimson, growing seven feet high; with a

* Dixon.

river fringe of willow and oleander and laurustinus, and beyond them small oaks and cedars. Then creeping mosses, sprinkled with little shining white flowers that twine in among them; and willow branches dipping and floating in the stream. Birds, too, in great numbers, rich in colour and song; and wild boars in the thicket, and the track of a tiger upon the shore. Then comes a place of sloping banks, covered lightly with grass and weeds and wild oats; with patches of yellow daisies here and there, and a line of purple blossoms fringing the base of the next terrace. And beneath and among all these, the scarlet anemones cover the ground like a mat: "a sea of scarlet bloom," with "little golden islands." ' *

' *Those* were the yellow daisies,' said Sue.

'Sometimes in such a place,' mamma said, opening one of her books, ' the wind and the flowers together make wonderful work: this is what some eyes have seen there: " When the wind, sweeping down the gorges of the hills, passed over the plain, a broad band of crimson marked its course; for the wild grain, light and elastic, bent low, and revealed the flowers beneath it, — presenting the appearance of a phantom river of blood, suddenly issuing from the earth, and again lost to sight, to reappear elsewhere, at the magic breath of the breeze." '

' Did *you* see that, mamma ? ' said Gracie.

' No, it was later in the season when I was at

* Lynch.

the Ghor, and then everything was burnt up. Wild oats as high as a horse's back, purple thistles that would overtop the head of his rider, all turned white with the fierce heat of the sun.'

'What becomes of the people then?' said Cyril.

'There are none there; no people live in the Ghor: there is neither village nor city in all its length and breadth. Wandering Arabs, or husbandmen from a distance, come and plant fields here and there; but these go away again, until the time of harvest. For when the summer heat sets in, the Ghor is like nothing you can think of but a furnace. Only everywhere there are two fresh, cool things in sight; the white-topped peak of Mt. Hermon, lifting its calm, glittering crown far off against the northern sky; and the green course of the river, winding along in the bottom of the valley: the stream itself you cannot see, except in little bits at a time.'

'I should think you could see it all, from such high ground on each side such a valley,' said Cyril.

'No,' said mamma, 'only a green line. From the foot of the mountains you ride across the sunburnt plain, among white sand-hills and scattered thorn bushes, till you come suddenly to the edge of a bank that overhangs the valley. You pick your way down by a winding path through the bushes to another broad terrace and cross that; then down another fifty feet or so into a complete thicket; and crossing that, you stand on the edge of a deep cleft full of trees, whose tops are on a level with your feet. Through this cleft rushes the Jordan. But in the rainy season, it rises up far above the edge of the cleft, and "overflows all its banks in the time of harvest." It is a beautiful jungle; with willows, tamarisks, white and pink oleanders, exquisite flowering canes, hollyhocks, marigolds, laurustinus and white asphodel. And in the thicket beyond, wolves and jackals and wild boars and tigers find cover, and are sometimes driven out by "the swellings of Jordan," as were the lions in former times. There are no lions now.'

'Mamma, how broad is the stream?' said Gracie, — 'and how deep?'

'According to the character of its banks. Where they are low and soft, the river spreads out broad and shallow, — eighty yards across perhaps, and but two feet deep: in another place it is six feet, in another ten, and narrower in proportion.'

'But I don't see,' said Cyril, 'how anybody could baptize people in such a river as that. They couldn't get to the water.'

'There are fords, you know,' said mamma, 'at places where the banks slope gently and the cane brake is broken away, and where perhaps some turn of the current has thrown up a bar. Such is the ford near Jericho. But even at the fords it is hard to cross sometimes, the current is so swift and strong; indeed it is impossible to cross safely unless you understand the river and choose just the right place.'

'*That's* like the Jordan of our hymns,' said Gracie, — 'I wondered at first why the name was used. And we cannot see the stream, till we are close upon it, — and then people either get over safe to the Promised Land, or are swept away down to the Dead Sea.'

'"And Jesus knoweth all the fords,"' said mamma softly, quoting her favourite Rutherford.

'Ah!' said Gracie with one of her glad exclama·tions, 'that was what the shining ones meant in the Pilgrim's Progress: "for, said they, you shall find it deeper or shallower according as you believe in the King of the place." But, mamma, I don't quite understand why all the flowers and freshness should be near the river. I mean I don't see how the two Jordans are alike in that.'

Mamma's eyes grew full. 'They are not all — at all times,' she said: 'sometimes the whole region is in bloom: but those flowers cannot stand "the burden and heat of the day." It is "the tree planted by the rivers of water," whose leaf shall not wither: and he who looks not on the things which are seen, but on the things that are unseen, he can say: "I shall be satisfied, when I awake, with thy likeness." No wonder the blossoms hide the stream!

'John had come "into all the country round about Jordan:" into "the circles of Jordan," — as the word is: like the "links" of the Scottish rivers. Not into the higher desert plain, but low down by the river, into the rich green "circles" that lay about its many crooks and bends. Beginning at the lower end of Jordan, John slowly made his way up, preaching and baptizing as he went; and had now reached Bethabara, beyond Jordan — that is, on the east side. Bethabara means "the house of passage," and the place must have been near one of the fords, — probably that one five miles above Jericho, where the great highway from Jerusalem crosses the river. It is supposed that Bethabara is the same with Bethnimrah — an old time place, two miles back from this ford on the east side; where there was not only a fine fountain belonging to the village, but by which also the Wady Sha'ib poured down its current to the Jordan. Bethnimrah means "the house of sweet water;" and in some old Jewish versions the name is spelled almost exactly like Bethabara. The ford here is about breast high.

'Here John was baptizing; and it seems the people had not believed him when he answered their musings about him at the lower ford, but had carried back an uneasy rumour which excited the learned ones at home. And now all the way from Jerusalem came priests and Levites, to ask him again, "Who art thou?"'

'Who were the Levites themselves?' said Cyril.

'The tribe of Levi was chosen from among the twelve tribes of Israel, and set apart for the especial outward service of God. Of this tribe was Aaron, the first high priest, and all the true priests of Israel after that were his descendants, and all his descendants were priests; but the rest of the tribe were called Levites. They could not do priestly offices, but they were the priests' assistants; they carried the tabernacle, they prepared the shew bread, they formed the choir; doing all the less sacred work of the tabernacle and temple service. They also were public readers of the law and instructors of the people. So just as we send ministers and elders to our General Assembly to arrange church affairs, there came priests and Levites to Bethabara to inquire about John and his preaching. "Who art thou?" they said. "And he confessed, and denied not; but confessed, I am not the Christ:" not the one whom you expect. And they asked him, What then? "Art thou Elias? And he saith, I am not."'

'Why, didn't they know his name was John?' said Cyril.

' Elijah, you know,' said mamma, 'or Elias — for the names are one, was a very noted, wonderful prophet in the days of the kings of Israel; and it had been promised that the forerunner of Christ should be like him. "I will send you Elijah the prophet," said Malachi; and the angel who foretold John's birth said that he should go before the Lord *in the spirit and power of Elias:* warning the people and denouncing sin as Elias had done. But the Pharisees, interpreting everything after their own fancy, supposed that Elijah himself was to come. He would appear three days before Messiah, they said; proclaiming in a voice that the whole world could hear, on the first day peace; on the second h ppiness; on the third salvation. This was so firmly believed, that if goods were found and the owner not known, people said, " Put them by till Elijah comes;" — at certain ceremonies a chair was always set for Elijah; and during certain prayers the door was always left open, that he might come in and announce the Messiah. And the very same sayings and customs are found among strict Jews, even at the present day. To meet this false notion of the people, John answered No.

'Then said the deputation " Art thou that prophet?" God had promised to raise up a prophet from the midst of the people, like unto Moses: standing between the people and God's anger as he had stood, and like him knowing the Lord face to face; for Moses was a great type of Christ. But the Pharisees seemed not to understand that this was but another name for the promised Messiah. " Art thou that prophet?" they said, — and again John answered No. In despair the priests and Levites asked once more — " Who art thou then? that we may give an answer to them that sent us. What sayest thou of thyself?"

'And as usual,' said mamma, 'John had nothing to say of himself. I am only a voice, he said, — a voice to tell the people of One mightier than L John was the perfection of a gospel preacher, — nobody and nothing but a voice through which God spoke; a voice to tell the people of Jesus,'

'Wouldn't be much need of writing out such sermons,' said Cyril drily.

'Mamma, why did he give such puzzling answers? — why didn't he speak plainer?' said Mabel.

'The simple truth is very puzzling sometimes,' said mamma, 'but not to those who are seeking it simply, and with the whole heart. These priests and Levites were full of their own notions and desires, rather than of the Lord's sure promise, or they would have understood in a moment. For John merely quoted from one of the old prophecies about the Messiah and his herald, — that "coming consolation of Israel," for which old Simeon had waited so long : —

'"Comfort ye, comfort ye my people, saith your God. Speak ye comfortably to Jerusalem, and cry unto her that her warfare is accomplished, that her iniquity is pardoned : for she hath received of the Lord's hand double for all her sins. The voice of him that crieth in the wilderness, Prepare ye the way of the Lord, make straight in the desert a highway for our God."'

'And yet they did not understand,' said Gracie.

'It was what they did not care to understand, — these were Pharisees, careful about their many prayers, little anxious about their sins. They were at a loss what to make of it all. "Why baptizest thou them?" they inquired; for this was one of the signs of a new teacher and leader, a new order of things; but if you are not Christ, nor Elias, nor yet that prophet, what revolution do *you* expect to bring about? And John answered, None. My baptism is but an outside form, and reflects no honour on me, nor gains any virtue from my hands. But even now there is One among you whom ye know not; coming after me yet preferred before me; whose shoe's latchet I am not worthy to unloose: seek him.'

'Mamma, what sort of a place is Bethabara now?' said Gracie.

'A wild enough place, if its site be really where I told you. Riding up the Ghor beyond the plain of Jericho, you cross the lower plain, and then descend about forty feet to "the channel of the winter floods:" a heavy thicket of trees and undergrowth, their lower branches tangled and matted with the refuse drift which the floods have left. From there — or through there — a path goes winding down to the water's edge, the view shut in by impenetrable forest above and below, and on both sides the river. But just at the ford there is a little clearing. Imagine a stream fifteen feet deep, rushing along among the trees like a mad thing; imagine a score of wild Arabs swimming and riding all around: imagine your bridle seized by one of those on horseback, who dashes off into the stream, while one of the swimmers keeps close at your side, holding you firmly to the saddle against the wild rush of the current: imagine all this, and you can form some idea of the winding, difficult ford of Bethabara.'

' And could John baptize *there ?*' said Mabel.

'John probably baptized at the fountain near the village a little way back. There are only ruins there now, and wild vegetation, and the abundant water; but the old highway from Jerusalem to the country beyond Jordan crosses the same ford still.

' And now at last Jesus began to shew himself openly to the people. Coming back from the wilderness, he crossed the river first to where John was baptizing, with the usual crowd about him. Men from villages near by, and others from northern towns miles away; Pharisees, who asked for baptism for its own sake, thinking that water and a form could wash away their sins; humbled penitents, who while calling themselves John's disciples, yet remembered that " without shedding of blood there is no remission." But whether caring for it or not, every one of them knew well that by special divine command, there were laid upon the altar at Jerusalem " two lambs without spot, day by day, for a continual burnt offering ; " and that this daily sacrifice had been offered for fifteen hundred years, foretokening him that should come. Past them even now, from time to time, went great flocks of sheep and lambs, going down to the ford, and thence up to Jerusalem for the temple use; and every cry from these innocent creatures must have stirred in many a heart the old mystery of the meaning of all this, — ringing out anew the words of the prophet : " Hath the Lord delight in the

blood of lambs ? " — " behold Lebanon is not sufficient to burn, nor the beasts thereof for a burnt
offering."

'It was the next day after the priests and Levites
had come with their questions, going away answered but not satisfied; and the usual day's
work was going on, when of a sudden "John
seeth Jesus coming unto him." And as if in a
moment the whole mystery were made clear to his
own heart, or speaking the joyful faith which now
saw its rest and abiding place, — in answer to the
many who had that day come with the query,
"what shall we do?" John said: "Behold the
Lamb of God, which taketh away the sin of the
world." Then was fulfilled the words of the prophet: — "Lift up thy voice with strength, — say unto
the cities of Judah, Behold your God!" John
speaks as if he had been weary for another sight
of that face which he had seen but once, — as if he
were almost heartsick at being so constantly taken
for his Master. "This is he of whom I said," he
cried exultingly, "after me cometh a man which is
preferred before me: for he was before me" — he
was from the beginning. And I did not know him
myself; but I came baptizing with water — calling
all men to repentance — that he might be known
in Israel. Then solemnly John bare witness of
him, for these were not the same people who had
been at the lower ford. "I saw the spirit descending from heaven like a dove and it abode upon
him." And I should not have known what this

meant, but He who sent me to baptize, the same gave me this for a sign: "And I saw, and bare record that this is the Son of God." This is he of whom it was written: "He is led as a lamb to the slaughter," — this is he of whom it was promised: "He shall bear their iniquities." "Look unto him and be ye saved, all the ends of the earth," — "Behold the Lamb of God, which taketh away the sin of the world."

'This thought, not new indeed, but now made plain, seemed to fill John's heart; he wanted to speak of nothing else, he could not rest till all eyes looked that way. The day after this, standing with two of his disciples, he saw Jesus walking by; and looking upon him his joy again broke forth, and he said: "Behold the Lamb of God!" And the two disciples heard him speak, and they followed Jesus. "A word fitly spoken, how good is it!"' —

'Who were the two disciples, mamma?' said Sue.

'One of them was Andrew, the other I suppose was John the apostle and evangelist. The story is told in the Gospel which he wrote, and John never if he could help it mentioned his own name. It was the beloved disciple I think, who now for the first time saw and loved his Master; drawn to him by the ineffable beauty which shone through the veil of his humiliation. Now first John saw that of which he afterwards wrote: "The Word was made flesh, and dwelt among us, (and we beheld his glory, the glory as of the only begotten of the Father,) full of grace and truth." Now began to be fulfilled these words: "As many as received him, to them gave he power to become the sons of God, even to them that believe on his name." Behold the Lamb of God! said John the Baptist,— and the two disciples heard him speak, and they followed Jesus.

' As soon as any one ever begins to do that,' said mamma, ' Jesus knows it. He knew it then, at once; and when they had followed a little way he turned and looked at the two, and said: "What seek ye?" Do you follow me for curiosity, or for variety, or for love, or for favours? And they answered him: " Rabbi (the Jewish word for master), where dwellest thou?"'

' That wasn't answering very exactly,' said Mabel.

' Yes, it was,' said mamma, — 'it was a perfect answer: We seek thee,—that is the one point on which a believer need make sure. He may be eager to learn the wonders of grace, he may be wearily seeking a change from the world's hard service; he *must* come begging for favours: but if he is truly seeking Jesus he need not trouble himself with any smaller questions; the Lord will surely say to him, " Come and see." So they came and saw where he dwelt. Not in any palace or castle or great house, but in some little hut in the village, or a cave in the distant hillside, or in a summer booth made of branches and reeds down

by the river. Such slight sheds are common
enough in the Ghor, where the fierce heat of the
sun demands a shelter, but where people rarely
stay long enough to put up a more substantial
house. "Come and see," says Jesus now to every
one of those who seek him; for "my kingdom is
not of this world." Think well, count the cost, —
I promise you only a shadow from the heat, a
covert from the storm.'

'"And they came and saw where he dwelt, and
abode there,"' said Grace joyfully.

'Yes, counting all things else but loss for the
excellency of the knowledge of him. It was the
tenth hour. The Jews at that time divided the
day between sunrise and sunset into twelve parts,
calling each one an hour: of course these hours
were of very different length at different times of
the year. The sixth hour would be always at midday, but the others would vary according to the
length of the day. If this was early in the spring,
as I think, the tenth hour would have been between four and five o'clock: and that day — the
rest of that day — the first two disciples abode
with Jesus.'

'Ah mamma! those were good times!' said
Gracie sighing.

'But hear what Jesus says to us in these times,'
said mamma: '"Behold, I stand at the door and
knock: if any man hear my voice, and open the
door, I will come in to him, and will sup with him,
and he with me." Only open the door in every

prayer, as they once did for Elijah; only in everything you do leave a place for Jesus : and "he that
shall come will come, and will not tarry." And
all doubtful things and questions "put by till he
come."'

Chapter XVIII

FROM JORDAN TO CANA.

And then the two disciples stayed with **Jesus** all the time, after that, didn't they?' said Sue.

'For a while,' answered mamma. 'But no one can stay with Jesus all the time in this world, except in heart; it is only in heaven that we shall be "ever with the Lord." Andrew and John were poor men, and had their living to gain; and now they were disciples, and had work to do for their Master. They might not spend all their time in studying his words, but with the joy of the Lord for their strength, and the hope of salvation for a helmet, they must go forth and bear the glad tidings to other hearts. "Let him that heareth say Come." "We do not well," said the starving lepers of Samaria when they had found food and treasure: "this is a day of good tidings, and we hold our peace."

'Even that night the work began. Before many hours had passed, as it seems from the story, Andrew's heart grew too full for quiet listening; and as if he could not wait to hear another word, "he first findeth his own brother Simon." Springing away from the little hut, he sought among the crowd that had come down to John's preaching for his brother, and then told him all in one word: "We have found the Messias."'

'And did Simon know what he meant?' said Mabel.

'Every Jew knew that name,' said mamma, — 'the Messiah — the Christ, as the Greek word is; the Anointed One. Every Jew knew that Messiah would come; but apparently Simon did not at once believe his brother's report, for it is said that Andrew "brought him to Jesus," — a little against his will perhaps, and doubting, as was Simon's way. And the Lord, reading his thoughts, gave him at once a token to steady his faith; a proof of the divine power into whose presence Simon had come: telling him not only his name and his father's name, but also his character and future work. "Thou art Simon " — "a hearer " now; but "thou shalt be called Cephas " — "a stone." Strong, sturdy, rough, by nature, in my hands thou shalt become a stone for the builder's use. For,' added mamma, 'it is with the Lord's Church now, as it was with the temple of old: a great many different materials are chosen and prepared and inwrought. There are "onyx stones, and stones to be set, glistering stones, and of divers colours, and all manner of precious stones, and marble stones in abundance."

'So the night passed; and "the day following,

Jesus would go forth into Galilee:" crossing the ford from the east bank of the river, and journeying on up to the Lake of Tiberias. "And he findeth Philip." I think it is likely,' said mamma, 'that Andrew and Simon had told the Lord about Philip, who was their fellow-townsman of Bethsaida —a little town on the Lake shore: told of him as their friend, and perhaps as one who was "waiting for the consolation of Israel." And the Lord, as he often does, was pleased to act upon information of which yet he had no need, and to receive the request of one friend for another. He went to find Philip, "and saith unto him, Follow me." Philip seems to have obeyed instantly,—he was one of those who came at the Lord's first call; and joining himself to the little company, the four went slowly on among the sweet Galilee hills, with wondrous talk by the way, until Philip's heart grew hot within him; and in the fulness of his new faith and joy he too hastened away to spread the glad tidings. "Philip findeth Nathanael, and saith unto him, We have found him, of whom Moses in the law, and the prophets did write"—the Shiloh, to whom shall be the gathering of the people; the Governor that shall rule Israel; the Prince of peace. He is not a foreigner, like these our present rulers; but according to the word that Moses wrote, he is "from the midst of us, and of our brethren,"—"Jesus of Nazareth, the son of Joseph."'

'And Nathanael did not believe, either,' said Gracie.

'Nathanael, I suppose, thought Philip enthusiastic: "Can any good thing come out of Nazareth?" he said: for Nazareth was a town of very poor repute among the Jews, and Nathanael — unwilling to check his friend's ardour too roughly, gently reminded him what a very unlikely thing he was saying. The mere name of Nazareth in that connection must prove him mistaken.'

'What was the matter with Nazareth, that they did not like it? — such a beautiful place,' said Mabel.

'I do not know certainly,' mamma answered. 'The people of Judæa held all those of Galilee in some contempt, as being less cultivated and speaking a ruder dialect than themselves; but that could not have been the thought in Nathanael's mind, for he himself was a Galilean. I think — indeed from other parts of the story I am sure — that they were a hard, unbelieving, unrighteous set; and thus it might well be that Nathanael, a strict-living and pure-minded Jew, disliked even the very name of the place.'

'Mamma,' said Gracie, 'I notice that the first thing all these disciples say, is, "We have found."'

'And therefore, speaking from the joy of their own hearts, they could answer fearlessly as Philip did, "Come and see:" they spoke that they did *know*. There is always great power in "I have found."

'Jesus saw Nathanael coming to him, and at

once told his character, as he had done Peter's.
"Behold an Israelite indeed!" he said, — for well
the Lord knew that "all are not Israel which are
of Israel." But in Nathanael was no guile, no
pretence; and the name of Jew, and all the outward forms of Jewish life and obedience, in him
were but the signs of true heart service. "Blessed
is the man unto whom *the Lord* imputeth not iniquity!"'

'But I don't like it in him that he just accepted
such a good character, without a question,' said
Mabel.

'You would have had him shew guile, to prove
himself guileless,' said mamma. 'My dear, a man
ought to know whether he is serving God with all
his heart. But Nathanael was puzzled how other
people should know it, — or at least this stranger,
who had never seen him before. "Whence knowest thou me?" he said. It is true, my heart is
fixed — but how do you know it? And Jesus answered, I know all about you. When you were
far from here, out of sight, "Before that Philip
called thee, when thou wast under the fig-tree, I
saw thee."

'Nathanael, I presume, was also a traveller that
day; having come down to the Lake on some special errand, from his home among the hills. And
when noontide came, he stayed his business for a
while, and sat down to rest and dine, not in the hot
town, but under the cool shade of a fig-tree on the
hillside. There are few things so pleasant as the

shade of a fig-tree,' said mamma, — 'the branches
are so very spreading, and the leaves very thick;
and the breeze plays in and out among them till
they are like a thousand little green fans. In that
hot climate it is far better than a tent. And there,
hidden in the shady solitude, Nathanael had said
his midday prayer as was the custom with all devout Jews; praying with his face toward Jerusalem, earnestly entreating that Messiah would come.
Noontide was long passed now, and Nathanael was
stirring about his business in the town, when
Philip called him and brought him away to Jesus.
What then did those words mean? — "When thou
wast under the fig-tree I saw thee." At once,
with a swift flash of recollection, Nathanael knew
they could have but one meaning; there was but
One in all the universe who could speak them
so; even He of whom Hagar said, "Thou God
seest me," — of whom David wrote: "O God,
thou hast searched me and known me: thou knowest my downsitting and mine uprising: thou un-
derstandest my thought afar off." In a moment
the whole truth was made clear to Nathanael; and
he believed, and instantly proffered his allegiance;
"Rabbi, thou art the Son of God: thou art the
King of Israel." Thou art he to whom God said,
Thou art my Son; he whom the Lord hath anointed to be "captain over his inheritance," and who
shall "set up an ensign for the nations."

'"Believest thou because I said this?" said Jesus
unto him: "thou shalt see greater things than

these." For so it will always be; and people will see more and more of the glory and love of Jesus, according as they believe. And then the Lord went on partly to explain his promise. You call me the King of Israel on earth, but hereafter you shall know that I am the only way of approach to heaven. Jacob in his dream saw a ladder set up between heaven and earth, and the angels of God ascending and descending upon it, — you shall see the glories of which that was but a sign. You shall see heaven opened to men; and every message of mercy, every breath of prayer, ascending and descending by me, the Son of man. Some people suppose that Nathanael had been musing on the old vision of Jacob that day, and so the Lord just answered his thoughts and longings by telling him what it meant.

'I think,' thus mamma went on, 'from the course of the story, that Jesus and his new disciples then left the Lake and journeyed on to a little village some miles away, where Nathanael lived. It is a wonderfully beautiful road, even now in these days of Galilee's desolation; first skirting the Lake for a while, through the rich plain of Gennesaret. This plain is "the ambition of nature," says an old Jewish writer; and there is a marvellous growth — and variety of growth — there still. It is a sort of level crescent among the hills; bordered on one side by the blue waters of the lake, with their broad fringe of rosy oleanders and tropical plants; while on the other rises the hillside,

gilded and fragrant with wild mustard, decked
with all manner of bloom. Then the road turns
westward, leaving the Lake, and climbing slowly
up the great gorge of Wady Hamâm, between
perpendicular cliffs a thousand feet high. till it
comes out upon the broad plain of El Bûttauf.'

'This lies higher up than Esdraelon?' said
Gracie.

'Much higher. It is the old plain of Zebulon,
stretching east and west along the back of the
Nazareth hills. In April the plain is carpeted
with young grain, and the hill-slopes covered with
grass: and both are enamelled with flowers.
White asters, and crimson; cyclamen, anemones,
convolvulus of different colours: the air full of fragrance, and the hillside clumps of trees and bushes
full of birds in full song. Across this plain, among
its water courses, its little hamlets walled with
gigantic hedges of prickly pear, the road winds
on; until at the further edge of the plain, on the
side of a little glen which slopes steeply down to
the level ground, you come to a ruined village. It
was never a very large place, probably, but with a
most exquisite situation; overlooking the rich plain
and its bordering hills; and was once flourishing
and full of people. Now, it is all desolate, — in
Kâna-el-Jelil, as the Arabs call it, there is not one
inhabitant nor one habitable house; and the whole
neighbourhood is so wild that the men of Nazareth
use it for a hunting ground, — coming there to
hoot bears, leopards, and gazelles. A little lonely

ruin the village is now; its very name called in question by some; and yet eighteen centuries ago it was chosen to honour above all the great cities of the world, for there Jesus wrought the first of all his miracles.'

'What do you mean by its name being questioned, mamma?' said Cyril.

'Another little town — Kefr Kenna — claims the honour for itself. But there is little trace of the old name in that: while Kâna-el-Jelil is the simple Arabic translation of Cana of Galilee. "And the third day there was a marriage there," — either the third day from the Lord's first going forth into Galilee, or the third from that on which Philip brought Nathanael to him. Cana was Nathanael's home; and Jesus and his other disciples had journeyed with him along the wild road of El Bûttauf to the little village among the hills. Some have fancied that Nathanael himself was the bridegroom on this occasion; and if so, or indeed if he were merely a near friend of the parties, he had probably gone down to one of the larger Lake towns to buy things for the wedding, when his friend Philip drew him away to see Jesus. However that may be, "both Jesus was called, and his disciples, to the marriage." The mother of Jesus was already there. It is the custom at these Eastern marriages for all the women friends of the bride to assemble at her house some days before the wedding-day, and there remain with her until she is married. They come dressed in their gayest robes, and spend the time in music and feasting, in going to the bath, in dressing and talking. Then on the day of the marriage the bridegroom comes with a party of his own special friends, and takes the bride back in procession to his house, where the marriage feast is spread.

'Among the women who were with the bride, and had now accompanied her to her new home, was the mother of Jesus. I never read these words,' said mamma, 'without thinking of a custom which is universal in Palestine to this day. It is thought a great honour there, as well as a great blessing, to have a son; and the mother at once drops her own name, and takes that of her first born. She may have been called Miraim before, but now she is *Um Daoud* — the mother of David: or perhaps she was Leah — and is now *Um Yuseph*. I always think of that, when I read these words: "the mother of Jesus."'

'Then if you lived in Palestine, mamma, would you be Um Cyril?' asked Sue.

'I should be Um Cyril,' said mamma smiling; 'and all you girls would have to submit to the fate of women in the East, which is to be thought of very small account. Mary must have been an intimate friend of the family, or perhaps even a relation, for she seems to have assumed part of the care and responsibility of the feast. And it fell out, that either through mistake, or because unexpected guests had come, the supply of wine fell short. Presently there was a call for more, — and

it is probable enough that none could be had nearer than the Lake cities, some twenty miles away.

'In this emergency, Mary — who you know had
laid up and pondered many things in her heart —
Mary bethought her of the divine power which
had been declared to be in her Son: there was an
easy way out of the difficulty, — she had but to
state her case. "The mother of Jesus saith unto
him, They have no wine."'

'And Jesus was displeased,' said Mabel. 'Why
was that, mamma?'

'I do not know that we can say *displeased*,' said
mamma, 'though he certainly rebuked her presumption. As to his form of address, that was
nothing in itself: "woman," was a common man
ner of speech; yet this was perhaps the first time
the Lord had used it to her. But it was needful
she should understand that the time of his subjec-
tion to her was past; he had gone forth now into
the world, to do the work which he came from
heaven to do: with human ties and human claims
he had thenceforth no concern. Still less might
she attempt to order or dispose that work, or to
hasten by even a moment God's set time. "What
have I to do with thee?" he answered in grave
reproof. You want me to work a miracle, — but
"mine hour is not yet come." When I put forth
my power, it will be at the bidding of no human
voice. Mary ventured no more. Shrinking back
from his rebuke, yet with her faith in his power —
even in his affection for her — untouched, she said

quietly to the servants: "Whatsoever he saith
unto you, do it:"—and there left it all.'

'Mamma, how pretty that is!' Grace said.
'And just like Mary.'

'It is beautiful,' said mamma: 'it is the simple
faith of a child of God, who acknowledging his
mistakes, and bearing humbly both delay and dis-
appointment, yet knows that not one of his re-
quests "is forgotten before God." In some way,
in the Lord's good time, the blessed answer to the
request will come. He expects it, he makes ready
for it,—saying to heart and hand, *Whatsoever he
saith unto you, do it,*—then quietly waits. And
such faith is never put to shame.

'The room where the feast was spread, was
doubtless much like what you can find at the present day in Palestine: such as I have myself seen
in a mountain village not many miles from Kâna-el-
Jelil. A long, high room on the second story,
with many windows of lattice-work instead of
glass; one end furnished with carpets and cush-
ions, and the walls rudely frescoed. In one corner
of the room at the uncarpeted end, was a shallow
stone basin let into the floor, and by it stood three
tall water jars. As each guest came in, he paused
for a moment by the basin, while a servant drew
water from the jars and poured upon his hands;
the water instantly disappearing through a hole in
the bottom of the basin. But in this room at
Cana, as it was a feast and the guests were many,.
"there were set six water pots of stone, after the

manner of the purifying of the Jews, containing two or three firkins apiece." We cannot tell exactly the size of these jars, for it is not quite certain whether the Greek word here is used for a Greek measure, or for the old Hebrew bath; but they must have held from ten to sixteen gallons each. The feast was now in full progress; and the jars, having furnished water for the washing of so many hands, stood empty in the corner. Then said Jesus to the servants, " Fill the water pots with water. And they filled them up to the brim."

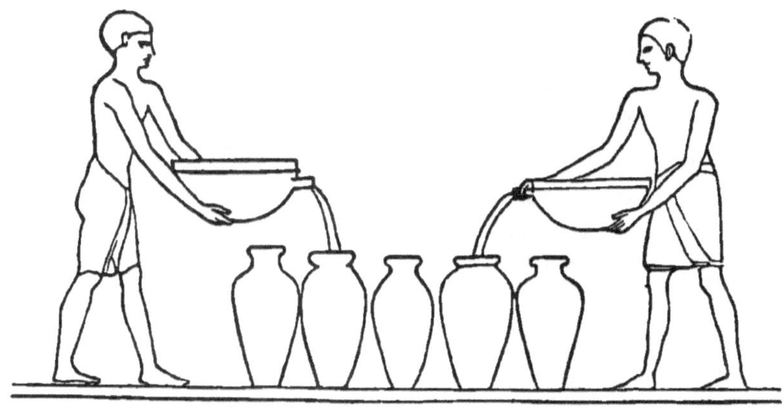

WINE JARS.

' Jesus, from his place at the table, noted them as they wonderingly obeyed his orders; going back and forth, up and down, between the water jars

and the distant fountain; until at last the bright
drops were brimming over, and the servants drew
near him for further orders. And he saith unto
them, " Draw out now, and bare unto the governor
of the feast." And again the servants, following Mary's directions, and yet more yielding to
the authority with which this new command
was given, obeyed. "And they bare it." Setting down the large vessels in which they had
brought water from the fountain, they took up
their small beakers again, and drew out, and bare
to the governor of the feast.

'The fact that there was "a governor" that
day, proves that it was a large assembly; for on
smaller occasions the master of the house himself
presided. But when the guests were many, and
of many sorts, some friend was chosen to act as
master of ceremonies; to arrange the guests, and
keep order, and see that all went well. To him
now came the wondering servants, with their pitchers filled from the water jars; not knowing even
yet, perhaps, the miracle which had been wrought,
— laughing privately, and nudging each other,
or else afraid of a rebuke. And when they had
filled his cup, the ruler of the feast tried first, as in
duty bound, what he was to offer to the guests.
"He tasted the water which was made wine," not
knowing whence it was; "but the servants which
drew the water knew." And so excellent was the
wine, that the ruler of the feast could not keep silence about it. He even called the bridegroom,

telling him what a strange mistake he had made. "Every man," said he, "at the beginning doth set forth good wine:" the cup before dinner, when a man's taste is pure, must needs be choice: and "when they have well drunk, then that which is worse" will do: "but thou hast kept the good wine until now." '

'Well did the ruler find it out?' said Cyril. 'And what did he say?'

'We are told nothing of all that,' answered mamma. 'The servants knew, and doubtless Mary also, at once; and they could hardly have kept so strange a thing long secret. But all we are told is that this was the beginning of the miracles which the Lord wrought while he was on earth; and that little Cana of Galilee was the first place where Jesus thus "manifested forth his glory," his divine power. And then, "his *disciples* believed on him," — those who had faith already, gained more; but of all the others there is not a word said.'

'Mamma,' said Sue, 'what is a miracle?'

'It is something which interrupts the course of natural events and causes; not produced by human power, but by the direct power of God. This was the beginning of those wondrous acts by which Jesus proved that he was indeed the Son of God. "And we beheld his glory," wrote one of his first two disciples; "the glory as of the only begotten of the Father."

'After this, followed by his mother, and his

brethren, and his disciples, some for love and some
for curiosity, Jesus went down to Capernaum, a
city on the shore of the Lake of Gennesaret.
" And he continued there not many days." '

Chapter XIX.

JERUSALEM.

THE city of Jerusalem, to which our scene now changes,' said mamma, 'stands at almost the highest point of the long back-bone ridge of Palestine. From the plain of Esdraelon, which lies you remember just south of the Nazareth hills, the ground rises up into that platform of high table-land — all broken into separate heights and valleys — which forms the wester wall of the Ghor, the eastern wall of the Shefelah Up and up, from the mountains of Ephraim to those of Judah, until at Hebron it reaches its greatest elevation of 3,029 feet above the level of the sea. Jerusalem, some twenty miles north of Hebron, is just a little lower, or 2,610 feet above the sea: perched upon a hill and among hills — " beautiful for situation, the joy of the whole earth." No other great city of the world was ever so placed; and although two or three of the neighbouring hilltops rise slightly above its own, yet as you come near Jerusalem its walls and towers stand out against the sky, having no background that is of earth. And never had a city such natu-

19

ral bulwarks. On every side the ravines are deep, and except on the north even precipitous, forming a complete trench around the walls; and beyond mounts up the circle of hills without a break, unless to the south-west, at the opening of the plain of Rephaim. Whoever would invade Jerusalem, must not only scale these hills, but also cross the valley, exposed to the fire and missiles from the town. "As the mountains are round about Jerusalem, so the Lord is round about his people from henceforth even for ever."

'The hill on which the city itself stands, is in fact five hills, welded together; the whole breadth between the ravines being about half a mile; and the sides of the ravines were always too steep for the city to spread down into them: it merely crowns the height. Through the middle of this hilltop platform runs a shallow ravine, dividing the city into two ridges: Mt. Moriah on the east, where once the temple stood, and on the west Mt. Zion, the old "city of David." '

'I thought Bethlehem was the city of David,' said Cyril.

'So it was, because David was born there. But this was "Ariel, the city where David dwelt," — the site of his palace was here. North of Zion is the smaller hill Akra, and still north of that, Bezetha; while Ophel is but a continuation of Mt. Moriah on the south. Zion was the highest of all. On these five stood Jerusalem, "builded as a city that is compact together;" and placed as it was in the highway between all the great nations of old time, it is no wonder that it was called by many the centre of the world. "The world is like to an eye," wrote one of the Jewish rabbins: "the white of the eye is the ocean surrounding the world; the black is the world itself; the pupil is Jerusalem; and the image in the pupil, the Temple."

'Besides its natural defences, the city was strengthened on all sides with walls. Where the ravine was deep enough to be quite impassable to an enemy, a single wall was thought sufficient; but in other places there were two or even three; and in the walls were twelve gates.'

'Mamma, just stop one minute,' said Gracie. 'things come too fast. I've been trying to compare it, as you went along, with the account of "Jerusalem which is above," — and I can't make out the mountain defences. There's nothing said about them in the Revelation.'

Then our mother said with a smile: '"We have a strong city; *salvation* will God appoint for walls and bulwarks." Can anything break through that?

'The marriage at Kâna-el-Jelil must have taken place in March, or early in April; for a little while after that "the feast of the passover was at hand, and Jesus went up to Jerusalem." At this time of year the city is in its beauty. Later in the season, the summer heats dry up the brooks and wither the flowers; but in spring, even within the city, every little clear space is like a wee flower-decked meadow, and the very walls themselves are rich with leaves and bright blossoms. And the hyssop has its place there still, as in the days of King Solomon; who "spake of trees, from the cedar tree that is in Lebanon even unto the hyssop that springeth out of the wall." '

'Mamma,' Gracie said, 'I never understood that promise before: "Neither shall the sun light on them, nor any heat." Nothing shall ever wither or fade, up there.'

I thought a quiver swept over mamma's face, but she went on steadily.

'In this spring-time of beauty our Lord Jesus went up to Jerusalem, — he whose hand had made it all, from the glowing oleanders along the river banks, to the small hyssop upon the city wall; but there was little else that looked fair to his sinless eyes. For the people he had made had lost the image of God, and the nation he had chosen were "gone away backward" from his service. It was the feast of the passover, — the special set time for remembering the Lord's mercies and the wonders he had wrought for the deliverance of his people, — and this was the state of things in Jerusalem. Going into the temple, the house "built in the name of the Lord," Jesus found there "them that sold oxen and sheep and doves." One whole end of the court of the Gentiles was turned into a common market, where were crowded vast flocks of sheep and lambs and kids; and their constant . bleatings, and the cries and shouts of the drovers, mingled with the solemn psalms of praise from the inner parts of the temple. In the next court, the court of the women, sat the money-changers.'

'But how happened all this?' cried Cyril.

'The priests allowed it, I suppose, by reason of some profit it brought to them; and the people liked it because it saved them the trouble of seeking their own offerings, and bringing them to the temple. By a very old appointment, every Jew paid into the temple treasury a yearly tax of half a shekel, — about thirty cents of our money, — and this must always be paid in Jewish coin, of precisely that value. It was the yearly "offering to the Lord," and was generally made at the time of

HALF-SHEKEL.

the passover. Now every one had not, perhaps, the right change; and the foreign Jews who came to the feast, and brought this tax for their countrymen at home as well as themselves, would have only foreign coin. And there in the court of the women were set thirteen great chests, — this one for the tax, and this for freewill offerings, and so on ; and by each chest sat a money-changer with his table.'

'Well, wasn't it really a convenience?' said Mabel.

'The Jews thought it so,' said mamma, — 'and they are not the only ones who have brought traffic into God's house, with great satisfaction. So the court of the Gentiles was used for a sheep market, and the court of the women became the city exchange ; and the two things by which God had ordered the Jews to remember that they were his people — the daily sacrifice and the yearly tax — they turned into means of dishonouring him, and defiling that holy and beautiful house which he had chosen to put his name there. The drovers made their profit, and the money-changers took their premiums, — other wares were soon brought to a place where buyers were so many ; and the great solemn feasts which God had appointed, became like common fairs, where people sold and bought and got gain.

'This Jesus found. And catching up from the floor some of the halters and leading strings which the cattle merchants had let fall, "he made a scourge of small cords, and drove them all out of the temple, and the sheep and the oxen." Then passing on into the next court, "he poured out the changers' money, and overthrew the tables." And he said to them that sold doves, "Take these things hence ; make not my Father's house a house of merchandise." '

'It was strange they should mind him,' said Cyril. 'People would dispute such an order now-a-days, fast enough.'

'Remember in the first place that their own consciences had not a word to say in defence. For every one of these traders must have been a Jew, — the lamb or the half shekel received through *Gentile* hands would have been held unclean, and not fit for either sacrifice or offering: and they *knew* they deserved to be driven out. But then as no one had ever attempted it before, they doubtless thought too that Jesus was a prophet, armed with special orders from on high. More than all, they felt — not knowing — the force of that Divine Power which "looketh on the earth and it trembleth: which toucheth the hills and they smoke." "Who can stand in thy sight, when once thou art angry?" The traders fled from the temple; and no man dared interfere in their behalf. Then the disciples of Jesus, standing by, saw what it was to be — like Elijah — "very jealous for the Lord God of Israel," for the honour of his name. They remembered that it was written, "The zeal of thine house hath eaten me up:" or as it is in another place, "My zeal hath consumed me, because mine enemies have forgotten thy words:" breaking forth and burning in a hot flame of indignation.

'The priests and Levites, on their part, and what other Jews were in the temple, looked on at first in silent wonder, — then came up to demand an explanation. They wore threatening faces, and deep anger was in their hearts, as they gathered round the daring stranger who had broken up their market and scattered their gains. "What sign shewest thou unto us?" they asked, "seeing that thou doest these things?" Great prophets who presume to lay down the law to the people, always give a token that they are sent from God, — what are *thy* credentials? Then answered Jesus and said unto them: "Destroy this temple, and in three days I will raise it up." '

'Mamma,' said Mabel, 'it seems to me that told them nothing, — how could they under·stand?'

'It told them all,' answered mamma. 'The temple, you know, was called the house of God; his presence was said to dwell there. "Will God indeed dwell on earth?" said King Solomon at the dedication of the first temple: "behold, the heaven and heaven of heavens cannot contain thee; how much less this house which I have builded." But now the Eternal Word "was made flesh and dwelt among us;" and within the veil of that human form, "dwelt all the fulness of the Godhead bodily." This was the first thing told by the Lord's answer: I am the true Temple, of which this other was but a sign.'

'And in heaven there will be no temple, · because there we shall see face to face,' observed Gracie.

'Then for proof,' said mamma, 'the words contained a special assumption of divine power.

"Am I a God, to kill and to make alive ? " said one of the kings of Israel when the leper came to him for healing : for well did every Jew know that to raise one from the dead was God's work alone. But " *I* will raise it up," said Jesus. And then, while declaring the awful Presence in which they stood; while proclaiming his boundless power; with it all he told of his boundless love as well — of the crowning finish of his work. You seek my life, he said, — but know that when I choose to give this temple of God into your hands, in three days after you have destroyed it I will raise it up. Not earth nor hell can hinder the work I came to do, — you people "imagine a vain thing." I will not only die, but live, for the souls of men. This would be the seal of the promised redemption; " for if Christ be not risen, our faith is vain ; we are yet in our sins." '

'But the Jews didn't know what he meant,' said Mabel.

'No,' answered mamma, 'because "by faith we know " — and they would not believe. They set themselves against his words. "Forty and six years," they said, "was this temple in building," — forty and six had passed since King Herod and the priests had begun their scarce finished work of rebuilding and repairs, — " wilt thou rear it up in three days ?

' "But he spake of the temple of his body." And even his disciples did not then fully understand. But long after, when the sign had come to

pass and the seal had been set, "when he was
risen from the dead, his disciples remembered that
he had said this unto them;" and then they "believed the Scripture, and the word that Jesus had
said." '

'What Scripture, mamma?' Gracie asked.

'O, so many, so many!' said mamma, her eyes
flushing with joy. 'Listen: "He will swallow up
death in victory," — "O grave, I will be thy destruction:" "Thy dead men shall live: together
with my dead body shall they arise." — "For if
we believe that Jesus died *and rose again,*" ' she
added softly, ' "them also that sleep in Jesus will
God bring with him." '

'And so "life and immortality were brought to
light by the gospel," ' said Gracie, — 'and I never
understood how, before! Mamma, that did indeed
tell all.'

'So came on the passover. And on the feast
day (the whole time of the feast was eight days,
but this was the special feast day, which began on
the night when the passover lamb was slain) Jesus
wrought miracles before the people; and many,
seeing them, "believed in his name." They believed that he was sent from God, and perhaps
even accepted him as the Messiah; but it seems
to have been for the most part only that sort of
acceptance which was willing to have him for king
over the nation, and against the Romans, — not
over their own hearts, and against sin. "And Jesus
did not commit himself to them," — did not re-

ceive their proffered allegiance; "because he knew all men." He had come to save his people from death — not to give them a splendid earthly career; and now paid no heed to these outward professions, reading the secret desires which prompted them. For "the Lord searcheth all hearts, and understandeth all the imaginations of the thoughts;" and the Lord alone.

'Among all those who were attracted by the splendour of his miracles on this occasion, but one is spoken of by name: "a man of the Pharisees, named Nicodemus." He was a man in high authority too — "a ruler of the Jews:" one of that Supreme Court of seventy-one members, the Sanhedrim, which was appointed to try idolaters, and false prophets and teachers, and erring priests. And hearing of the wonderful miracles performed on this feast day, and of the teachings of him who wrought them, I suppose the Sanhedrim thought it was time to look into the matter. Was this a false, or a true prophet? — they were in doubt what to say. So one of their number, either to satisfy himself or sent by the rest, came to Jesus by night to talk with him.'

'He was afraid to go by day,' said Cyril contemptuously.

'He did not want to commit himself,' said mamma. 'His own mind was not made up, and it would be a terrible thing for a strict Pharisee, a member of their High Court, to be seen going to visit a false prophet. Therefore he came by night;

and with smooth words professed more faith than I think he felt. "Rabbi," he said, "we know that thou art a teacher come from God: for no man can do these miracles that thou doest, except God be with him." '

'He didn't know that one name of Jesus was " *God with us,*" ' said Gracie.

'I do not quite know what he knew,' said mamma. 'I may do Nicodemus great injustice, but those first words of his never sound to me honest. They seem more like a snare than a compliment. And you see the Lord passed them by as mere words, and sent a searching arrow of truth down to the very depths of the Pharisee's heart. " Verily, verily," — with the strongest, most doubly sealed assurance, — "I say unto thee, Except a man be born again, he cannot see the kingdom of God: " — except you become as a little child, utterly humble and weak and ignorant — a new creature, it is in vain for you to inquire about me. You will examine with " eyes which see not," and " a heart which cannot perceive."

'The clear, keen reply startled Nicodemus out of all his prepared speeches, " How can a man be born when he is old ? " he asked quickly and with a touch of scorn. Men are children but once in their lives. And I think he really did not understand, for the Lord's reply is gracious in its explanation. Again with that solemn doubling of the assertion, Jesus answered: " Except a man be born of water and of the Spirit he cannot enter into the

kingdom of God." There must be a new life not of
the body but of the soul, "by the washing of re-
generation, and the renewing of the Holy Ghost."
Marvel not at this, — you cannot reason it out,
" Dost thou know the balancings of the clouds, the
wondrous works of him which is perfect in knowledge? how thy garments are warm, when he
quieteth the earth by his south wind?" So sover-
eign, so silent, so unseen, is the action of the Spirit
of God in men's hearts.

'And Nicodemus, with all his old learning pow-
erless and broken, answered: "How can these
things be?"

'Are you a teacher — "a master in Israel?"
Jesus answered him, — come out to judge *my*
teachings, — "and knowest not these things?
We speak that we do know, and testify that we
have seen;" and you — teaching you know not
what — "receive not our testimony." The learned
ruler is ignorant, the righteous Pharisee scorns the
truth. If you doubt these things which are done
every day on earth, how shall you believe if I tell
you of the wonders of heaven? Yet I alone can
tell them; for no man hath ascended up there,
save he who came down from thence : the Son of
man, whose presence even now fills heaven and
earth. And then, using an image well known
among the Jews, Jesus went on to tell for what he
had come. " As Moses lifted up the serpent in the
wilderness, even so must the Son of man be lifted
up." '

'I don't know what serpent that was,' said Sue.

'It was the brazen serpent,' said mamma. 'Long before that time, when the Israelites were dying with the bite of fiery serpents in the wilderness, God appointed a wonderful means of cure. "Make thee a fiery serpent," he said to Moses, "and set it upon a pole : and it shall come to pass, that every one that is bitten, when he looketh upon it, shall live." '

'But how could *looking* at the serpent cure the people ?' said Sue, with her head a one side.

'Because so God had appointed; and that brazen serpent which Moses lifted up in the wilderness, was a wonderful type of the Lord Jesus; the people who looked upon it, believing, were healed; but those who would not look, just died as they were. Jesus had not yet finished his work, but he told Nicodemus what it was to be. "Even so must the Son of man be lifted up :" lifted up on the cross: "that whosoever believeth in him should not perish." Jesus says to all the world, "Look unto me, and be ye saved;" but it is only those who look that live. And whosoever will not believe, is condemned already. "And this is the condemnation, that light is come into the world," — and they will not see, they will not believe, — they "love darkness rather than light, because their deeds are evil." '

'And did Nicodemus believe ?' asked Cyril.

'I do not know; we are told nothing more of him in this place, nor indeed much anywhere. But the Lord's words sound as if there were a great struggle in the Pharisee's heart, — as if self-righteous pride, and pride of learning, were even then contending against the truth. "You must be born again." Jesus told him, — then left him there, to be blinded or guided by the light, as he might choose.'

' "Light is come into the world," ' — Gracie repeated. 'Mamma, that is almost as terrible as it is joyful.'

' There's my verse, too, in that chapter,' said little Sue, tracing her small finger along the page. ' "God so loved the world, that he gave his only begotten Son." I like that best.'

And our mother answered, sweet and grave, in the old words of St. Paul to the Ephesian church : ' "Be ye therefore followers of God, as dear children." '

Chapter XX.

FTER these things," ' said mamma, ' when the days of the passover were ended and the people had departed to their own homes, Jesus came with his disciples into the land of Judæa. Perhaps he too had gone back to Galilee after the feast, returning now again into Judæa; or else it means only that he went forth from the city walls of Jerusalem into the open country. The land of Judæa — or Judah, got its name thus.

' When Solomon died, and his son Rehoboam came to the throne, then came trouble as well. Jeroboam, a young Ephraimite whom Solomon had employed on some of the public works about Jerusalem, set himself up for king as soon as his master was out of the way; and then the whole nation was divided. Part followed Jeroboam, styling themselves the kingdom of Israel; while those who were true to David's line and to his rightful heir, were called the kingdom of Judah. For at first almost all the tribes went after the Ephraimite usurper, and Judah alone was faithful to her king.

Afterwards the little tribe of Benjamin renewed its allegiance, and then to these two the inheritance of Dan and of Simeon was annexed; so that the kingdom of Judah at last embraced the whole southern end of Palestine, from the mountains of Ephraim quite down to the desert of Sinai.

'But from that time the people had no rest; and the next two hundred and fifty years were filled with strife and dissension, with jealousies and civil wars, between the two kingdoms that had once been one. Then the king of Assyria came up against Israel, took its cities and carried the people away captive into his own land. Because they "had sinned against the Lord, and had feared other gods," the Lord permitted this.

'The kingdom of Judah stood firm for a hundred and fifty years longer; and God sent them messengers to warn them, "because he had compassion on his people, and on his dwelling place: but they mocked the messengers of God, and despised his words, and misused his prophets, until the wrath of the Lord arose against his people, till there was no remedy." And then it came to pass, "through the anger of the Lord," that the king of the Chaldees came and took Jerusalem, and burned the temple, and broke down the walls; and slew many of the people, and carried away the rest captive, with Judah's king; "to fulfil the word of the Lord:" leaving only the poor of the and in the deserted fields and vineyards.

'It was all conquer and be conquered in the
20

East, in those days,' said mamma; 'and within
thirty years from that time the king of Chaldea
was himself overcome by Darius the Mede; and all
he had became part of the great Persian empire
and possessions.

'The better to govern and tax the people, Darius
divided his empire into twenty rulerships or satrapies; and the fifth satrapy included all Syria, of
which Palestine is a part.'

' What are satrapies ?' said Cyril.

'Provinces governed by satraps, — a satrap is
the Persian name for a certain sort of a ruler.   But
the Jews — or Judæans — disliked the name of
province; and those who were allowed to come
back after their long captivity, called it the Land
of Judæa, — this southernmost portion of the country, more than seventy miles long from the desert
to Mt. Ephraim, and sixty miles across from sea to
sea.

'Next the desert, on the south, Judæa was just
wavy pasture-land; on the west lay the rich plain
of the Shefelah; while on the east, stretching
along the Dead Sea, was the wilderness of Judæa,
— wild, rugged, and uncultivated, — where John
came preaching.

'Midway between these two was the hill country: a table-land of rolling hills, with deep cut
water courses, with numberless springs and wells,
..n dark hidden caves among the rocks.   Every
hillside was terraced, every height crowned with a
village or a walled town.   This was in the days of

its glory. The land of Judæa was some of the wildest of all Palestine ; the haunt of wild beasts ; and held by a race the strongest, the most distinguished of all the tribes, and the largest of all. Judah was foremost in the wars with the Canaanites for " the promised possession," — " Judah is a lion's whelp," said Jacob, when he gave prophetic blessings to his twelve sons. So tradition says that the standard of the tribe bore that device, with the motto: " Rise up, Lord : let thine enemies be scattered; " — fit words for the valiant race that should be called " the lawgiver," that should bear the sceptre for ever. " For it is evident that our Lord sprang out of Judah : " he who " must reign, till he hath put all enemies under his feet." As the channel of all the blessings we have or hope for, " God chose the tribe of Judah." '

' Mamma,' said Gracie, ' was Zacharias thinking of the standard, when he said those words about being " delivered from the hand of our enemies " ? '

' Perhaps, — it is our standard of victory. When, — as John saw in the Revelation — the knowledge of God was hid, and his mercy shut up; there was found no man in heaven or in earth who was worthy to open the sealed book of the destiny of this guilty world, nor even to look thereon; for the seven seals of justice were upon it. And then, ' the Lion of the tribe of Judah prevailed, to open the book and to loose the seals thereof." '

'And there was deliverance in the breaking of every one of the seals!' said Gracie.

'Was that my Jesus, mamma?' said little Sue.

'Ay,' answered mamma; '"for in the midst of the throne stood a Lamb as it had been slain. And He came and took the book." All was given into his hands, for the sake of his precious blood; and now in every trouble, in every danger, in every fear, we may say: "Weep not: the Lion of the tribe of Judah hath prevailed."

'He was on earth now, and came into the land of Judæa with his disciples, and he tarried there, and baptized. Not with his own hands, as did John the Baptist, but the people who received him and believed his word, were baptized by his disciples "in the name of the Lord."'

'Well, John had not stopped baptizing?' said Cyril.

'No, John was not yet cast into prison, and as long as he was free he was at work. The feast of the passover was held in April, and it was probably in early summer — perhaps in the end of spring — that these next events took place. At that season the heat of the Ghor is fierce and almost unendurable, so that John sought other places where he might preach and baptize. Just now he was at Ænon, — "the springs" — near Salim. Nobody knows where this was, — and so of course different travellers follow different fancies, and bring home various reports. Some think Ænon is away up in Samaria, in a springy valley between Shechem and

the river Jordan, — but the Bible words seem to
me to say that John was in Judæa. The most
probable place, I think, is that spoken of by Dr.
Barclay, — the Wady Farah, a deep ravine about
six miles north-east of Jerusalem. The Arabs call
it "the **valley of delight;**" and certainly there is

"much water" there. The Wady lies two thousand feet above the Jordan, a narrow, shady ravine,
with thick overhanging leafage of fig trees and
grass and tall reeds and bushes; the rocky sides in

some places very high and near together. "A bold
stream runs down the glen, widening out from time
to time into clear bright pools, and fed by half a
dozen springs which burst forth from among the
rocks."* At different parts of its course the
stream is crossed by old aqueducts, once well
built and handsome, but ruined and broken now;
and on the rocky face of the ravine are hermit
chapels and cells, remaining still, though the narrow paths of ascent to them are worn and washed
away. A few of these grottos, high up on the
cliff, are used by Arab shepherds for their flocks.
Wady Farah opens out of another Wady, which
begins its course on the east slope of the Mount of
Olives.'

'But where is Salim?' asked Cyril, — '"near
to Salim," it says.'

'And Salim is just as unknown as Ænon.
Travellers who think they find Ænon up in Samaria,
tell of a village near by, where there is a Moslem
tomb called after "Sheckh Salim;" while others
point out a Wady Salim or Selam which runs into
Wady Farah, in which are the ruins of an ancient
city of that name. We cannot tell; but wherever it was, John the Baptist was there, with his
disciples. It would seem as if some of the people
went back and forth between the two places of
baptism, comparing and disputing; for there arose
a question between them and John's disciples
about purifying: was John's baptism good? was

*Barclay.

it worth anything?—or must men follow this other teacher? Such seems to have been the point, rather than minor ones, for John's disciples were stirred for the honour of their Master. They came to him, sorrowfully and reproachfully, shewing how his own words had in part done the mischief. "Rabbi, he that was with thee beyond Jordan, to whom thou barest witness, behold the same baptizeth, and all men come to him."'

'I suppose they had learned to love John, and they *hadn't* learned to love Jesus,' said Gracie.

'Yes, it was that doubtless in some, and in some merely the pride which would uphold their own teacher. To this day, I believe, in the wild country east of Jordan, there is a little band of people who call themselves John's disciples. But no price could lure John from his loyalty to his Master. "A man can receive nothing," he answered humbly, "except it be given him from heaven:" all my success, all my power, has been from God. I am but a man, giving as it has been given to me: but this other is the Lord. Ye yourselves know that this is what I have always told you, and with great joy I tell you now. "He that hath the bride is the bridegroom: but the friend of the bridegroom, which standeth and heareth him, rejoiceth greatly because of the bridegroom's voice."

'In most Eastern marriages,' said mamma, 'the parties never see each other for a whole year after they are betrothed: and all intercourse between

them, all messages, are by means of another person, called the friend of the bridegroom. But
when the day of marriage comes, and the bride is
brought home by the bridegroom, and he sees her
and talks with her face to face, then the friend of
the bridegroom "rejoiceth greatly," hearing the
bridegroom's voice. His own part of the work
has been faithfully done, and all things are now
in the hands of him to whom they properly belong. "This my joy therefore is fulfilled." So
spoke John the Baptist, so speaks every faithful
minister: thinking it little while people flock after
him, but rejoicing greatly when they turn to follow
Christ. "He must increase," said John in the
gladness of his heart, "but I must decrease. He
that cometh from above is above all." "And what
he hath seen and heard, that he testifieth," —
whereas I am of the earth and can only speak of
the earth. John's words sound here as if he
must have been with the Lord when Nicodemus
came on his visit of inquiry, and so have heard
the whole conversation; he repeats so nearly several things that were said. And it may well have
been; for if John, like other devout Jews, went
up to the passover, he would have been certain to
spend every minute that he could with Jesus; and
could thus tell of his own knowledge not only what
he had heard but what he had seen: "No man
receiveth his testimony."'

'But it was not *no one*, literally,' said Mabel.

'Not literally; but the proportion was so small

that it seemed like none. You know how we say, " everybody does this," — " nobody likes that ; " using the words in precisely the same way. " Who hath believed our report ? " said the prophet Isaiah, speaking beforetime of the ministers of Christ. But lest his disciples should put a wrong meaning upon this, John went on immediately to tell them of the honour, the wisdom, the glory of those who do believe. " He that hath received his testimony, hath set to his seal that God is true : " he is permitted to become a witness for God.'

'I don't understand that, ma'am,' said Cyril.

'From the beginning of the world, you know,' said mamma, ' or at least from the day of Adam's first sin, God had promised a Saviour ; one who should be strong enough to destroy the evil spirit that had overcome Adam, and powerful enough to take away the curse which thenceforth came upon all the world. But the time was not yet. Again and again was the promise renewed ; from age to age the glad words rang out : " There shall come forth of Zion a deliverer," — " I have laid help upon one that is mighty ; " and some believed and looked forward, some doubted and forgot. Then Jesus came, he in whom " all the promises of God are yea and amen ; " and every one who received him, rejoiced in the fulfilled word of God. " He hath visited and redeemed his people, *as he spake* by the mouth of his holy prophets since the world began," said Zacharias

"He hath holpen his servant Israel," said Mary, "*as he spake* to our fathers." "We have found the Messias," said Andrew, — "We have found him of whom Moses in the law, and the prophets did write," said Philip. And to this day, every one who receives Jesus, sets to his seal that God is true : that his utmost promise of an all-sufficient Saviour is fulfilled.'

'But we don't seal things,' said Mabel. 'We only sign them.'

'We do when the matter is of great importance,' said mamma. 'But in the East seals are used in all cases, and no document is thought true and binding without one. Every man has his seal, — a bit of stone or metal or porcelain, — and he wears it in a ring on his finger, or hung round his neck or upon his arm. And each seal is graven with not only the owner's initials, but also with a motto; and often with words telling his ancestry as well, serving the same purpose as an English coat of arms. In using the seal, it is sometimes pressed down upon a morsel of clay, sometimes merely dipped in ink and then stamped upon the paper. And if a wandering Bedouin is too poor even to have his name cut on a piece of stone, he dips the end of his finger in the ink, and with that stamp seals his contract.

'This is the way now in the East, and it was just so in former times; the king had his signet of authority, and the subject his seal of honour; and there is a beautiful old custom connected with this matter of the seals, which I want you to understand. When a bond or treaty was between a king and his subject, and each must set his seal, the two seals might not stand close together. The king placed his on the inside of the bond, and the subject placed his on the outside, so that when the paper was rolled up or folded, only the latter would be seen. Just so is it in the bond between the Lord and every believer; according to the words in 2 Tim. ii. 19: "The foundation of God standeth sure." For on the inside, hidden from all eyes, is the King's seal, having this motto: "The Lord knoweth them that are his;" while on the outside, visible to all men, is the seal of the believer, and its motto: "Let every one that nameth the name of Christ depart from iniquity." Even a child can be a witness for Jesus and his truth; but then he must affix his seal.'

'That is one of the very finest things we have heard yet!' said Cyril.

'With what reason they might all do this, John went on to tell them. It was but to receive the testimony of him who is above all: "for he whom God hath sent speaketh the words of God." He hath not the Spirit by measure, as I have, and all the prophets, — "of his fulness we receive;" for in him all fulness dwells. "The Father loveth the Son, and hath given all things into his hand:" the government shall be upon his shoulder, the uttermost parts of the earth be his possession. It is no question now of purifying, of baptism, of

works : — "*He that believeth on the Son hath life;
and he that believeth not the Son shall not
see life ; but the wrath of God abideth on him.*"
For now was come the full explanation of what the
prophet Habbakuk meant · "The just shall live by
his faith."'

Chapter XXI

JACOB'S WELL.

'Mamma,' said Cyril, coming in as he often did with a question : 'if all men came to Jesus to be baptized, how was it that no man received his testimony ? '

'It was the old story,' said mamma : ' "They do honour me with their lips, but their heart is far from me." There is no seal set by such a profession.

'Certainly many came: "The Pharisees heard how Jesus made and baptized more disciples than John," — to whom had gone out "all Jerusalem and Judæa." But it was not the Lord's pleasure that their curiosity or ill will should be gratified then ; the time was not come : neither would he in any way interfere with John's work. For eight or nine months after the passover, as it seems, he tarried in the land of Judæa ; and then when the talk and stir concerning him began to increase and take shape, " he left Judæa and departed into Galilee. And he must needs go through Samaria."

'When God puts a " must needs " in the course of our daily life,' said mamma, stroking Sue's fair head, as yet touched with only the daily sunshine, 'it is never because there is no other way by which he could lead us; there may be many. But this is his chosen way, the best. And in our Lord's own human life it was the same: the "must needs" means only choice, wisdom, and purpose, — never necessity.'

'Then it wasn't the only way to get to Galilee,' said Cyril.

' Not at all: three roads lead from Jerusalem to the north. One crosses the Jordan near Jericho, and passing up on the east bank recrosses the river just below the Lake of Tiberias. Another strikes off westward towards the sea, then takes its northward course through the Shefelah and the plain of Sharon. The third, shortest and most direct, winds up and down along the central ridge of hills, right through the heart of Samaria. This is the common road at the present day. But in former times it was a very unpleasant road to a Jew; for the old jealousies had not passed away with the rival kings and separate kingdoms, and still Judah vexed Ephraim and Ephraim envied Judah. Indeed there were some new reasons for this. When Judah was carried away into Chaldea, the poor of the land were left; and at the end of the long captivity hundreds of the weary exiles were permitted to come back to their own land. But with Samaria the case was different. Her cities were completely stripped of inhabitants, and her whole land left desolate.'

'Well I don't see how even a powerful king could do that,' said Cyril.

'It was no unheard of thing in Eastern wars,' said mamma. 'Herodotus tells of an island "stripped óf its men;" of others where the inhabitants were "hunted out;" and concerning Samaria, Josephus — the old Jewish historian — says that "Shalmanesar transplanted all the people." Her king "was cut off as foam upon the water," "the thorn and the thistle came up upon her altars," and the land lay empty for forty years. Then another king of Assyria brought men of five different nations and cities, "and placed them in the cities of Samaria instead of the children of Israel." These people were idolaters: they fancied that every land had its own particular god; so when troubles and misfortunes came upon them in their new abode, they sent word to the king of Assyria, saying: "The nations which thou hast removed, and placed in the cities of Samaria, know not the manner of the God of the land: therefore he hath sent lions among them." In answer to this, the king sent back one of the captive priests who had been carried away, to teach them "the manner of the God of the land;" and he "came and dwelt in Bethel, and taught them how they should fear the Lord," the God of the whole earth. But they were unwilling scholars, and only added His name to their long list of idols. "Every nation made gods of their own:" from that day on, "they feared the Lord, and served other gods," —

and when fear and service *divide* a man's heart, it makes bad work.'

'I suppose the people of Judah didn't admire such proceedings,' said Cyril.

'Not at all. A hundred years later, when the exiled Jews came back to their own land, these new Samaritans made great professions of friendship, and even offered to help rebuild the temple of God at Jerusalem. But the Jews would have nothing to do with them, in any way; and then the Samaritans threw off their friendly mask, and became openly what they were already called, "the adversaries of Judah and Benjamin." Then a fresh source of quarrel came in to make matters worse. About four hundred years before the gospel times, a certain Jewish priest, dismissed from Jerusalem for misconduct, got permission from the Persian ruler to build a temple in Samaria; and now, with rival temples as well as rival blood, the feud grew deeper and stronger. Pilgrims passing through Samaria on their way to the Jerusalem feasts were refused hospitality, were even sometimes waylaid and ill treated; so that many were driven to take the roundabout coast road, or that which lay east of Jordan, instead of the direct route. But the Lord had now a special purpose to accomplish, — "and he must needs go through Samaria." '

'The great highway from Jerusalem to Galilee, once broad and in good condition, is now little more than a bridle-path, and a difficult one in many places : for donkeys and mule drivers make it to suit themselves. Once it was thronged with pilgrims, with husbandmen, and at times with Roman legions, — once, very long ago, "the land was full of horses, neither was there any end of the chariots;" but now "the highways lie waste; the wayfaring man from distant lands ceaseth:" there is little passing through for business or for gain; and the traveller journeys on alone, without even a chance villager in sight. Journeys amid the hushed scenes of Judah's glory; among ruins that mark the old gathering places of the thousands of Israel: for "Israel is an empty vine," and "Judah mourneth."

'If the Lord was at Jerusalem when he departed into Galilee, it was probably from the Damascus gate that he set forth; following the road

across the upper end of the Kedron valley, and
then up to the height of Scopus, where departing
travellers take their last look at the holy city, as
passover pilgrims from the north were wont to
take their first. The hill is strewn with their fare-
wells and their greetings, in the shape of hundreds
of little stones heaped up together, three or four
in a place ; marking spots where the lingering foot
tarried, whence the eager foot sprang on. From
Scopus the wild path crosses a broad, desolate
plateau which stretches on northward for about a
mile, and then drops gently down yet further into
the valley beyond. Few trees, few cultivated
spots are seen ; the way is lined with limestone
rocks and ruined villages ; but every step is among
the sites and associations of Old Testament times.
Here, close by the little village of Shâfât, is the
hill where once stood Nob — a city of the priests ;
and in the narrow valley beyond Shâfât, David
waited for Jonathan, who came bringing word of
Saul's unconquerable hate to the son of Jesse. On
the steep, barren " Tuleil-el-Fûl " — the " hill of
beans," as Arabs call it, — was Saul's own city,
Gibeah of Benjamin : it is a shapeless mass of
ruins now. Then comes Er-Ram, — a wretched
Arab hamlet, but built up in part with fragments
of columns and great hewn stones : this was the
old Ramah of Benjamin.

'Then comes Bîreh, the ancient Beeroth ; and
from Bîreh the road descends into a lovely Wady
or water course ; the sides terraced at first, but

then growing wilder and steeper, and overhung
with grey cliffs. In the spring every possible spot
here is green with wheat. Next up the high
bank of the ravine, and with a sharp turn round
the brow of the hill; and there at your feet is one
of the exquisite picture-views of the Holy Land.
The glen you have just left, creeping softly out
from among its heights, is met by another that
opens in from the east; and the two join forces,
and wind off together among the distant hills.
On every side now there is cultivation. Olive trees
scatter their grey light and shade over the bed of
the glen, and fig trees stand among the higher
rocks; and highest of all are vineyards, mounting
on terraced steps to the very top of the hill. This
is part of the inheritance of Joseph's son Ephraim;
whose land was blessed of the Lord "for the precious things of heaven, and for the dew, and for
the deep that coucheth beneath, and for the
precious fruits brought forth by the sun, — the
chief things of the ancient mountains; the precious things of the earth and the fulness thereof."
And the old blessing seems to linger among these
hills even yet.

'You can imagine the little band of disciples
following their Master along the rough, worn road,
— resting beneath a tree here, or stooping to
drink from a wayside spring further on, though
the scene was not as lonely then as it is now.
Now, it seems as if everybody was hid, or hiding;
and if you catch sight of a swarthy Arab face peer-

ing out from behind the rocks, you have not the least wish to improve the acquaintance. Yet the unseen villagers carry on a great deal of fine husbandry here and there. Beyond the valley of which I spoke just now, there is a rugged platform of high ground, stretching a mile or more east and west, and bristling all over with great peaks and points of limestone. The patches of soil between them are nowhere more than two or three yards square; and yet skill, and patient labour, have turned the whole height into a fig orchard. The loose stones are all gathered into heaps, and the fig trees send down their roots into the clefts of the rock, and twist and thrust their branches in and out among the rough peaks, and fling the shadows of their broad leaves like a veil above the whole. The path rushes down from here into the bed of a winter brook, and after stumbling along there for half a mile, it joins two other dells, —making what the Arabs call a "Mussullabeh," or place of cross glens. Very wild, very lovely: the sides terraced in part, while here and there the white limestone cliffs gleam out, and shew the pierced openings to their old rock tombs. Then you pass a height crowned with an old ruined castle; and so come to Ain-el-Haramîyeh — the Robbers' fountain.'

'Mamma,' said Sue, 'if *I* came there, I should run away pretty quick.'

'Many other people have thought just so,' said mamma; 'and many have done it too: even men, if they are alone, often like to hurry past the Robbers' fountain by daylight. For the place has a well-earned bad name; and every year adds to the list of bad deeds committed in that fair little dell. Yet it is probable, I think, that here the Lord spent the night which divided his two days' journey into Samaria.'

'What could make you think that, mamma?' said Mabel.

'It is just at a convenient distance, — travellers who are *not* afraid often camp there; and then the place is so winsome in its prettiness. The stream rills down through a fringe of fern leaves, filling two or three hollows in the rock with its sweet water; and there is a fresh carpet of green turf; and crocuses and anemones and cyclamen bloom and gleam among the herbage, and in every crevice of the rocks. The surrounding hills are (many of them) terraced to the very top, — thirty-six terraces — rising one above the other — on some; and each one filled with olive trees and figs.'

'But where could anybody sleep, that didn't have a tent?' said Cyril.

'On the grass, or upon a rock, — Jacob's stone pillow has never gone out of fashion in those lands; and with a mantle for covering, and a Syrian sky for canopy, one may easily rival Jacob's sleep, if not his dreams. If it were so, that the wayfarers rested that night at Ain-el-Haramîyeh, then it must have been early morning when they proceeded on their way. Up and up among the

terraced hills, rich in the season with olives and
figs and vines and corn; the birds in their morning burst of joy; and on everything the beauty of
the dawning light. A little later in the season these
hills and valleys are blazoned with the hues of a
thousand flowers; but it was early winter yet, and
only the fair little white crocús, and purple cyclamen, and blue veronica were in bloom, with here
and there an anemone before its time. It seems
as if that must have been a wonderful morning
among the hills of Ephraim, — as if they must have
echoed with the old doxology: "Praise ye the
Lord from the heavens: praise him in the heights,
— mountains, and all hills; fruitful trees, and all
cedars; beasts, and all cattle; creeping things, and
flying fowl." Only "the young men and maidens"
were silent; and "the old men and children"
knew not who it was that passed by.

'From this point the way grows less lonely.
Files of camels, with their tinkling bells, come in
sight; and mules, and donkeys; and armed Arabs
pass you on the road, and flocks with their shepherds are in the valleys, and peasants — in their
gay red, white and green dresses — are in the
fields. So on past Shiloh — now Seîlûm — where
once the ark of God was placed, and all the tribes
came up to worship; the road widening and im-
proving, and taking its course now and then
through the green plains which interlace the
Mounts of Ephraim.

'Passing thus on from point to point, you come

at last to the foot of a high, bleak ridge, up which
the path goes winding to the very top. A toilsome half hour's climb it is, but then what a view!
The plain at your feet is seven miles long, unbroken with fence or wall, but tufted here and
there with olive trees. A low, fringing ridge of
hills bounds it on the east, but on the west the
heights mount up in barren supremacy; and on
the very highest point of all, there stands a small
white Moslem *wely*, or tomb: the landmark of
Mt. Gerizim, the place-keeper of the old Samaritan temple. Mt. Ebal rises just beyond; and
in the cleft between the two lies Nablous or Shechem. Far, far to the north — eighty miles away
— is the blue cone of Hermon with its crown of
snow.'

'Hermon is Lebanon, isn't it?' said Gracie.

'Hermon is the highest peak of the eastern
Lebanon range, — or of "Lebanon toward the
sunrising," as it is called in the Bible; the Anti-
Lebanus of the modern maps: it is the "goodly
mountain" which Moses so longed to see. When
all the lower country is parched and sunburnt,
there are always bands of snow upon Hermon.'

'You said the other day, ma'am,' said Cyril,
'that Lebanon *once* blessed all the land with
springs and rains. Why don't it now?'

'God has made use of many second causes to
carry out his curse,' answered mamma; 'but that
the people called down themselves. Here, on these
two hills by Shechem, the tribes once stood, and

heard read out the blessings and the curses which
should be their portion, according as they were
faithful or not to Him who had brought them up
out of Egypt. " If thou wilt not hearken unto the
voice of the Lord thy God," said Joshua, " to observe to do all his commandments," — " all these
curses shall come upon thee."

' " Thy heaven that is over thy head shall be
brass —

' " The Lord shall make the rain of thy land
powder and dust —

' " The fruit of thy land, and all thy labours, shall
a nation which thou knowest not, eat up; and
thou shalt be only oppressed and crushed alway —

' " Thou shalt become an astonishment, a proverb,
and a byword —

' " And ye shall be left few in number."

' So read out the Levites, standing on Mt. Ebal,
and all the people said, Amen, — and the weight
of that " amen," is on the whole land now. " All
nations shall say, Wherefore hath the Lord done
thus unto this land ? " — " Then men shall say,
Because they have forsaken the covenant of the
Lord God of their fathers."

' From the high ridge which overlooks the plain
of el-Mukneh, Shechem itself is not in sight; but
as you go gently down into the plain many little
villages peep out here and there from their hiding
places among the rocks. Not one is set upon the
level ground, but each has climbed the hillside,
some further, some less far.'

'That's a queer arrangement,' said Cyril.

'It is one of safety and defence,' said mamma; 'for the people are wild and quarrelsome, though they have little to fight for, and nothing to fight about except some old family feud or late affront. In general this is the course of Arab quarrels. Somewhere, at some time, somebody was hurt by some one else; and as blood revenge never dies out among the children of Ishmael, so every relation of the man who did the deed, lives thenceforth in peril. He may be little more than a beggar, and his very rags scanty, but he goes armed to the teeth : a long gun in his hand, a short sword in his belt; perhaps pistols and a club as well. All these he carries about with him; and watches his goats on the hilltop, or drives his plough in the plain, with these sharp companions. Fierce enough he looks, with rags and weapons in such unequal proportions; his red cap or Tarbûsh made very long, and hanging down at one side over a white turban; a swarthy face, and wild eyes. Perhaps the first blood drawn in the quarrel between two families was shed four hundred years ago — and ever since then the law of blood revenge has been at work, striking now on one side, now on the other. Such are the people about Nablous — the old Shechem.'

'But things weren't so in the Bible times?' said Mabel

'Very much so, some things. Moses appointed cities of refuge to which a man might flee from the avenger of blood, and Shechem itself was one

of these cities. People and nations in the East
may pass away, but the customs of a land remain.'

'Nice customs they must be, to live among !'
said Cyril.

'But I don't see how they can do their work,
ploughing or anything, dressed so,' said Gracie.

'They do it Arab fashion,' said mamma, 'which
is seldom very thoroughly. No Arab likes work.'

'And was it all just so, when my Jesus must

needs go through Samaria?' asked Sue. 'The roads and the flowers, and everything?'

'The people were different, Sue, for Judæa was full of Jews and Samaria of Samaritans; and there were more people, and they were less wild than these poor Arabs; and the land was in better cultivation. But it was the same old road, going over the same hills: and though many a town was then standing which is now in ruins, and though the villagers were doubtless better dressed, yet all that made less difference to his eyes than to ours; "for as in water face answereth to face, so the heart of man to man." And "the Lord looketh upon the heart."

'Passing down the west slope of the ridge, and then along the green plain of el-Mukneh, Jesus came to "a city of Samaria, which is called Sychar, near to the parcel of ground that Jacob gave to his son Joseph." Now that parcel of ground, as we are told elsewhere, lay *before* Shechem, — and as "before," in Eastern speech, means "to the east of," therefore Jacob's field must have been just east of the city, — either part or all of the plain of el-Mukneh.'

'What made them use "before" in such a queer sense?' said Mabel.

'It is an old habit of words, begun in very early times, and kept up in some places to the present day. A man reckoned the points of the compass with his face towards the sunrising. Then the east was before him and the west behind; the south lay at his right hand and the north on his left. " If thou wilt take the left hand," said Abraham to Lot, in their division of lands, " then I will go to the right." '

' And was Sychar Shechem ? ' asked Cyril.

' That is one of the vexed questions among Palestine travellers and learned men. The name Sychar is used nowhere else in the Bible, and some think it was merely a nickname of reproach — meaning " foolishness " or " drunkenness " — and given by the Jews, in their national hatred, to the great Samaritan city. I must confess, it seems to me little like the sweet, grave dignity of John's style of narration, to use such a byword ; and I am more ready to believe (with others) that Sychar was one of Shechem's suburban towns ; perhaps represented still in the little village of Aschar, or traceable in the scattered foundations that lie among the old trees of the olive grove about half an hour east of Nablous, near the mouth of the valley. It is hard to tell : modern writers are divided, and old authorities seem confused and contradictory ; but whichever opinion may be true, Sychar was near Jacob's parcel of ground, and " Jacob's well was there."

' The wells of an Eastern country,' said mamma, ' like its customs, are permanent things ; outlasting the cities by which they stand, or the nation they may supply. The valley of Nablous is full of springs — there are some eighty just in and about the town itself, with others further down the

valley; and still the old well of Jacob holds its
place, — one of the few sites in Palestine which
are not even questioned. The well is on the point
of a low, rocky spur of Mt. Gerizim, that stretches
out from the hill just where the Shechem valley
opens into the plain of el-Mukneh, and was perhaps the western limit of Jacob's "parcel of a
field." On one hand the level plain, with its corn
and olives; on the other, the ascending valley,
rich with all fruits and gay with all flowers almost
that grow, and musical with the song of night-
ingales and other birds. The valley of the Nile
itself is hardly richer than the vale of Shechem.
And above all, the soft, tremulous atmosphere, the
faint haze, which is so seldom seen among the
parched lands of the East, hovers over Shechem
and its eighty springs.'

'And Jacob's well, mamma?' said Gracie.

'Jacob's well, as I said, is down at the mouth
of the valley, in the clear heat of el-Mukneh; for
it stands but twenty feet above the plain. A
round, smooth shaft, carefully laid in mason work
for a few feet at the top; the rest a straight bore
in the solid rock, nine feet across and seventy-five
feet deep. Once it was more than a hundred, but
travellers have done their best to fill it up.'

'Fill it up !' — exclaimed the children.

'Truly yes,' answered mamma: 'some fling in
stones to test its depth, and some for the wise
pleasure of hearing them clink and splash as they
go down; and so the old well that Jacob dug is

gradually filling up by Gentile hands. Travellers
are not the only ones in fault, however; for the
Arabs in their quarrels, and the Moslems in their
rule, have from time to time helped on the work.
The old church above the well is no loss, nor the
vaulted room where once the monks set up an
altar; but their stones have been so rudely dis-
lodged and thrown about, that the well mouth is
now but a dark opening in a heap of rubbish.'

'And was there a church there when Jesus
came?' asked Mabel.

'Not then, nor for long, long after. Then, there
were but the old worn curb-stones of the well, and
perhaps the great stone for its cover.

'Here, then, on the border of the well, Jesus
sat; "being wearied with his journey." It was
about the sixth hour, or twelve o'clock; and the
midday sun beat down with a pitiless heat, which
no dweller in western lands can imagine. Jacob's
well is a good six hours' journey from Ain-el-Haramîyeh, and from that — or some neighbouring
place — the Lord must have walked since break
of day. He was wearied with his journey, — there
is no one of all our infirmities with which he cannot be touched.

'Shechem itself was not in sight from the well;
but numberless smaller towns and villages looked
out from their stations among the hills. El-
Mukneh was barren as yet, — with barley just up,
and wheat not sown; and the host of spring flowers all biding their time. The red earth of the

plain, and the grey olive trees, and the long road through Wady Mukneh, were shining in the noon-tide glare: over all an intensely blue sky; and up against the blue the old time-honoured and re-nowned peaks of Ebal and Gerizim. Such was the scene where Jesus sat alone at midday, being wearied; and his disciples were gone away **into the city to buy meat.'**

Chapter XXII.

THE WOMAN OF SAMARIA.

HERE cometh a woman of Samaria to draw water." — If I begin our talk to-day with shewing you a picture,' said mamma, 'you must understand that it is not meant for a fancy sketch of the old scene : our Lord Jesus came not of Arab blood, neither had the woman of Samaria any kin to these her swarthy successors. But as while the people change, the old customs remain, this picture is probably as true to the well-side groups in former days, as to those which may be seen now at every Palestine spring and fountain. In way and manner it is, I presume, a perfect illustration of our story.

' " Jesus therefore, being wearied with his journey, sat thus on the well," — for the wells are the halting places, all through the East ; " and there cometh a woman of Samaria to draw water." Women are the water drawers there, still ; carrying sometimes a stone or earthen pitcher to be filled at the fountain, if the water rises near the surface ; or else a skin bucket and rope to let down

22

into the well. And from the earliest times till
now, the traveller resting by the well-side said to
the women who came to draw, "Give me to
drink." '

' Jacob himself did once,' said Grace.

' And Abraham's servant,' said Cyril.

' Generally the request is gladly met; and the
woman "hastes," as did Rebekah, to let down her
pitcher and draw for the thirsty stranger. But
sometimes national or religious hatred will change
all that. Only a short time since an English
wayfarer at a spring just beyond Nablous, asked
water of a woman who was there with her pitcher,
and was sharply refused. "The Christian dogs
might get it for themselves," she said. With more
civility of words, yet with maybe the same sort of
feeling, spoke the woman of long ago : " How is it
that thou, being a Jew, askest drink of me, which
am a woman of Samaria ? " for the Jews had no
dealings with the Samaritans.'

' Even in such little things ? ' said Cyril.

' Even in such little things. The separation was
complete, the hatred very bitter; there was even a
special and solemn curse poured out against the
Samaritans in the public service of the temple at
Jerusalem. No Samaritan might give evidence
against a Jew, his oath would not be taken in a
court of law; no Jew might visit or even salute
a Samaritan; nor eat with him, nor sleep with
him, nor drink from his cup: merely to touch it
would have rendered him " unclean." No wonder

the woman was surprised when the Lord said to her, "Give me to drink." How is this? she answered.'

'I don't just see why he did ask her,' said Cyril. 'He must have known she wouldn't give it to him.'

'Whoever would win people to the truth,' said mamma, 'must let them feel that he neither shuns nor shrinks from them. Not, "Stand by thyself, I am holier than thou;" but, "Come with us, and we will do thee good," is the Christian motto. Before Jesus spoke of her faults or hinted at her need, he first set aside by his example the proud Jewish scorn and loathing of these poor strangers: he was willing to drink from her cup, he was willing she should do him a kindness. Or if not, still he would do her one. How gently he answers her refusal, how pityingly he sets forth her blind ignorance, — and oh, they are some of the saddest words that can be said to a poor human soul: "If thou knewest" — "if thou hadst known." To meet Jesus and *not* know him; to have God's hand held out, and not even see the gift that it offers!'

'Mamma, what gift did my Jesus mean?' asked Sue.

'The unspeakable gift, — the gift of himself. "God spared not his own Son" — "Jesus gave himself for our sins." If thou knewest, thou wouldst have asked of him. Yes, so it would be always; but people do not know, because they will not believe.'

'"Thou wouldst have asked — and he would have given," ' Gracie repeated.

'What is living water?' said Mabel.

'An unfailing, living spring. Not the rain water, caught in muddy pools and hollows; nor those deceitful brooks which vanish away when the sun is hot; nor the deep cistern water, stored up by human care; but the stream which bursts forth unfailing, from a far-away source which no eye can see; prepared by his hand who "sendeth the springs into the valleys." There is a play upon words here, as well as that speaking by a figure which all people in the East love. I asked living water of thee, said Jesus to the woman, and have been refused; but if thou hadst known who it was that spoke, thou wouldest have asked of him, and thy request have been granted.'

'How had he asked her for living water?' said Mabel. 'I thought it was out of the well.'

'And well water was always called *living*, as distinguished from that of pools or cisterns. A *well* in the East is fed by springs. So the woman at first took the Lord's words quite simply; yet answered with more respect than she had hitherto shewn: "Sir, thou hast nothing to draw with, and the well is deep." It is an old, peculiar mark of Jacob's well, unchanged to this day. In most Palestine wells the water rises to within easy reaching distance, but here the mere surface of the water is often more than seventy feet down, and you can only draw with a very long cord. It is

one of the tokens by which Jacob's well is known,
to this day. " From whence hast thou that living
water ? " asked the wondering Samaritan ; standing with her skin bucket in her hand, gazing at
the thirsty traveller who had asked (for a Jew) so
strange a thing, and then as strangely turned the
request round upon her. " Art thou greater than
our father Jacob ? " she said, half curiously, half
in scorn. He not only dug the well, but he drank
of it, — and his children, and his cattle : canst
thou get living water without digging, and with
nothing to draw ? '

' Jacob wasn't her father, though,' said Cyril.

' The Samaritans are not the only people who
have laid claim to a more noble descent than was
theirs by right. Dwelling in the land which had
once really belonged to Jacob's sons, they too
called themselves his children ; heirs of his hon
ours and his blessing. There was some mixture
of Israelitish blood among them, I suppose, —
some scattering offshoots of the tribes whom Shalmanesar had " transplanted ; " and perhaps the
renegade priest who built the Samaritan temple
may have carried over a few people with him ; at
all events, " children of Jacob " is their chosen
name, even now, when there are not two hundred
Samaritans in all the world. " Art thou greater
than our father Jacob ? " said the woman, — and
Jesus answered yes. " Whosoever drinketh of
this water shall thirst again : — but the water
that I shall give, shall be in him a well of water
springing up into everlasting life." '

'The wells of salvation and Jacob's well, side by side,' said Gracie.

'Yes, and it is hard for us to imagine the peculiar power that such words would have upon any dweller in Eastern lands; where water is life; the supply often uncertain and scanty; and where soil and climate provoke the most overpowering thirst, so that people will drink eagerly such water as we would not touch with the tips of our fingers. The mere sound was full of cool refreshment: "A well of water, springing up into everlasting life." And behind this figure, so perfect to Eastern ears, there lies a meaning for all who dwell in the length and breadth of this wilderness world; where even brethren sometimes "deal deceitfully as a brook," and "the pleasant places are dried up:" for, "Whosoever drinketh of the water that I shall give him shall never thirst." Never thirst,' — mamma repeated: 'it is one of the promises of heaven. Yes, and he that cometh to Jesus "hath the promise of the life that now is," as well; and for him the Lord will open springs in the desert, and pour floods upon the dry ground. "Behold, my servants shall drink, but ye shall be thirsty."'

'How quick the Lord's words came true!' said Gracie, — 'how soon she "asked of him." The minute she understood just a little bit what he could give.'

'She knew but very dimly yet,' said mamma; 'the truth and the figure were all mixed up in her mind. Yet one ray of the Lord's double meaning seems to have shot down, "quick and powerful," to the hidden needs of her heart. "Sir," said the poor woman of Samaria, a suppliant before him whom she had but just turned away, "give me this water, that I thirst not, neither come hither to draw." Children, that is one of the great life prayers of the Bible! And whenever, in all your life, you are attracted by worldly honour or pleasure or gain, — those reservoirs that men have built up or hewn out, — go pray this prayer of the poor Samaritan. Come not thither to draw! — not though every great one of earth trod the path before you. The works look strong, but they are but "broken cisterns;" and the streams sound sweet, but "when it is hot they vanish away." He that cometh to Jesus shall *never thirst;* and "whosoever will, let him take the water of life, freely."'

'And was that what the woman of Samaria meant, mamma?' said Gracie.

'No, I think she hardly knew herself what she meant. But smitten with the sweet sound of the words, drawn on by the heart longing for better things which even those furthest from God feel now and then, — the request sprang to her lips: an echo of the old cry for the Desire of nations. A request such as many a one makes; mere longing, backed by no purpose. It was a light thing to ask for the water of life; but to procure it for her, to have it in his gift, cost the very life blood of him to whom she spoke.'

‘ She knew nothing about that,’ said Mabel.

‘ And the Lord did not tell her then: the first thing was to deepen and clear up her sense of need. With a few simple words that no one else would have understood, he brought her sinful life to her remembrance, proving that he knew it all. “ Go, call thy husband,” he said, — and again the word was “ sharper than any two-edged sword ” — “ a discerner of the thoughts and intents of the heart.” The woman of Samaria felt the blow, — yet for a moment made as though she felt it not, trying bravado. “ I have no husband,” she answered sullenly. But she had to do with one whose eyes are on all the ways of man. “ Thou hast well said, I have no husband,” Jesus answered her with grave rebuke. “ For thou hast had five husbands; and he whom now thou hast is not thy husband.” Five times had she been married, and when for the last time she was separated by death or by divorce, she had gone off with yet another man to whom she was not even married. “ In that saidst thou truly,” was the Lord’s comment. You have confessed your own sin.’

‘ So much for trying to answer God,’ said Cyril.

‘ When God speaks to a sinner in reproof,’ said mamma, ‘ there is but one reply: “ Behold, I am vile: what shall I answer thee? I will lay my hand upon my mouth.” But at first the poor woman of Samaria — like many another — tried to stand her ground. Staggered by the stranger’s clear knowledge of all her life, she made another unwitting confession: "Sir, I perceive that thou art a prophet," — this is all true: but then she sheered off from heart work and heart questions, and took refuge in outside disputed points. The old, old fashion, which will never die out! Such is my life, she acknowledged; — but, "Our fathers worshipped in this mountain; and ye say, that in Jerusalem is the place where men ought to worship."'

'What mountain was that?' said Mabel.

'Gerizim; the old mount of blessing; on a low spur of which she stood at the moment, by Jacob's well. Here, on the very top of the mountain had stood once the rival temple of Samaria, and though that had long been destroyed, yet still the Samaritans prayed towards Gerizim, even as did the Jews towards Jerusalem. A false Jewish priest had built the temple in the first place; and when it had stood on its high lookout for two hundred years, another Jew — John Hyrcanus, high priest and ruler at Jerusalem — came with his forces and levelled it with the ground. A hundred and thirty years had passed since then, but still the people kept up their old feeling, and said, "Our fathers worshipped in this mountain;" and now that near two thousand years more are gone by, still the top of Mt. Gerizim is a sacred place. There is but a handful of Samaritans left in the old inheritance of Ephraim (there are none elsewhere), but year by year they keep the feast of

the passover on the crest of the old mountain;
there slay their sacrifices, and mark their foreheads with the flowing blood, and eat the paschal
supper in the old fashion: girded, and staff in
hand. During all the days of unleavened bread,
they camp out upon the mountain top, and twice
more in the year go there in solemn procession for
other feasts; and still they say to strange travellers
from a distance: "Our fathers worshipped in this
mountain."

'So spoke the woman of Samaria in answer to
the Lord's searching words; and thought, I dare
say, that she had cleverly turned the conversation
away from herself, in a way no Jew could withstand: the rival "mountain of the Lord's house"
was one of the bitterest points in all the feud.
But Jesus, in his divine wisdom and patience, at
first passed by the question; and told her that all
outward forms were as trifling as her excuses were
vain. "Woman," he said, "the hour cometh,
when ye shall neither in this mountain, nor yet at
Jerusalem, worship the Father:" even now has
that hour struck. God dwelleth not in temples
made with hands, — he is a Spirit: and must be
worshipped in spirit and in truth. These outward
signs, these numberless ceremonies; a chosen
place, a particular building; shall all pass away.
No name or profession will answer now; no sacrifices, no feasts, no dress: the reality is come, of
which they were but signs, and the signs are for
ever done away. The worship of God must be
with a new heart, not with old forms.'

'And then he took up the other question,' said
Cyril.

'Yes, for no point of *real* truth is unimportant.
You know not what you worship, he told her:
"salvation is of the Jews."'

'Mamma,' said Gracie, 'her answer sounds as
if she knew *that* already.'

'Yes, so I think. She did not deny his asser
tion, but at once explained it by some established
fact. "I know," she said, pondering his words,
and eager perhaps to prove that she did know
something, — "I know that Messias cometh."
Ah!' said mamma, closing her books, 'these are
pitiful words! — why are disciples so unlike their
Lord! Ignorant as you say we are, — you Jews!
who have never tried to teach us anything, —
"when Messias cometh" — your own Messias —
"he will teach us all things." And Jesus answered: It is true. Ask, and you shall receive.
"I that speak unto thee am he."'

'Mamma, was she glad?' said Sue. 'Did she
believe?'

'I think she believed his words fully. For
what Jew was ever like this? — With no scorn of
her, for he asked to drink of her cup; with no
hatred to Gerizim, for he said that the Jerusalem
worship too should come to an end; with no enmity
to her race, for he spoke to her of God and salvation; while all other Jews believed that a
Samaritan was beyond the reach of heavenly grace,
an outcast in both worlds. But whether she was

glad or not, depends upon what heart answer she gave to his words. For in a whole life long, there is no such breathless moment as that in which the soul first comes face to face with this: " Behold, *now* is the accepted time." '

Chapter XXIII

FROM SYCHAR TO GALILEE.

'I WONDER,' said Mabel, 'what sort of meat the disciples got, when they went away into the city?'

'None at all, I fancy, of the kind you mean,' said mamma: "such meat is but little used in the East in ordinary. There are no butchers' shops full of ready-killed beef and mutton and veal, for fresh meat spoils directly in that hot climate; so the rich people kill a sheep or a kid as they want it, just long enough before dinner for the cook to do his work, and the poor live upon other things. "Rise up, slay, and eat," is the Eastern rule of custom; now, as it was long ago.

'Arab chiefs can do this, and Moslem rulers; and their hosts of retainers make clean work of anything that remains from the master's table. But the common people, who have no flocks of their own, nor money to buy a whole sheep or kid for a single dinner, live almost entirely upon bread and fruit and vegetables. In some places they have fish as well, in others locusts. The "meat" with which the disciples returned to Jacob's well,

was probably a supply of thin cakes of bread,
dried figs, raisins, with a few late olives or early
oranges. There might have been cucumbers too,
and honey. With these simple stores they came,
and much to their amazement, found their Master
talking with one of that despised race who were
publicly cursed in every Sabbath service at Jerusalem. They had begun to learn, however, that
his ways were not like their ways; and "no man
said, Why talkest thou with her?"'

'Well how had they bought all their things
without talking?' said Sue. 'That's what *I* want
to know.'

'Ah that was a different case. They would
buy and sell together, these people who hated
each other so bitterly, — it was only the words
and offices of kindness that were forbidden. Like
the barrier set up between the Jews and other
nations in later times, — in the dark ages of
Christendom, — "We will buy with you, sell with
you, get gain with you; but we will not eat with
you, drink with you, nor sleep with you."

'The disciples marvelled, but did not speak.
And the woman, on her part, as if their presence
broke the spell which had held her fast, left her
pitcher at the well — sure token that she would
come back again — and went her way into the
city, to declare the marvel which had sunk so
deep into her own heart. "Come!" she cried, —
"come, see a man which told me all things that
ever I did: is not this the Christ?" — he who is
to "tell us all things."'

'But he had told her very little,' said Mabel.

'So much, and such secret things, that she knew he knew all. And she spoke with such utter conviction and assuredness, that — woman though she was — the men of Sychar gave heed. People in the East are easily drawn together by any story or report of a new thing. They have not much to do — or do not much — and are always ready for novelty or amusement, in whatever shape. So at once, as it seems, "they went out of the city, and came unto him," — trooping down the beautiful valley — the loiterer from the city streets, and the merchant from his shop, and the rich man from his noonday nap. The tiller of the field quitted his plough to join them as they came along, and the herdsman left his flock of kids on the hillside, and hurried down to see where the others were going.

'Meanwhile, the disciples, now once more alone with their Master, set out before him the provisions they had brought; and then, finding he gave no heed, they "prayed him, saying, Master, eat." They had left him weary, faint perhaps for want of food, and now coming back with their supply, met only preoccupied looks and answers : "I have meat to eat that ye know not of," he said unto them. Then said the disciples, whispering together, "Hath any man brought him aught to eat ?" Jesus knew all their thoughts; from the proud wonder that he would talk with a Samaritan, to the slowness of heart which could not yet

understand who their Master really was nor for
what he had come. "Jesus saith unto them, My
meat is to do the will of him that sent me," — it
was their first lesson in active Christian life.'

' It *sounds* just like a reproof,' said Mabel.

' He is a very perfect man to whom the Lord's
example does *not* come as a reproof, when placed
side by side with his own. See how it was here.
The disciples had gone away into the city, they
the people of God, among people that dwelt in
darkness, worshipping "they knew not what;"
and had passed along, greeting no man, saluting
no man, with no word of kindness or teaching for
any. Then came back to their Master, to find
him rejoicing that he had declared the truth to
one soul out of that very city : his own human
need forgotten and pushed aside in the strength of
his divine love. "Ye should remember the words
of the Lord Jesus," wrote the apostle Paul, "how
that he said it is more blessed to give than to receive." And what was that will he came to do,
that work he made haste to finish ? — "To bind
up the broken-hearted, to proclaim liberty to the
captive, and the opening of the prison to them
that are bound." Already had "the pleasure of
the Lord" begun to prosper in his hands; his ear
could catch the clank of the falling fetters from
souls that were bound; his eye could see the
weary servants of sin, coming forth to be "the
Lord's freemen." "Say not ye," he added to his
wondering disciples, "There are yet four months

and then cometh harvest? behold, I say unto you,
Lift up your eyes, and look on the fields; for they
are white already to harvest." '

'But I thought harvest *didn't* come till spring,'
said Mabel.

'So thought the disciples — and were probably
quite bewildered at their Master's words. They
had hardly begun to think, I fancy, of the work
they were to do with him: neither did they real-
ize the mighty power of God, with whom one day
is as a thousand years. They said — as often we
do now — "Yet four months, and then cometh
harvest." So much ploughing, so much planting,
so much waiting, and then the return. At their
feet lay the broad plain of el-Mukneh, winter-
bound: the wheat not sown, the barley just starting, — all brown and bare, and shewing small sign
of even the "blade" — much less of "the full corn
in the ear:" harvest was four months away. And
little as they saw of its golden glory in that wintry
plain, still less could they even imagine that other
harvest of which their Lord spoke. Only he who
knoweth the end from the beginning, could watch
the little band of despised Samaritans that now
began to come straggling down the old Shechem
valley, and even think of that glorious "fulness of
the Gentiles" which should by and by come in.
"White already," to the Lord's eyes, is many a
field which we call barren.'

'But don't people *have* to wait?' said Cyril, —
'missionaries, and all that? I thought they just
had to wait and work till the time came.'

'Wait and work?—yes,' said mamma, 'so they must. But sometimes I think the waiting gets more than its share; and that if men believed more fervently the power and love of God, they might take their faith for a sickle instead of a plough, and go boldly forth into the barren fields and find them "white already." Then should it oftener be true than now: "A nation shall be born at once." "Concerning the work of my hands," said the Lord by his prophet, "command ye me:" it is a broad promise.

'"And he that reapeth receiveth wages"—to him shall be given the "Well done," the "rest from his labours," the "recompense of the reward;" and besides, he "gathereth fruit unto life eternal." He does not go alone to his welcome on high, but the souls that he has gathered to Jesus on earth, shall be with him every one; and over them shall Master and servant rejoice together. People talk of "new fields of labour"'—said mamma,—'and I suppose in all that great field, the world, there is not one spot where good seed has not been sown! God has wrought with men always, since the world began; sending them prophets, sending them messengers, sending his Spirit into their hearts. And now when new workers go forth, and of a sudden the rose and the myrtle spring up where there were thorns and thistles before, still is the old word often true: "I sent ye to *reap*,"—"other men laboured and ye have entered into their labours." Burn away the matted turf from any spot of ground, lay open to the sunshine the muddy bed of any pond, and suddenly there will be a new crop of leaves and plants, unlike anything — it may be — in all the region round about. Every soil is *full* of seed. Work for God need not always be so slow as men imagine; and people do not need cold knowledge half so much as they want active warmth and air.'

'Then there is something good in people's hearts,' said Mabel.

'Good seed and native growth are two different things,' said mamma. '"The heart is desperately wicked," said a missionary, preaching in India: "and who can bring a clean thing out of an unclean? not one." Then up rose a wily Hindoo, and said smoothly: "Doth the lotus flower grow out of the mud?" Now the lotus has an exquisitely fair and fragrant blossom, like our water lily, but its roots are planted far down in the dark bed of the river.'

'That was clever of the Hindoo,' said Cyril.

'Very clever, — but truth has no need to fear the cleverest things that can be said against her. "It is true" — answered the missionary, — "the lotus flower grows in the mud. But first there must be a good seed planted, and then the sunshine must warm it, and the floods keep it moist; and when at last the stem springs up to the surface of the river, still the dew and the light must cherish and strengthen it, or there will be no fair blossom. Even so must God's grace work upon

the good seed planted in any heart." A nd while
he is the Great Husbandman, we his serv ints may
be under-gardeners and reapers, if we will.'

'Mamma,' said Gracie, 'when the turf is burnt
off, as you say, are they flowers that spring up ? '

'Not all,' said mamma. 'Rank weeds, and
good plants run wild, and delicate blossoms. I
have found a frail little garden flower in just
such a new growth on cleared ground, far away
from where any garden had been within my knowl·
edge. Who planted it ? — who dropped the good
seed in many a wild human plantation? Nobody knows now; but one day the sower and the
reaper shall rejoice together, in the presence of
Him who sent them all.'

'The Samaritans were very ready to believe, I
should think,' said Cyril, studying the verse.

'Many of them were: many believed even at
the saying of the woman, "he told me all that ever
I did." And they came down to Jesus, and "besought him that he would tarry with them."
They had asked favours of the Jews often before,
but I fancy this was the first one that ever was
granted: "He abode there two days." And his
surprised disciples had almost as much to learn as
the Samaritans themselves.'

'O I wish it was all written down!' said Gracie,
— 'that "word" at which "so many more be-
.ieved"!'

'Yes, many more,' said mamma, 'And these
not by hearsay, but they knew for themselves.

"We know," they said unto the woman, "that this is indeed the Christ, the Saviour of the world,"— "Not of the Jews only, but also of the Gentiles.

'Well *I* wish we knew whether Sychar was Shechem,' said Mabel.

'It has but little to do with the interest of the story or of the scene, after all,' said mamma, 'whether Sychar was Shechem — or only one of the daughters of Shechem. The old hills are the same, — Mt. Ebal spotted with the openings to its rock tombs, as if it might have been the necropolis of ancient Shechem; and Gerizim, with every stone and ledge used as a terrace, and every foot of soil planted with figs and vines. And far up on the top of Gerizim are the Samaritan "holy places:" the old site of their temple; the ground where year by year they kill and eat the passover lambs; the broad, smooth slope of rock towards which they pray.'

'The people didn't change much then, after all,' said Cyril.

'Not as a people. "Many believed"—but more it seems did not; for the old hatred to the Jews, and the violent molesting of pilgrims, soon went on again after the former fashion. And in later times the Samaritans have been very hostile to the Christians at Nablous. They are a tall, handsome set of men, the few that are left now; living with greater strictness of forms than the Jews themselves, and intermarrying with no strange nation. You can distinguish them in a e.it by their red turbans; while the Jews green, and the Christians yellow, and the Moslems white.'

'Mamma,' said Gracie, 'how do you think the fields there look now, to the Lord's eye ?'

'Full of glory,' said mamma; 'for the day cometh when he "shall be gracious unto the remnant of Joseph," and "Joseph shall have two portions," and "shall inherit the land." Then, "when the Lord bringeth back the captivity of his people, Jacob shall rejoice and Israel shall be glad." "Israel shall blossom and bud, and fill the face of the world with fruit."

'Two days the Lord abode in Sychar, and then passed on into Galilee; perhaps taking the road which goes direct through the hills from the plain of el-Mukneh; although it has seemed to me more likely, from the words here, that he went the somewhat longer route by Cæsarea and the plain of Sharon. This road is good all the way — no small matter in Palestine winter travelling; and it comes out across the back of the Nazareth hills, without passing near the town itself: "For Jesus himself testified, that a prophet hath no honour in his own country." But "the Galileans received him," — the people of the province generally, who had been up to the passover, and had seen the miracles which the Lord wrought there. It was eight months ago, now, but they had not forgotten the wonders of that time. "So Jesus came again into Cana of Galilee," which lay just on, or very near, this highway from Cæsarea to the Lake.'

'The Lake of Gennesaret,' said Gracie.

'Yes, or of Tiberias, — the Sea of Galilee. Down by its quiet shores, near twenty miles away from Cana, stood Capernaum, a. beautiful Eastern city. Unlike all cities in this part of the world, to look at; but like them all in the life-changes and trials, the heart-hopes and fears, that were hid away even within its palace gates. A nobleman dwelt there, — probably one of Herod's State officers, for the word signifies a servant of the king, — and the nobleman's son was sick. The father, I think, was one of those who had seen the Lord's miracles at Jerusalem ; yet in the strength of his prosperous life, gave little heed to the help that was laid on One so mighty. But now of a sudden all other help had failed ; and having heard that Jesus had returned from Judæa, he went at once to find him. "In their affliction," said the Lord, "they will seek me early " — or eagerly. No other messenger would do, he must go himself: "he went unto him, and besought him that he would come down, and heal his son : for he was at the point of death."

'Now however submissively we may ask for all other things, boldness is one of the first lessons we must learn, in coming to Jesus for his help : we must take no denial ; even if the Lord (as in this case) meet us first with a reproof. You, he said to the nobleman, believe only when you see won-ders : much as you thought of my miracles on the feast day. you have forgotten all about me ever since. But the nobleman, with his whole heart fixed, seemed scarce to hear the Lord's cold answer: he attempted no excuse, he made no denial, but only repeated his cry for help. "Sir," he said, "come down ere my child die!"'

'I think he was very bold indeed,' said Mabel. 'He might have seen that the Lord didn't want to be troubled with him.'

'But that is *never* true,' said mamma. 'The Lord only wanted to draw out his faith, to have one life and death cry for help, and then it was instantly answered. The poor father himself was not in more haste than the pitying Saviour: there was not a moment lost. "Go thy way," said Jesus; "thy son liveth." At once, now, already he is healed; for Jesus can always do for us abundantly, above all that we can ask or think. "Come down," the nobleman had said; thinking that long hours must pass before the sick one could be relieved: but Jesus answered, It is done. "His word runneth very swiftly."

'Children, you see in this story — and you will always find it true — that when one comes to Jesus with this sort of resolved boldness; saying, with Jacob, "I will not let thee go except thou bless me;" then there is always faith to receive the blessing. A half cry is followed by a half belief But he who letting go of everything else,

> " Ventures on Him —
> Ventures wholly," —

has burned his whole shipload of doubts. Won

derful were the words spoken to the noble of Capernaum, but the man believed them all; and obeyed as soon as he believed, "He went his way." Jesus did not go with him, as he had asked, but 'dismissed him alone, with only his new-born faith — and that word which cannot be broken — for companions. So he went, — riding his mule along the old plain of el-Bûttauf; with fears peeping out of every bush before him, yet hiding their faces as faith came trembling by. For faith will be a coward sometimes, and oftener before fear than before danger; and not all the glory of the face of Jesus, could keep out of mind that poor dying face at Capernaum.

'But "the Lord knoweth our frame," — and will not let faith be tried a moment longer than it is able to bear. "As he was now going down," the nobleman saw men before him on the road, and presently knew them for his own servants. What had they come to tell him? I think perhaps faith trembled very much, as the men drew near, and laying each his hand upon his mouth, bowed almost to the ground before their master. And the nobleman, after the fashion of the East, greeted them gravely: "The Lord be with you!" — but the servants answered: "The Lord bless thee! Thy son liveth."'

'O wasn't he glad!' cried Sue. 'And so am I.'

'It wasn't really any news to him, though,' said Mabel.

'The strongest faith is wonderfully glad to be

proved right,' said mamma; 'and the nobleman, in his joy, did not forget his faith, but at once sought to strengthen and confirm it, going over the whole proof in detail. At what hour did he begin to amend? he asked, — and they said unto him, " Yesterday at the seventh hour the fever left him. So the father knew that it was at the same hour in the which Jesus said unto him, Thy son liveth;" and coming home, he told the wonder and the grace to all around him. " And himself believed, and his whole house." '

'Well certainly *that* boy wasn't sick for nothing,' said Cyril. 'But how was it "yesterday" — if Cana was so little way off?'

'Eighteen miles is a large half-day's journey; and as it was already afternoon when he set out, and as the Jewish day ends at sundown, it must have been "yesterday" before he could well meet his servants. But also, the road across el-Bûttauf is very wet and marshy in parts, at certain seasons; and the travelling very slow and even dangerous. Mr. Thompson declares it was " the most *nervous* ride " he ever took, with the horses in mud and water up to the knees, and a treacherous quagmire on each side of a barely two-feet-wide path. So it may well be, that the Capernaum noble passed the night at some village on the road, and that it was early morning when his servants met him; but we are not told.'

Chapter XXIV

BETHESDA.

'I AM so very glad to get to this chapter,' said Grace, as mamma opened her Bible at the fifth of John. 'Now we shall hear all about the pool of Bethesda.'

'I wish I could tell you all about it!' said mamma, — 'or indeed anything certain. But we will take the story first, in its simple Bible words : no human opinions can alter that.

' " After this," — some time, longer or shorter, after the second going to Cana and the healing of the nobleman's son, — " there was a feast of the Jews ; and Jesus went up to Jerusalem." '

' Always a feast ! ' — said Cyril, — ' the Jews made a great deal of their feasts, I think.'

' There were three in the year of which they *must* make a great deal, — three for which every man must go up to Jerusalem : then there were various others of less importance. John is generally so particular in telling the name of each feast, — " the Jews' feast of tabernacles," " the feast of the dedication," " the passover, a feast of the Jews," — that many people have supposed this

nameless occasion was one of small importance.
Others — because Jesus then went to Jerusalem —
think that it was one of the three great feasts: the
passover which came four months after he was in
Samaria, or the feast of Pentecost, just seven weeks
later still. But there was no law nor rule *against*
going to the common feasts; and for all that appears, this may as well have been the feast of
Purim, in March, as the passover in April: it was
simply "a feast."

' "Now there is at Jerusalem by the sheep
market, a pool, which is called in the Hebrew
tongue Bethesda, having five porches." There
were many such pools in and about Jerusalem in
former times; great open reservoirs, carefully built
and lined with water cement, which the underground streams passed through and filled as they
rambled on their way. For Jerusalem was rich
in her secret water sources. Whatever the Greek
name of this pool may have been, it was called in
the Hebrew tongue, Bethesda — the house of
mercy; for it had five porches: five places of shelter from sun and from storm.'

'I don't see how a pool could have porches,'
said Cyril.

'There is hardly a word told us about Bethesda
which may not be understood in different ways,'
said mamma; 'and so the very porches are de-
batable things. One idea is, that they were open
spaces between the pillars of a colonnade. But as
the same Greek word is used elsewhere for Solo

mon's porch, which we know was a colonnade itself, the meaning seems rather that the pool lay — like the court of an Eastern house — surrounded with a flat-roofed corridor; five-sided perhaps, or having five deep aisles or archways of entrance. "Cloisters or colonnades round artificial tanks are common in the East."* "In these lay a great multitude of impotent folk, of blind, halt, withered, waiting for the moving of the water." I am not sure that there are really more diseased persons in Eastern lands than in our own, but sure I am that one sees more of them. There, where people live out of doors, misery is not hid away as here; and now by this broad swimming pool, or bath, lay a great multitude. Impotent folk — cripples with no power in their limbs; and withered — whose limbs had shrunk and perished from an accident, or from paralysis; and halt, and blind. Blindness is fearfully common in the East. The light soil, the white rocks, the cloudless glare of the sun, do terrible work. In Jaffa they say every tenth person is blind; and other cities are yet worse off. And physicians are few there, and public charities almost unknown, except such a bath here and there as these open pools. But this pool was peculiar: the sufferers did not step in at once, but lay there waiting for the moving of the water. "For an angel went down at a certain season into the pool, and troubled the water." '

'O I wonder what angel *that* was!' said Sue.

*Smith's Bible Dictionary.

'I wonder what he did to the water,' said Cyril
'For it says that whoever stepped right in after
that, was cured. Do you suppose they saw him ? '

'No, I suppose they saw only the troubled — or
disturbed — water,' said mamma.

'But then,' said Mabel, 'how did they know it
was an angel ? '

'People had seen angels so often in those days,'
said mamma, — 'had seen them work out God's
various purposes of love or of judgment, — that
they really believed in that constant employment
of angels in earthly matters, which in these days
men forget or lose sight of. For their ministry is
just as real, although now it is invisible. In the
old times it was sometimes visible, sometimes not.
The destroying angel went silently and unseen
through Egypt at the dead of night, to slay all
the first born; but David saw the angel that
smote Jerusalem with pestilence — saw him with
his drawn sword in his hand. So Elijah probably
saw the angel that brought him food and touched
him on the shoulder, bidding him arise and eat;
but I suppose it was not till the morning **dawned,**
that Daniel knew of a surety that God had sent
his angel and shut the mouths of the lions —
taken away their power or their will to **do him**
mischief. Zechariah saw the angel that talked
with him go forth, and another angel went out **to**
meet him, bringing a new message.'

'And is all that — are all such things — **really**
true now ? ' said Mabel.

'**Ay**, and will be while the world stands,' said mamma. ' " The chariots of God are thousands of angels," — bearing his power, his blessing, and his care, to the ends of the earth!

'An angel at certain seasons disturbed the waters of the pool; and then whoever stepped in first was made whole. Among the people that lay there waiting, was one who had been a cripple for near forty years. He "had an infirmity" — perhaps like that of the man whom the apostles healed at the Beautiful gate; a weakness of the feet and ankles, so that he could not move at all — or but very slowly — without help. His friends or neighbours had brought him to Bethesda, I suppose, and left him in one of the porches. He was out of the way there, and safe; and if he could but work himself along into the water, might get cured. They had done all that could possibly be expected of *them*. Not so thought Jesus. He looked at the man's patient face, his helpless attitude, and knew how long he had been "in that case;" and then spoke to him the very words that now he says to many a sin-bound sufferer. " Wilt thou be made whole?" he said: Are you willing? do you desire it? The poor cripple meekly answered him with the difficulties of his case. "Sir, I have no man, when the water is troubled, to put me into the pool:" I am ready, but helpless; "while I am coming, another steppeth down before me," and the chance is lost. Is that all? the Lord answered him, — ready and willing but very weak ?   Know then that I am strong : " Rise, take up thy bed, and walk."

' " He that has no helper," is one of the Lord's chosen ones,' said mamma, her voice faltering a little. ' The man, with his eyes fixed upon that look of pity, his ears drinking in the music of that voice, just gave himself up to him who is mighty to save. With the command went forth the power, and was received by the poor cripple as he obeyed. Such words from any other lips would have been mere mockery, — " rise up and walk," to one for forty years scarce able to creep. But with his eyes fixed upon Jesus, the man forgot himself, — and all things are possible to one that so believeth. " Immediately he was made whole, and took up his bed, and walked." '

' Well he must have been strong,' said Sue, ' to carry his bed ! '

' It was a very light one,' said mamma. ' Palestine beds are generally nothing more than very thin mattresses, or very thick quilts, spread upon the floor. The rich pile several together, but the poor use only one, and often only a mere mat: these beds are rolled up and put aside in the day. Such a bed a well man can walk off with easily enough. The cripple here rose up at once, in the power of his faith and of the Lord's grace, and rolling or folding together the mat on which he had lain so long, he left those sorrowful porches of Bethesda, and with a light foot mounted the hill and entered the streets of Jerusalem.'

'Mamma, how could he leave Jesus so soon?' said Gracie.

'Jesus was not there, — it tells afterwards that he "had conveyed himself away, a multitude being in that place," — he did not see fit then to stop and heal them all, as he did many another time. And the cripple may have thought it was the angel of the pool himself who had appeared to heal him, and then vanished so suddenly out of sight. So with his bed upon his shoulder, he went with a glad, free step along the city streets; "and on the same day was the sabbath." Then said the Jews who met him, "It is the sabbath day : it is not lawful for thee to carry thy bed." For the old law about keeping the sabbath was very strict; and to the wise and blessed regulations given by Moses, the Jews had added new ones of their own; observing them all, not in the spirit of love and obedience, but of self-righteous pride. And now they had no eyes nor ears for the miracle which had been wrought, nor stopped to find out whether the man was merely on his way home, but brought their charge unqualifiedly : It is not lawful.

'The cripple, on his part, disputed not the law, but gave the authority which had for once set it aside : "He that made me whole, the same said unto me, Take up thy bed, and walk." And he himself had no more thought of questioning than he had of disobeying. Then said the Jews, somewhat scoffingly, "What man is that which said unto thee, Take up thy bed and walk?" But the cured one could not tell them : Jesus had vanished from his eyes. He went on to his home — or some place where he could leave his bed, and then went into the temple to offer his thanks : for he knew that every good thing came from the hand of God, by whatever other hand it might have come to him. He was probably too poor to offer the sacrifice of thanksgiving according to the law, — a man not rich enough to hire some one to put him into the healing waters of the pool, could hardly find money on a sudden to buy a sheep, and fine flour, and oil, — but he went to hear and join in the public praises of God, and to see the evening sacrifice laid on the altar, and to hear the sounding of the silver trumpets of joy. And standing there, suddenly he heard again that voice which had made him whole; speaking words of counsel now, of grave warning, "Behold, thou art made whole," it said, — look at the goodness of God, think of it, study it, — then take heed : "sin no more, lest a worse thing come unto thee."'

'What *could* be worse?' said Mabel.

'The consequences of slighting God's mercy,' said mamma. 'Better to lie a lifetime by the pool of Bethesda, waiting to be healed and always disappointed, than to use recovered life and health and strength in any way but the service of him who gave them all. The man made no answer, that we are told, — perhaps had a half thought still that it was an angel, — but as he left the temple he pointed out his wondrous physician to the people who stood by, and learned his name. "And therefore did the Jews persecute Jesus, and sought to slay him, because he had done these things on the sabbath-day." If any one of the Lord's followers ever thinks it a strange thing to be "persecuted for righteousness' sake," ' added mamma, 'he would do well to study these words.'

' "Such things " ! ' — Gracie repeated. 'Why no one but Jesus could do such things ! '

' No one; but it was specially because they were done on the sabbath, that the Jews made a clamour; for that self-righteousness which dwells in the border of a garment, the name of a day, or the name of a church, had need to keep up all its defences. The Jews settled with themselves that they would kill him, and perhaps even then made threatening demonstrations; but Jesus answered with a calm assertion of his authority, his right to rule. "My Father worketh hitherto, and I work." — "Who can say unto him, What doest thou ? " — "His work is perfect " ! '

' I wish we knew where the pool was,' said Mabel.

' I think there is hardly a pool in or about Jerusalem, which is not called (by somebody) the pool of Bethesda. No one knows where it was, — no one can say certainly that it is not even now hidden beneath the ruins of the old city; but I will tell you what different people think.'

' Where is the sheep market ? ' asked Cyril.

' Passed away with other things of that old

time.   You notice that the word "market" is in italics, — a sign that it was supplied by the translators of our English Bible.   Other learned men say the word should be "gate," or "pool;" but the Greek text says only, "by the sheep."   It may have been the gate where the flocks for the temple sacrifices were brought in ; it may have been the enclosure where they were penned ; or even that "pool of the sheepskins" mentioned in Nehemiah, where the fleeces taken off in the temple were washed.   Somewhere — near some one of these — was a pool; and every traveller to Jerusalem makes new search for it in vain.   Some think it lay near what is now called St. Stephen's gate, on the north side of the city, — forming part of the great Birket Israel — a fosse or reservoir that is seventy-five feet deep and three hundred and sixty feet long.   Dr. Barclay believes it hid under "the immense banks of rubbish" that are piled up close by the spot where the temple once stood. Dr. Robinson chooses the Fountain of the Virgin ; a little cave-pool, twenty feet down in the rock of Ophel, where one would say a "multitude" could scarce have found even standing room.   "It may well be doubted," says Dr. Porter, "whether this fountain or the Pool of Siloam farther down is the true Bethesda ;" and of all visible sites, Siloam seems the most probable to me, where the waters of the fountain of the Virgin flow out and find ampler room.   It stands lower down the hill, yet was "doubtless once within the city walls ;" and its Greek name of Siloam interferes not at all with its being "called in the Hebrew tongue Bethesda." The water is sweet tasted, slightly brackish at times; and according to some authorities varies in flavour at different times of year. It is of great fame still as a pool of healing and (according to some old writers) had once the same irregular flow that is found still at the upper fountain.'

'That is the Fountain of the Virgin?' asked Gracie.

'Yes, — the Dragon's fount, as the Arabs call it. They think a dragon lives at the fountain head, and that when he lies down to sleep the waters are shut off; but when he rouses up and goes away on an excursion, then they flow again. For the flow is most irregularly irregular. Sometimes for a day or two the basin will be almost dry; and then on a sudden up comes the water, — gurgling out from under the steps, covering in a moment any foot that may stand there, and making a perceptible wave all across the basin. Then in fifteen minutes more it is all quiet and low again, and the water after rising ten or twelve inches, sinks down to its old level, flowing off by the underground channel to Siloam. Sometimes this happens two or three times a day, sometimes once in two or three days, or at longer intervals yet. There is a stone-built dam at the end of Siloam now, which prevents this irregular tide from being perceived there, but in former days, the water

rushed down through the narrow winding passage
from the Virgin's fount, and brought its noise and
stir even into Siloam's quiet pool. And some
people have thought,' added mamma, 'that this
was the "troubling" of the water, spoken of by
John. Not, as others charge, to get rid of the
miracle, or of the angel's work; but merely supposing that the angel who had care of that particular spring, did at certain times direct a flow
of healing water — from some mineral spring, perhaps — into the fountain, and thence to the pool.
But as the flow lasted but a very few minutes, the
strong virtue of the water was soon diluted and
lost; and thus it was only he who *first* stepped
in that was healed.'

'Mamma,' said Sue, 'does every spring have an
angel?'

'I cannot tell you much about angels,' said
mamma smiling. 'John, in the Revelation, tells of
"the angel of the waters," as well as of the one
"standing in the sun," and the other "flying in the
midst of heaven;" and for aught I know, every
part of the world may be under the care and ruler-
ship of angels: they may be the Lord's under-
governors.'

'But does any mineral spring heal *all* diseases?'
said Mabel.

'Not all diseases were there to be healed; the
people were all "*impotent* folk" — cripples. However, we cannot decide these difficult questions
without more discoveries in Jerusalem, and more

knowledge than we shall maybe ever have in this
world. Intermitting springs are found here and
there, in other places; and so are healing springs,
and angels are at work around us all the time.
And though we may never know just where this
one poor cripple lay, when the Lord made him
whole; we are sure that every day and in every
place the sick, the weak, the broken-hearted may
come to Jesus and be healed; for *he* is the **same,**
" yesterday, to-day, and forever." '

Chapter XXV

THE KING AND HIS HERALD.

'MAMMA,' said little Sue, 'I thought God never did anything?'

'O Sue!' said Gracie.

'Well I did,' said Sue. 'Because it says in the first chapter of Genesis — no, it's the second chapter — that when the world was all finished God rested.'

'He rested from the work of creation, — *that* was ended, for our world,' said mamma; 'but not his work of care and of mercy. You cannot look at a thing, Sue, but tells of God's work; you cannot live an hour without feeling it; you cannot even read a common newspaper without finding proofs of it in a thousand ways.'

'In the paper?' said Mabel.

'Mamma,' said Sue, 'please begin with what the things tell that we look at.'

'They all tell of his work of creation,' said Cyril, 'but how of any other, mamma?'

'When our neighbour built his sawmill in the valley,' said mamma, 'and it was all completely finished, what did he do then?'

'Why he began to use it,' said Cyril. 'O I see!'—

'And how did he begin to use it?—did he just set the mill in motion and then leave it to itself?

'No indeed,' said Cyril, 'pretty work that would have made! He watched it all the time. There was first the right log to choose and put in place, and then to get the right thickness for the board, and then to let on the water and set the saw going, and then to stop it all at just the right minute.'

'All true,' said our mother; 'and what a man does in his imperfect way with a machine, that God does with the universe: but *his* rule is perfect,—absolute in power, wonderful in working. It is unseen,—"I look on the left hand where he doth work, but I cannot behold him;" it is unceasing, and beyond and above all human comprehension. "When I applied my heart to know wisdom, and to see the business that is done upon the earth, then I beheld the work of God, that a man cannot find out the work that is done under the sun : because though a man labour to seek it out, yet he shall not find it; yea, farther; though a wise man think to know it, yet shall he not be able to find it." And he who wrote that, was the wisest man that ever lived. "Man goeth forth unto his work until the evening,"—but "there is that neither day nor night seeth sleep with his eyes." "My Father worketh hitherto, and I work."'

'But *how?*' said Cyril. 'Tell us some of the ways, mamma, please.'

'In every way. "He sendeth the springs into the valleys," "he maketh grass to grow upon the mountains;" the cedars of Lebanon are of his planting. He forms the light,— he makes darkness, and it is night. He thundereth marvellously with his voice, he directeth his lightnings unto the ends of the earth. By the breath of God frost is given, and he saith unto the snow, Be thou on the earth; likewise to the small rain, and to the great rain of his strength. He stayeth the proud waves. The clouds are turned about by his counsels, he quieteth the earth by his south wind, "he casteth forth his ice by morsels: who can stand before his cold?"'

'And then, mamma?' said Gracie,—the children all listened eagerly.

'Then, he upholdeth all things by the word of his power. The hawk flies by his wisdom, the young lions seek their prey from God. "The eyes of all wait upon thee, and thou givest them their meat in due season; that thou givest them they gather." Even in the wilderness where no man is, God causeth it to rain, "to satisfy the desolate and waste ground; and to cause the bud of the tender herb to spring forth." "Canst thou guide Arcturus?" said the Lord to Job. "Canst thou lift up thy voice to the clouds, that abundance of water may cover the earth? Canst thou send lightnings, that they may go and say unto thee, Here we are? Who can *stay* the bottles of heaven? — Wilt thou hunt the prey for the lion?

Who provideth for the raven his food?"—and Job answered: "I know that thou canst do everything."'

'Now, mamma, tell about *us*,' said Sue.

'It is all as true for us, as for the smallest blade of grass or the brightest star,' answered our mother; '"in him we live and move;" "he giveth to all men life and breath and all things." He maketh herbs to grow for the service of man, and the year is crowned with his goodness. He sendeth forth his breath—we are created; he turneth man to destruction. "I kill and I make alive," said the Lord; "I wound and I heal." "I form the light and create darkness, I make peace and create evil." He leadeth his people like a flock, they are guided by the skilfulness of his hands. In every least thing of their lives, as in the greatest, this is true. For their sakes "he maketh the storm a calm;" "he upholdeth those that fall;" the Lord looseth the prisoners, he relieveth the fatherless and the widow; the poor crieth unto him, and he that hath no helper: his tender mercies are over all his works. The preparation of a Christian's heart, the answer of his tongue, is from the Lord: he may plan out his way, but the Lord directeth his steps. "Except the Lord build the house, they labour in vain that build it; except the Lord keep the city, the watchman waketh but in vain." "He putteth down one and setteth up another;" "he giveth power to get wealth;" the whole disposing of each lot is of the Lord. "He withdraweth man from his purpose;" "he instructs him to discretion;" "who teacheth like Him?"

'And as in all these private, personal affairs, so with those that are public and national. The heart of kings, as of other men, is in his hand: he bringeth counsel to nought, he breaks in pieces mighty men without number and sets others in their stead: he ruleth by his power forever. He makes peace; in war it is he who "takes off the chariot wheels" and overwhelms the army: and a king is not saved by the multitude of an host, for "there is no restraint to the Lord to save by many or by few." By him kings reign: "I chose David," he says of one, — "I girded thee, though thou hast not known me," he says to another; and always and ever, "He will work, and who shall let it?" "His counsel shall stand, and he will do all his pleasure." Every good gift, of mind or life or circumstance, comes from him; but also, "Shall there be evil" — that is grief, judgment, discipline — "in the city, and the Lord hath not done it?" "My Father worketh hitherto," said Jesus, "and I work."

'The Jews, well read in the Scriptures, understood these words at once; and knew that they were an assertion of divine right and power. But that mystery of God in which simple faith can rest, is a mere stumbling block to rebellion and unbelief. There is no one point for which so many have refused Jesus as this, — that he made himself equal with God. Tell a Jerusalem Jew now

that Jesus was divine, and often he will drown
your words, crying out " The Lord our God is one
Lord!" And multitudes more, in other lands,
both Jews and Gentiles, who acknowledge the
prophet, the righteous man, refuse "Immanuel;
God with us."

'In answer, the Lord went on to declare unto
them something of that mystery which they dis-
dained, — the separate divine persons, the one
God: telling first the oneness, and then the personal distinctness, and then the equality, and then
again the oneness: thus beginning and ending as
it were with their own watchword, " The Lord our
God is one Lord."

'He is one: "The Son can do nothing of himself," — " but what things soever the Father doeth,
these also doeth the Son likewise;" and yet are
these two not the same; for in human affairs the
Son is invested with supreme authority. The Father hath given all things into his hand. Equal
in power, he raiseth the dead; while by him shall
all men be judged at the last day. "God is judge
himself," said the Psalmist, speaking beforetime
of that day: "He cometh to judge the earth."
There could be but one meaning to these words
of Jesus: the Father " hath committed all judgment unto the Son; that all men should honour the
Son even as they honour the Father." Yet God
had declared long before, " My glory will I not
give to another," — therefore this was not another,
but was one with himself; for " he that honoureth

not the Son honoureth not the Father which hath sent him." And the hour is coming, said the Lord, when you shall *know* my divine power; for the dead shall hear my voice. Even now at my command disease takes its flight, and the dead in sin are made alive unto God. I am one with him. It will be my voice that shall arouse the sleepers, at the last day, and mine that shall have authority to pass judgment on them all: calling some to the resurrection of life eternal, and some to that of eternal death. A just judgment, — according to the will of the Father, with whom I am one.

'If you take not my word for all this, — a man's evidence for himself is not always accepted, — there is other proof, and other witnesses. "Ye sent unto John, and he bare witness unto the truth." I need no such testimony — but I remind you of it for your own sakes. A greater witness tells who I am: even the works that I do; "and the Father himself, which hath sent me, hath borne witness of me." Through me has been every manifestation of him.'

'It was strange they did not believe, then,' said Gracie.

'The Lord went on to tell them why they did not, — what were the real difficulties in the way. For then as now, want of proof, and doubts about mysteries, and all such things, are but like sham earthworks, mounted with Quaker guns. The real fort of resistance lies far within: "men love darkness rather than light." It is the light — not the mystery — against which they wage war. You boast of the strictness with which you keep the law of God, said Jesus to his scowling listeners, but his word does not abide in your hearts : you neither know nor love it, — or you would believe in me. " Search the Scriptures," — study again those books of the law and the prophets of which you talk so much ; for it is those very writings that testify of me. And yet, " Ye will not come unto me that ye might have life," — for life is their portion who hear my word. I need no honour, as I need no testimony, from men ; but I know that you fail to give it, only because the love of God is not in you. It is because I come in the name of the Lord, that you do not receive me. But let another come in his own name, working and speaking for his own sake, and you will listen to him. How can you believe — having no eyes for any but worldly honour ? And the charge against you will come from that very Moses in whom you trust. If you *believed* his words, you would have received me ; " for he wrote of me." He wrote that the seed of the woman should bruise the serpent's head ; that the Lord should raise up a Prophet from the midst of you, whom ye should hear : he told of the Star out of Jacob, of the Angel of the Covenant. " But if ye believe not his writings, how shall ye believe my words ? "

'They had the proof in their own hands, the knowledge was within their reach.'

'What made the Lord say John *was* a light?' said Cyril. 'John wasn't dead yet, was he?'

'John's light shone no more in public. It is only "the lamp of the wicked" which "is put out in obscure darkness," and John was drawing nearer to the perfect day; but it was within the walls of a prison. And this was the cause. Herod Antipas, son of the first Herod, and tetrarch of Galilee, had married the daughter of Aretas, king of Arabia; while his half brother, Herod Philip, had married Herodias, his own niece. But after a while, when Herod had been staying at his brother's castle, Herodias agreed to leave Philip and come to live with him; which she did.'

'What became of the other wife?' said Mabel.

''The daughter of Aretas? — she heard of this new arrangement, and fled away, and went home to her father; and Aretas afterwards made war upon Herod, to avenge his daughter's wrong. Such was the state of things, while John went up and down, preaching the baptism of repentance. At one of his riverside sermons, Herod himself was present: so it seems, from the words in Luke; perhaps commanding those very soldiers who came to John, saying, And what shall we do? And John, "bold as a lion," told Herod very frankly what *he* should do, speaking at once of Herodias, and saying, "It is not lawful for thee to have her." Herod doubtless was very angry; and would perhaps have put John to death on the spot, but "he feared the multitude, because they counted him a prophet;"

and even tyrants must regard the multitude sometimes. Herod pocketed his wrath, and went his
own way, leaving John to go his. And by and by,
there came upon the wicked king a sort of awe and
liking for the fearless preacher, "knowing that he
was a just man and a holy." He even tried to
bring about a good understanding between John
and his own conscience; "he heard him gladly"
— truth was quite a refreshing novelty at Herod's
court — and even "did many things" at his bidding. But if Herod's conscience was pacified, so
was not the anger of Herodias, — she never forgave
John for his words about her; and she fumed and
teased and worried Herod, — until at last, tired
out, against his own better feeling, "Herod sent
forth and laid hold upon John, and bound him in
prison for Herodias' sake, his brother Philip's
wife." To "all the evils he had done," Herod
"added yet this above all, that he shut up John in
prison." '

'*That's* what his hearing him gladly was worth,'
said Cyril.

'That is the way a great many people enjoy
stirring sermons, said mamma: 'they are a variety.
And the "many things" which people do in conse-
quence, serve as a sort of salve to an uneasy conscience; healing the wound "slightly." John had
been "valiant for the truth," and now he was to
be "faithful unto death," and then to receive his
crown. The light which had burned and shone so
long for God was sinking down behind the dark

outlines of the world, its work all done; for high
and clear and bright rode now "the Star out
of Jacob," — that "true Light," to which John
came for a witness: and the shadows began to flee
away.'

NOTES.

Note I. BETHLEHEM — THE MANGER. — Since my last sheets of copy went to the printer, I have with wonderful pleasure found evidence to support my decision of at least one vexed point — the manger at Bethlehem. I had studied and thought it out, until certainly if I was not tired of the subject, the subject had tired me; and now just as the volume is out of my hands, comes new evidence, from Young's new translation " according to the letter and idioms of the original languages." I need but put the two versions side by side, to shew how they explain each other.

" She brought forth her first born son, and wrapped him in swaddling clothes, and laid him in a manger; because there was no room for them in the inn." Luke 2 : 7.

" She brought forth her son — the first born, and wrapped him up, and laid him down in the manger [*lit.* laid him up *or* back in the feeding-place] because there was not to them a place in the guest-chamber [*lit.* place of ' loosing down their baggage']." Luke 2 : 7. — YOUNG'S *Trans.*

I should add, that the two sentences in brackets, are from Young's " Companion " to his own work.

Note II. BETHLEHEM — DAVID'S WELL. — As I have (perhaps needlessly for this volume) touched upon

David's well, 1 must give the grounds of my assertion that the well is still there. And first, on the other side from Dr. Robinson.

" We were able to find no well at Bethlehem, except one connected with the aqueduct on the south. * * That to which the monks give the name of the ' Well of David,' is about half or three quarters of a mile N. by E. of Bethlehem, beyond the deep valley which the village overlooks ; it is merely a deep and wide cistern or cavern now dry, with three or four narrow openings cut in the rock. * * They assured us, that there is no well of living water in or near the town."— *Bib. Researches,* i. 470, 473.

"About a quarter of a mile north of the gate of the modern village is a ' well,' which is now pointed out as that for whose waters David longed when in the ' hold' of Adullam. It is a cistern, as the Hebrew word would seem to indicate."— J. L. PORTER, *in Bib. Cy.* i. 354.

" It is in a rude enclosure, and consists of a large cistern with several small apertures. It bears marks about it of having been long in use ; and its position seems perfectly to agree with the sacred narrative. * * The word used to express it in the original Hebrew is not a fountain, but corresponding with the Arabic *burah,* a pit or cistern."— DR. WILSON's *Lands of the Bible,* i. 399.

" A fountain round which a bevy of the Bethlehemite maidens may be seen congregated at most hours of the day." — STEWART, *Tent and Khan,* p 333.

" About half a mile from it (the town), and at the top of the opposite slope, a road leads to the left. Into this we first turned aside. At the corner where the roads meet, there is a garden or orchard, chiefly planted with fig trees. This, tradition says, was the farm of Jesse, the father of David. Close by this there is a field where there is a very old well, and where the ruins of some old town are observable under the surface."— BONAR'S *Land of Promise*, p. 112.

" It is the supply of water and the well that decide the site of an Eastern city ; and while the walls and even the whole position of the place, as at Nazareth, may be changed, the fountain and the well can never move." — TRISTRAM'S *Land of Israel*, p. 148.

Note II   BETHLEHEM—THE MASSACRE.— The precise number of children slain depends of course not merely upon the population at that time, but also upon how far Herod's executioners knew and carried out the king's intent to slay merely all the *boys*. The following bits of history may be of interest in this connection.

" It has been too often the cruel policy of despots of the East to consolidate the foundations of their thrones by the slaughter of all who had claim or power to dispute their authority. Jehu furnishes an example. The history of Abyssinia also records an instance of a tyrant ordering the destruction of nearly 400 children ; and an eminent writer quotes the case of a king of Pegu who fancied that a nephew's claim to the throne would interfere with his plans, and therefore he sought to kill the child ; and when he discovered that the youth was secreted by some of his nobles, he commanded that all the children of the grandees, these children amounting to about 4,000, should be put to death — a massacre much more terrible than that committed by the enraged King of the Jews. Herod's cruel spirit appears to have descended to his son, for we are told that he put 3,000 of the leading persons in the nation to death, in order that he might punish some supposed offence." — *Sunday School World, September,* 1864.

Note IV. Sychar. — " A village like Askar answers much more appropriately to the casual description of St. John, than so large and venerable a place as Shechem." — Smith's *Bible Dictionary.*

" If we admit the identity of the present well of Jacob with that mentioned by John, there can be but little doubt that Sychar was a small Samaritan town not far from that spot. — Thomson's *Land and the Book,* ii. 206.

" The form of expression is somewhat peculiar. It would seem to convey the idea that the city was an obscure one, or else that, while Sychar was its popular name, it had another. The common opinion is that Sychar is only another name for the better known Sychem or Shechem."

"But the well is a mile and a half from the site of Shechem, now Nâbulus; and the question arises — If Sychar and Shechem were identical, could it be described as *near* the well, while at such a distance. The word is indefinite. It is difficult to say what distance would be called ' near.' "

" The testimony of ancient geographers does not tend to remove the difficulty. Eusebius writes: ' Sychar, *before* Neapolis.' "

" According to the Bordeaux Pilgrim, who travelled in A. D. 333, by Neapolis, at the base of the mountain, stood *Sichem,* beside Joseph's monument — and a thousand paces farther was *Sychar* " —J. L. Porter, *in Bib. Cy.*

While Dr. Robinson says — " It is hardly necessary to remark upon the confusion and inconsistency of all this." — *Bib. Re.,* ii. 291.

Many more opinions, for and against, might be given, but these are enough.

Note V. THE PINNACLE OF THE TEMPLE. — No view taken now of the valley of Jehoshaphat can give more than a faint idea of the old sheer depth of descent. The walls surrounding the Turkish mosque have nothing of the height of the old Temple porch; and the valley itself is filled up with rubbish. The workers under the English " Palestine Exploration Fund " have already begun their researches along the southern front of Mt. Moriah, bringing strange things to light. " Shafts and galleries have been driven through the mass of rubbish which covers the base of the Temple rock, and have revealed the enormous depth to which it has accumulated. Through the *débris*, the cyclopean walls supporting the Temple have been traced to a depth varying from 60 to 90 feet, and the wall itself has been shown to have reached at this point a height of from 170 to 180 feet; a curious justification of a passage in Josephus, in which he describes the dizziness with which the spectator looked down into the valley beneath.   •

* * * Thirty feet below the vaults which have been known to exist at its south-eastern corner, a passage has now been found leading into the solid substance of the wall and indicating probably large sub-structures."— *Saturday Review, in Littell's Living Age, No. 1231.*